Adia's Ballad

Marc A. Beausejour

S.H.E. PUBLISHING, LLC

Adia's Ballad

For information contact : www.shepublishingllc.com | info@shepublishingllc.com | Tel: 219.515.8032

Library of Congress Control Number : 2024931397

ISBN : 978-1-953163-92-9

Edited by: Leslie E. Stern

Second Edition : February 2024

10 9 8 7 6 5 4 3 2 1

To everyone who's striving hard to accomplish their hopes and dreams. Don't ever allow anyone to tell you that it's impossible. All things are possible with God and as long as He's in your corner, you'll never lose.

Acknowledgments

First of all, I would like to thank my Lord and Savior Jesus Christ. If it wasn't for Him, I wouldn't be motivated to continue writing. It seems like only yesterday, I was just starting my first book, and now I'm on my fourth book. I thank my good friend and editor, Leslie Stern who is an extraordinary author in her own right, teaching and mentoring me. I thank my parents, Jean and Lineda Beausejour who has put up with me more than they had to and their continued support. Last but definitely not least, I would like to thank all my friends, readers, pastors, and supporters that I've been blessed to come across during my twenty-nine years on this planet. You all played a part in the inspiration of my stories, and I hope I can continue. Thank you.

Introduction

What is a ballad? A ballad is defined as a poem or a song narrating a story in short stanzas. Ballads have been around for hundreds of years, and they have aided in telling stories that otherwise may have been forgotten over the course of time. There are traditional ballads which were considered legendary and have been the base of many folklore songs that have lasted for generations. In the modern world of pop culture and music, a ballad is usually a sentimental song that a singer incorporates in their compact discs, mixtapes, or upcoming albums. Portions of ballads have been etched on gravestones to remember those who have passed on and those are the ballads that usually transform the deceased into sources of inspirations for others who have aspirations to become legendary and to be remembered for the impact they make upon mankind.

In this story, we will look at the story of a young lady, who, after losing someone very dear to her, turned to music for her salvation. This story, set once more in various parts of New York, is not based on real characters or events. Based on the background and scenery of this tale, there is profanity, racial slurs and certain situations that are not suitable for children and may be sensitive to some people. So as the young lady approaches the microphone, take heed as you read her story.

Prologue

The subway tracks creaked as the passenger train pulled into the Forest Hills station, slowing down as the wheels, controlled by an engineer's brakes, screeched before coming to a halt. A throng of passengers waited for the train car doors to open. For the first minute, people thought there was a delay as the doors stalled but in the next minute, they opened, and the passengers eagerly boarded the train. Among those who boarded the train was fifteen-year-old Kira Brown, who entered the retracting doors near the middle of the subway car. Her older sister, Chanté and boyfriend Wallace Jermaine entered the train through the door near the back of the same subway car. Chanté rolled her eyes impatiently.

"Why she can't neva' walk in the same direction we walkin' in?" she complained to Wallace.

Wallace laughed as Chanté glared at him in jest. "Aww, leave her alone. She ain't causing trouble to nobody. She'll be aight," he replied.

"Whatever. You ain't the one who gotta live with her." Chanté retorted. The one trait she hated about her sister was when she tried to act like an adult.

Although they were only two years apart in age, Chanté still felt she had seniority over her younger sister. She couldn't bear to hear her parents laud her with compliments on how well behaved she was and how mature she was for her age. It could also be Chanté's jealousy emerging and she wouldn't doubt it. Kira had always been the cute young one. Chanté had been the "rough around the edges" type of girl and it was not the type of attitude her parents favored. They didn't even like Wallace when he picked them up to go to this concert at Radio City Music Hall. Kira's favorite gospel artist, Adia, was in town and she had been yearning to go to the concert for weeks. Chanté didn't have any problems with Adia. In fact, she actually thought she had a pretty voice and a body that most men coveted. It just annoyed her that Kira had been talking up the event for weeks. Whether she kept playing Adia's newly released CD or she constantly commented that she wished she had a ticket to see her, Kira was simply aggravating.

It annoyed Chanté so much that in order to shut her up and show her parents how supportive she was of her perfect sister, she used her babysitting job money, and the rest of her savings to purchase two tickets to the concert. The tickets weren't cheap either, costing sixty dollars each and even then they weren't getting the best seats in the building. It didn't matter to Kira, who stared excitedly out the window of the underground as an intricate part of New York's MTA system.

Looking at her sister staring dreamily out into the dark tunnel, Chanté shook her head. "Look at her. She so juiced up for this concert, it ain't even funny." she retorted.

Wallace, who had been busy checking his social networks on his cell phone, stopped just long enough to wrap his left arm around Chanté .

"Baby, you need to stop worrying about yo' sister now, fo' real." he told her.

"I know but she's been annoying me with all her CD's of Adia." Chanté replied. "Don't get me wrong, I'm feeling her too, but that girl got some serious baggage," she added

Wallace shook his head, indicating that he understood what she was saying. The train rolled on, stopping only to pick up passengers at other stops. Wallace smiled at Chanté but the smile was far from innocent. It was one of those sly grins that he would give her whenever he was acting mischievously.

"I'm just going so I can see if Adia's body shape is legit. Anybody can look like a gorgeous chick with all them photographers photoshopping everything." he said.

Chanté looked at him. "So that's why you agreed to go wit' me? To check her body out?" she asked jealously.

Wallace realizing that he had gone too far, attempted to backtrack slightly.

"No that's not the only reason. I just wanna see what she bout to do. I give it only a couple weeks. She ain't about to be no gospel singer a few months. I mean how could anyone change it up that fast?"

Chanté didn't need to hear about Adia's transformation from one of the most well-known R&B acts in the US to singing gospel, since it was on every music broadcast. As they passed the Lexington Ave train station, Kira knew that they were only a few train stops away.

She asked Chanté , "Do you think Adia will have time to go sign autographs?"

"Oh hush, chile!" Chanté said, although she sounded amused.

What made Kira different from all the other little girls that looked up to Adia? She had to admit, from the time Adia began her singing career, she has dealt with a bevy of issues. Adia had been cheated out of millions of dollars by her former record label and had been forced to deal with many personal issues. "Damn shame what she let happen to De'Von", she thought as she reflected on the artist who had been involved in a relationship with Adia before their relationship had taken a turn for the worst. Chanté had enough dirty laundry to air about Adia for days.

Yet Adia had the gall to profess that she changed her life for the better and that she had decided to change her direction in music, fooling young girls like her gullible sister. Kira didn't seem to care about what Adia had been through. She still idolized her. Sometimes Chanté felt that Kira would rather have Adia for an older sister.

"You do know all the stuff that she did right?" she asked her sister. Kira shook her head.

"It doesn't matter what she did. If Adia got a second chance, everybody could get one. She dealt with so much in her life but she still went above all that. I would've thought you of all people would understand that." she replied, challenging her sister.

Wallace who came over to sit next to Chanté and Kira, scoffed upon hearing Kira's statement.

"If you want my opinion, her first album that she came out with was way betta' than what she's coming out with now." he retorted as the train arrived at a station that read in large block letters at the side of the tunnel ROCKEFELLER CENTER.

"Why do you think that? Maybe cuz she had less clothes in the music videos?" Chanté asked.

Wallace smiled sheepishly. He didn't want to mention it out loud, but secretly, he agreed with Chanté. As they approached the station, the train came to a stop once again, and the doors opened. Chanté, Kira and Wallace exited the train and headed up the stairs of the Rockefeller Center train station. The next stop was Radio City Music Hall, a theater that had history of famous acts, stage plays and its share of legendary performers gracing the stage. It was about seven twenty-seven that evening. In another hour, Kira would be watching her favorite artist.

It was May 19th 2011. The neon lights at Radio City Music Hall were barely illuminated as people began entering the famous venue. Within a couple of hours, masses of people were swarming through the doors and gateways. There was a tangible buzz in the air as the hall filled with excited ticket holders and music fans, all whom anxiously awaited the beauty and elegance of Adia.

The golden curtain covered the stage as promoters, hosts, and backstage assistants made final preparations for the show. Sitting on a stool off the side of the stage was Adia. Her head was demurely bent down in prayer. She could feel the rapid thumps of her heart as she calmed her nerves. Chewing the last bit of flavor of the Juicy Fruit gum she had been nervously chewing for the past hour, she resorted to popping the gum in her mouth. Adia's mother had always hated it when she popped her gum. It made an annoyingly tedious sound that could drive anyone up the wall. Adia was wearing one of the signature sweaters from her own line and jeans with designer shoes, Adia's hair was tied back in a straight ponytail. Before she went on stage, she had her usual hair and makeup preparation done by her make-up artist, Charli Tatum. Charli had a wealth of experience from working with female artists in the past and she did a great job making sure that Adia's makeup was on point and reflected the beauty in her cheekbones and her eyes. Adia was always grateful to have Charli with her. During their time together, Charli became more than just someone who worked for Adia. She became a trusted friend and always knew the right words of encouragement to say whenever Adia felt down.

While she sat praying, Adia heard singing on the other side of the back stage, which resembled harmonized singing. Adia smiled to herself. She knew those voices. They belonged to the background vocalists and singers, Marvin, Tasha, and Susan.

"They always go above and beyond for me. I love them," Adia thought with a smile. Susan, noticing that Adia was all alone in the corner, stopped singing with her fellow vocalists and walked over to Adia.

"Everything ok, baby?" Susan asked in a way a concerned parent asked their children. She was only ten years older than Adia but to Adia, she was maternal.

"Yeah, I'm ok mama. Just thinking," Adia replied. She always called Susan 'mama' as a term of endearment.

"Ok, well I just want to make sure you're ok, honey. We go on in a few minutes, so we got to get to our places." Susan said.

"Ok, thanks mama." Adia replied and she got up from her chair and walked over to the center of the stage. Light and sound technicians made sure that all final checks on the venue.

Finally Adia stood up and approached the curtain, ready for her upcoming performance. 'You got this, girl,' a voice in her head told her. But the voice in her head wasn't her own. The voice sounded so strange, yet so familiar. Hearing voices in her head was nothing new for Adia. In the course of her brief career, she had some great moments, but she also had regrets. She knew there were people whom she had let down, people she had hurt. Often times she found herself thinking back to those days.

'How foolish I was. I almost lost it all....my friends and my dream,' she thought. She wouldn't blame any of those friends if they never spoke to her again.

Sean, Vanessa, Shania, De'Von; the list went on. Rolling her sweater sleeve up to her shoulder, she places her hand on two tattoos she had on her right shoulder. One was a tattoo of a Bible verse, Philippians chapter four verse thirteen, to be exact. Another tattoo bore the initials of a dearly departed relative who met her end far too soon. L.A.M. 1985-2003. After that, she was convinced the voice was that of her late sister. As the curtain opened and music played to the sound of applause, Adia was determined to show them a different side of her. She wanted her songs to tell her story. She wanted to show them Andrea McAfee.

Chapter One

Dr. Jan Ralwinski sat calmly in her high-backed chair, smiling warmly at her patient, who was sitting in the comfortable recliner across from her. Out of all the patients she has seen over the years, there was no one with whom she has grown closer than the young woman who was lying across from her.

She had known Andrea McAfee for close to six years and watched her grow from a shy, self-conscious little girl into a smart, independent, and outspoken young lady. Dr. Ralwinski clearly remembered the very first meeting she had with Andrea back in October 2003, a few weeks after she endured one of the most devastating tragedies in her life. She first learned about Loree McAfee through her parents, Amos and Alisha McAfee who started seeing her after losing their eldest daughter in a senseless act of gang violence. Many people considered Dr. Ralwinski as a shrink or a psychiatrist, but she preferred to think of herself as more of a grief counselor. It was true, she has dealt with many cases of death and loss of loved ones, but most had become disenchanted with reality from their ordeals. This was not so with the McAfee family. Although they were naturally stricken with sorrow, they were a very resilient family and she commended them for their heartfelt attempt to keep on living despite losing a key member of their family. Andrea was no exception.

A fish tank, about three feet long sat against the wall. The tank contained five fish: two GloFish Tetras, an angel fish, and two colorful clown loaches. Although the fish and the tank were the property of the office where she worked in Forest Hills, Dr. Ralwinski had made it her personal responsibility to feed the fish on a daily basis. She recalled the first meeting with Andrea, after she was introduced to the doctor by the parents.

"Hi Andrea, my name is Dr. Ralwinski, but you can call me Jan or Janet if you want," she had said. She always wanted to make her patients, especially the younger and the more vulnerable, feel at ease.

"Ok." was all that came out of Andrea's lips at the time. The doctor directed her into the office.

She knew Andrea was shy and would not speak her mind right away. Her shyness gave her away immediately when she saw Andrea looking around at the psychiatric diplomas, degrees, and other credentials.

'She looks so alone and lost', she thought when she finally invited Andrea to sit. There was a sofa in the room, a large recliner, a smaller chair, and the high-back chair the doctor used. It was a kind of test to see where her patients chose to sit. If they sat closest to her, they were open. On the far end of the sofa, they were distant. The small chair meant they felt small and insignificant. The large recliner would be chosen by a patient who felt competitive with the doctor. During Andrea's first sessions, she chose the smallest chair.

It didn't take a doctor to realize that Andrea had been quite close with her sister and while she was still numb from the tragedy, she also had a very hard time trusting others. So Dr. Ralwinski was aware of how important it was to gain Andrea's trust. That first meeting was painfully awkward on Andrea's part, until she noticed the fish tank.

"Are those yours?" she had asked.

"They most certainly are. I feed them and take care of them every day," she replied, showing Andrea the different multi-colored fish.

The doctor smiled as she saw Andrea's eyes sparkle with awe and excitement over the fishes in the tank. "If you want, I could let you feed them one day," Dr. Ralwinski said.

"Really? You'll let me feed them?" Andrea asked, surprised.

"Of course, dear. I'll show you how to feed them." Dr. Ralwinski said and she went over to the fish tank with Andrea, explained how to sprinkle the fish food on top of the tank and also explained how the filter in the tank had to be changed at least twice a month so the water could remain clean.

Just like that, the ice had broken between the doctor and Andrea and for the first year or so, when she was visiting almost daily, she would feed the fish before their sessions. The grief counseling sessions began with little more than just asking Andrea how her day went and discussing whatever Andrea wanted to talk about. Before long, Andrea saw Dr. Ralwinski as more than just a psychiatrist or a common doctor. She saw her as a friend, someone in whom she could confide whenever she wanted to vent about her school or her friends.

As the years passed and the more Andrea matured, the closer their bond became. Here it was, six years later; the year 2009, and although Andrea still fed the doctor's fish, she found herself sitting on the sofa right next to Dr. Ralwinski, indicating trust and personal contact. Dr. Ralwinski always allowed Andrea some time to gather her thoughts and start the conversation but her session with Andrea was nearly over and she had an appointment with another patient who was waiting in the lobby. Dr. Ralwinski decided to initiate the conversation.

"So how's school going?" she asked. Andrea continued to look up at the ceiling. She remained silent for a moment before replying.

"School's ok, I guess. Senior prom's coming up soon." she said. The doctor smiled, raising one of her eyebrows.

"So have you decided who you're taking to the prom yet?" she asked with a laugh.

Andrea shook her head. "I don't even know, Jan. These guys out there now are just so, I don't know, basic. They keep trying to stay tryin' to spit the same rap game to me. Besides I don't even know if anyone's gonna ask me go with me anyway, you know what I'm sayin'?" she asked.

Dr. Ralwinski couldn't comprehend Andrea's words. Andrea was a very attractive young lady. She was fully developed with long legs and beautiful brown complexion and thin lips. Whenever Andrea smiled, anyone could feel her warmth and sincerity. She couldn't understand why nobody would want to go to the prom with her.

"What about Sean?" she asked, referring to Andrea's longtime friend Sean Hawkins.

Andrea looked at Dr. Ralwinski. Surely she couldn't be serious. Sean was like a brother to Andrea because they had known each other for so many years. She put him in the same category with her other friend Vanessa Roberts, who was almost a sister to Andrea. Of course nobody would ever replace Loree, but if anyone came close, it was Vanessa. They told each other secrets, they knew each other's tendencies, favorite foods, bad habits, and ideal men. Sean did not fit the description of their ideal men.

"Nah, it would be like going with my own brother. Besides, he's probably going with someone else anyway." Andrea replied.

She knew the doctor was trying to help her, but she hated how everyone expected her to be her older sister. She couldn't be Loree, no matter how hard she tried. She may have had her beauty but it was her personality that was totally different from Loree. It made her uncomfortable when people made comparisons between the two. Loree had been her own person and had her own identity. Andrea was still in search of that identity and was still attempting to find herself.

"But the prom's not going to be for another month so I've got plenty of time to choose," she added.

"Yes you do. Don't rush things. Always take your time. Just focus on school and saving up for college." she advised Andrea.

But the prom wasn't Andrea's only problem.She was experiencing a very unique problem, one that might have had other people thinking that she was mentally unstable.

"Jan, I've been hearing her again," she said abruptly.

Dr. Ralwinski stopped smiling momentarily and looked Andrea right in the eye. Jan knew full well who Andrea was talking about.

"You heard your sister again?" she asked. Andrea nodded her head, positively answering the question.

In the last few years, Andrea had been experiencing moments where she would have visions of her sister; in dreams or odd times when she felt she heard Loree speaking to her as if she was still alive.

"I know it sounds crazy and all, but I keep hearing her voice. It could be a dream or reality. Last night when I fell asleep, she appeared again and she was giving me a message. I couldn't hear the message, her voice was muffled, but she was speaking to me frantically, like she was warning me about something, but I don't know what she's warning me about," Andrea explained. The doctor nodded her head. "Do you believe in life after death, doctor?" she asked.

Dr. Ralwinski has always believed in a higher power, but not to the extent that Andrea seemed to believe it. Dr. Ralwinski was always a proponent of evolution, natural selection, and natural death. In her opinion, when someone died, they were gone. But from previous experiences, she knew that people coped with death in different ways. While some people slipped into a state of obscurity and helplessness, others would claim that their loved ones would come back as spirits or ghosts and communicate with them. It all sounded absurd, but Doctor Ralwinski knew Andrea long enough to know that she wasn't going crazy or insane. Andrea probably sensed the doctor thought she was crazy too, but she continued anyway.

"So I'm sleeping right? And suddenly I'm in some kind of dream state where the room is all white. I don't see anything. No tables, no chairs, nothing. All I see is a door with a gold knob. Before I can breathe out a word, the gold knob turns and I see her come out. She's wearing a long white robe or shroud, I couldn't tell because it was kinda blurry," she explained. "But it had to be Loree. I recognized her voice. There she was, alive and clean, no bullet holes, no blood..." Andrea's voice trailed off, as she felt the all too familiar lump in her throat and her eyes welled with tears. It took her a moment, then once she composed herself, she continued. "She came close to me but we didn't make any contact or anything. She was telling me something, but even though she was close, I couldn't make out what she was saying. It was some freaky stuff but at the same time, in a weird way, it felt good knowing that she was watching over me," she continued.

"Honey, you know that dreams are our thoughts or our innermost desires coming out in a state of sleep. They show that you are still thinking of Loree." Dr. Ralwinski said. She reached into her office desk drawer for a prescription pad. "I think you should take this medication. It helps with depression and anxiety." she added.

Andrea took the prescription the doctor handed her. "So you think I'm crazy, huh?" she said furtively.

Dr. Ralwinski smiled. "Not at all, Andrea. When we lose our loved ones so early in our lives, we always wish they were still with us. I'm just concerned about your health and making sure you are getting enough of sleep and exercise," she said.

Andrea stood up from the couch. She walked over to the small wall mirror the doctor had in her office. A lost, insignificant girl looked back at her. Both she and her parents agreed that she did not resemble her sister. Loree was lighter in skin tone and she was more developed at age eighteen than Andrea. Andrea was slimmer but she still displayed flashes of her late sister's attitude and individuality. She didn't know why but she hated when people compared her to Loree, in their attempts at comforting her. She would always smile and say thank you out of courtesy but the comparison still bothered her.

I'm not Loree and I will never be Loree. She wished people could understand it and let her heal and move on. Dr. Ralwinski walked over to Andrea and placed her hand on her shoulder gently. She knew the session was over.

"Make sure you get plenty of rest and if you ever need to talk about anything, feel free to set up another appointment, ok?" she said. Andrea nodded to show that she understood, before she picked up her school bag and walked to the bus stop to get home.

Early the next day, Andrea and Vanessa were walking to school. On the way there, Andrea noticed her friend seemed distracted. She had headphones plugged into her Mp3 player and she seemed to be enjoying whatever music was playing more than being with her. This frustrated Andrea, since she had been talking to Vanessa about one of her co-workers at Johnson's, a clothing retail store located in Forest Hills.

"Girl, are you even listening to me? So I'm working over by the lingerie section right, and this chick Gloria comes walkin' up to me tellin' me that they need assistance over at the cash register," Andrea vented. "I'm like 'Girl you see me busy ova hea', why you can't call anybody else up front? Better yet, you get behind the register and ring someone up once in a while," she continued.

Vanessa laughed. "Damn girl, you probably shoulda told her ass off right there. That's what I would've done," she replied while still dancing to the sounds from her mp3 player.

"Girl, who are you listening too? I wanna know who you turnin' up for," she said grabbing one of Vanessa's headphones.

Vanessa reached out in an attempt to grab her headphones back. "Come on, Drea why you gotta be like that for?" she protested, even though she was laughing.

Andrea carefully placed one of the headphones in her ear, listening to the flowing rap lyrics:

She callin' me Papi cuz she like how I flow/Rub it nice and slow like Usher, she already know/Runnin' game all day, she gone be callin' me T.O./I ain't the type of nigga that be sweatin' any hoe.

Andrea listened to more of the song. His flow was legit but he was no different than any other rapper who was out there rapping about how many times they had sex. But for Vanessa's sake, she pretended to like the music.

"He's nice. Who this be?" Andrea asked. Vanessa looked at her friend with a shocked expression.

"Don't tell me you don't know who this is. You supposed to be the music expert and all that, and you don't even know one of our own?" she asked.

Andrea shook her head. "Nah I never heard this kid before," she said. Vanessa rolled her eyes. "This is De'Von Franklin girl. He ain't all well known yet, this is one of his first albums that he made," she replied.

"Oh ok. Well he can flow alright. But who does he have singin' the break, cuz they couldn't hold a note if it had a handle." Andrea replied.

Vanessa stared at her, her eyes enlarged in what seemed as a failed effort to suppress her laughter over the cut of Andrea's jib toward De'Von's background singers.

"You know he signed over at that new label, Metro Records. They big all over Queens and I hear they be all in the clubs and bars looking for talent," she replied. "You know, if you sing at one of them amateur nights that they have, you never know who could be there from Metro," she added.

But Andrea shot the idea down quickly. One of Andrea's special gifts was that she had an amazing singing voice. Unfortunately the only people who knew about her voice were Vanessa, Sean, and a few other classmates of hers, not counting her church.

"Nah, I ain't on a level like that. Besides, I sing for myself whenever I feel some type of way," Andrea said.

Vanessa didn't believe it for a second. "You got a great voice. Whenever I visit your church on Sundays, you always be getting all the solos," she said.

"Yeah but that's different to me though. I'm singing for the pastor and his congregation, who won't judge you, no matter how bad you sounded," Andrea replied.

At the same time, when they crossed an intersection, they were joined by their friend Sean Hawkins who came up and surprised them from behind, wrapping his long arms around their shoulders in jest. Sean was wearing a Yankees authentic jersey and Nike athletic shorts topped off with a New York fitted baseball cap. The overhead hug came too quick and sudden for Andrea, who recoiled.

"Uh-uh somebody is way too happy this morning. What happened, did you finally get some?" she asked. Sean's smile and jovial expression disappeared when Andrea made a subtle, but effective jab at his virginity.

"I see you got jokes. Nessa, tell Stella ova' there she need to get her groove back," he joked back. Andrea laughed, rolling her eyes at him.

She could remember when she first met Sean in junior high. He was a small, chubby boy who was always laughed at by the other kids. Even Vanessa and Andrea poked fun at him for a little while. But at some point during their time in the sixth and seventh grades, they became friends. They later became great friends after Andrea lost Loree and just as she was beginning to lose a grip on life, Sean and Vanessa eased her pain. They heard her silent cries and pleas for compassion and understanding and without hesitation, they responded. When nobody else, other than Dr. Ralwinski, was there for Andrea, Sean and Vanessa stood by her. They had been inseparable ever since and as they matured over the years, they'd watch each other's transformation.

Vanessa, who had grown out of her stutter and her lisp early on in their relationship, had grown into her body and became a beautiful woman with olive-colored skin and long braided hair. She had also developed a talent for doing hair and has done Andrea's hair on many occasions. Sean eventually shed his fat and developed muscles and athletic attributes, lending his talents over to play basketball for junior high school and eventually at Richmond Hill High School. Sean played junior varsity basketball his first three years at the school and finally broke through the varsity ranks at the school, averaging eleven points and six rebounds a game. As the season wound down, the Lions' record did not qualify them for the state tournament but Sean had enjoyed a breakout year. Unfortunately, he found himself under the shadow of the only two other players to average more than him, Jake Alstead and Michael James. Both players had received their letters of intent and were going to Lehigh College and Iona College on scholarships. Sean had yet to receive his letter of intent. Although he has attempted to shrug it off and pretend that it wasn't a big deal, secretly he was concerned that he was being passed over and his opportunity would never arrive.

Andrea and Vanessa were Sean's biggest supporters, attending all of his home games. However, Andrea felt that Sean was being too melodramatic about his scholarship situation. Another situation that annoyed Andrea about Sean was the fact that everyone kept insinuating that either they were dating or that he was dating Vanessa. Neither of the alleged rumors were true but Andrea eventually figured out that a boy couldn't hang out with two girls and just be friends in other people's eyes. So as far as she was concerned, they may as well have kept on talking. It hadn't helped that Sean had developed physically so rapidly; so much so that other girls came to Andrea, asking her if Sean was seeing anybody. At first she would respond on his behalf but eventually she would say that she didn't know and they needed to ask him themselves.

"Well Vanessa, let Sean know I'm gonna get my groove back right after he gets his swag back. Oops, my bad. You gotta have something first before you lose it," Andrea replied, while Vanessa laughed.

"What you laughin' at?" Sean asked Vanessa. "Who you listening to, anyway?" he asked her again before waiting on a response for the previous question. Vanessa rolled her eyes.

"I'm listening to this track called 'stay out my business," she replied while Sean made a face and Andrea laughed. "Nah but I'm listening to De'Von though," she replied.

Sean's eyes lit up. "De'Von? Oh nice! That boy dope though," he said.

As they approached the doors of Richmond Hill High School, Andrea let out a sigh. She knew she was about to enter through what she called the wolves den. She called it that for obvious reasons; the boys that hung out at the front of the doors would be waiting to catcall and make thirsty wolf sounds at her. Sometimes she wished she didn't look so appealing.

"Yo' ma wassup? When we gon' chill?" "Lemme hold yo' bag for you." It was very annoying.

As she turned around to respond sharply to one of the boys, she felt a hand on her left shoulder. Turning around, she saw the hand belonged to the assistant principal.

Chapter Two

Andrea followed the assistant principal to her office, walking up two flights of stairs en route to their destination. Many of the kids were too busy talking and joking around to notice that Andrea was being led to the office, although a few kids whispered, and speculation arose. Andrea couldn't understand it herself, as she walked into Mrs. Martinez's office. She felt dread rise up within her. She never had any disciplinary action imposed on her at Richmond Hill and she held a steady 3.7 GPA. What could Mrs. Martinez possibly want with her? Once Andrea was seated in her office, Mrs. Martinez closed the door behind her.

"Good morning, Ms. McAfee. I bet by now you're probably wondering why I brought you here," Mrs. Martinez said in a stern voice.

Many of the staff members at Richmond Hill dressed very casually, but Mrs. Martinez was strictly business; wearing a green blouse with a gray skirt and black pumps. She was new to Richmond Hill, having been an assistant principal for only two years. According to most of the students, Mrs. Martinez was a strict disciplinarian, and she had a zero-tolerance for laziness or incompetence in the school. As a result, she was also the most feared staff member by most of the students. Andrea, however, did not bear those feelings toward Mrs. Martinez.

"I'm not sure Mrs. Martinez. Did I do something wrong?" she asked, making it come out as more of a plea rather than sharp retort. 'Maybe if I suck up just enough, she'll lessen my punishment,' she thought.

But Mrs. Martinez smiled and nodded her head. "Not at all, Andrea. Quite the opposite actually. I called you up here to present you something," she replied. A wave of relief washed over Andrea and she let out a silent sigh of relief.

"I understand that you have filled out some college applications and a few of the college applications that you submitted to our office required a letter of recommendation," she continued.

Andrea closed her eyes as she shook her head. How could she have forgotten to submit a letter of recommendation with her college applications? She thought she fulfilled all the requirements of the applications. "I'm so sorry, Mrs. Martinez. I must've overlooked that part of the application process," Andrea said, realizing that it was probably too late to submit a letter of recommendation at this time.

"No need to worry about that Andrea. You are one of our top students at the school and have excelled in your classes despite the odds that you've faced. So I've taken the liberty of writing you a letter of recommendation to any college of your choice," Mrs. Martinez replied, smiling.

Andrea didn't know what to say at first. There had to be over a thousand kids at the school, maybe two hundred seniors. There were probably over fifty seniors in the school who may have had a better GPA than Andrea. Surely she didn't deserve the letter of recommendation from the assistant principal herself, unless the letter was a product of the one single characteristic that she couldn't stand: remorse. One part of Mrs. Martinez's statement remained in Andrea's conscience:

Despite the odds that you've faced. She knew that Mrs. Martinez couldn't bring herself to say it, but she knew what she meant to say when she was giving her the letter. We know that you and your family have endured through the tragic loss of a family member and because you've suffered through it and worked through it, we want to help you in your time of need.

Andrea was not one to be rude or ungrateful when people were so overprotective of her or her family. It was nice the first few months, maybe the first year but Andrea soon realized that she didn't want to live the rest of her life having people feel sorry for her. She didn't want anyone to look at her with pity and use those emotions to skate through life. Andrea was still coming into her own; and she wanted to grow up as a normal teenage girl like everyone else.

"Mrs. Martinez, thank you very much, but I don't think I can accept that letter. I didn't really earn it," she explained.

But Mrs. Martinez insisted. "Don't be silly, Andrea. You have earned it. You were a merit honor student for two years, you've had semesters where you've made straight A's, you were in the beta club, and took some SP classes," she explained. "As far as I'm concerned, there's no other applicant I would choose," she reassured Andrea.

Andrea looked in her eyes for a brief moment. One trait she had learned from her sister was the ability to read a person just from examining their eyes. She remembered when she had been eleven years old and while Loree was out with some friends, Andrea had snuck into Loree's desk drawer and borrowed Loree's favorite hoop earrings. Andrea wanted to wear them for school the next day and knowing that Loree had plenty of other earrings, she wouldn't notice them missing until the next day and by that time, she would have already returned them. Unfortunately Loree returned home earlier than expected and for some odd reason, wanted to wear those particular earrings. When she looked in the drawer and they were missing, she turned to Andrea.

"Drea, where my earrings at? The hoop ones I had?" she asked.

"I don't know where they are," she replied. She didn't know how Loree did it but she saw the guilt reflect in Andrea's eyes. Loree had quickly crossed the room they shared and looked under the bed where she found them.

"Mmhmm. I thought so. If you gonna steal my style and lie about it, do it right next time," Loree said. Andrea was confused.

"How'd you know?" she asked. Loree laughed, instead of getting angry with Andrea.

"Girl, it was all in yo' eyes. They talked before you did," Loree replied with a snicker. The jokes, the laughs, and the conversations with Loree seemed so long ago. Now Andrea was staring at Mrs Martinez's own pupils to see if they were lying. It looked genuine enough. As the warning bell rang, Mrs Martinez handed the letter back to Andrea.

"Thank you for the letter, Mrs. Martinez. I appreciate it," she said sincerely to the assistant principal before she walked back to her class.

Vanessa waited for Andrea to exit her Mentorship class when the bell rang. Since they didn't have any classes together on their last semester at Richmond Hill, Vanessa had always taken the time to walk outside of the classroom to wait for Andrea so they could walk through the school to discuss their day. Vanessa knew that once they got outside the school, Andrea's father would be waiting outside to pick her up because he would drive her straight to Forest Hills, Queens to drop her off to work at Johnson's. So when Andrea walked out of the classroom, Vanessa confronted her about the unexpected summons from the assistant principal.

"So what did Mrs. Martinez want?" she asked Andrea as they made their way to the front of the school.

"Nothing," Andrea replied. "It's not like I got in trouble or nothin' like that. It had something to do with college," she added.

She didn't feel like telling Vanessa that Mrs. Martinez offered her a sympathy gift in the form of a recommendation letter. She wanted to move on and build a future of her own someday instead of being a person that everyone pitied.

"Where Sean at?" Andrea asked, eager to change the subject.

"Girl, you know where he at. He be stayin' at that gym all day after school," Vanessa replied.

"He still goin' hard for that scholarship, huh?" Andrea asked. Vanessa nodded her head to confirm Andrea was correct in her assessment. "Can't say I blame him though. Everybody trying to get that free money to get up out of here," she added, and in truth she could sympathize with Sean.

Andrea loved her family and her friends and her support system but aside from those elements, her neighborhood had little else to offer in terms of opportunity. Most of what Queens offered was dead-end jobs and staying out in the hood, dealing drugs or hustling to make a living. After Loree's death, she remembered how hard it was to function as a family those first few weeks. Andrea's mother, Alisha, emotionally withdrew from the rest of her family members, unable to eat or sleep and put her own health at risk. Andrea would never forget the countless times she found her mother kneeling down next to what used to be Loree's bed with her face buried near the foot of the bed, tears soaking it. Andrea's father also grieved Loree's death but in the aftermath, he began to pursue Loree's killer. He had hired detectives and hounded police officers from all of New York to track down the alleged shooter. When the police apprehended David Anderson, who had been Loree's boyfriend at the time of her murder, Amos McAfee was convinced that David was the prime suspect in Loree's death. He wanted nothing less than the book thrown at him when his day in court came. But to his dismay, David had been exonerated in court when key witnesses took the stand and convinced the jury that David was innocent. To state that Amos was upset was an understatement. He felt the justice system had failed him and the NYPD was not vigilant in keeping the streets clear of gangsters, thugs, and drug-dealers.

The situation reached a point that Amos considered moving out of Richmond Hill to move his family away from what he perceived to be a crooked justice system, violent gangs, and more importantly unbearable grief. A father should never have to bury his daughter the way Amos buried Loree. Since the funeral and the court case, Amos rarely smiled. His previously jovial personality was replaced by a moody, surly one. It made him irrational, insensitive, and unpleasant to those who had once been his friends. Worse than his obstinance with others, Loree's murder made him fiercely overprotective of Andrea, who lived the next six years without enjoying the normal privileges that other kids her age took for granted. She couldn't have sleepovers and she wasn't allowed to be outside after nine o'clock at night. There was a set schedule in the McAfee household. Since Amos and Alisha worked day shifts in customer service and sales for different major companies, they were always home at the same time, so dinner was served promptly at six-thirty. Andrea had never been in jail or solitary confinement but she couldn't imagine either of those places being more restricted than her own home.

Happily, Andrea accepted a job opportunity to work at the new retail department store, Johnson's. Andrea saw the job it as an opportunity to escape from the prison that was her home, at least for a few hours. It took plenty of convincing and compromising with her parents to be able to work. Andrea knew here parents worried that Andrea could meet the same fate her sister. Andrea finally appealed to her father until he broke down and finally gave her permission to apply for the job. Even though Amos wanted to protect his youngest daughter, he also wanted to teach her responsibility and discipline. After Andrea had worked at Johnson's for a year she had to admit that despite her initial excitement to be out of the house, the job was beginning to get under her skin. The employers would hire staff who wouldn't do their job and Andrea would end up covering for them. This really angered her but she wouldn't say anything out loud. She kept quiet and performed her duties but secretly she wanted more out of life. Aside from her regular appointments with Dr. Ralwinski, every Friday, she only had her job and school and it was getting monotonous.

As they exited the school doors, Andrea waved goodbye to Vanessa who began walking the opposite direction to get home. When Andrea turned the curb, she saw her father, Amos, waiting for her in their small Honda Civic. She got into the car and greeted her father.

"Hey Daddy, what's up?" she asked. Amos, who wore a stoic glare on his face, changed his reaction almost immediately, although it was only for a brief second.

"Hey, baby how was school?" he greeted back with a smile. Andrea shrugged. "School was school. Nothing special happened today. How was work?" she asked.

"Work was good today," Amos replied.

"That's good," Andrea replied back. In her mind, this was not how a real conversation with her father should be but all she got was general courtesy and few words.

Her father's curt conversations became awkward to Andrea. She longed to have a real talk with her father so she could have a substantial relationship with him. Andrea just didn't have anything in common with her father since her sister's death. She loved him as much as ever but there would always be a part of her father that she would never be able to reach. He would pick her up from school as he always had and would drop her off to work at Johnson's Department Store. Andrea didn't have to clock in until four thirty, so she had plenty of time. She worked only part-time and was due to leave at nine o'clock that evening. She worked three days during the week and one Saturday or Sunday a week.

After one year of working, Andrea realized there were some employees there who barely tolerated her. One of those employees was Gloria Herrera, who was hired around the same time Andrea. Gloria also worked at the merchandising and floor support at Johnson's. Both girls were trained to work the cash register if the store ever got too busy. Despite the fact that Gloria was slightly older than Andrea by a couple of years, she was never diligent in accomplishing her task. It angered Andrea because she knew Gloria was slacking off on purpose to encumber Andrea with more work. Nevertheless, she was thankful to have a job because it kept her away from her home, where she would have to live in depression and awkwardness. Andrea's parents did attempt to maintain normality in their home but there was simply too big a void left by Loree's passing. Loree had a gift of easing any tension in their home and definitely between their parents; a gift that Andrea never possessed. It wasn't that they didn't try to gain a relationship with Andrea. It was all too soon and the time that could have been used to get closer to their second daughter was instead spent in grief and bereavement.

As they drove along the road, Amos stopped at a red light and while waiting, he saw a group of boys exiting a 1-Stop store, which was the local corner store. The boys walked out laughing and talking, dressed in T-shirts, fitted caps, du-rags, and jeans that sagged so low, a portion of their undergarments showed. The boys stopped walking just a few yards from the store and hung out, leaning against the wall of another establishment.

Andrea started to roll her eyes, because she knew what was coming. The image of those boys would be planted in Amos's mind to the point where he would begin criticizing and judging the individuals. Sure enough, Amos started talking.

"Damn, why can't these boys dress like they got some type of sense? Rolling their pants down, just standing there like everything's ok, when they know they gonna draw attention to themselves," he angrily remarked.

"Daddy, it's no big deal. They ain't doin' nothin' wrong," she said, wishing her father would be quiet. But Amos wouldn't quit.

"You don't think so but contrary to what people tell you, perception is reality. How these boys dress defines who they are. You dress like you're a hoodlum, then that's who you are," Amos said flatly.

"Daddy, you don't know that. It's not fair to judge someone like that, without knowing who they really are. Just chill, all right?" Andrea replied sharply.

"I know exactly who they are. Homeboys with no home training, that's who they are," Amos said.

Andrea couldn't think of anything else to say, because she felt like she was in an argument she couldn't win. Her father seemed to realize the fight had left his daughter, because the next words that he spoke were calm.

"Andrea, you have to start opening your eyes to the world around you. If you meet a boy, he can't be displaying this type of image. Is that a picture of a man who's going to take care of business at home or at work, if anyone ever hires them? I don't think so and I don't want you mingling with these types of boys," he said firmly.

Chapter Three

Amos arrived at Johnson's Department Store at four-thirty in the afternoon. Andrea scanned the parking lot. The lot was not filled to capacity, so she knew the store wasn't busy yet. She had worked there long enough to know the shopping rush wasn't until seven or eight o'clock. Adults would do their shopping during the daytime but as soon as dusk would settle, the store would be crowded with teenage kids, shopping for the most up-to-date fashions and popular clothing brands. Whether they were trying to look fresh for a date or a night at a club, the store was never short of customers at the time the streetlights illuminated. Some of these kids were from Richmond Hill High School but most of them came from other high schools such as Forest Hills High School, Jamaica High School, and Andrew Jackson High School. This influx of young shoppers most likely explained the young employees hired to work for Johnson's. Their jobs ranged from cashiers and sales, which was Andrea's current position, to clerks, warehouse workers, and cart workers. It wasn't the greatest gig in the world, only paying a dollar more than the minimum wage set for employment at the time but to Andrea, it was a paycheck. She had been working as diligently as possible to save most of her money because, despite the letter that she received, she knew college life wasn't cheap. Before she stepped out of her car, her father stopped her.

"Do you have your work badge today?" he asked, smiling slightly. Andrea rolled her eyes and laughed. Her father knew how forgetful Andrea could be at times and more often than not, she would leave her work badge at home. Luckily, today wasn't one of those days.

"Got it right here," she said, taking it out of her purse.

"Ok baby, have a good day. I'm coming to pick you up at nine-thirty sharp, ok?" Amos said as he pulled away from the open parking lot. Andrea waved goodbye as she entered into the store through the employee entrance. Johnson's had two floor levels. The boys and men's apparel along with other miscellaneous items were sold on the first floor. In the middle of the store was a two-way escalator, one which went to the second floor and one that descended to the first floor. All of the cash registers and check-out locations were on the first floor. Andrea walked over to the employee computer database to punch in for the day. She walked over to another room, which served as the breakroom and had the employee restrooms. There was a small locker room across from the restrooms. Andrea located her locker and turned the combination for her locker to open. She placed her purse inside her locker and closed the door, making sure the lock was secure. God, please don't let it be a busy day today she thought as she set out to perform her first duty of the day.

Two hours into her shift, Andrea was assigned to the men's department, hanging up new Nike apparel. She used the small stepladder from the janitorial closet and used it to hang all the medium and small sized sweatshirts and hoodies that she carried. The lower rack was being cleared to place t-shirts, athletic gear, and shorts with summer season arriving. As she worked on hanging the apparel, her co-worker, Gary Thompkins, came over.

"Yo Drea what's up?" he called up to her. "Better be careful up there, hanging that stuff cuz I don't wanna see you break your neck," he added jokingly.

Andrea laughed. "What's up, Gary. Nah, I'm straight. I ain't got too much more to go anyway," she said as she reached down toward the small cart that contained the rest of the sweaters.

"Here, lemme help you with that," he offered, handing one of the sweaters to Andrea.

"Thanks, Gary I appreciate that," she said. She didn't know why more guys couldn't be like Gary. Not only was he incredibly sweet and charming but he was very mature and responsible.

Andrea didn't know Gary very well, but she knew he couldn't be any older than twenty years of age. He attended Queensborough Community College as a full-time student aside from working at Johnson's. Tall, dark, and very handsome with a great smile that showed perfect teeth; Gary was the type of guy Andrea would be interested in. There was only one obstacle that prevented Andrea from pursuing any type of relationship with Gary; he had a girlfriend. Andrea knew about her because she had seen her visit him at work and sometimes while they had lunch breaks, she would stop by and join Gary for lunch. Not that his girlfriend wasn't pretty, but Andrea always felt Gary could do so much better. The one trait Andrea did not share with other girls was the fact that she wasn't clingy or needy. She always felt other girls needed to control their man in fear of losing him to another woman. Andrea thought it was just insecurity. She remembered when Gary introduced everyone to his girlfriend, whose name was Regina. However, when Gary introduced Regina to Andrea, it was clear that the two girls would not warm up to each other right away. Andrea had always kept a strictly business relationship with Gary, although she would joke around with him at times. Regina had clearly felt threatened by Andrea, and she must have warned Gary to stay away from her because in the last couple of months, Gary hadn't exchanged more than a few words with Andrea, and this was the first time Gary actually initiated a conversation.

"So what time do you get off?" she asked him as he passed her another sweatshirt.

"I get off in a couple minutes actually. So I don't appreciate the fact that you still got me working," Gary laughed.

"You offered to help me, remember? Don't go puttin' this on me now," Andrea replied laughing also.

"Oh, that's exactly what I'm bout to do. It's all your fault," Gary said laughing as he passed up more sweaters to Andrea.

Gary and another co-worker, Cindy Henderson, who worked up front at checkout were the only two that made working at Johnson's worthwhile. She felt that if they weren't there, she probably would have died of boredom. Regina was only one part of the problem Andrea faced at Johnson's; she wouldn't be the only problem Andrea would face at Johnson's. The other dilemma was walking in her direction as quickly as possible. With her hair braided so tight, it was a surprise that it didn't cut off the air supply to her scalp, Gloria Ramos made her way to the men's section. At first she acted as if Andrea wasn't there.

"Hey Gary, what's up? Front's getting real busy now. Are you still on the clock?" she asked him.

"Actually I'm just about to get off now," Gary answered her before heading back to the employee break room.

Gloria turned to Andrea and before the words even came out of Gloria's lips Andrea knew what was coming.

Not again. She knows I'm busy and she's still gonna call me up to checkout? She foul for that she thought.

"Andrea, leave that stuff there and come up front. They need extra cashier assistance," Gloria said.

Sighing deeply, Andrea stepped down from the ladder and headed to the front of the store. Gloria technically wasn't the manager but because she was floor support, she still had authority over the other workers. Andrea didn't like it but she knew it wasn't her decision to make.

The checkout rush lasted until just about the end of Andrea's shift. Andrea felt as if she had rung up more than two hundred customers. Cindy, who was standing at the register just across from Andrea, gave her a weary shake of the head.

"Whew, it's almost ova' thank God," Cindy said as she leaned over her register. She had the same shift as Andrea, who got off a little after nine o'clock.

"I know, right?" Andrea agreed. She looked around. The store was nearly empty and the janitors were beginning to clean the fitting rooms and sweep the floors.

At that moment, the radio speaker, which played songs from s specific station, belted out a soulful ballad, one that Andrea knew very well. Andrea couldn't explain it but she had a certain feeling that overwhelmed her whenever the song played. Before she could stop herself, Andrea was singing the song, eyes closed, her spirit enveloped around every single note that came from the radio. Even though there were still a few customers there and even though Cindy was watching, she didn't care. Andrea was lost in her own world. Cindy was indeed watching and she marveled at how well Andrea hit the high notes and how cutting and precise her voice was when she sang. Her soprano was piercing and she stopped only long enough to notice Cindy and another customer look at her.

"I'm sorry," Andrea said as she prepared to ring the customer up.

"Don't be sorry at all," the customer said. She was a kind, elderly lady. "I'll say, in all my sixty-seven years, I have never heard a voice quite like yours. You need to think about doing something with that one day." she said. As the old lady walked out the door with her purchases, Andrea saw Cindy shaking her head in agreement.

"She's right, you know. You should do something. Maybe audition for American Idol or something," she said.

Andrea smiled and she sensed herself blushing. She was no stranger to hearing positive praises and accolades about her voice, due to singing for church but Andrea wasn't sure that a singing career was the one for her.

"You really think so?" she asked.

"Of course you should audition that voice. Why not?" Cindy asked.

"I don't know," Andrea replied. "I never thought of singing as a career. What if I'm not good enough to make it anywhere? I mean, the subway stations are full of what ifs and could've beens. I just want to have a career more solidified," Andrea replied.

She struggled on deciding what she wanted to do after high school. Then after the tragedy, she considered working on a degree in psychology, after the way Dr. Ralwinski had worked so brilliantly with her. Dr. Ralwinski has supported Andrea in her goals and she also felt that Andrea would be a great psychologist one day. Her parents didn't quite share the same vision she had regarding her future. But it was okay with Andrea if they didn't agree with her. It was her life, not theirs.

"Nothing more solidified than a singing career, especially if you get signed to a label. Once you get that million dollar contract, you'll have enough to take care of yourself and your family," Cindy said. "And you can finally get outta hea," she added in low tones.

Andrea looked at the clock and saw it was nine-twenty seven. She had to clock out so she could leave. Her father would be arriving in a few minutes. She waved goodbye to Cindy and headed to the employee break room and locker room. As she was working on the lock combination to get her purse and her call phone out, Gloria walked into the locker room.

"Hey girl, getting ready to leave?" she asked.

No I'm only in this locker for my health. I'm planning on sleeping here tonight. What do you think? Andrea thought, rolling her eyes.

She did not want to engage in any small talk with Gloria. She noticed that Gloria addressed her as if they had been friends forever, when the truth was that Andrea couldn't stand to be in the same room with her.

"Yeah, my dad's coming to get me in a few minutes," she replied as plainly as possible. As she took out her belongings and prepared to leave, she heard Gloria call her name.

"Andrea, I heard you out there today, singing. You have a good voice and all, but wrong place wrong time. This ain't Soul Train. So please save it till you get home," Gloria said.

Andrea stopped in her tracks. Was this what Gloria came to tell her? "Sorry, Gloria I just know that song and I guess I got carried away. It won't happen again, okay?" Andrea replied as she began walking toward the exit.

"I'm just trying to help you. If Mrs. Snell caught you doing that, you could get written up. Consider it free advice," Gloria said as she turned toward her own locker.

Andrea nodded but at the same time, she wished Gloria never talked to her at all. She wishes she could sing like me. Her voice is probably so scratched up, it sounds like nails running through a chalkboard Andrea thought laughing silently to herself as she headed out into the cool night.

After Amos picked Andrea up from work, they arrived at the small duplex house where they lived. Alisha was already at home and Andrea picked up the scent of dinner. Her mouth immediately watered. She ate only a salad for lunch at work but it sure didn't beat the macaroni and cheese, collard greens, and chicken legs that her mother cooked.

"Hey honey, how was work today?" she asked Andrea.

"Work was good Mom, but that smells really good. Is it too late to grab me a plate?" Andrea asked.

"Not at all, please help yourself," Alisha answered, smiling.

"Thanks Mom. I ate lunch on my break but it didn't do me any justice. I'm starvin' like Marvin," Andrea said.

As she took her food, Andrea couldn't help but feel glad that her mother was in the kitchen cooking again. She remembered how difficult it was for her to even lift a spoon, much less a pot to resume cooking after Loree's passing. Since her mother had begun seeing Dr. Ralwinski regularly and communicating with the members at First Baptist Church of Elmont, ministered by Reverend Morgan Whitefield, Alisha slowly had started to pick up the fragments of her life and had resumed working and doing chores at home. Andrea remembered how long her mother had been out of touch with reality, she and her father had to rely on fast food or eat Chinese. Alisha also had trouble eating during that time and she dropped weight at an alarming rate. She had been hospitalized a few times due to her malnutrition and the doctor, along with her family, convinced her to keep moving through life because her friends needed her and her family needed her.

Alisha also sought advice from Pastor Whitefield and a particular series of pamphlets he had created from the married couples' ministry on keeping the family together despite tragedy. Alisha had been reading the pamphlets and adhering to the advice the pastor gave her. Amos, on the other hand, did not find the series particularly helpful or beneficial to him. He still attended the meetings and church services but only because his wife attended them. He had long since lost faith in any type of pastor, since an incident involving his former pastor from a different church became the subject of nasty rumors of unfaithfulness, infidelity, and secrets. Amos decided that he would still go to church but would not depend on its representatives for help of any kind. He would pray for help and if God did not feel it in His good graces to help him, then he would have to figure out another way.

As Andrea devoured her dinner, her father sat across the table from her. At first Andrea didn't notice because she was so busy eating. Then, as if she could tell someone's eyes were on her, she looked up and her father's eyes met her.

"What? Am I eating too fast?" Andrea asked, slightly embarrassed.

Amos laughed. "No, it's not that, although it wouldn't hurt to slow down a little bit," he chortled.

Andrea smiled sheepishly. "I guess I could slow down a little bit," she said. Pacing herself even more, Andrea still noticed her father gazing at her.

"Andrea, I just wanted to let you know that we are proud of you. You are working hard at school and you're maintaining at your job," Amos said. "I have to admit, I had my doubts at first about you taking on school and work but you have proven me wrong and you've taken care of business," he added.

Andrea smiled at her parents. This was the first time he had ever said that. He was actually proud of her. She hadn't heard either of her parents say it and to hear the actual words gave her a boost.

"Thanks Daddy and thanks Mom. I'm trying," she replied.

Amos placed her hand on Andrea's shoulder. "Keep up the good work," Amos said. After her late dinner, Andrea went to her room to start on homework. Walking into her room always held an eerie feeling. Andrea had always shared a room with Loree, so it was extremely strange, even to this day, to walk into the room and not see Loree lying on her bed or walking in after one of her party nights. Loree had posters of her favorite music pop and R&B artists hung up on the wall. Andrea's love of music was born and bred by her late sister. Although Loree couldn't sing as well, she still warbled with the artist on play on the radio. At one point Andrea was jealous of Loree and she wasn't shy about admitting it. Loree was beautiful, had light brown eyes, and a great figure.

The only edge that Andrea had over Loree was the voice. She always had the vocal talent and she had earlier memories when her Sunday school teacher would select her to choose the song of the day and when she sang it, she noticed the other kids had to strain their voices to be able to attempt to reach her range and it was just too difficult for them. After working on her homework, Andrea looked at the clock it a little after midnight. She took a shower and slipped on her pajamas. As was her custom, she knelt down on her knees and she prayed.

"Dear Lord, thank you for this day that you've made. Thank you for my parents that you've blessed me with, who would go through anything for me. I pray that tomorrow's a better day and that I make that day much better than today. I pray that you forgive my sins and please help me stay focused on my goals. Please tell Loree up there that I said hey and I'm still thinking about her each and every day. Amen," she concluded before turning her lights off and turning in for the night.

That very night, Andrea had an odd dream. This time she wasn't in a room with just a gold knob like in the previous vision. She stood on what looked like a stage, with a black curtain behind her. The seats, which would normally be filled with people, were empty. Andrea did not see a single soul out in the audience. A single microphone stand was set in the middle. Andrea found herself wondering what she was doing there when she heard a voice coming from the right side of the audience. At first she couldn't make out the sound of the voice but then her stomach dropped as she recognized the voice.

"This ain't Soul Train! This ain't Soul Train! Go sit down some-where!" Gloria's voice blared out across the theater, echoing and with each repetition of the statement, the screeching got louder and her ears started to ache as the microphone produced feedback.

Looking closer at the microphone, Andrea realized that Gloria's voice was coming from the microphone. Then, inexplicably, the microphone started to move on its own. It leaped off the stand and started to inch toward Andrea. "You ain't nothin'!" it said.

Andrea couldn't believe what she saw. As she continued to back away from the moving microphone, a figure emerged from the other side of the stage. Drawing the curtain back, Andrea saw who it was right away. There was no heavenly glow or white flowing robes on her but Andrea saw Loree as she had been in life. Loree calmly walked over to the microphone and without questioning why it was moving on its own or why it was talking, she unplugged the microphone from the back, cutting off the power. Then, almost carelessly, Loree threw the microphone over her shoulder and almost ghostlike, turned toward Andrea. Andrea was frightened but at the same time, she felt a sense of warmth.

"Don't worry, Drea. I'm here. It's me. Gimme some love, girl," Loree said, smiling. Andrea walked over to Loree and was surprised that she could hug Loree. She felt her warm embrace as her arms wrapped around her sister. Tears flowed from Andrea's eyes.

"I miss you so much," she said.

Loree smiled. In appearance, they looked the same age but Loree still stroked Andrea's hair like she used to when Andrea was little. "I miss you too, baby. You're gonna do good but don't lose yourself," she said. Andrea looked at Loree's eyes, puzzled. What did she mean "Don't lose yourself?"

Chapter Four

"*What you mean by that, ReRe?* What you mean 'Don't lose myself?'" Andrea asked but no sooner had she tried to ask the plethora of questions on her subconscious mind, the dream sequence began to shift. Loree began to dematerialize as Andrea's vision of the stage and seats blurred.

"Wait, Loree, don't go yet, please!" Andrea beseeched Loree as her sister became more transparent as time went by until she was no longer there. "Come back Loree, please!" Andrea pleaded but to no avail as she was left as empty and alone as she had been for the last six years.

Suddenly her cell phone alarm blared, waking her from the wonderful dream. Sitting up in bed, she yawned and headed over to the dresser drawers and shelves to look through her clothing, until she found a picture of Loree smiling at some forgotten joke. Andrea stared at the photo, almost laserlike, until her eyes welled up with tears. Six years couldn't take the pain away or bring her back. Every day her sister was gone she was rendered incapable of speaking and had created an alternate universe in certain moments; especially when the late-night encounters with Loree became more frequent.

"What were you tryin' to tell me, sis?" she whispered to the photo. If anyone had walked in her room, they would've thought Andrea had lost her mind. Andrea knew she had to come to grips with the fact that she couldn't allow the visions to control her life. Who knew? It might not have been Loree speaking to her. She remembered being in church and Pastor Whitefield taught a sermon about how the devil could disguise himself as an angel of light to deceive others. How did she know the devil wasn't just playing with her mind?

'I'm over here talking to a picture; an inanimate object. Satan ain't playin' with my mind, I'm playing with my own mind. Maybe I'm going crazy for real,' she thought as she got up from her bed and walked over to the bathroom.

After washing her face and brushing her teeth, she looked into the bathroom mirror and for a fleeting second, she saw Loree again; her brown eyes donned her favorite eye shadow and were staring intently at her. Blinking again, she saw only her own reflection staring back at her. Heading back to her room, she mentally prepared for school before she remembered that it was Saturday. No school today. However she still had to go to work that afternoon and money never fell on anybody's lap if they stood still and did nothing. She decided to make herself productive by stripping her bed and bagged her clothes to take them to the laundromat which was located only three blocks from her home. As soon as she finished, she went home and looked through her school bag for any school assignments that she had to complete. After ten minutes, her cell phone rang. Looking at the caller ID on her phone, Andrea recognized the caller.

"Hey Vanessa, what's up girl?" she greeted her friend.

"I'm good, girl. What's up with you? Why you sound so tired?" Vanessa asked. Andrea didn't want to go into the details of the dream to Vanessa.

"I just didn't get a lot of sleep last night. I'm just tryin' to wait until I have to go to work," she replied.

Andrea couldn't see Vanessa on the other side of the receiver, but she was ready to bet that Vanessa was shaking her head. She didn't know why that gesture bothered her. She knew that Vanessa believed it was sympathy for Andrea's pain, which she couldn't possibly because she has never lost anyone close to her. Life was difficult for everybody, and Andrea was no exception.

"So my dad's gonna be at work a lil' longer than usual. Do you mind getting your mom's lovely Honda to come pick me up and drive me to work?" Andrea asked.

She heard a sound on the other end of the phone that sounded like Vanessa sucking in her teeth. "I don't know if my Mama's lovely Honda got any gas in it or not," she replied in the same tone of sarcasm that Andrea used to ask her the favor. "Besides, I didn't know you worked on Saturdays too," she added.

"I don't work on too many Saturdays, but they got me on schedule today. It's all good, cuz I ain't got nothin' to do today anyway," Andrea answered.

She didn't hear Vanessa respond right away, so she assumed Vanessa was thinking it over. "I can pay the gas money, girl. It ain't a big deal. Come on, please?" Andrea asked.

She didn't mind taking the public transportation system to work but if she could avoid paying for bus fare or paying to take the subway, why not take advantage? Finally Vanessa agreed to give Andrea a ride to work.

"But you betta' not have me waitin' on you outside yo' house for 3 hours, you feel me?" Vanessa asked, laughing.

"I won't do you like that 'Nessa, believe me I'm good for it," Andrea replied laughing as well.

"Mmhmm. That's what you said last time. I'm serious Drea". You my girl and all but trust, I will start charging cab fare," Vanessa said.

"Shut up 'Nessa. Ain't nobody tryin' to pay you cab fare. You betta go sit down somewhere with that," Andrea laughed.

She said goodbye to Vanessa before hanging up and falling back down on her bed. She was not looking forward to going to work because she knew that because it was Saturday, the store would be busier than usual. She just hoped the time went by quickly so she could earn that extra money. Looking through her purse, she found the pink headphones that she had been trying to find. Searching on her phone's browser, she continued looking until she found the exact artist she wanted to hear. She scrolled down the playlist of the hottest contemporary artists and her eyes fell on a familiar artist. She clicked on one of the songs from the artist and before long she had De'Von Franklin on repeat. After listening to a couple bars of one of his songs, she couldn't help but marvel at his rhyming skills, wordplay, and the street element that he brought to the music. It also didn't hurt that he looked like a cross between Boris Kodjoe and Common, yet he didn't look like he was a day over twenty-three years of age. The boy was just a chick magnet and it was no wonder Vanessa liked him. As she listened to De'Von, she soon learned who he was through his songs.

The stretch limo that had been previously parked on the side street of Madison Avenue in Manhattan pulled out of the parking lot. The chauffeur took a small handkerchief out of his side pocket to wipe the perspiration from his face. He had to stand outside in the New York heat for what amounted to a little over an hour. His employer and one of his friends were inside one of the shoe outlets, searching for a specific brand of sneakers. After looking unsuccessfully for the sneakers, De'Von Franklin and his friend and confidante Sam "Slam" Watkins walked out the store in deep dudgeon. Two bodyguards walked out before De'Von and Slam made it to the limo. A group of fans, consisting mostly of young teenage girls, were yelling at the top of their lungs when De'Von emerged from the store. The fans were not at a frenzy, but they were begging De'Von to sign their posters and trying to get pictures taken with him. Not too long after that, the two men and the bodyguards managed to make it to the limo just in time. As the limo drove through the busy streets, De'Von looked back through the rear window and saw some fans trying to get a picture of the limo, a few were attempting to catch up with it, but eventually fell back.

"Told you they ain't got the Flights ova there. Besides if you keep droppin' by these stores, these hoes gonna get you one day," Slam said, smiling.

De'Von smiled back. He wore dark designer shades, not only to block out the rays from sunlight, but to exude his status. He had every right to do so. Being a boy who grew up in the Bronx and didn't have much coming up, the one gift he had was rapping. His free-styling ability caught the ear of one of the executives of Metro Records, which was a label still in development and production. They already signed a few female R&B singers and they needed a male rapper to compliment the latest sound in the music industry. From that moment forward, De'Von was signed and he got his first album completed. Few of the executives at Metro believed the album would make any money for the studio. Within months, De'Von made all the doubters eat their words by being nominated for best new artist of that year. Unfortunately he did not win the award but with an album that hit gold-record status, his reputation increased and his record sales grew. De'Von was a man in high demand and he enjoyed every minute of his newfound fame. Now he was looking for sneakers to wear and none of the stores carried the ones he sought.

"Well, where else can I find 'em, bro?" he asked Slam. Slam was already on the job, checking his phone for any possibilities of the sneakers being available online. Looking over Slam's shoulder as he perused his phone, De'Von saw that Slam had a very unique and explicit wallpaper background on his phone that displayed a beautiful and mostly naked black model. Aside from a small cloth or blanket covering her lower area, the model was completely naked. Looking at his friend, De'Von knew Slam had a serious model fetish.

"So I see you got your model of the week," De'Von said.

"Oh you already know!" Slam confirmed. "Her name's Veronica. She likes long walks at the beach, she's down to earth, loves to go out to lounges and strip clubs, and she a closet freak. She says she a pro between the sheets. We bout to find out," he added confidently.

De'Von shook his head. The picture looked clean and professional, as if it had been photographed recently. It just looked too good to be true.

"Man, you don't even know that chick. You probably just took a snapshot of page twenty-five off King Magazine," De'Von said laughing.

Slam was more than a friend to De'Von, he was a roadie and a hype man. Everywhere De'Von performed, Slam would be everywhere on the inside, talking to girls at the concert, even setting De'Von and himself up on some nights with girls. In Slam's mind, there was no such thing as a groupie. There were women who just wanted to enjoy the company of successful men, and Slam and De'Von were more than eager to oblige in those instances.

"Anyway, you see where else we can get the Flights at?" he asked.

Slam continued searching for outlets where the ideal sneakers could be found. "Yo, there's this spot ova at Forest Hills. Johnson's is the name. Check it out," he said as he showed De'Von the retail store and confirmed that they had the Flights that he had been seeking.

"Damn, all the way in Forest Hills though? I ain't bout to drive all the way to Queens, man," De'Von replied.

"Come on, man. You been waiting to get these Flights for four weeks. Here's your chance. Don't blow it," Slam said.

De'Von thought about it for a moment. As much as he wanted the sneakers, was it worth driving all the way to Queens? "Yo, I just don't wanna have to mess wit' all them hood rats that be staying out there," he said.

Slam smiled a little because he knew what type of girls De'Von liked. "They ain't all hood rats, bro. They got fine-ass women in Forest Hills too man," he said.

"You don't know the type of women I be into," De'Von thought as they entered the freeway. He sincerely hoped the sneakers were there and hoped he wasn't wasting his time driving to Queens.

As Vanessa pulled up to Johnson's parking lot, Andrea felt her heart drop at the sight of the throng of teenagers flocking to the entrance of the store.

"Oh Lord, you can't be serious," Andrea sighed apprehensively as Vanessa pulled up to the parking lot.

The peak rush normally didn't begin until five or six o'clock, yet these kids were still crowded as if some big-name rapper or celebrity was expected to arrive with an entourage that was ten guys deep. Andrea shook the absurd idea away from her mind. It wasn't as if Johnson's never had a music star or actor visit before and she was sure there were a couple stars who shopped there. But there were better chances of pigs flying over Shea Stadium than a mainstream artist visiting Johnson's. Andrea sighed again as she took out her badge and prepared to go to the employee entrance.

"Ok, Ma. Don't work too hard," Vanessa laughed as she dropped off Andrea and made a U-turn.

"Trust me, I won't even stress this," Andrea replied as she waved goodbye to her friend and entered the employee door to prepare to go to work.

Placing her purse in her locker, another familiar song played on the radio. But this time, Andrea didn't break out into song. She listened to the song and sat transfixed, as though she would never move again, never feel joy again, never smile again. It was a song about guardian angels. A beautiful song sung by one of her favorite female gospel groups, called Virtue. She loved the song so much because it was serene; it was comforting and soothing. It also happened to be the song that was playing on her radio six years ago when her mother received the news that would send the family into a tailspin. Loree was fighting for her life in Queens Hospital Center. Although they arrived as soon as they heard the tragic news, her family always held out hope that she would pull through and for a while, Andrea held out the same hope for her sister. But as the hours passed, Andrea had a feeling that Loree was already gone. The only thought that ran through Andrea's mind was the song "Angels Watching over Me". That was all she could think about for days. Loree was not on Earth physically, but she was an angel. She was with all the heavenly ethereal beings, and she was watching over Andrea. The recurring dreams that Andrea had about Loree only confirmed what she felt.

She recalled a time when a local neighborhood girl named Tatiana had given her a hard time whenever she would play outside with her other friends. Andrea had only been eight years old at the time. Tatiana was loud, brash, and whenever she didn't get her way, she became confrontational. One day, the girls on the block had been jumping rope and Andrea wanted to join in on the action. The ability to jump rope as a child was an acquired art combining talent, footwork, coordination, and timing. Andrea was very good at it and whenever the girls had a double-dutch rope session going, Andrea would jump in, on time and avoid the rope as it circled in a rhythmic motion. She kept the pace up fairly well for about five to seven minutes. Suddenly the rope stopped and tied up Andrea's feet, almost causing her to fall. At first she thought one of the girls turning the rope lost rhythm by accident, but when she turned back she saw Tatiana standing there, looking satisfied.

"Awww did I mess up widdle Andrea's jump roping? I'm sowwy," Tatiana said disdainfully.

Andrea was only thankful she had been able to stop herself, so her feet didn't get entangled in the rope. She stared at Tatiana angrily.

"What's your problem?" she asked. Tatiana, who was ten years old at the time and taller than Andrea was and towered over her.

"What's your problem?" Tatiana mocked Andrea's words as she stepped up to Andrea. "What you gonna do about it?" she added threateningly.

Andrea did not back down but she felt her fear rising. Tatiana was the definition of tomboy in the neighborhood, and nobody messed with her. She could make Andrea regret that she ever spoke back to her. But before anyone else spoke, another voice shouted across the street.

"Hey! You messing wit' my lil sista?" Loree and a couple of her friends were on their way back from a barbecue.

Carrying a rib and corn plate, Loree turned the corner just in time to see Tatiana hovering over Andrea. Tatiana stood exactly where she was, not moving an inch.

"It's none of your business," Tatiana replied harshly. Loree had been taken aback by the comment.

"Hold this for me," she asked one of her friends as she handed her the plate and walked over to the girls. Loree stood a couple of inches over Tatiana. "Little girl, you best not try me today cuz I guarantee you I will make it my business. If you eva' step to my sister again, I will snatch yo' pigtails from yo' head, you hear me?" she said.

Tatiana's eyes flashed with fear but only for a second. She stared Loree straight in the eye and took one look at Andrea before walking away. Tatiana never messed with Andrea again and before long she moved out of the neighborhood. Andrea had never forgotten that moment and there had been so many more times when Loree had stood up for her. More than ten years later, Loree was still watching over her, if only in dreams. Andrea only wished she could decipher what Loree had meant when she said, "Don't lose yourself."

"Andrea! Andrea! Earth to Andrea! Girl, what planet are you on, right now?" Gloria asked, sitting just inches away from Andrea. She was totally lost in her thoughts, and she never heard Gloria call her name.

"Sorry, I just got a lot on my mind right now," she replied.

"I feel you, but you need to check that, cuz we mad busy, in case you ain't noticed," Gloria said smartly, before she opened the locker room door to step out. Rolling her eyes, Andrea put her badge on and walked to the back of the store to search for new merchandise to display on the shelves.

While Andrea worked at sorting out merchandise, the limo carrying De'Von and Slam parked outside the store. The throng of kids gathered around curiously, wondering who was in the limo. Their curiosity turned into shouts of surprise and realization when they saw one of their favorite artists exit the limo, surrounded by the three bodyguards who flanked him. The girls were yelling, and the guys were throwing up their hands in exultation, welcoming the famous artist to Forest Hills. De'Von and Slam smiled. They made the choice to not get caught up in the excitement of the moment so they would be distracted from their mission. De'Von would have gladly remained outside to sign autographs, but he felt it would be counterproductive to what he wanted to accomplish. He entered the store and with the crowd still following him, he walked up to Cindy who was at her register. Cindy, who was reading a magazine, barely looked up before she recognized who was standing opposite her.

"Oh my gosh, you're...you're De'Von Franklin," she stammered.

"That I am, baby. Check this out, I'm looking for the Flights. They said that ya was the only one that had 'em hea," De'Von said, in his smooth, silky voice.

Cindy looked at De'Von, still transfixed by his aura and his presence, surrounded by his bodyguards. "Oh the Flights? Yeah, we should still have some pairs in our shoe section in the back," she replied. "If you want, I can walk ova there and see if we got more," she added.

"Nah I'm good. I'll find 'em. Thanks," he said, opening his wallet and giving Cindy a hundred-dollar bill.

At first, Cindy was going to refuse the money. Technically, the employees weren't allowed to receive tips, but De'Von and his entourage were already making their way to the back of the store before Cindy thought it through. She silently pocketed the money, secretly planning to keep it as a memento instead of spending it. Meanwhile De'Von reached the back of the store. To avoid the swarm of kids from pushing through the small aisles, De'Von ordered his bodyguards to create a barrier to prevent anyone else from entering the shoe section until he found the athletic footwear he sought. After searching for a couple of minutes without any success, Slam turned to De'Von, shaking his head.

"Yo, I don't think they got them shits here, dog. Let's bounce," he said.

"Damn!" De'Von said in frustration. He was prepared to take Slam's word and leave the store before word spread throughout the borough that he was in the store and cause Johnson's to be over capacity. Just when he was about to make this decision, a store associate walked out from one of the side fitting rooms. She had been in the back cleaning the fitting rooms and clearing off the clothes rack and was completely unaware that she was in the presence of a rising music star.

She is fine. Girl's got legs fo' days, De'Von thought as he approached her.

Sensing someone behind her as she was putting a pair of Stacy Adam shoes back on the shelf, Andrea turned around. Standing before her was a guy standing over six feet tall, wearing Ray-Ban sunglasses, a fitted NY

Yankees cap, and three gold chains across his neck with a couple of gold rings. She only saw that face once before and it was on a cover of a CD case.

"Excuse me miss, I was looking for a pair of Flights. You got any more?" he asked. A million thoughts were running through Andrea's head at one time.

Oh my goodness, it's De'Von Franklin. I can't believe it's him but it's really him. Ok Drea, calm down. Don't let him see you nervous or sweating. You gotta play it cool. Act like you not even interested in him. Besides, he human just like everyone else. Once she had given herself a little pep talk, Andrea was sure she didn't appear to be star-struck. To her surprise, she found that she was able to answer De'Von's question without fainting. "Yeah, we do have more. You didn't see 'em at the rack?" Andrea asked.

"Nah, I couldn't find 'em there," he replied. Andrea looked at the sneaker shelf and sure enough, she couldn't locate the Flights either.

"One of the other employees must have forgotten to stack them the other night. I'm sorry, I'm sure we got some in the back room here. What's your size?" she asked.

De'Von was taken aback by how confidently this girl was answering him. She didn't seem impressed by his status or his money. As a matter of fact, she sounded as if he was bothering her. Maybe he needed to break the ice with a joke.

"Too big to handle," he replied, grabbing his crotch area abruptly while his friend laughed.

Andrea laughed also. The crude joke was off-hand but it was funny.

"Come on, for real now, what's yo' size?" she asked again.

"Nah, I'm a twelve though. You got any twelves?" De'Von asked smiling at Andrea, showing off his pearly white teeth. Now Andrea was in a state of near-meltdown mode. Somehow she still managed to play it off.

"Yeah we should have some size twelves. Lemme take a look," she said. As soon as Andrea left to go to the back merchandising area, De'Von turned to Slam.

"Yo, you see shorty right there? She can get it," he said. Slam didn't see Andrea the same way his friend did.

"Yeah whateva' man. She's aight, but I'm tryin' to get these shoes so I can roll up outta hea." Slam said.

"What's wrong wit' you, dude?" De'Von asked indignantly. "I'm sayin' she look fine tho. I might have to swing that," he added. Meanwhile in the merchandise area, Andrea searched until she found the Flights in size twelve, as she came out with the gear.

"I forgot to ask what color you wanted but I saw black with orange streaks. That's the only one we got in size twelve right now," Andrea said.

De'Von looked at the sneakers. "Hell yeah, these look fly. That's exactly what I'm lookin' for," he confirmed.

"Alright cool. If you give me a second, I can ring you up over here," Andrea offered as De'Von tried on the sneakers. They were a good fit. Slam was only too happy to pay for the purchase and leave.

With the mass of kids still following them, Andrea walked over to the register and rang De'Von up and as he paid for his sneakers, he said slyly, "By the way, I didn't get your name, baby."

Andrea laughed. "Don't worry about it. By the time you leave here, you ain't gonna remember it anyway," she replied back, just as slyly.

As De'Von and his entourage walked out, Cindy walked over to Andrea. "Girl, how were you able to hold yoself together? Don't you know who that was?" she asked.

Andrea shrugged. "Another satisfied customer?" she replied as they both laughed.

"Girl how come you ain't call me??!! You know I love me some De'Von Franklin!" Vanessa shrieked over the phone later that evening when Andrea finished work.

Andrea made sure she didn't waste any time calling Vanessa to tell her about the unexpected celebrity visit.

"Please girl, I was at work. At the end of the day, De'Von ain't payin' my bills or upgradin' my life," Andrea replied.

"Whateva girl. Go 'head and be a hater all your life," Vanessa said.

Andrea scoffed. "Ain't nobody hatin' on him. I'm just not star-struck like these other lil chickenheads out there," she replied.

"So now I'm a chickenhead, is that what you tryin to say?" Vanessa asked in a challenging voice.

"Girl please, ain't nobody callin' you no chickenhead. You shoulda seen it. There was mad people that was all up in his grill tryin to feel up on him, just to get an autograph. Chicks were damn near cryin' they eyes out. I thought it was funny," Andrea said, laughing.

She could hear Vanessa make a sound of sarcasm that Andrea heard through the receiver.

"Well what you expect? That boy got a net worth of seven million. I'm surprised waterfalls ain't fell out yo' eyes. He worth more than we'll eva' see in three lifetimes," she replied.

Andrea laughed. She couldn't believe what she was hearing. Vanessa was not normally the superficial type, yet here she was, swooning over a complete stranger who she'd probably never meet.

"I feel you girl, but he still human. He still bleeds when he gets cut. He still coughs when he gets sick," she said.

"Mmmm, girl don't you worry about him gettin' sick. I'm all the antidote my baby needs," Vanessa said.

Andrea held the phone a few feet away from her ear, staring at it as if it was a repulsive slug. *That's it. I'm convinced my girl is sick. She need help,* she thought.

"But fo' real though, you know you and I go way back right. You can keep it a hundred wit' me. What was your first impression of him when you saw him?" Vanessa asked.

Andrea's mind flashed back only a couple of hours ago, when she was face to face with hip hop/R&B's newest artist. She couldn't deny that there was a certain genuine personality about De'Von. He was not one of those celebrities that acted brand new or stuck their noses in the air just because they made a bit more money than everybody else. There was warmth about his smile, his humor and his laid-back personality and she might have been of a fool for thinking it but she also believed he was trying to play games with her. Maybe he was just joking around and that was the way he spoke to all his female admirers but maybe, just maybe, he was genuinely interested in her.

"I thought he was cute. Typical homeboy attitude. He didn't brag about the ducats he was makin'. He had a friend with him too, girl, so you know he was tryin' hard to save face," she replied.

"Girl you know how they all gotta have they wing-man wit' em. And they say we travel in packs," Vanessa retorted.

"I know, right," Andrea agreed, laughing. There was silence between the two girls for a moment. Then Vanessa asked the question that had been running through Andrea's head for most of the afternoon.

"If you had a chance to go out wit' him though, would you?" she asked.

"Yeah I would. Only problem is that he would have to get past my daddy. To that, I would tell him good luck, cuz you know how my dad is about these guys. One look at De'Von and he would flip," Andrea replied.

She didn't hear Vanessa say anything that time because she knew Andrea was right. "Hmmm, so that means my path to De'Von is clear and I won't have anyone standing in my way," she told Andrea, jokingly.

"Girl please. You'll find a way to screw that up, anyway," Andrea said. "Anyway I gotta go to bed. I got church with fam in the morning. I'll talk to you later," she said before she hung up and prepared for bed. This time, Loree did not appear to Andrea in her dreams.

As the McAfee family made their way to First Baptist of Elmont, they could already see the church members filing inside. They had arrived just in time for the morning worship to begin. As the family parked, Andrea was silently wishing that her family could enter the church before the pastor noticed them. She looked at the church entrance. Normally Pastor Whitefield would stand at the front entrance of the door, greeting people as they entered. Andrea loved her pastor, but she didn't know how many times she could bear Pastor Whitefield asking her to sing a solo after he had preached. It wasn't that she didn't like singing but at this point, it had Andrea wondering if the pastor was using her whenever those thoughts ran through her mind. As the family approached the empty doorway, she thought she was in the clear until she heard a loud booming voice from the other end of the entrance hall.

"Brother McAfee and Sister McAfee, how you all doing this fine morning?" the pastor greeted, walking over to shake hands with them.

Pastor Whitefield was a short, yet stout man with his hair receding and showing streaks of gray. He was dressed in a black and blue striped suit and a black tie, which he normally covered with choir robes before he preached. In appearance, Pastor Whitefield was a sharp contrast to Andrea's former pastor from another church. Pastor Hillman was six foot four and was built like a pro football player.

"We're doing good today, pastor. How's Vivian doing?" Amos asked as he shook the pastor's hand.

"She's coming along just fine, brotha. She's taking her treatments one day at a time," Pastor Whitefield replied.

Vivian Whitefield, the pastor's wife, was fighting breast cancer and although she had been in remission the cancer returned to her body more aggressively. Since the return of the cancer, she had been taking chemotherapy for the last couple of months. Andrea admired her pastor's courage to still stand up and preach and spread the Gospel, despite his wife fighting for her life. In a way she found herself fighting to stay positive despite the negative thoughts and discouragement that surrounded her on a daily basis.

Turning to Andrea, he asked "So sista Andrea, would it be too much trouble if I asked you to sing a solo today after the sermon?"

It was exactly what Andrea feared. She hadn't prepared a song for the church. Normally she would be prepared with a bevy of gospel songs to choose from, but at the moment, she didn't have any ideas.

"Pastor, I don't know what I'm gonna sing, though..." she stammered but Pastor Whitehead stopped her.

"Hey, don't worry about it, sister. Just sing what God puts in your heart. When it comes to the Lord, the best plans are executed without our immediate preparation. You have to trust Him in all things," Pastor Whitefield comforted.

As they entered the church, the choir began singing and Andrea still found herself unsure what she was going to sing. As the service continued and Pastor Whitefield approached the podium to preach his sermon, she still found herself undecided. Finally, Pastor Whitefield called her name and Andrea approached the stage. A thousand eyes stared at her, anticipating her next move. Beads of perspiration started to form on Andrea's head. She closed her eyes and attempted to remember Pastor Whitefield's words:

"Just sing what God puts in your heart."

Then, as if God gave her the very song sheet, she started to sing "His Eye is On the Sparrow." When she finished the song, she opened her eyes. The church hardly had a dry eye in the building. Silence ensued at first; then the applause and the roar of approval followed.

Chapter Five

As soon as the pastor finished his sermon and served the final prayer to end the service, there remained a buzz around the congregation of the church. The joy was not due to the sermon that was just preached but the spectacular solo performance that headlined the Word of the day. Even Pastor Whitefield couldn't deny that Andrea stole the show, and he was not the least bit jealous. Andrea was even surprised to hear the pastor laughing and bragging to the members of the deacon board.

"I knew she could bring this house down. She came up to me, acting like she was nervous, but I knew better. God works in mysterious ways, but it ain't no mystery that the girl can SANG!" he exclaimed to those around him as they laughed and cheered with him.

Andrea herself had a bit of difficulty moving around because she couldn't escape the throng of church members that came to shake her hand and greet her, compliment her on having "the voice of a generation," as one man put it. Andrea humbly accepted her kudos and out of kindness, shook everyone's hand who wanted to greet her, but she wished it would stop. She really didn't want to draw too much attention to herself, and she made a mental note to ask the pastor not to put her in that last minute situation again. As her mother and father drove her home and all the church members having gone their separate ways, the McAfee family drove home through awkward silence. Finally it was Alisha that broke the silence.

"Andrea, you did such a marvelous job today," she complimented.

"It was no big deal, Mama. Come on, you've heard me do solos before," she replied.

"I know but there was something about your performance today, honey. It's not like anything I've heard from you before," Alisha continued. "It was like you felt something in you, compelling you to go on and reach the highest level of splendor. It was as if someone was driving you," she added.

Andrea looked at her mother's reflection through the front windshield mirror. She was silently pleading with her mother not to go that route, because she had a sinking feeling she knew where the conversation would end up. Unfortunately, Alisha confirmed her suspicions.

"You know, Loree would be very proud of you if she was here," she said.

"Well she's not here though, Mama. So can you please stop going there?" Andrea replied with an uncharacteristically rough edge to her tone. Although her father was driving, he stared through the mirror back at Andrea. Alisha stared at her daughter as well. Andrea finally realized that she may have overreacted. "I'm sorry, Mama. It's just that I hear about Loree almost every day. I just wish I could go through one day without hearing her name. I miss her as much as anyone does but I'm not trying to hang Loree's name over every little thing I do. I...I'm sorry for yelling at you the way I did but I just got too much in my mind right now," she apologized.

As their car parked in from of the apartment building, Andrea got out of the car and walked up to the door, not bothering to address her mother or her father about the argument they had in the car. A few hours later, Andrea was on the phone with Vanessa.

"So your solo really was all that?" Vanessa replied when Andrea told her about the performance at the church.

"It was ok. I'm not saying it was off the chain or nothin' like that. But Nessa, they were literally clapping and standing up while clapping. I was getting more love than I can remember, girl." Andrea said.

She thought she heard what sounded like the sucking of teeth on the other line. "Girl, you coulda told me that you was about to sing a solo today. I coulda brought my camcorder and taped it to send to American Idol or something," Vanessa retorted.

"Really Nessa, so you would've exploited me like that without askin' me if it's cool or not?" Andrea replied.

"Of course I would've asked but even if you said no, I would've talked your ear off into letting me doin' it anyway. The world needs to hear you, girl. You are way too talented to act like you can't sing, come on now," Vanessa said.

Andrea thought about what her best friend said. To her, singing was an escape from the reality of her hard-knock life. Her parents had decent jobs, but they were still living paycheck to paycheck. Singing couldn't guarantee her a luxurious life. There were plenty of potential singers who gave up their futures, their lives, their homes, and bet on a future as an artist, only to be the ones knocked down by the cruel reality of life. Singing was not going to guarantee the bills being paid and it wouldn't keep the city from shutting off their electricity or water if they weren't. Singing was not substantive, and Andrea knew she had to lean on her study in college and her major.

"There are talented people everywhere, Nessa. What makes you think I'm gonna get a chance in this city?" she asked.

As Andrea saw it from personal experience, the odds were never in her favor, at least not in this lifetime. If she could make a dollar off every note that she sang, she would sing until she passed out, as long as she landed on a huge pile of cash.

"Never say never, girl. Think about all the girls who were discovered here. Lisa Velez, Mary J. Blige, Jennifer Lopez, I mean if it happened for them, maybe it could happen for you," Vanessa reasoned.

Good ole Nessa, always tryin to stay positive in a negative world, Andrea thought. "Well, when hell freezes over and pigs start flyin', maybe I'll take your word at face value," Andrea said, laughing.

She heard laughter on the other end. "Girl, you a hot mess. Lemme get off this line before I get caught up playin' with you," Vanessa laughed before she hung up. Shaking her head, Andrea hung up her phone before laying down on her bed.

A deep bass instrumental played a rhythmic beat that was heard throughout the hallways of Metro Records. Sounds eminated from one of the recording sound booths where Metro artists recorded. Producers checked levels and managed the quality of music that was developed from the booth. Eight people were in the booth. Some were producers and sound technicians and the rest of the audience consisted of other artists who were watching De'Von working on one of his songs from his upcoming album. Hypnotized by the beat, the lyrics, and the sophistication of the treble and metronome beats that accompanied the song, the audience bobbed their heads as the beat rang out. Slam was smiling as he watched his friend work behind the booth.

Pretenders hatin' cuz they know I got tha' juice/ I get loose, stay slayin' fools, breakin' all da rules/Niggaz fleein' cuz they see me risin' high/They lookin fo' dat ecstasy, but I hit em with the sly/Let 'em try cuz I got that endless supply/ Won't stop da hustle till the hustle gotta die.

Slam was seen bobbing his head to the rhythm as the part came where the hook, or break had to fill in the score. Miesha Hammon, another recording artist for Metro, was the one chosen to provide the hook for the song. Unfortunately, her vocals could not match what the producers and De'Von wanted in the song, and De'Von showed his frustration during the recording.

"Hold up, hold up, cut this shit man. What was that?" he asked, looking at Miesha.

"What was what? What's the problem?" Miesha asked, her face showing signs of confusion. The music playback stopped and the producers attempted to find out the issue.

"What's wrong, man? Why'd you stop the take?" one of the producers, Craig Barton asked.

De'Von shook his head. "I'm just not feelin the break, man. No offense," he said quickly to Miesha, hoping to spare her feelings. They had been an item but they called it quits weeks ago. Unfortunately, Miesha took it more seriously than De'Von anticipated.

"What you mean, you ain't feelin' da break?" she asked, glaring across the booth at De'Von.

Unlike him, Miesha, wasn't new to the game. Having recorded since she was sixteen, twenty-four-year-old Miesha did not think that De'Von had any right to criticize her voice. De'Von looked at Miesha, an incredulous look on his face. He wouldn't tolerate anyone raising their voice to him.

"You ain't heard me da' first time? I said I wasn't feelin' it, so you need to fall back," he said.

"Man, you need to fall back wit' them wack verses and stop testing my patience. I only agreed to do this shit for Craig and if you got a problem with it, I'mma roll up outta hea. I don't need this," Miesha bit back.

"I don't give a damn. While you gone, you need to find a voice before you step to the mike," De'Von replied.

Craig ran inside the studio before the confrontation got out of hand. It was their twentieth take on the same track and he understood that tempers were flaring and these artists were volatile.

"Guys, guys! Look this is a paid session ok? We can't be over here wasting time, wasted time is wasted money," he explained.

"Tell that to Pretty Boy ova there. He think just cuz his last album blew up, he all that. He musta forgot who introduced him to tha game," Miesha replied.

De'Von looked across the studio from Craig to Miesha. "So what? You sayin' I owe you something now? You need to go somewhere with that," he replied.

Putting his hands over his head in exasperation, Craig left the recording booth and stood outside the studio. One of the other producers, a man who also happened to be the talent consultant for Metro Records, named Julio Vargas decided to try his hand at easing the tension. Of all the producers in the studio, no one understood the artists better than Julio. He claimed sole responsibility for signing both Miesha and De'Von. He recognized these were talented recording artists who were selling records by the millions and it was his job to be sure these artists stayed together. He knew the survival of Metro Records relied on these two potentially platinum selling artists. Julio stepped into the booth.

"Ok Miesha go take ten ok? You're doing great baby, don't worry," he reassured Miesha. Once Miesha left the studio, he turned to De'Von, who stepped away from the recording microphone to gather his thoughts.

"Everything ok, champ? Is there something you wanna talk about?" he asked. De'Von shook his head.

"Nah man, I'm cool. I wasn't tryin' to blow her shine, man. She cool and all but I just wasn't feelin' her in this song," De'Von replied.

Julio, in a big brother fashion, put his arm around De'Von. "I know you're under a lot of pressure, man. The second album is always difficult cuz your fans are always expecting the best," he said.

"And I wanna give 'em the best," De'Von said. "But I need someone with that special sauce to add to this entrée, man. Her voice just ain't cuttin' it," he added.

"De'Von, she's the only artist we can get right now to collaborate with you. We have seven other artists on tours and Yolanda's at home with her family on maternal leave," Julio explained, describing one of Metro's artists who had just given birth to a baby boy and was resting. "So Miesha was really the only one who could sing this hook for you, other than that, we just don't have anyone else available," Julio repeated.

"Then let's just continue recording the other songs in this next album and just leave this one alone until we can sign someone who can kill dis' hook," De'Von said.

Julio thought about the idea. "Ok fine with me but let's try to stay productive here, ok. We gotta get this thing out as quickly as possible," he said. He knew that the longer De'Von took on any song another artist would come out with new music and his sales would suffer dramatically.

"Alright man. Look I'm takin ten, too. I'll be back," De'Von said, walking out of the booth. Slam waited outside the studio and when De'Von made his way out of the doors, Slam made his way outside as well.

"What's up man. Why'd you'd stop the take for?" he asked.

"I just wasn't feelin' it man. Miesha's been in da game a hell of a lot longer than everyone around hea' and I get that but my next album gotta be fire man. If I'm not feelin' it, how's everyone else gonna react when the album drops?" De'Von asked.

"I feel you bro, but you can't beef about that all day. Gotta make do with what you got," Slam replied. De'Von gave Slam a look that said You supposed to be on my side. I thought you was my boy. Slam saw the look of vain sarcasm on De'Von's face. "What man? I'm just sayin' it ain't the end of da world, man. Anyway, I got you tonight son," Slam said, his eye gleaming mischievously.

De'Von looked at his friend. He didn't like the look that Slam had on his face at that very moment. It was the traditional Slam scheme look. "What you do now, man?" he asked.

Slam took out his phone and flashed what appeared to be an ad. "So I put this ad online for your biggest fans to come to your studio to hear you rap live in studio," he explained.

De'Von glared at Slam. No wonder, security had such an overwhelming job on their hands trying to keep the excited fans away from entering the studio earlier in the day. He thought there were more girls than usual during this session.

"Anyway, I did a lil drawing where I put the names of fifty shorties in a hat and the two that I draw out, will be our company for this evening," Slam added.

"You did what?" De'Von asked, his mouth open in surprise. He couldn't believe it. He had no problems entertaining the ladies and he was thankful to Slam for that opportunity. But picking out of a hat? There were doubts running through De'Von's head.

"Man, you a snake, bruh. So where the hat at? Let's do it," he said, wanting to get it over with quickly.

But Slam smiled even wider. "Nah, I already finished the drawing kid, and the winners are outside waiting on us right now," he said, unable to hide the anticipation and glee on his voice.

De'Von couldn't believe it. One part of him wanted to be angry at Slam for exploiting his fame to obtain women, yet the other part of him was curious and wondering where this would lead. Slam gestured to De'Von to follow him outside to the front of Metro Records. Two girls, one black and one Latino were waiting. Summer hadn't arrived but these girls were dressed as if they were ready to go to Cancun, Mexico or Panama City Beach. Wearing short-crop top tees that bared their midriff and short skirts that revealed their legs, they seemed ready for the evening. De'Von smiled at Slam.

"light, so I see you ain't screw this one up. Which one's mine, man?" he asked.

Slam smiled. "Mamacita's mine, so you got Ms. Brownskin. But they both bad, wouldn't you agree?" he asked.

"I gotta agree with you dog. Let's go. How I look, am I clean?" De'Von asked as he went out to meet the women.

The two young women, who could scarcely believe that they were actually outside the studio where De'Von worked, got themselves worked into a total fervor. When he finally walked outside to greet them, De'Von gave them a moment to gather themselves from their excitement about meeting him.

"Oh my God, it's De'Von. I must be dreaming, for real," the young black girl said. She wasn't too young, she didn't look older than twenty years of age. The Latino girl looked like she was about the same age. Both had black hair that fell in curls over their shoulders.

"Yeah, yeah, it's me in the flesh, baby. What's happenin'?" he greeted them, with his normal laid-back personality.

"Well, we just won a date with you. I can't believe this is happening. Wait till I tell my friends about this. They are not gonna believe this," the Latino girl said excitedly.

"Well they do say that all good things come to those who wait. May I take the time to tell ya'll that ya look very, very sexy?" De'Von complimented.

"I second that," Slam interjected. "Welcome ladies, to the front of the studio. Hea's the king of Metro Records himself, De'Von Franklin. So what's ya names?" Slam asked.

The two girls still seemed too excited to be in the presence of a millionaire and De'Von's aura made them temporarily speechless. However they eventually composed themselves long enough to introduce themselves.

"I'm Roxanne Sanders and this is Christina Aldana. We are your biggest fans," Roxanne said excitedly. "So where are we going?" she asked.

"Well, we goin' to go get a bite to eat and then we gonna chill for tonight. Is that cool?" Slam replied.

"Yeah that's cool. Oh my God, we are going out with De'Von and his friends. This is just wild," Roxanne said.

De'Von gestured to the three of them and they walked to a section of the studio, where there were parking spots for directors and producers and singers. Parked on one of the parking spots, was a new Mercedes-Benz, sleek and black in design. De'Von wanted to show his new friends how he got around at times.

"Normally, I take the limo to get to where I'm going, but today's a real treat. We get to ride in da Benz today," De'Von said as he unlocked the car. The girls were still wide-eyed and in their phase of excitement as they entered the new car. Slam looked at De'Von, his face crestfallen.

"Hold up, you ain't tell me that you was gon' break out da Benz. So it's like that, huh?" he asked.

"It's dinner and a movie right? We just gonna show these ladies a good time after dinner, maybe ride around Times Square a couple times, then steam up da windows lata' you feel me?" De'Von said slyly as he dapped Slam.

"I feel you, man. Let's roll," Slam said as he got into the car and waited for De'Von to get inside the driver's seat, talking to the girls as they excitedly chattered about the rare opportunity they were experiencing at that moment.

Within the next hour, De'Von's Mercedez Benz, followed by a black Ford Coupe which was driven by his two bodyguards, Alton and Rex, arrived at the Red Star Chinese Restaurant on the corner of 112th and east 115th Street. Stepping out the car, De'Von, Roxanne, Christina, and Slam entered the busy restaurant. Slam had already made reservations, so the host directed them over to their reserved table located near the center of the restaurant. As they walked over to the table, De'Von noticed a small annoying detail; Roxanne was very touchy-feely. Normally De'Von didn't have an issue with women wanting to touch him but Roxanne had this very unnerving habit of grabbing his arm and pulling him close to her as they were walking to the table. One of De'Von's pet peeves were needy and clingy women; women who loved to lay claim on him as if he was exclusively theirs was a huge turn-off for him and it was his misfortune that he was out on the date with a long nailed, long fingered clinger. Still he wanted to spare her feelings, he allowed her to continue holding him until they reached their table. Roxanne looked around excitedly.

"Wow, I've never been here before. I mean I've eaten Chinese food before but I've never been to this one. Look at the windows, it's so beautiful! Wow and the designs are something else…." She kept on going and going about the restaurant and soon De'Von realized that Roxanne had another negative trait going for her: she was an incessant chatterbox. She talked for minutes at a time and De'Von would find himself thinking *Come on girl, ain't you gonna take time to breathe between sentences?*

Again he spared her feelings because he knew that Roxanne and Christina probably never been to these restaurants in the city. Thankfully, while Roxanne continued talking his ear off, the waiter finally arrived with the menus.

"Order whatever you like ladies, it's all on us," Slam said proudly. De'Von looked at Slam, shaking his head. Sometimes he loved to act like he was the one running the whole show. He must've forgotten who the performer was and who the sidekick was. As they placed their orders, Roxanne turned to De'Von.

"This is so cool! I'm having a good time but I always though you was a club banger. I thought we were gonna go to some hot spots out hea' and turn up," she said.

Roxanne had not been lying. De'Von did enjoy going to clubs to perform and on nights he wasn't performing, he would just kick back in the VIP section with some of his fans, taking pictures, popping champagne. He was surprised how much of his celebrity life Roxanne seemed to know.

I gotta start watchin' out for them paparazzi. Before long, these girls gonna know me more than I know myself, he thought, and that was one event that he couldn't let happen.

De'Von was not looking to settle down. His goal was to make music and relax for as long as he could. He didn't see marriage in the near future for him. As far as he was concerned, a wedding ring was nothing but a piece of gold that bound a man to certain servitude and lockdown forever. It was not for him.

"What is this? Lo-Mein? Egg-Foo Yung? What the hell is this stuff?" Roxanne asked.

De'Von began looking around. Some of the customers were beginning to get distracted by Roxanne's outspokenness and although she wasn't doing it on purpose, it was bringing unneeded attention to De'Von. Thank goodness the waiters quickly returned at a crucial moment, bringing out their food just minutes later. De'Von ordered the chicken fried rice while Slam and Christina ordered identical dishes on what looked like lo mein noodles. Roxanne's order arrived and she ordered a special type of seafood dish with a side of shrimp egg rolls. As they ate, Christina would occasionally glance at Rex and Alto who stood in front of their tables.

"So do these guys go everywhere ya go?" she asked.

"Well you know how it is. When you as big as De'Von is in this game, you gotta have backup. You neva' know who could be comin' after yo' paper," Slam replied. De'Von nodded his head in agreement.

"So how long have you two known each other?" Christina asked.

"We grew up on Morris Park Avenue down the same block. We went to the same middle school and high school together," De'Von answered. "We'd be chillin' and sleepin' in the same classes and freestylin' with other cats who were tryin' to step to us. When Julio found me and signed me, I came back fo' my boy. The rest was history," he added.

"So what you mean to say is that he just riding wit' you just to get yo' paper too?" Roxanne asked with her mouth full. Slam laughed as if what Roxanne stated was complete nonsense.

"Nah, it ain't like that. Slam's ma dude, we were boys before I eva got to this money. If there's anybody that knows how I be, it's him," De'Von answered.

"Appreciate da' love dog," Slam said, smiling.

"No doubt," De'Von replied. Roxanne and Christina looked at each other and by the looks that they gave each other, it was pretty clear that they weren't buying the idea that Slam was really De'Von's friend and that he was there for reasons other than money.

De'Von knew that there were people that questioned his friendship and loyalty to Slam but if there was any intrinsic fact he knew about his childhood friend, it was that he always had his back. When nobody else cared, Slam had been the only one who had befriended him back in middle school when the future looked bleak to him. De'Von had decided back then that whatever rewards he might reap out of this game, Slam would share in those rewards. He needed the support, especially after a difficult time in his life but he couldn't allow himself to think about those obstacles during this dinner. As they ate Chinese food, De'Von did not know when the conversation shifted to matters of the bedroom. Either the waiters must've spiked the beverages with love potion or the girls were really excited. Either way the questions started to get strange.

"So what's your favorite bedroom position?" Roxanne asked De'Von.

De'Von nearly spit his drink out when he heard that. It was a question so far out in leftfield that he didn't know how to respond to it at first. Finally he said, "Whatever position suits the lady," he said in his smooth, debonair voice.

Roxanne let out a little squeal and she and Christina were trying too hard to contain their laughter. After the exchanged sexy gazes between Slam and De'Von, they both excused themselves to go to the restroom. As soon as they were out of earshot, Slam turned to De'Von with a devilish grin on his face.

"They ready, bruh. I'm being fo' real. They ready, homie," he said. But De'Von shook his head.

"Nah, man not this time. Ain't no way you convincing me to do this. It's just dinner and a movie," he said.

Too many times, especially when they went on a tour, Slam had found a way to get De'Von the girls he needed to relax him and give him a good time. Most of the time De'Von did not complain but he couldn't keep playing these silly games with these girls.

"Look at 'em though. Dog, these girls are ripe and we got 'em wrapped around our finger. Hopefully they can wrap something a lil' bigga' tonight," Slam said, grinning widely.

At that same moment, Roxanne and Christine came back to join them at the table. "So what do you got planned after dinner?" Christina asked Slam and De'Von.

Slam looked at De'Von with a look that indicated he was extremely confident with his plan. "Well we were thinking about watching a movie after this....." he started.

The sun's bright rays flickered through the blinds of the Holiday Inn hotel the following morning. De'Von was awakened by the chirping of birds and bustling people outside. Lying next to him was Roxanne, sound asleep and unabashedly naked under the sheets.

The only time that girl is ever quiet is when she's asleep. I got skills, De'Von though as he stretched his arms slightly and yawned.

He hadn't planned on the previous night unfolding as it did. The girls agreed to watch a movie with them and immediately following the movie, they drove to the Holiday Inn. Slam had called a few more people and they had a brief and very impromptu party filled with games, food for guests, and of course alcohol. Martinis, Patron, and Hennessey flowed all through the night and although De'Von wasn't drunk, he wasn't sure if he could say the same about Roxanne. If De'Von thought she was slightly reckless when she was sober, he clearly hadn't seen the crazy person until she got drunk. Being the gentleman that he was, De'Von guided her to her hotel room and was prepared to bid her goodnight, until she grabbed him by the shirt and dragged him inside her hotel room. They made crazy, wild, sexy love that night and De'Von had to admit, although Roxanne was a little bit strange and possessive, she knew how to work her curves.

That girl was pullin' moves that I ain't seen no other girl pullin'. But I still gotta give my pipe game credit though. I had her screamin' and moanin' my name a million times like she was countin' sheep and I knocked that ass out, he thought with a strange twisted sense of pride. Being careful not to wake her up, he pulled on a pair of pants and put on a tank top, before walking to the balcony. He was not very high up since the hotel room was only on the third floor. Then he walked outside the hotel room into the hallway. A few minutes later, Slam emerged from his room and wore a smile as big as De'Von's. Walking over to De'Von, he dapped him.

"Man I can't believe I let you talk me into this," De'Von said, although he was smiling.

"C'mon son, quit cryin. You was stressed out after the studio session and I just help you relax. I did you a favor, bro, least you can do is thank me," Slam replied.

"Thank you?" De'Von said, as if mocking. "You set me up wit' a girl who might need a muzzle the next time she go out wit' anybody and you want me to say thank you?" he asked.

"But you got some, didn't you?" Slam asked. De'Von laughed.

"Yeah I got some. Lemme tell you though, the only way I got that girl to shut up was when I was doin' her, and even then she was still screamin' my name," he replied.

Slam laughed with glee as they gloated on their activities the previous night. "How was yo' girl?" he asked Slam.

Slam was wearing his Nike T-shirt and athletic shorts. "Man she just found out last night why they call me Slam," he replied lazily and the two young men sat back in silence for a moment before De'Von finally said, "Thanks, man."

Slam shrugged it aside, as if he refused to acknowledge any credit given for setting his friend up on a complimentary one-night stand.

"So you gonna keep seeing dis chick?" Slam asked. De'Von shook his head.

"I can't see it, son. I mean, her swerve game was nice but I ain't serious about...." his voice trailed off.

Police sirens could be heard from a distance and they appeared to be getting closer. De'Von rushed to the window at the end of the hallway upon hearing the sound. A small brown Nissan Acura was at full speed followed by three police cars in hot pursuit. Nobody except Slam and his mother knew why the police sirens bothered De'Von. Nobody knew why his anger broiled whenever he saw the blue and white cop cars.

Slam walked up to him. "Chill dog, it's over. Don't even sweat that," he said. But it wasn't over, because of Mason Franklin.

Chapter Six

It was the summer of 1999 as teens and Bronx residents made their way over to Nakia Bolden's small residence in East Tremont, New York. It was the day before Independence Day and Nakia held a barbecue gathering outside of her home in a small yard that would have been over capacity if she didn't open the outer fence. The yard was filled with high school and college students, finally relieved that school was over and they could relax and party with their friends. The music blared over the loudspeakers that were set up by DJ B-Roc, the local town deejay who was called to play for the event. As the smoke from the grill rose up into in the air, wine coolers, juice were being poured or opened and beer cans were being popped. A small table was set up to the side and on that table three young men were playing an intense game of dominoes.

At the other end of the yard, a girl with a short pixie hairstyle was frantically looking around, obviously searching for the boy who had stood her up on a date only few nights before. She was accompanied by two other girls who were helping her find the culprit. Little boys were playing stickball, riding bikes, playing with water guns, and playing basketball. The sky which had been bright and sunny earlier that day, started to show signs of dusk that began its slow descent. At last Tina, the girl with the short pixie hair cut found the boy she had been seeking. She pushed through the crowd of kids who were laughing, talking, and drinking. They were enjoying the day with their dates, while she remembered waiting for two hours outside the cinema for a date who never arrived. She approached the boy, who was sitting on the domino table playing with a few older boys. He was wearing a Yankees cap, with a New York Knicks jersey and baggy jean shorts. Unfortunately he was so immersed in his game that he didn't notice the angry black girl who stood over him. One of the older boys playing dominoes, noticed her.

"What up Tina?" he asked in a slow seductive voice.

"Don't play wit' me Wayne. I ain't in the mood fo' it today. I need to speak to dis fool right hea'," Tina replied, slapping one of the boys in the back of his head.

The boy turned around, no doubt angry by the blow to his head. "Damn girl, what's wrong wit' you?" he asked.

Tina rolled her eyes, as if she couldn't believe this guy had no clue as to why she would be upset with him. "You think you slick, Mason? You had me waitin' on yo' ass for two hours outside the movies. What you bout to tell me now? You had to watch yo' lil' brother again?" she asked, exasperated.

Mason Franklin turned around to face Tina, a sheepish grin on his face. "That was yesterday? I forgot baby, I'm sorry. I'll make it up to you tomorrow, I promise," she said.

At this, Tina shook her head. "Uh-uh, I don't think so. That was yo' last chance," she said.

Mason still looked at her with the foolish grin as if he knew what he did but he hoped to sweep it under the rug.

"C'mon Tina don't be like that. I know I didn't call you last night, I was busy. I was at the studio puttin' some tracks in," he explained.

Tina wasn't going to fall for his smooth routine this time. "You spend all this time tryin' to hook up wit' me and when I finally clear my schedule for you, you stay playin'. I spent all this time waitin' for you, hopin you'd come around but you ain't neva' gon' do right, so I'm done," she said before turning her back on him.

Mason watched her walk away, flanked by her other friends. "Damn shorty, you forgot to call her? That ain't cool dog," Wayne said.

"Whateva' man. I was takin' care of business. You know what I'm sayin?" Mason replied. "My boy got me connections to send that demo tape to Uptown records. Wit' moves like that, you know I ain't got time to be playin', bro. When I start gettin' that guap, then she gon' remember who I am," he added.

After playing dominoes for a few minutes, DJ B-Roc stepped up to the mike over the turntables. "Yo, yo, yo, to all da Brooklyn heads and Bronx heads in da house, I got my man Mase ready to step up to da mike, to spit some shit fo' ya. Give it up!" he shouted, playing an instrumental.

Upon hearing his name, Mason got up from the domino table and stepped up to the microphone. His words and lyrics came quick and swift:

Rollin' fates like I'm rollin' craps/Dishin' back slaps ,the real facts, best of the blacks/Comin' at yo' door hard as I'm playin the card/shootin' aces like Iverson, I'mma tough-ass guard/As I shift wit the gift that I lift beyond the rift/ Imma kick it to da lil homie Dev so he could rip.

At this time a little boy, no more than eleven years old ran up to the microphone. Mason had been rapping so intensely that nobody noticed little Devon Franklin as he approached the stage.

Lil freak providin' da link of da week/ Baby I got da chain that these bustas seek/Stompin' weak MC's mo' than half my age/Lightin' up da stage where you see me wit' my lyrical gauge/ I'm front page on Daily News, Jet Magazine and the Post/You wanna be da star but I'm still da games' host.

The song continued as Mason and Devon alternated between verses to the delight of the crowd, who were beside themselves with shock. Some of them were familiar with Mason's raps because he was accustomed to rapping at parties and events. This was the first time he had collaborated with his little brother. Devon and Mason worked on the timing and delivery numerous times before they performed together at the barbecue. When it was over, the crowd shouted themselves hoarse and the standing ovation applause could be heard for miles.

As people greeted Mason and Devon after the barbecue was over, they were giving him accolades such as "I had no clue your brother could rap like that," and "Yo, dat lil man can spit. He need to be in da booth wit you forreal homie,"

But Mason always responded the same way. "Yeah he nice, but lil man gotta stay in them books and get outta high school first."

Mason graduated high school and was ready to continue his education at Brooklyn Technical College but he felt the music industry beckoning. His mother, already disappointed at the career choice he had made to his music rather than his education, persuaded him never to pass his influence of music as a career to Devon. Unfortunately for her, Devon had already picked up certain characteristics of Mason's rap style, his wordplay, his rhyme scheme and his attitude. He was already entertaining his classmates at school during lunch by rapping and coming up with small freestyle verses. It appeared that Mason was headed for certain success with his music career. However, there was a side to Mason that few knew about. Mason was into drugs. He didn't dip into too deep but he was big on smoking marijuana. Music was his only way out the drug game.

As he walked home from the barbecue with Devon, Mason said, "Yo, Dev, you killed it today, son. But you gotta come in a lil earlier aight? Gotta get that timing right, boy."

Normally Devon would find a rebuttal to his criticisms but he agreed with Mason. "Ok. I got you Mase," he replied.

Mase put his arm around his little brother's shoulder. "It's important that you take all this advice I'm givin' you man. One day, you'll be the only MC in the family. I won't be around forever. Be careful who you roll wit' cuz these cats ain't all cool with you," he said. At the time, Devon listened but he never understood what his older brother was trying to tell him. It wouldn't be too long until he found out.

The next night around midnight, Mason received a call on his cell phone. It was Brian Watts, his good friend. He was also involved in the street drug hustle and quickly made a name for himself. This placed Brian and those who associated with him in danger because not only did aggressive drug users know him but he was a familiar face for law enforcement to track down. Brian called Mason because he needed money, having spent all his money on the game and paying others who were selling for him. He needed some ready cash to keep him going for the week. Mason debated about meeting Brian at the street corner nearly five blocks away. Brian had helped him on many occasions and Mason never wanted to owe anybody any type of favors, so he got out of bed, snuck past his brother, who was still asleep and slowly opened the window. He raised it until the opening was just large enough for him to sneak out. His plan was to go to the street where Brian wanted to meet him and loan him some money so he could reciprocate for all the times Brian assisted him. He knew he took a serious risk, because the corner was known for rabid drug users and dealers, all of whom posed a threat to Mason. Mason slowly snuck out of the window quietly so that he wouldn't wake Devon. Walking to the street corner where Brian waited for him, Mason saw a couple of young boys who were either talking with friends or focused on other people. Mason walked up to Brian.

"Come on, bro. You mean to tell me that you couldn't meet me at my crib and you can meet me out hea?" Mason said.

Brian shrugged. "Couldn't take that chance, son. Too much at stake. So how much you got man?" he asked.

Mason pulled out his wallet and began to count his money. As soon as he verified that he got the exact amount requested, Mason gave Brian four hundred dollars. Brian grinned as the money was counted into his hands and his hopes of getting out of the block without drama were becoming a reality. All of a sudden, Mason heard the blaring of police sirens a couple of blocks away. The car sped over to the two boys.

"Shit," Mason heard Brian say. The officers stepped out of their car. "Good evening gentlemen. Lovely evening tonight, isn't it?" one of the cops said.

Mason, at that moment, was unsure how to answer the question. He wasn't sure at if the cops were speaking sarcastically or if they actually wanted him to answer the question. It was no secret that the law enforcement in New York was not well liked by some citizens in the area. They were perceived to be biased, cruel, and abrasive. Both cops were standing there, waiting for a response.

"Is there a problem officer?" Mason asked. He noticed the other officer glancing sideways to make sure the street was empty.

"As a matter of fact, we have a huge problem. We suspect that there have been residents of this area involved in a drug-selling ring. May I ask you to empty your pockets, please?" the officer said as they both approached the two boys. As Brian and Mason complied to what they were instructed to do, one of the officer's face had wide eyes as he suddenly recognized Brian, from a prior incident.

He whispered something to his partner, as Brian and Mason stood there, pants pockets turned out, the cop said. "Gentlemen, I would like to ask you both to place your hands behind your back. You are both under arrest," he finished.

"For what?" Mason asked angrily.

"For associating with a well-known leader of a drug syndicate. Where are you storing 'em?" the officer asked.

"Storing what, man? Look ain't nobody slangin' rocks. Why you messin' wit' us for?" Mason asked angrily.

"Shut up," one of the officers replied. Mason couldn't believe that he was being arrested for no reason.

It would surely break his mother's heart. He couldn't let himself go down without a fight. He didn't know what led him to react the way he did but he couldn't do this to his mother. He couldn't go to jail. He had too much riding on him. He looked at Brian and when Brian's eyes met his, they knew what they had to do. When the police officer's back were temporarily turned, Mason and Brian took off running at high speed.

"Freeze!" one of the cops yelled as he began to pursue Brian. The other officer ran after Mason.

Brian ran toward the south end of the street and by jumping fences and running down through the subway, he was able to elude the officer. Unfortunately, Mason was not so lucky. It was his misfortune that the officer that was pursuing him was Officer Jack Shores, who was one of the fastest runners in the division. It didn't take long for him to catch up to Mason and when he finally caught him, Mason threw his elbow back, in hopes of catching Officer Shores off balance, but the determined officer held on. Mason swung back at the officer, connecting with his cheekbone. The impact was so severe, it cut open the right side of his face. Seething with anger, Officer Shores proceeded to pull out his firearm rather than his radio to call for backup. Before Mason knew what hit him, he heard the sound of the bullet being blasted from the gun's pointed barrel and he felt the bullet rip through his carotid artery. The sound was so ear piercingly loud, it woke Devon who was nearly five blocks away. A sharp pain ran down through his neck and down his arms and then he realized he couldn't feel his arm. Something was wrong.

Realizing that Mason was not sleeping on his bed, Devon snuck out of the home and only made it one block away before the other residents ran toward him. They appeared frightened and didn't stop, even after seeing him. Devon continued walking forward toward the streets where he knew danger was lurking. Officer Shores was standing over Mason, who was mortally wounded and unable to control the blood flowing from his neck, Devon ran toward his brother, but an older man grabs him by the shirt collar and pulls him back

"Son, don't be stupid," he said. As soon as the ambulance and paramedics came to the scene, Devon, finally saw through the dark moonlight, that his older brother was lying on the ground, barely able to form words as his life continued to pour out of him.

"MASE!!" he yelled, running to his brother. He broke through the yellow tape and got to his brother's side before the inevitable occurred.

Mason Franklin was pronounced dead at the age of eighteen. Devon cried for what seemed like hours and his mother, who was told the somber news at the door by another officer, broke down and was inconsolable in her sorrow. As details of Mason's death began to circulate, Devon, who initially thought that Mason must've been shot by one of his sellers, found out that the police, who were sworn to protect and serve the citizens, were responsible for the death of Mason. Nearly ten years had passed since that horrific night, but every time De'Von heard police sirens and saw officers, he felt the same wave of anger rush in him. They had taken his brother away from him and it was a crime that Devon would never forget or forgive. The family eventually filed a lawsuit against the NYPD and investigation was launched. But as primitively angry as Devon was, nothing sowed his anger more once he found out that Officer Shores was not indicted for the murder.

So the man who killed my brother gets to walk on some white privilege bullshit and left my mom and I heartbroken for years. If I can, I would make sure that crooked-ass cop get what he deserved, De'Von thought.

 As De'Von and Slam watched the police car chasing after another car, he was revisited by the primal rage of watching his brother die in his arms. Slam placed his hand on De'Von's shoulder.

"I know, man. I feel you. There's nothing you could've done, dog," he said.

"I was right there, he heard me callin' him. I always thought he was gonna be ok," De'Von said as he looked out the window, shaking his head. "It's all because of the damn police. It's been ten years, man. I try to let it go, you feel me? I try to shrug it off, but he was fam," he continued.

It wasn't as if De'Von owed Mason, but Mason had always set a standard for De'Von to meet. He had been the oldest, the smartest, and the best rapper in all of East Bronx. It wasn't easy for De'Von to fill his brother's shoes after he died but he kept the dream going. After the funeral, De'Von vowed to make it in the music business and accomplish what Mason never had the chance to accomplish. His goal was to finish what Mason essentially started and not only survive doing it but to thrive. When Julio eventually discovered him and signed him to Metro Records at the age of eighteen, De'Von knew he was there to carry the legacy of his fallen brother while carving out his own. The first action he took was to capitalize the "V" in his name, adding an apostrophe. He made the choice to make this change because of the significance of entering an adult game. He was no longer a little boy, waiting for queues from his brother or from anyone. He controlled his music and every single song on his album had one stipulation; De'Von would be given free reign when it came to the writing and the production of his rap music. It had been an unforgettable ride, from recording his debut album, to having the album go gold, to being nominated as best new artist that year. While De'Von was proud of his accomplishment, he hoped he wouldn't fall into the same trap as many singers did; following up a great album with a poor one. He was determined to represent not only Mason and himself but all of the Bronx.

The bell rang at Richmond Hill High School, signaling the end of the final period of school. Andrea walked out of her mentorship block and headed to the school doors. Rolling her eyes, she knew what she would have to deal with and sure enough when she walked out the school doors, the boys started on her right away.

"What's up baby? Yo ma, I'm feelin you, what's up this Saturday? You tryna chill?" they were asking.

Exasperated, she turned around to face the boys. They just never had any tact and were quick to pursue women way out their league. One of the boys, a very interesting individual with a round face, lazy eye and a very unappealing smile with crooked teeth, was bolder than the rest and he walked over to Andrea.

"Listen Ma, forget the rest of these jokas behind me. Check it, I know I've been comin' on a lil' strong from time to time. I would like the opportunity to take you out on da real and if you give me that chance, I promise you'd have more fun rollin' wit' me than these dudes behind me. So what you say?" he asked.

The other boys watched with close attention as they awaited the response from Andrea. Andrea appeared to be thinking over the invitation and for a moment, the guy thought he had a chance.

Andrea replied sweetly, "Well, lemme think about it," and took a second to think before adding, "Yeah I thought about it, and nah I'm good. Good luck finding someone down wit' you though. There's someone out there for everybody."

Walking down the stairs, she laughed to herself as she imagined the whole scene unfolding behind her. The guy's friends were probably laughing at him, a few of them were probably calling her names while dissing her for being too good for them.

"Hey girl, wait up," a voice yelled behind her. Andrea turned around and saw Vanessa heading toward her.

"My bad for not waiting but I had to get out of there quick," Andrea said. Vanessa turned back at the boys.

"Ugh, I don't blame you at all. The one wit' the jacked up teeth tried to hook up wit' me," she replied.

Andrea looked at her. "You too? That fool tried to ask me to dinner this Saturday," she said. Vanessa laughed.

"What did you say?" she asked.

Andrea made a small sound. "Girl, what you think I said? I told him to point his suckas somewhere else," she replied. "If these dudes made as much effort in actually passin' classes as much as they do tryin' to spit game, they probably would have a chance wit' a real one," she added.

"Like Gary, maybe?" Vanessa asked, slyly.

Andrea turned to her, laughing. "Nah, don't even go there, girl. He got a boo already," she said.

Vanessa shrugged. "So? He don't really like her anyway, and I don't be goin' to Johnson's that much anymore, but I bet he be runnin' your mind," she said.

Andrea laughed. There were a lot of girls in the world, but there was only one Vanessa. She couldn't think of another girl, besides Loree, who knew her inside and out.

"If Gary had a twin brother who was single, believe me I'd give him my time and then some," she confirmed as they walked home.

As soon as Vanessa turned the opposite direction to head home, Andrea opened her front door with the keys.

Thank God I'm off work today, she thought as she walked to her room and fell face down on her bed. School was beginning to drain her energy. She wished it could be over already. Opening her book bag, she started to work on her assignments for the day. After an hour and a half, she heard her parents come home. Then the phone rang. After a couple minutes, her mother knocked on the door to her room.

"Phone's for you," she said.

"Who is it?" Andrea asked. She knew it wasn't Vanessa or Sean because they had her cell phone number. Slowly, Andrea took the phone, hoping it wasn't Johnson's calling to let her go. "Hello?" she asked on the receiver tentatively.

"Why you sound so surprised, girl?" a familiar voice replied on the other end.

Andrea's heart skipped a beat. It was Shania Hillman, a friend of hers and her late sister. Andrea always considered Shania somewhat of a sister, even before Loree's passing. The countless sleepovers, the dates where they went places, and the fact that Shania was her first Sunday School teacher at the church ministered by her father Michael Hillman. Although the McAfee family no longer attended the Rock of Jacob Baptist Church due to a fall-out between her father and Pastor Hillman, Shania remained in contact with Andrea, through the first year without Loree. Once Shania left to go to college, she found it more difficult to stay in close contact with Andrea. Andrea was never angry with Shania. She knew that Shania had her own life and she was dating a potential first round NBA draft pick in Trevor McClain, who was currently overseas playing for an Italian basketball club. Shania had graduated college with a Bachelor's in psychology and became a social worker in the city of New York.

"What's up girl? It's been a minute," Andrea replied.

"I know, girl. I feel like a corporate robot working all day," Shania said.

"Girl, who you telling?" Johnson's ain't no joke neither," Andrea replied.

"I feel you," Shania agreed. "So how's school going?" she asked.

"I'm ready for it to be over with already," Andrea answered, laughing. "I can't wait to graduate," she added. "So how's yo' big balla doin'?" she asked.

"Oh, Big-Head's doing fine. Last time I talked to him, he tried to sweet talk me in Italian. Ultimate fail," Shania said, laughing.

Andrea laughed as well. "He also asked me something else," Shania said, then she was silent for a moment. It took exactly fifteen seconds for Andrea to figure out what Trevor asked his girlfriend.

"Oh my God, he asked you to marry him!" Andrea said excitedly.

"Yeah he did, and I said yes," Shania confirmed enthusiastically.

Andrea was beside herself with joy. She recalled the earlier days of Shania's relationship with Trevor and how unsure she had been about her future with Trevor. Trevor had been a self-professed player, both figuratively and literally, and settling down had not been not part of his big plan. Shania had changed Trevor's way of thinking because she had stuck with him through all the difficult times in his life. Andrea knew it was only a matter of time before they decided to tie the knot.

"I'm so excited for you guys. That's really great. Awww, my boo's about to be a basketball wifey," Andrea gushed as Shania laughed.

"Uh no, we both gon' be workin' on our careers. I ain't bout to be a stay-home wife, suckin' up all da bread. If that's who he thinks he's gon' marry, he got da wrong one," Shania replied.

"I know that's right," Andrea confirmed as they both laughed.

After a minute, Shania continued. "Anyway, I wanted to hit you up, because I was hoping you could be the maid of honor," she asked.

Andrea was speechless for a moment. Shania was one of the most well-known girls in the Richmond Hill area, from her father's history as a former high school football star her own history as a track star. She was sure Shania had many friends and influences in her life. Why would she choose Andrea?

"Really? Me?" Andrea asked with uncertainty.

"Yeah, girl, you know there's no one else I'd rather have then you. You're still my sister," Shania replied.

Andrea leaned back onto her bed, where she had been previously sitting. It was true that they were like sisters, but Andrea had a feeling that if Loree was still alive, she would have been the maid of honor in the wedding. Andrea began to feel the familiar sense of inadequacy she had felt the last six years whenever people performed actions or rewarded her because of Loree. It was just like Ms. Martinez who had written her college letter of recommendation when she wasn't obligated to do so. Andrea's first impulse was to refuse the offer but this was her second sister. She couldn't let Shania down, no matter what she thought about the intention of the offer.

"Ok, 'Nia, I'll do it," Andrea said.

"Girl, I appreciate it so much. Thank you," Shania replied.

"When's the wedding, by the way?" Andrea asked.

"Well, we were shooting for the summertime. We decided to get married in August," Shania replied.

"That's perfect," Andrea said. In essence, it was the ideal time for Andrea. Although she was unsure which college she would attend, she was certain that the wedding would be scheduled before school began.

"Ok, cool. So I'll let you know from our wedding planner, when we are doing the rehearsals," Shania said.

"Cool. Is the wedding gon' be at the Rock of Jacob Baptist Church?" Andrea asked.

"Of course it's gonna be there. Where else would it be?" Shania asked, as if she couldn't believe that Andrea asked that question.

Andrea couldn't believe she asked such a question, either but she wasn't so sure her parents were going to support it. Andrea's father still thought Pastor Mike was a disgraceful liar and a cheater and no happy occasion, such as a wedding, would be able to change his mind.

"Ok that's cool," she replied.

"Great, well anyway I'll talk to you later and I hope you don't work too hard," she said.

"Ok, bye Shania! Tell Big-Head I said what's up," Andrea said, referring to Trevor. Shania confirmed she would before hanging up.

Walking downstairs to the kitchen to drink some water; Alisha who was preparing dinner; asked, "So how is Shania doing?" she asked.

"She's doing great Mama. She's getting married this year," she answered. Alisha's eyes widened.

"Oh wow, that's great! I'm so happy for her. Is it the young man that she has been dating?" she asked. Alisha recalled seeing Trevor a few times when they would go out shopping with Andrea.

"Yes Mom, it's Trevor," she confirmed. "Anyway she called because she wanted me to be her maid of honor," she added.

"Really? What did you tell her?" she asked.

"I told her I would do it," Andrea replied.

"Oh, I'm so happy for them and congratulations on being her maid of honor," Alisha said.

Looking around, Andrea saw Amos watching television, so she proceeded to speak with her mother on a hushed tone.

"Do you think Daddy will want to go?" she asked. Alisha, who was initially confused why Andrea was whispering, finally got the hint.

"I don't really know, honey. You remember how the last meeting went between them. It just didn't end very well. So I can't say that your father will be there," she confessed.

Andrea knew all too well what meeting her mother was referring to. Six years before, after Loree was tragically gunned down, Amos walked into Pastor Mike's office, hoping the pastor would help testify against Loree's alleged killer and ex-boyfriend David Anderson. When the pastor refused to do so and requested that charges not be brought against David, a shouting match ensued between the two men and Andrea had the misfortune of being in the room. Since that time, they never attended Rock of Jacob Baptist Church again.

Chapter Seven

Music executives and producers sat around a large square table that stood in the center of the meeting room. There were about thirty members of Metro Records' employees, and they sat talking to themselves as they waited for the CEO of Metro records, Garamond Morgan, to arrive to start the monthly performance meetings. These meetings were held every month to discuss sales, promotions, and revenue generated from the sale of albums, tours, and special appearances. Up until previous months, Metro Records had experienced major breakthroughs such as De'Von's early album and Miesha's most recent album. However, the past month's meeting indicated that Metro Records was beginning to experience periods of deflation and a staggering drop in sales. This decline was what prompted the CEO to visit the facility to address those issues and to form a plan to increase Metro Records' sales. The music game was terribly competitive; the other record labels smelled blood and were closing in quickly on Metro's numbers and sales. Mr. Morgan's plan was to discuss the existing artists at Metro and determine their marketability. Among the producers included in the meeting with the CEO were Julio and Craig. Both men were whispering apprehensively as they waited for Mr. Morgan's arrival.

"I can't believe De'Von blew off the rest of his studio session. That guy just doesn't understand the importance of deadlines," Craig said quietly to Julio, shaking his head. "I tell ya, these kids nowadays got no respect for studio time," he added.

"I'm sure he had a good reason to miss the rest of the session. It's no big loss. Besides his next album was already eighty percent completed," Julio replied.

"But the man ain't gonna give two cents about eighty percent. He was right. We should start hiring adults instead of kids. Why should we be stuck with hiring kids when we should be looking for other talented, middle-aged performers?" Craig asked.

Good question. You got me there, Julio thought. Suddenly the doors of the meeting swung open and two more executives walked in, followed by Mr. Morgan.

"Good morning gentlemen," Mr. Morgan greeted. The producers, who had been talking amongst themselves, stopped at once. There was utter silence in the room aside from Mr. Morgan's voice.

"As you all well know, we have endeavored to make Metro Records one of, if not the most, successful record label in the US. We had a discussion last month concerning the alarming rate at which our sales and profit have been sinking. Gentlemen, we have a problem. Juco, our recording label competitors across town in Jersey, has begun to increase sales. Uptown records are still the kings of New York and let me not get started on Virgin Records," Mr. Morgan said.

Julio and Craig listened as the President of Metro Records continued to address the producers.

"We have got to be better models and better people. With that said, where are Julio and Craig? I want to address those two men," he said.

Both Julio and Craig lifted their hands to indicate that they were available. "So I seem to understand that we are moving along with De'Von's next album, is that correct?" he asked them.

"That's correct sir," Craig replied.

"How far have you gotten in that project, gentlemen?" Mr. Morgan asked.

Craig seemed to be at a loss for words, so Julio answered for him. "We are nearly done with his album however, Mr. Franklin was not pleased with the feature session with Miesha," Julio explained. "One of his tracks requires a unique sound fit for the song and Miesha just doesn't seem to fit what he was looking for," he added.

"What's wrong with Miesha?" Mr. Morgan asked. "She's an exceptional young lady who has been working with us for years. What issues does De'Von see in that?" he asked testily.

"Well sir, what we meant to say is that while we do respect Miesha and her career, we feel she is not the right voice for a particular track," Julio replied.

"Well what do you suggest we do, Mr. Vargas? I have a list of possible tour dates that I would like to get scheduled underway as quickly as possible. De'Von is scheduled to tour over forty-five venues in a span of four months. We need this album finished so it can be in stores, so we can't afford to be wasting time," Mr. Morgan said. "Time is money, gentlemen. I give you two weeks to figure this out and complete the album. If this album isn't completed in the allotted time, I will not be holding De'Von solely responsible, but I will be holding you gentlemen responsible as well. Is that understood?" he asked.

"Yes sir, that's understood," Craig said.

As Mr. Morgan continued to lay out his agenda for the future plans of Metro Records, Julio sat and contemplated. Where was he going to find a singer that better suited and complimented the raw edge that was brought by De'Von? As soon as the meeting was over, Julio walked over to Craig.

"Well, that wasn't as bad as I thought it would be," Julio said. "But we still got two weeks to get his album out. It's obvious Miesha ain't the type of flavor I'm looking for in his album. We need to get a fresh voice. Someone who ain't afraid of the spotlight and someone who's gonna put pressure on these other labels out there," he said.

Finally, as if lighting struck, Craig had had an idea. "Why don't we scope out some dancehalls, clubs, or other places to find a singer that fits what Mr. Franklin was looking for," he said.

Julio shook his head because he knew it was a task that was almost impossible. They needed to find an amateur female with a voice that could speak to the modern generation, and he wanted a young lady who was very confident and was willing to help take Metro to the next level.

"What are the chances that we would find a young lady with that type of vocal capacity?" Julio thought out loud. He heard Craig make a scoffing sound.

"In this city? Good luck wit' that," he replied.

After school, Andrea and Vanessa started on their way back home, when they heard someone calling their names. Looking back, they saw that it was Sean jogging towards them. He was wearing the school's warm up track pants and a Nike T-shirt as he ran toward them, his long legs taking long strides.

"There's a sight for sore eyes. Where you been at this whole time?" Andrea asked.

"I was at the gym puttin' in work as usual. Gotta stay ready," he replied. "Besides Coach P thinks I got a good chance to make it to a D1 school," he added, referring to the coach of Richmond Hill High School men's basketball team, Nate Plummer.

After six full years as the head coach for his alma mater, Nate helped sparked a resurgence in Richmond Hill basketball and had the kids ready each year to make a run for the state championship. Early on during his tenure, many people in the area had doubts about Nate's credibility as a coach. Many of those doubts had surfaced from his mysterious background and his prior offense over which he had been arrested due to threatening another man with a firearm. But just like many other historical moments in the annuls of time, once the situation was over

Nate's past faded and he was hired as head coach for the basketball team which proceeded to experience six straight years of winning records.

"So I bet you about to go home and blow up yo' mailbox lookin' for that scholarship, huh?" Vanessa asked.

"Nah, I'm good about that now. I've been working out and recording some of my workouts. I'm about to send them to a couple schools that I applied for. No more sittin' and waitin' fo' me. I'm 'bout to make it happen," Sean replied confidently.

"Well that's good," Andrea said. As they continued to walk the block, a police car that was driving through the busy streets, slowed down and came to a complete stop in front of them. Such a sight would have dismayed many young black students, but Andrea, Vanessa, and Sean were familiar to these regular police stops because of one person who drove the squad vehicle. A black patrolman emerged from the driver's seat and approached the three teenagers.

"You guys are supposed to be at home at this time. What are you doin' out in these streets?" he asked in a stern voice. Andrea and Vanessa tried to hide their laughter, fully aware of the officer's identity.

"What's so funny? This is no joking matter," he said.

"Yeah, yeah Officer Hawkins, we on the way home now," Andrea replied. A smile slowly broke out across Officer Hawkins' face.

"Well I gotta make sure I do my job, right?" he asked, laughing. The only person who didn't find the whole situation amusing was Sean.

"C'mon Pops, did you have to stop like we did something wrong though? You know people gon' be watchin'," Sean said.

Officer Hawkins laughed again. He missed the days when his son was once proud of him being a member of the New York Police Department. It seems the older these kids got, the more concerned they became with their public image and their so called "rep." He remembered a time when he had one of those.

"I know. I just saw you walking and I wanted to find out how the workouts are going," he said.

"Workouts are good, just gotta keep workin', like you," Sean said.

"That's my boy," Officer Hawkins said. He was a big, heavy set man who had once been an athlete himself in his high school days. "So, you want me to give you a ride back home in the squad car?" he asked Sean.

"Nah Pops, I'm good," Sean replied, shaking his hand. "Besides, people gonna think I'm a perp or something," he added.

"Nah, they won't say nothin'," Officer Hawkins replied. "Streets are quiet today. We had a speeder earlier but nothin' too serious," he added.

"Not yet at least," Sean corrected. If there was anything Sean knew, it was that 101 Avenue and Lefferts Blvd could pop off at any moment.

"Well, what about you girls? You need a ride?" he asked them.

"We're ok. Thanks Mr. Hawkins," Andrea replied.

"Ok. Well, I'll see you girls later. Sean, I'll see you later at home, son." he said before entering his vehicle and driving off.

"Thank God," Sean said as soon as the car drove out of sight. He hated when his father did these brief impromptu visits while on duty. It was embarrassing and awkward.

"What's wrong with you?" Vanessa asked.

"Nothin' I just hate when my pops be pullin' this shit. Sometimes, he don't get the fact that I ain't a lil kid no more. If people knew that my pops was a cop…." he started, before trailing off.

"Why does it even matter?" Andrea asked reasonably. "Your father's one of the good cops out there," she added.

"You think niggas out hea' care if my pops is a good cop or not? To most of 'em, he still workin' fo' da' man. He still five-oh. All they gon' see is the badge," Sean said.

Andrea and Vanessa looked at each other. They remembered when Sean was proud of his father for being a police officer and looked up to him as a hero. Only since they entered high school had Sean begun to believe that the police officers in New York City were corrupt and out to make more trouble against them as young adults. To the other students, Sean's father was merely a part of an oppressive system that meant to keep them all down. Sean realized that not only was his father's job dangerous but it was filled with rumors and scrutiny that affected his entire family.

Down in a basement-like structure underneath a home in East Tremont, three men were sitting together, playing craps. A hip hop beat was blaring from the speakers that sat next to a makeshift mini-home studio. It was a deep base sound that had the boys bobbing their heads to the beat. The song wasn't original, it was the instrumental to a track by a well-known artist that had been released a couple of years back. The men were a rap group – or crew – and they had goals of being signed to a major label. The assumed leader of the group, Tico Jones, headed the trio. He was accompanied by two other young men, John Jay or JJ for short. The other boy was name Nick Brown, who was often called NB on a couple of their demo tracks. The basement and equipment belonged to Tico, who rented the home but had to work two jobs to pay the bills. Life was not easy, especially for Tico who had two sons, both born out of wedlock, to two different women. After legal custody battles and child support payments, the two kids lived with Tico, where they currently slept. It was a little bit before one o'clock in the morning and Tico was becoming anxious.

They had finally gotten a demo CD to one of the other men on the block by the name of Tony Wadell, who worked at Metro Records and was introduced to Tico through JJ, who grew up only three houses away. Tony promised them that he would get the demo to the other producers for consideration but they hadn't heard a word yet. Tico was beginning to sense deception on Tony's part and being from the hard streets of the Bronx, he hated being taken for a fool. He had never served jail time but he had been arrested under suspicion of assault. Due to lack of evidence, the police were forced to release him but they were never convinced that Tico was completely innocent. Tico gave the police no further reasons to doubt his character and he continued to mind his own business.

With his two kids, Ricardo and Marissa depending on him, he had to make this happen. Tico was a neighborhood rapper who grew up the same way as De'Von. Although the two had never crossed paths, Tico felt that he should have been signed instead of De'Von and that the system was working against him. Tico also felt that his struggle would one day be the pathway to his success and he counted the days that remained before he could grant his kids whatever they wanted. The basement was filled with the scent of marijuana and the smoke rose to the ceiling, where the three men were playing craps.

"Yo, Tico where Tony at? You ain't tell him to meet you hea?" JJ asked, as he prepared to roll the dice.

"Hell yeah, I told him to meet us hea today," Tico replied." Anyway, that's yo' boy, and I'mma hold him to what he said. If he even think about playin' wit' me, that busta's gon' wish he neva' met me," he added.

"Man, he'll come through. Chill wit' all that noise," NB replied, as he counted his take after the game.

All three men, throughout the course of the game put money down, for the purpose of the game. Suddenly they heard a knock at the basement door. Although they figured it was Tony, the crew was still suspicious of any visitors and each right hand reached for the guns at their sides. Tico walked to the door.

"Who dis?" he asked in a deep tone.

"Man, its Tony. Hurry up man, open the door," Tony said.

The basement light, which was already dim, became dimmer when Tico opened the door, allowing Tony to walk in. The silhouetted figure saw Tico holding the gun.

Chuckling silently he said, "Damn, all ya paranoid like this? Ya could drop em, man." It took about a minute, but once the men were reassured that it was Tony, they put their firearms away.

"So what's up wit' the demo? You played it for'em?" Tico asked. Tony scratched the back of his head, which was done whenever Tony was ready to give an excuse.

"Well not exactly. This week had been a busy week in the studio and I just ain't gotten around to play it yet," he replied.

JJ and NB just shook their heads, as if they knew Tony was going to give an excuse. "Well, what you waitin' for man? I ain't got time to waste," Tico said.

Tony sat down on the small couch that stood next to the table. "I'm waitin' fo' the right time, homie. Look, the CEO of the company came and visited the label. He had a meeting with basically all the producers," he attempted to explain.

But Tico wasn't ok with the setup; as a matter of fact, he was beginning to feel that he was being set up.

"I don't care what's going on, we had a deal. I mean, they got De'Von in there and I know I could flow much betta than him," Tico exclaimed angrily. "I gave you one job to do, man and you couldn't even do that. Now I'm sick of this waitin' around man. I promised to leave the street hustle game alone but if that's what I have to do to put food on the table, then that's what I'm gonna do. Look man, I'm tryin' to stay clean, but you keep playin'", he said.

"Look, things been crazy the last couple of days, with the meetings and other things man. But trust me, I ain't forget about ya'll," Tony reassured.

"Better not," Tico threatened. "Tony, you my boy but if I can't trust you to make this happen, I'll no longer have a use for you," he added.

"You'll get in. Trust me. Check this out," Tony said, pulling out a sheet of paper. It was colored blue and there was a picture of an outside velvet rope entrance with a picture of a microphone. Tico snatched the sheet out of Tony's hand. The paper was apparently an invitation for an amateur night that would take place at the Fusion nightclub and lounge within the next week. Although Tico read the invitation, he saw it as no more than a waste of his time.

"What the hell is this?" he asked harshly. "You givin' me this invitation for some amateur night? I didn't come to you about performing in front of some people in South Queens, I came to you to get me a contract. I'm really losin' my patience, son and you don't wanna go there," he added, his voice rising dangerously.

"Just read the whole damn thing. Did you even look at the bottom of the paper?" Tony asked. Tico glanced at the bottom.

He was able to see that the first place winner of the amateur night at Fusion could win cash prizes and a possible recording contract with Metro Records. "And your point is?" Tico asked.

Tony sighed. Not only were these guys paranoid, but they were also lazy. "Look man, all you gotta do is show up at this amateur gig, blow the stage up, and you get the contract you been lookin' for. Unless you afraid to go live wit' yo' material," he replied.

He knew that at this point, he was goading Tico on to take the challenge but he may have barked up the wrong tree. Tico grabbed Tony roughly by his shirt collar. "Who said I was afraid?" he asked menacingly.

Many men would have been intimidated to find themselves in Tico's grip and intimidating stare, but Tony seemed very smug, almost comfortable. "So if you ain't scared, you'll do it, right?" he asked. Tico still holding onto Tony, looked back at his boys.

"Hell yeah, man. Let's tear it up on amateur night," NB agreed. JJ voiced his sentiment as well, asking Tico what he had to lose by participating in the amateur night.

Tico released Tony and thought about it for a moment. He has performed in front of a few people previously, but this was a club full of people. What if nobody liked him? What if he froze up on stage? Then he could kiss the opportunity goodbye.

Still looking at Tony menacingly, he said, "Ok, I'll do this. But if I don't win, you better be workin' overtime to make sure my demo gets to the right hands. Cuz if you come back hea' with nothin' but air in yo' hands, you'll be sweatin' bullets, foreal, you feel me?" Tico threatened.

"Man don't even sweat that. You'll win," Tony replied.

"I know I'll win. Even if I don't win the contest, I still betta get my contract, right?" Tico asked.

"Yeah don't worry. I'll take care of it," Tony agreed before walking back outside, closing the door after him.

Holding the invitation in his hand, Tico rejoined his two friends. "I don't know about yo' boy. I feel like he sleepin' on me. If he don't wake up and get his shit together, he gonna be sleepin' fo' good," he said in hushed tones.

It seemed that everyone in his block was getting a chance. He vividly remembered the level of anger he felt when he saw De'Von's face at the VMAs, nominated as a Best New Artist just last year. De'Von was nothing more than a stroke of luck; who happened to hail from the same hometown as he did and was just lucky enough to get his shot.

My day will come too, watch me. If he thinks I'm just gonna sit there and watch him get rich, he got another thing comin. He ain't nothin' but a wanksta, he thought as he continued managing his beats and playing craps with his friends.

Coming back home from work, Andrea placed her bookbag down on her room floor. I got so much homework to do, it ain't even funny. They need to make homework optional for seniors, she thought as she opened her chemistry book.

After a couple of hours working on formulas and answering experiment questions, she laid down on her bed resting her pounding head for a moment. She reflected on the day's events at school. With the prom approaching next Saturday, the school has begun the frenzy of trying to sell as many tickets as possible. Vanessa had already purchased her ticket and she had even picked out her dress. She had a date for the prom; Jimmy Davidson who played defensive end on Richmond Hill's football team. Elated as anyone could be, Vanessa put all the pressure of finding a date squarely on Andrea's shoulders. At first, Andrea was reluctant about even going to the prom. If she went, she would be the first, since Loree never had the chance to attend her own senior prom.

Although Andrea tried to block out any type of flashbacks about Loree because it would have her in tears again, she couldn't help but wonder to herself. How would it have been if Loree had been given the chance to go to her senior prom? No doubt she would have gone with David, her hot quarterback boyfriend; that issue was a no brainer but what would she have worn? Andrea temporarily placed herself in Loree's shoes. She knew Loree loved to wear black sheer dresses and the more the dress bared her shoulders, the better. She could've seen Loree and David in matching black tux and dress. She also could've seen her late sister wear a champagne colored dress and she knew David would not have any issues with wearing that particular color at all, which was why she never believed David was responsible for her sister's murder. Even if her parents thought he had, Andrea was never convinced. There were times when she heard Loree argue with David about petty issues but they would make up as soon as the next day because they were so much into each other. He would've done whatever her sister wanted. While lying in bed with those thoughts, she heard her phone vibrate. Checking the screen, she saw that it was Vanessa who sent a text message.

Log into your Facebook account. I gotta show you something, it read.

What's so important that I gotta log into FB for? I just finished doing HW. I'm bout to KO, she replied back.

After a minute her phone vibrated again. Chick, just log on! It's gon' be quick I promise, Vanessa replied.

Wondering why her hard-headed friend could never take a hint, Andrea gave in and logged into her Facebook account. The profile picture she had posted a year ago was still there. The profile picture reminded her that her hair was shorter and she was a little slimmer than she presently was, with a weak attempt of a smile.

If only people knew what my smile was hiding, she thought. With thoughts of changing her picture, she scrolled her mouse up to the top of her screen where she saw the notification sent by Vanessa. When Andrea clicked the notification, the bright blue colored scheme loaded. Fusion nightclub was holding an amateur night where she was among about sixty other people who were tagged in the photo. Shaking her head, Andrea was simply annoyed. She couldn't believe Vanessa had acted so impulsively again. She just refused to accept that Andrea didn't want to perform. Reaching for her phone, Andrea texted Vanessa again; this time putting an angry face emoji with her message.

Call me NOW!!! Andrea made sure to put emphasis on the exclamation points that she used. Her phone rang. Andrea answered the phone

"Vanessa, what is this? Why you got me tagged in that picture for?" she asked.

"Why not?" Vanessa asked, in question. "Girl you got dem vocals and it's time to show the world what you can do wit' em," she said.

"Girl you know I don't like singing in front of crowds," Andrea argued back.

"But you do it at yo' church all of da' time," Vanessa argued.

"That's different, though girl," Andrea argued back. "When I sing at church, it's because the pastor knows I can sing and I'm just helpin' him out," she added.

"Well girl, now it's time to help yourself out. Read the rest of this invitation," Vanessa countered as Andrea's eyes scanned to the bottom of the invitation.

The first place winner would win a cash prize of a thousand dollars and a recording contact with the label of their choice.

"Girl, I've told you a thousand times, I'm not doing any amateur night, or singing for nobody. I'm sorry but you gon' have to listen to me one of these days," Andrea said.

"Ok, ok, I got you. Just think on it, at least," Vanessa said.

"Besides, I think I gotta work that day anyway so it's out of the question," Andrea said.

"Ok whateva, but anyway did you get a date for the prom yet?" Vanessa asked, shifting gears suddenly.

"As a matter of fact, I do have a date," Andrea answered. She thought she heard Vanessa gasp in surprise.

"Get outta hea'. Who asked you?" she asked. Andrea hoped that Vanessa would be ready for her response and not judge her choice.

"Quentin Stevens asked me," Andrea replied. There was silence on the other line and Andrea thought for a moment that Vanessa was no longer on the line.

Vanessa finally replied, "Quentin? You mean the quiet boy that sits behind us in chem class?" Andrea wondered why it took Vanessa so long to reply when she answered the question. Vanessa had clearly been trying to put a face to the name.

"Yeah him. So what?" she asked.

"Nah girl, you know I ain't got no problem with that. He cool. He just don't be talkin' too much. But that's good," Vanessa said.

Andrea chuckled while her best friend tried to cover her tracks. She had to admit, the whole situation was awkward, because prior to that, Andrea had never spoken to Quentin. He was so quiet in the corner of the classroom that he barely answered questions whenever the teacher asked. He dressed normally in South Pole shirts, jeans, and Nike sneakers. He wore thin glasses and was relatively clean-cut. As Andrea recounted earlier that day, when chemistry class had ended and the kids filed out into the hallway, Quentin strode up to Andrea. Andrea had never really spoken with him before but she remembered greeting him every time he walked into class.

"Hey Andrea, what's up?" he asked casually.

"Nothin'. What up wit' you?" Andrea replied just as casually.

"Chillin'. You know, countin' down till graduation," he replied.

"I know, right?" Andrea agreed. "I can't wait to get up out of hea'," she added.

"Right," Quentin said. "Yo, so I was just wondering if you had a date for prom yet?" he asked, in slow tones.

Andrea smiled. Aww that's sweet. He probably was shy and worked up nerve to come ask. I don't have a date anyhow and he's cool and kinda cute, she thought. "Nah, I ain't got a date yet," she answered.

"Neither do I," Quentin said. "So would you like to go to prom together? If it's cool wit' you?" he asked, scratching the back of his head, which wasn't itching.

"Sure, yeah. I'd love to go wit' you," Andrea replied.

"Word?" Quentin asked, looking shocked. It was as if he was surprised that Andrea agreed to go with him.

"Yeah, I'll go wit' you," she said again.

"Cool. So I could pick you up in my car or we can do limo group, whatever's good wit' you," he said.

"We can do a limo group. My homegirl's goin' with Jimmy who's on the football team, so we can roll wit' them," she suggested.

"Yeah, that's cool," Quentin said. "So what color you wanna do?" he asked, referring to dress and tuxedo colors.

"How about blue?" Andrea suggested.

"Yeah, that works," he said. After arranging to meet the group at their designated location, they parted ways.

"So does Sean have a date?" Andrea asked Vanessa that night.

"Girl he goin' with LaShondra Jenkins," she replied.

"Nuh-uh! Lashondra?" Andrea asked. If there was one bit of information Andrea knew about Lashondra, it was that she got around more than the Metro Transit Authority. Boys had dunked on her more than all members of the basketball team combined.

"Hopefully he can handle her. Me, personally? I thought he could've done much better than her but you know how she got her men all hypnotized," Vanessa replied. Andrea shook her head. She wished Sean could see past the beauty and notice real quality in girls.

Chapter Eight

It was a little bit after midnight on the darkest street of East Tremont and De'Von was running as hard and as fast as he could. But he didn't know from what he was running. Panting in huge gasps, he felt his legs tighten and get heavier, but he couldn't stop running. Looking behind him, he couldn't see anyone pursuing him. Streetlights illuminated the dark sidewalks and side streets as De'Von continued to run.

Why am I running? The answer came in the form of a blurred figure with a dark cap running after him. The figure seemed to be clutching an object in his hand. It wasn't until a few seconds later that De'Von saw that the object was a gun, and it was pointed squarely at him. With a renewed sense of fear and a burst of adrenaline, De'Von ran even faster and more swiftly but the figure kept pace doggedly and began to catch up to De'Von. As the footsteps became louder and louder, De'Von looked behind him and right before his eyes, the figure began to shape-shift. What he thought had been a stranger in a hooded sweatshirt began to transform into a figure more ominous to De'Von. A shiny police badge appeared just under his left breast and his hooded sweater tightened over his body. The hood seemed to have shrunk behind his head. A dark blue tie and police uniform transformed from the dark figure and the face which had appeared to be so dark that facial features couldn't be seen was now replaced with a face of a middle-aged white male.

He continued to run after De'Von yelling, "Freeze! Freeze you black piece of shit!"

De'Von did not comply to the voice of the officer and the officer, the insubordinate action, pointed the gun directly at his target. De'Von only had time to look back at the pursuer before the officer fired three bullets into De'Von. He felt the sharp, inconceivable pain that De'Von could only assume were bullets, which ripped through his upper body and lower leg. The world suddenly became blurry as De'Von, mortally wounded, fell on the sidewalk. One of the bullets, penetrated his lungs because De'Von couldn't breathe and his blood spilled over to the sidewalk.

The police officer stood over a dying De'Von and said, "Think you real slick, huh boy?" he said, holding the gun to De'Von's head. "We don't need any more of your kind here in these streets," he said before grabbing his gun and shot it at De'Von, from close range.

The bullet nearly entered De'Von's temple, guaranteed to destroy him, before De'Von woke up from the nightmare in a cold sweat. As he took a cleansing moment to stretch and rise out of his bed, he looked in the mirror. The nightmare had been so vivid, he was sure he had really been shot in reality. As he lifted his tank top, he traced over the spots where the policemen shot him.

Mase is that you, bro? What were you trying to tell me, son? Was that how it all went down?

Staring at his chest, De'Von couldn't get over how real the bullets felt, nor how painful they were. It was agony upon agony that he felt. Was it possible that his dream was a re-enactment of that fateful night? He wasn't sure but he knew that the pain he felt in the dreams was the same as Mason endured and it was all because of them. The crooked police establishment who thought of Mason as just another stupid black boy who resembled nothing but the troublemaking kind they preyed upon. De'Von blamed himself for not having been awake that night to prevent Mason from heading outside. Maybe then he could have prevented the tragedy.

Walking over to the nightstand in his room, he stared at the huge mirror. He was no longer the suave, attractive, toned, and tall rap star he had become. Instead he saw the little eleven year old boy who still waited for his older brother to arrive home from school so they could practice rapping. He saw the traumatically shaken boy who held his brother as he died in his arms as witnesses and law enforcement struggled to separate him from Mason's body. He was looking at a young boy who had similar dreams with his brother and had it not been for Julio and the producers of Metro Records, he would have probably ended up dead as well. But it wasn't over. The pain his family felt would never go away. Feeling the fatigue slip away, De'Von decided to call his mother at her home.When he dialed the number, he thought his mother wasn't home, for the phone rang five times. Finally he heard somebody pick up on the other end. "Hello?" the voice of Delores Franklin answered over the receiver.

"Hey Mama, it's me," De'Von replied.

"Pooh-bear, is that you? I haven't heard from you in a while baby, are you all right?" she asked.

De'Von chuckled. "You're the only one who can get away with callin' me that, Mama," he replied. "But I was just callin' up to check on you," he added.

"Mmmhmm, at two-thirty seven in the mornin'? You sure bout that, baby?" Delores asked.

De'Von couldn't believe how perceptive his mother was. She must've known that De'Von wouldn't have called unless he was in trouble or wanted to talk. "Yeah, I'm sure," he replied with a voice that indicated clear uncertainty. He knew his mother could read between the lines and she would know what he was thinking. "I know it's late but I just couldn't sleep again tonight and I just thought I would call...." His voice trailed off. His mother knew exactly why he called and she knew it wasn't because of her.

"Been thinking about Mase, have you?" she asked.

"Yeah, Mama. I know it's been ten years but it feels like he never left. It feels like he still here," he explained to her, trying hard to keep his composure but it was extremely difficult.

His mother realized how tough it had been for her youngest son. She still kept the baby pictures of De'Von along with Mason.

"Mama, I just can't believe he got shot down in cold blood, and by who? A racist-ass cop who be takin' lives from other folks. If I was there Mama, I would've stopped him from going outside. I should've said something," he said.

"Boy, I want you to close your mouth and listen to me right now," Delores scolded her youngest son. "Honey you ain't the only one who's missing Mase right now. Do you know how many sleepless nights I've had? No one feels worse about it than I do," she said.

De'Von couldn't bring himself to be as calm as his mother. Surely she had not forgotten how his brother's life had ended….or had she?

"Mama, haven't you ever wanted to strangle the life out of the sorry bastard that did Mase in?" he asked.

"Honey, believe me, I wanted to do that and much more, especially after he was not indicted and they ruled it a 'justified killing'. I wanted that man dead, Pooh. But I realized that if I needed that, it would make me no better than all the bad, nasty people in this world," she replied.

"Mama, I can't forgive him for what he did. There are times I be in the studio and I act like it's all good outside, but inside, I don't know what to do," he said.

"Honey we have to learn to forgive those who hurt us. It's what the good Lord would want us to do. Love is the greatest weapon we have against hate," she replied.

"But Mama, I can't see nothin' but hate for the police and what they did to my brother," De'Von replied. "Do you think they give a damn about us? Do you think they're tryin' to protect us? We're better off dead to them. Believe me Mama, I won't give a cop no satisfaction of even getting close to me, cuz if he do, I'm liable to do whatever, whenever," he added.

"Pooh, we shouldn't think that way. If we allow hate to consume us, it will consume us until the end," Delores said.

De'Von looked up at the ceiling that shone brightly from the moon. "I don't care, Mama. I just don't see it your way. I'm tellin' you if a cop eva crosses me...." he started before his mother started back on him, more roughly this time.

"What will you do? Don't be stupid! The police run this town," she snapped, without hesitation, but De'Von who was determined not to listen to the 'wells of mercy' speech. This was not one of the churches in which he had grown up before the horrible murder happened. If God had been involved at all, why hadn't he done anything to save Mason's life? As far as De'Von was concerned, God was just as guilty as the police officer.

"Just know that if they step to me, I will defend myself, I don't care who it is," he said in definite tones.

There was a long silence. His mother did not reply for a minute. Then she said, "I know how much it hurts, son, but you have to allow yourself to heal," she replied. With that, she said goodbye to De'Von and hung up. De'Von sat on the edge of his bed, thinking about what his mother said and about the dream that had plagued him.

Saturday finally arrived and that meant it was the day of the high school senior class prom for Richmond Hill students. As all the boys and girls made their last minute preparations for the event, Andrea and Vanessa were already prepared and Andrea could not have been more relieved. During the week, Vanessa had taken Andrea shopping for prom dresses and after visiting at least six locations, they found them. Vanessa selected a sizzling hot strapless red dress while Andrea went for a light blue dress that had one strap surrounding an artificial blue flower.

One of us has to be the sensible dresser, Andrea thought to herself as she paid for her order. Although she had different fashion sense than that of Vanessa, she loved her unique sense of style.

Looking down at her lovely blue dress spread across her bed, Andrea realized that she was actually looking forward to the prom. The night promised to be eventful, with Quentin picking her up from her house at six-thirty. Andrea called Quentin ahead of time to warn him about her father's temperament but Quentin seemed to laugh off the warning.

Ok, don't say I didn't warn you, she remembered thinking. The plan was for Quentin to pick up Andrea, then they would go to Vanessa's house, where they would all take pictures and hang around until the limo arrived. Once the limo came, they would ride together to downtown Manhattan to go to the Financial District; a landmark event venue with a dining and dance hall. Although the prom was scheduled to end at eleven or even close to midnight, Andrea knew many of the students, most of them drunk by that time, would be renting rooms at the Radisson Hotel only a block away. A few brave souls would attempt to drive home but they would do it at their own risk. Supposedly the group's limo driver was rented for the evening, so he would be there to drop them all back at Vanessa's home if they chose not to stay in the hotel.

Andrea stepped out of the bathroom where she just finished showering and putting on her undergarments, then she began to slip on the beautiful blue dress. She realized she needed some help to zip her dress up from the back, so she called to her mother. Alisha came upstairs and zipped up her dress. After carefully applying her makeup and jewelry, she was ready. Alisha stood behind her daughter as she looked in the mirror. With her normally straight brown hair curled and the dress fitted to her curves, Andrea resembled a beautiful black princess. The moment was too much for Alisha, who couldn't hide her emotions. With tears welling in her eyes, a smile broke out across her face.

"Aww come on Mama, don't cry on me now," Andrea said, although she was smiling as well.

"I know baby, but you look so beautiful. You've grown to be a beautiful young woman," she said. With that, she beckoned Andrea to come closer to her, so she could fix her hair and adjust the dress some more.

"Ok, I have to get Amos to see this. Don't move, ok?" she asked as she ran out the room.

"Mama, it's ok…." Andrea started to say but her mother already left.

She looked at herself in the mirror again. She couldn't believe it was really her. Her makeup was just right, her hair was just right, and she not only looked beautiful but she felt beautiful. She couldn't shake the warm feeling rising within her at that moment. It was a feeling that no matter what the world thought of her, she was always beautiful and she was always loved. She could almost see her sister come in the room, wearing all white, like she had in her dreams. She could see Loree standing behind her the same way her mother had stood behind her just moments before. Andrea closed her eyes as she felt Loree gently touch her hand.

"You look so pretty, Drea. Tonight is your night to let all your worries go. Enjoy yourself and bask in your beauty," she seemed to whisper in Andrea's ear.

"I will, sis." Andrea replied quietly.

"Don't fall for any hard-headed boys and don't force anything," Loree said.

Andrea smiled a bit. "He's a nice guy, Loree. We don't have to worry about him," she replied.

Loree smiled the same way she had in Andrea's dream. Andrea looked up and her mother re-entered the room, accompanied by her father.

"What do you think, Daddy?" she asked. Amos nodded his head approvingly.

"You look great, baby. I may have to have an extended talk with this Quentin fellow," he said.

"Come on Daddy, he's only my date for the prom. We're only friends. He's very responsible and nice. Give him a chance," Andrea said.

Amos smiled at his daughter. "I'll try, I promise I'll do my best," he reassured Andrea.

Andrea walked over to her father and gave him a hug. "Daddy, you will always be the first man in my life. Nobody will ever replace you," she said. Amos smiled so widely, it looked as if he might weep himself. During the touching moment, the doorbell suddenly rang. Andrea looked at the clock across the hallway.

"That must be him," she said, heading to the door. Amos gently stopped her, wanting to answer the door himself. As he opened the door, Quentin stood in his light blue tuxedo, dressed over a white pastel shirt and matching shoes. Andrea saw Quentin from the living room. Quentin, who normally liked to let his hair grow out to the point where it was disheveled, had actually gotten a proper haircut.

"He is cute honey," Alisha whispered in Andrea's ear.

"Mom!" Andrea said in hushed tones. Man, she's so embarrassing, she thought.

"How are you sir? My name's Quentin Stevens," he introduced to Amos, extending his hand for a handshake.

"I know that son," Amos replied, leaving Quentin's hand extended. After a few seconds, Quentin put his hand down to prevent himself from looking foolish. "Now, because it's my daughter's wishes, I will let you off with a kind warning son. I'm entrusting my daughter to you for tonight. It's a huge responsibility that I don't take lightly. I was a young man once too, so I know what goes on after these proms," he said.

"Daddy!" Andrea exclaimed, her eyes widening in shock.

"Now, I hear you're a nice young man. Prove it tonight by having my daughter home right after prom," Amos continued, ignoring his daughter.

"Yes sir, I'll bring her home after prom," Quentin said.

"Ok, enough of that. Time for pictures!" Alisha exclaimed as she went to get her digital camera.

When Quentin attempted to put the corsage on Andrea's wrist, Alisha exclaimed, "Not yet, honey. Not yet. I want to take a picture of you as you're putting it on," Andrea rolled her eyes. Her parents were way too enthusiastic about this event. After ten agonizing minutes of taking pictures, they were finally allowed to leave.

"Ok Quentin, remember what I told you now. I'm counting on you," Amos told Andrea's date.

"Ok. Yeah he got it, Daddy. Sheesh," Andrea said in exasperation as she closed the door behind her. They walked toward Vanessa's house, they didn't talk for a few minutes. Finally Quentin broke the silence.

"So yo' girl stay around here?" he asked.

"Yeah she only live a couple blocks," Andrea answered.

"That's cool," Quentin said. "You look great, by the way. I didn't get a chance to really say that at yo' house cuz your pops was givin' me da third degree," he added laughing.

"Thanks and yeah, my bad. I warned you about him though," she said laughing also.

"It's all good. He's just lookin' out for you," he replied.

"Yeah right, but sometimes I wish he'd be a lil chill and give me some space," Andrea said.

"You should try livin' wit' my fam. Trust me, a week wit' my three brothas and my lil sista, you gonna be runnin' back to your folks," he said.

"Really? I love kids so that wouldn't be a problem to me," she said.

"So you'll take 'em then?" Quentin asked, laughing.

"Slow yo' roll, man. I ain't say all that now," Andrea replied, laughing.

She couldn't believe how loose Quentin was. He was not a bad guy at all but then again, she never assumed he was bad. It was the fact that she never heard him say so much as a word the whole year. She was not a close friend of his, so she didn't know who he normally spoke with on a regular basis. Finally they arrived at Vanessa's small duplex-styled house. She rang the bell. After a second, the door flew open.

"Damn girl, what took you so long?" Vanessa asked. She was wearing her red dress.

"My bad, girl. You know my parents. They were takin' like a hundred pictures before we could even leave," she replied, entering her house.

"This must be Quentin," Vanessa said, shaking Quentin's hand.

"What's up?" Quentin greeted.

As they entered her living room, they saw the rest of the group; Vanessa's date Jimmy, the defensive end on the football team and Sean with his date, Lashondra. Jimmy stood nearly six foot five and was two hundred and thirty pounds of muscle. He seemed to be the type of fellow who knew he had the strength to break a person's back but had a playful side, a humor that some would deem inappropriate. Lashondra was a fair skinned girl, with thin lips, a shapely body and long hair that flowed down her lower back.

They talk about me wearing a weave all da time, and this girl got more than one hundred pounds of Brazilian on her head right now, Andrea thought as she greeted Lashondra.

They were not particular friends and it didn't take long for Andrea to recognize they probably never would be friends. Lashondra loved to talk about the latest gossip, whether it be airing an ex-boyfriend's dirty secrets or talking about another girl she didn't like. Andrea was not perfect, she has done her share of gossiping over the years but Lashondra seemed to take the talking game to whole new level.

Another aspect of Lashondra that Andrea found very disturbing was her wardrobe choices. Lashondra would go out of her way to attract every boy in Richmond Hill High School using provocatively low-cut clothing that showed miles of cleavage. She was unapologetic about her clothing decisions. It was reminiscent of the old days in Richmond Hill High, when a group of conceited girls known as the Black Barbies walked the hallways. Andrea would never forget how her late sister had high hopes of becoming one of the Black Barbies. However, Loree smartened up and realized that they were just as fake as their name, dropped them, and befriended a better quality of people. A rumor started that Lashondra had an older sister, who had been a member of the Black Barbies during their heyday in the early 2000's. Whether the rumor was true or not, Andrea couldn't see herself being friends with Lashondra because they would have nothing in common. It was a cruel way to think but Andrea didn't trust Jimmy and she certainly didn't trust Lashondra. Since they were dating her two closest friends and since Sean and Vanessa obviously couldn't see clearly because they were dictated by their lust, Andrea would have to keep quiet about her thoughts.

Vanessa's mother, who had been cooking in the kitchen, emerged with a digital camera.

"Ok everybody, while you're waiting on the limo to arrive, let's get some prom photos!" she exclaimed.

Instructing everyone to go outside, she lined the boys at a side angle, standing together, while their dates stood in front of them. After what seemed like forever and a million snapshots, the black stretch limo finally pulled up at Vanessa's house. The kids took one more photo with Vanessa's mother and after they got into the limo, they decided not to focus on what was behind them but rather what was ahead of them. Andrea looked around her. She had never been inside a limo before. There were long couch-like chairs, a television, and a refrigerator for keeping drinks cold. As soon as the group entered the limo, they were on their way to the Financial. The teens talked about different topics before they started to talk about future plans.

"So what school you goin' to, after you get outta here?" Sean asked Jimmy.

"Aw man, you know I'm goin' to Navy, on that football scholar-ship man," Jimmy declared proudly. "What about you? Where you goin'?" he asked.

"Man I got my options bro. Seton Hall, St. John, or Syracuse. You know what it is," Sean answered while lying back on his seat. Jimmy turned to Quentin.

"What about you, homeboy? Where you goin' after graduation?" he asked

"I'm actually goin' to Morehouse College. I already got accepted," Quentin answered.

Jimmy nodded his head, although judging by the slight smirk and the impatient eye roll; indicated that although he asked the questions, Jimmy couldn't care less about anyone who didn't share the same athletic goals that he did. Vanessa and Lashondra were checking out the television set that was in the limo.

"Yo, check this out!" Jimmy exclaimed as he reached into a small bag that he carried with him. Inside the bag were two bottles of Hennessey cognac. "We finna turn up in dat bitch tonight!" he stated, and the rest of the kids exulted in the prospect of drinking Hennessey at the prom.

Reaching into one of the compartments, Andrea and Quentin found a few plastic cups. The Hennessey had a hot tinge to it that went down smoothly. They all took a cup on the ride to the Financial District, and although she was not the one to be drinking multiple shots of Hennessey, Andrea couldn't help but drink two more short glasses. As the ride went on, they entertained themselves by turning on the television and watching Martin, which was Andrea's favorite show. She enjoyed the scenes when Martin Payne would ridicule one of his friends, Tommy, whenever he hinted about going to the place where he was employed that remained a mystery to the viewers. During those moments, Martin would say, "Tommy, you ain't got no job man!!!" to the roar of laughter from the audience.

As they watched, Sean found himself looking out of the window into the busy Manhattan streets. "Yo, this is legit, son. Now I know how it feels to be De'Von Franklin for an hour," he said laughing.

"Man, you ain't no De'Von. He makin' over six figures and you ain't even worth a dolla," Jimmy said, laughing. "But I feel you though. Nigga be makin' bank. He need to cut me in. Shit," he added.

"Yeah, that would be nice," Sean agreed. "Don't worry though, I'm gonna be countin' dem ducs in a couple years once I start ballin' D1," he said.

"What, you think you gon' go pro?" Jimmy asked with a snort of disbelief.

"You already know, man. Ain't no stoppin' this on da courts," Sean replied confidently.

Finally the limo pulled up next to the Financial District venue and ballroom, where the events of the prom were scheduled to take place.

"Yo, check it out," Quentin said. All six teenagers looked out of the window. Billions of lights streamed out of the building and a huge banner hung just inside the doorway arch, with the words RICHMOND HILL SENIOR CLASS PROM 2009 written in huge gold letters across it.

They could see the multitude of kids making their way inside. As the limo driver walked over to the passenger door to open for them, Andrea marveled at the extra effort that her school put toward the event.

Looks like they do care about us after all, she thought as she gracefully stepped out the limo.

Out of the three boys that exited the limo with their dates, Quentin was the only one who displayed chivalry by holding Andrea's hand to help her out of the limo. Sean and Jimmy were too preoccupied in their own excitement to help their own dates out of the limo. Lashondra and Vanessa had to exit the limo themselves, while trying to avoid getting their dresses caught under the car door. A photo booth with a professional photographer was in the room to the left for those who wanted to have a picture taken. Quentin was reluctant to take more pictures but not wanting to disappoint Andrea who was eager to take pictures, walked inside the booth. As they walked inside the ballroom, they saw one side had the dining tables and on the other side was the dance floor. There was also a small stage in the front of the room with one microphone in the center. Behind the microphone was a large screen, similar to those in movie theaters, with a projector that played all the notable moments of the senior year. Andrea knew that later during the evening, Carla Turtino, the class president, would announce the prom king and prom queen. Although she made it perfectly clear that she had no interest in being nominated, somehow her name made its way onto the list of nominees. She had a distinct feeling that it had been Vanessa who had entered her as a possible candidate for prom queen. Sean was also nominated for prom king, as was Jimmy. As they sat down to enjoy the refreshments, the music began playing. A few of the prom guests and their dates stepped to the floor and began dancing. Andrea and Quentin looked at each other for a moment before they started laughing. They both had the same thought. The first musical selection was not the one they expected. It was a pop song that had been on the music charts for weeks and they weren't too happy about it.

"Ayo, why don't ya play some real music? Don't nobody wanna listen to this pop bullshit," Jimmy said aloud, clearly inebriated.

Andrea could tell that Jimmy was beginning to look more drunk every minute but it was clear that Vanessa was ignoring all the early signs of obvious inebriation. Finally, the DJ switched the song to a well-known hip hop song and more people finally decided that the song was worth dancing to. Sean led Lashondra out to the floor and she wasted no time getting busy with her dance moves in front of Sean. Jimmy and Vanessa walked behind them, Jimmy holding Vanessa around her waist as Vanessa began moving her hips in an enticing fashion. Andrea was waiting for the one of the other boys who were eyeing her to ask her to dance, because she didn't think Quentin wanted to dance. She was surprised when he stood right in front of her with his hand outstretched.

"Care to dance?" he asked.

"Yeah, ok. Let's go," Andrea replied and they stepped onto the floor.

Andrea started to move her hips and she was surprised to see that Quentin was actually quite coordinated on the dance floor. She was afraid that her date might embarrass himself, thus embarrassing her but Quentin looked like a totally different guy on the dance floor. He no longer struck Andrea as some quiet book worm. Soon a slow ballad played over the system and Quentin took Andrea's hand and held her close to him, not forcefully and not reluctantly. He took her hand as they both danced to the slow song. All of a sudden, Andrea felt warm and comfortable in Quentin's arms. He moved well, he acted maturely, and he spoke well. Not to mention that he was focusing on his future education instead of the latest clothes or the latest trends. He was the ideal gentlemen to Andrea.

I don't know. I might give Quentin a chance after prom, she thought. She was getting so caught up dancing, that she didn't notice that Vanessa and Jimmy had disappeared from the dance floor. Sean and Lashondra still danced but when Andrea looked around, her friend was nowhere to be seen. Deciding to skip the next song, Andrea excused herself from Quentin and walked outside the ballroom. At first she thought that Vanessa was in the ladies room, so she started her search there but she quickly heard loud voices in the hall and saw Vanessa and Jimmy arguing out in the hallway.

"Look, I like you and all, but I ain't ready fo' all this yet," Vanessa explained.

"Girl c'mon quit playin'. You been teasin' me all day. So now I'm bout to show you another member of my team," Jimmy replied as he started to lift Vanessa's dress up. His lips found their way over to her lips and he kissed her. The problem was that Jimmy didn't know when enough was enough. "C'mon girl let's take this somewhere else," he said to Vanessa. Pulling her arm, against her wishes, Jimmy forcefully led her outside.

"Let go of me!" Vanessa exclaimed. Andrea couldn't believe what she was seeing. She was not going to allow her friend to be violated.

"Aye, what you doin'?" she blurted out as Jimmy and Vanessa stared back at her.

Chapter Nine

Realizing that he was no longer alone in the hallway with Vanessa, Jimmy started to walk toward Andrea. His eyes were hazed, unfocused, and almost in a slumber-like trance. He was beyond drunk.

"Ain't none of yo' concern. This is between me and my date, so why don't you go back to Urkel ova' there and lemme handle mine," he replied, still hanging on to Vanessa.

Jimmy had a strong grip and no matter how much Vanessa struggled, Jimmy seemed to get stronger while holding Vanessa's hand.

"Let me go!" Vanessa protested as she still struggled under Jimmy's vice grip.

"Damn baby, I thought you wanted to go have fun," Jimmy said.

"Get a clue, Jimmy. She ain't tryin' to get wit' you so let her go now," Andrea demanded.

"Why don't you make me? If you got da nerve…" Jimmy replied arrogantly. Andrea knew that Jimmy was much larger and stronger than her, but she wasn't afraid of him. Andrea started to grab Vanessa's other arm but one of the side doors opened and Quentin walked in through the doors.

"Everything good?" he asked Andrea.

"No, this fool right here just got denied by Vanessa, but he can't take a hint," Andrea said angrily.

Turning to Jimmy, Quentin decided to try talking with Jimmy. "Aye yo, c'mon, man. Let it go. She don't wanna stay with you, bro. Just let her go, son," he said.

"Check it out, poindexter. I ain't finna wait any longer-erer," Jimmy slurred. "She act like she the special one, true but ya holdin' me accountable. I only want what's mine," he continued. "She ain't yours to determine," he snapped back to Quentin.

"I get you dog, but don't go out like this man. It ain't worth it," Quentin reasoned but Jimmy was still ready to defend his case. Finally he decided to let the matter go.

"Whatever man, ya not about that life, anyway. I'm on my way back to da floor," Jimmy replied before going back onside the ballroom, finally letting go of Vanessa.

Andrea walked over to her friend to check on her. No bruises, no cuts, and no signs.

"You ok?" Quentin asked.

Andrea looked at him. He didn't have to appear the way he did to save Vanessa from Jimmy's aggressive attempt to abuse her. He certainly wasn't obligated to put himself in the middle of a potentially volatile situation. Yet he had.

"I'm ok, Drea." Vanessa replied to them both. "But it's over. My date with Jimmy is a wrap. He can go find another cheap hoe to violate, but I ain't wit' it," she said, with tears spilling down her cheeks. Andrea placed her hand on her best friend's back.

"Do you want to go home now?" Andrea asked. Vanessa thought for a moment.

"Yeah let's go. Making sure that I'm as far away from that guy would be a straight up priority to me," Vanessa said as they walked by the two front doors leading them back into the dance floor.

As midnight drew closer, many of the students started leaving to go home or to go to the hotels where they hoped to continue the festive moment. However, the mood was anything but festive for Andrea and her friends as they prepared to leave. Vanessa had to find out in the most brutal of ways that Jimmy was not who he seemed. He made no attempt to make amends for his attack on Vanessa and he continued the night partying as if nothing even happened. Andrea tried to savor some enjoyment but after watching her friend nearly get raped, she couldn't bring herself to stay another minute at the prom. She did remain to hear the class president yell out the names of the prom king and prom queen but she didn't hear her name called out. She couldn't even recall who won because it just wasn't important anymore. Sean and Lashondra were also mysteriously nowhere to be seen. Noticing the way Lashondra put herself out for Sean earlier had her convinced that they were possibly in a hotel suite, where Lashondra was adding Sean to her infamous man list. She saw Quentin talking to a couple of boys at the doorway, probably classmates or good friends. Before long, Andrea found herself contemplating the same question over and over again; where did she stand with Quentin? Quentin proved to be the ideal prom escort. He was funny, charming, quiet, and brave with a just enough crazy. She didn't know what made Quentin come out the way he did towards Jimmy, knowing that the crazed defensive end might have seriously hurt him. Quentin was calm and confident, which had allowed him to confront Jimmy.

Turning to Quentin and Vanessa, Andrea said, "Let's go." Gesturing for them to follow her out of the pavilion into the parking lot, Andrea looked around for any sign of Jimmy. Probably went to get a hotel room for the rest of the sorry saps that brought with his sneaky self, she thought.

She regretted not having enough time to warn the girls who were with him. As they made it outside, she took a last look back at the Financial District. The night would have been amazing had Jimmy not been there. Climbing into the limo, the driver offered to take them home. There was a vast difference between how they had arrived and how they were leaving, both physically and emotionally. The drive back to Queens was terribly quiet and equally awkward. As the limo driver pulled up next to Vanessa's house, all three of them exited the limo.

"Go home and get some rest, ok? Don't go near him anymore. If he so much as touches you, let me know," Andrea informed Vanessa.

Quentin was waiting for Andrea but he managed to inform the limo driver that he would walk Andrea home so that the driver wouldn't need to wait. After the limo left, Quentin and Andrea walked together toward her house. At first, Andrea and Quentin walked in silence, as they had early in the evening. After a few minuetes, Quentin decided to break the ice again.

"Yo, sorry bout yo' girl. She gonna be all right?" he asked as they crossed an intersection.

"Yeah she'll be ok. Vanessa's tough. I'm just glad I got there in time," Andrea replied.

"Yeah, but what if you didn't?" Quentin asked. Andrea looked at Quentin. She couldn't even bring herself to imagine what could have happened if she hadn't stumbled across them.

"Well, thankfully I was there and so were you," she replied.

"Yeah, that man's got issues. Once all that alchy's in his system, he was almost hard to stop," Quentin replied.

As they continued to walk towards Andrea's home, Quentin decided to lighten the mood. "So, other than Jimmy, I thought the night was fun. What you think?" he asked. Andrea laughed, one of the few times she had laughed since Vanessa's ordeal.

"Yeah, up until Sir Drunk-A-Lot screwed it up, it was straight. I had a great time," she replied as she saw her house looming in the distance.

"So great that you wouldn't mind doing it again, sometimes?" Quentin asked slowly. Andrea looked at him.

Her intuition told her that Quentin was a truly dependable guy and a smart guy and he was cute in his own way. All signs pointed to a possibility of a second date between her and Quentin.

"So wait, are you asking me out on a date?" she asked.

"I guess when it comes down to it, yeah. You wouldn't mind grabbin' something to eat or anything next Saturday, would you?" Quentin asked with a hint of hesitation in his voice.

Andrea was faced with a different challenge. She wouldn't exactly call herself shallow, but a great body tone had to be a plus. She looked at Quentin, He did appear to have a good body but she would never be able to tell of course, until the presumed relationship blossomed. Going out with Quentin would send not only strong signals but a statement that told society regardless of who people appeared to be, that it was possible to find a down-to-earth person. All signs pointed to Quentin being that person. Andrea simply had too many other obligations. Time simply would not permit Andrea to enjoy much social life.

"Quentin, you are the best date eva' and believe me, if the time was right, I would take you up on your offer," Andrea said. "But things are just so crazy for me right now, so it probably won't be a great idea," she added.

She saw the instantaneous effect the response had on Quentin. The light in his smile seemed to disappear.

"Oh ok, that's cool," he replied. "Maybe some other time," he added. Andrea felt badly for cutting it off with Quentin but it had to be done.

As they arrived at Andrea's home, Quentin said goodbye to Andrea and headed off toward his own home. Sighing with relief, Andrea opened the door to her home and the lights were all off. They both must be asleep, she thought as she took off her shoes and got ready to turn in for the night.

On Friday night, Tico and JJ listened to one of their demos on a playback in Junction Studios, located a few train stops away from Bed-Stuy. The studio, which was owned by a close friend of JJ's, was used primarily for recording commercials. He offered to help Tico, JJ, and NB record demos in his studio because although Tico had a sound system and a single recording booth, the technology was not as refined as the recording booth inside Junction Studios. The beats were more defined, the transitions were crisp, and the microphone feedback wasn't as dominant as it was in Tico's basement. The only downside to this setup was that it cost Tico nearly a thousand dollars for a few hours of session time but to Tico, it was well worth it. He needed to create a back-up plan in case the whole amateur night performance didn't go in his favor.

He would have another demo on the side ready to give to BHR Inc. BHR (Big House Records) was another big recording company in the tri-state area. They were known for signing not only newcomers but performers who were at the top of their game. They were also notorious for being in heated competition with Metro Records, both on the charts and financially. Although their feud had not escalated outside the music industry, there was no love lost between the artists who performed for each label. So far, Metro held the upper hand in new artists, marketability, and respectability; from the CEO down to signed artist. Tico wanted to believe Tony but the more he thought about it, the more he realized that Tony didn't have anything to gain regarding Tico's future. If Tico didn't make it for Metro, he was sure BHR would ask him to join their label and he would do so without hesitating. He had his kids to feed, he couldn't drop the ball now. He was too close. As the beat, along with Tico's voice playing in the background, all the boys were ecstatic about how well the track was coming along. While the song played, they heard another sound. It was one of the back doors near the side of the building. JJ went upstairs to answer the door. After a couple of minutes, JJ walked Tony down to the studio. Tony seemed to bob his head while listening to a few tracks by Tico.

"So is dis what ya performin'?" Tony asked

"You already know," Tico confirmed. "Check this out," he added as he placed some instrumental percussion tones in addition to the drum beat that he was playing.

"That's exactly what I'm talkin' about kid. Ya gonna have to bring ya A-game tomorrow cuz I peeped the number of contestants in this amateur night and you got some heat comin' ya way," Tony warned.

"Don't sweat it dawg, we got this," JJ stated confidently.

"Is that so?" Tony asked, looking at the three men with a raised eyebrow that seemed to say that he didn't believe them.

"Anyway, I got something for ya. Something to give ya a lil taste of that high life, you feel me?" he continued, as he reached into the pockets of the hooded sweatshirt he was wearing.

He pulled out stacks of one hundred dollar bills, held by a rubber band. There were no questions or comments on where he had attained a huge sum of money but the moment he took the money out, Tico, JJ, and NB looked at him as he counted the money within the stack to make sure he had the right amount. After that he handed the money to Tico.

"There you go, man. As per our agreement," he said as Tico counted the money. "Now remember, most of it goes toward the cost of the studio sessions and whatever's left can be split between ya" Tony added.

Tico took the money greedily, not bothering to ask its owner how he acquired the money and instead accepted what he thought was a well-deserved reward for his investment and hard work.

"Appreciate it, bro. You know these studio fees ain't cheap. Gotta stay greasin' elbows, ya feel me?" he asked rhetorically.

"Yeah man, but stay ready. I got ya' in Fusion tomorrow but that don't mean I can guarantee a victory for ya'll. Ya betta' kick some ass at this amateur night, represent BX and let em know what time it is," Tony said as the boys gave each other high fives and daps.

"Hell yeah," Tico said exuberantly. "It's about time we show these people what real music is. They've been suckin' off De'Von Franklin's raps for years. It's time to change the game for good, you feel me?" he confirmed to his comrades. They all agreed with Tico and Tony upon making absolute sure that they practice to solidify their sound.

Andrea was at work on Friday night when Vanessa walked inside Johnson's Department Store. Generally when Vanessa went to Johnson's, she intended to buy a pair of shoes or maybe a dress that might be a bit was too revealing. This time Vanessa didn't go the the store to shop for her or her family. She went there solely to find Andrea. As soon as she found her, Vanessa waved to Andrea and she walked over to her best friend.

"Yo' what you doin?" Andrea asked, as she walked over to the front of the store.

"I got some big news," she said excitedly. It was pretty clear that Vanessa had recovered from her encounter with Jimmy at the prom.

Andrea had been frightened for her friend because she saw the gazes that burned through her whenever she walked down the hall. Jimmy was a popular guy and there was no doubt that the story of the senior prom incident had probably been twisted to make Jimmy appear to be the victim and Vanessa had been a nobody who was out to take advantage of Jimmy because of his status. Sean, who had his own share of rumors swirling about him and Lashondra, had defended Vanessa on many occasions. Andrea found herself defending her friend as well because she didn't want to leave Vanessa on her own to be attacked by the ruthless student body. Finally after nearly a week, the rumors died down and life went back to normal. Andrea and Vanessa would often see Jimmy in the hallway but never spoke to him. Andrea didn't mind because she had never trusted Jimmy to begin with but she certainly wished the prom had ended as well as it had begun for Vanessa's sake.

"Ok so what's the big news? Lay it on me," Andrea said impatiently.

"Ok remember the invitation I showed you for the amateur night at Fusion?" she asked. For a moment, Andrea had forgotten about the invitation. Then she remembered the multicolored poster shot on her Facebook wall.

"Yeah, what about it?" she asked.

"Well, you got any plans tomorrow afternoon?" Vanessa asked.

"Yeah. I gotta work, you know that," Andrea replied.

"Well, now you got new plans. You're singing at Fusion tomorrow," Vanessa said. Andrea glared at her friend. Did Vanessa just inform her that she was singing in Fusion?

"Yo, it's too late for these games, Vanessa. Quit playin," Andrea replied.

"I'm not playing. Check the list of performers," Vanessa replied.

Andrea signed into her Facebook account on her phone and she was surprised to see her name tagged as one of the performers. Andrea's mouth dropped open. She knew she hadn't agreed to perform. She had distinctly told Vanessa she wouldn't. They couldn't have possible randomly picked her, unless someone signed for her.

"Vanessa, I told you I wasn't going to do this thing,"she said. "Who signed me up for this?" she asked.

There was silence on Vanessa's part and Andrea knew exactly what the awkward silence meant. She decided to confront the matter.

"Vanessa, tell me you didn't sign me up for this nonsense," Andrea said.

"Ok ok, so maybe I might have signed you up as a participant but look, it ain't no big deal," Vanessa replied.

Andrea couldn't believe it. "Vanessa, why did you sign me for this now? I told you I'm not singin," she replied.

"Why not? What have you got to lose? You got a bomb-ass voice waiting to be unleashed, girl. I know you can win this and who knows, you might pick up a record deal," Vanessa said. Andrea shook her head. "Besides my cousin works at Fusion and I told her about you, so she helped put you in," she said. "There are so many people who want this hea'." Vanessa added

"Ok, but we still have two problems. First of all, I can't ditch work and second of all Fusion nightclub and lounge is for folks twenty-one and older so there ain't no way they gonna let us in," Andrea replied.

"Don't worry about that. First of all, your job lets you leave early on Saturdays if it's dead and as far as getting inside, like I said, my cousin works for them. She knows about all the secret doors and backdoors that we can use to get in," Vanessa explained.

Andrea wasn't sure. She couldn't see any promise in this endeavor and didn't know if it was worth the risk. Sensing Andrea was thinking it over, Vanessa continued.

"Look Drea, we got a chance to change things. I know you could win this. Don't you want your family's situation to change? Don't you want better for them?" she asked.

"Of course I do, but what if I don't win?" Andrea asked.

"C'mon girl you got this. You're the best," Vanessa countered. Andrea wasn't certain but at that moment, she had to reconsider.

Maybe Vanessa was onto something. What would she have to lose by singing in the amateur night? There was also the matter of the award money which amounted to over a thousand dollars for the first place winner. Unfortunately, the major obstacle that stood between her and realizing her full potential was her work schedule. Andrea did know there were times when they would allow some of the employees to clock out early if it was too slow at the store. Despite the fact that Saturdays were usually busy, sometimes it could be the slowest day at work.   Knowing Pat Davis, the night floor manager, was very lenient she might actually let Andrea to leave work early.

"Ok, let's do it," she agreed.

"That's my girl," Vanessa said, smiling.

"But you sure yo' cousin's gonna be able to get us inside the club? Last thing I need is to cut my hours short, then we roll up in there and we get bounced," Andrea said.

"Trust me, my cuz got it taken care of already. Just be ready, drink plenty of tea, mami and go out thea' and slay 'em," Vanessa replied.

Andrea turned her face in disgust. "Ugh, I hate tea. Why you tellin' me to drink tea?" she asked.

"For the voice, baby. You gotta keep the voice fresh," Vanessa said in a flattering sales-pitch voice.

"Get outta hea'!" Andrea laughed as Vanessa walked out of the store.

A wave of anticipation as well as a wave of apprehension washed over Andrea. She was going to be singing in front of a crowd that was not going to be consisted of only church folks. She would be singing in front of real people; judges and more importantly, recording executives from Metro Records and BHR. She couldn't believe it. She secretly hoped that she would just give a good performance and not choke or freeze up like she had the previous Sunday at church. Unlike the church crowd, these folks would not take it lightly and they would not hold back their criticism of an artist who had performed poorly. As she continued working, she considered which song she would sing that night.

The line to Fusion Lounge in South Richmond, New York stretched to the end of the block early Saturday night. People waiting to enter the club had come from Queens, Long Island, Bronx, and Brooklyn to make their way into the lounge. The bouncer, Fred Dre', stood a full six-foot-eight inches tall and weighed almost three hundred pounds in body mass. His tall, domineering presence struck fear in those who dared to try and enter without proper identification. Fred watched half of the entrance, while the other half was reserved for celebrities, judges for the event, or studio execs. As Julio and Craig pulled up in front of the lounge, they saw immediately how crowded the lounge was going to be.

"Man, this line is crazy. They should've known betta than to schedule this thing on Saturday," Julio said.

"What fo', man? They makin' crazy cash in thea' bro," Craig replied. "Rule number one when it comes to business; always attract your major demographic on days when that demographic is available and what better day to schedule this than on Saturday?" he asked.

"That's what I'm sayin," Julio replied, cutting Craig off. "Many of these kids may not be in our demographic. Look how young some of these kids are. I doubt half of 'em are over twenty-one years of age," he added.

"Well, that's why we got good ole Fred hea' separating them sheep from the goats. Trust me, I know Fred. Nobody can get around him," Craig answered confidently.

After Julio and Craig paralleled-parked in the next block over, they made their way to the lounge's entrance. Fred saw them approaching, and his wide face, which had been stoic and emotionless, broke out into a large grin.

"Craig, my main man what's up, boss?" he said as he hugged Craig.

"What's up Big Fred?" Craig replied.

"Man, same ole, same ole you know what I'm sayin'?" Fred answered.

Unbeknownst to Julio, Craig and Big Fred grew up on Jamaica Avenue together, attending the same schools from elementary all the way to high school. But since Craig had started working for Metro, he had been unable to get back in touch with Fred or any of his old friends from the block.

"Man, how come you never come out to da block, son?" Fred asked.

"You know how it is, man. Workin' all day and barely got nights off. I might come out dis year, though. Just keep my Miller Lite cool," Craig said.

"You already know," Fred answered.

"Oh yeah, this is my boy Julio. We work at Metro together," Craig said, as Fred and Julio shook hands.

"Well, table's all set up for ya, so ya can roll on in and I'll clean the rest of this out," Fred said, gesturing to the line of people trying to get in.

Craig and Julio entered the lounge. The billboard's top pop music was already playing and people were either dancing or just sitting down in groups of three or four per table as they waited for the event to start.

"Let Fred know he's doing a good job out there. I want to hear a talented adult tonight, cuz the last thing I wanna do is sign another kid," Julio said.

"Come on, man. New York's got some talented kids out there though, you can't front on that," Craig replied.

But Julio was serious. He felt that he already had his hands full with De'Von when he had signed him at barely eighteen years of age. The worst part about the process had been clearing waivers and getting consent from his mother because he was still under age at the time. He didn't want to go through the same process again.

"We'll see what kind of talent they got, right?" Julio asked in response as they sat down and ordered a bottle of Merlot for their table.

Sneaking in from the shipping and receiving area in back, Andrea, Vanessa, and her cousin Irene walked through the crowd and found some alternative couches near the back of the lounge to sit down and watch the other performances. Andrea had managed to persuade Pat into allowing her to leave Johnson's early due to the store being quiet, just as Vanessa had predicted. Irene had picked them both up from Johnson's and drove them over to Fusion Lounge, where Irene parked near an open alley that would lead to the backdoor for the lounge. While they were driving, Andrea felt that familiar sense of apprehension and dread. What if they got caught sneaking inside the club? What if they ran into someone they knew from school or from the block? What if her father found out? Those questions among others, ran through Andrea's mind but the question that had been paramount in her mind was the most important one. What would she sing once her name was called? She delved into her musical memory. All she was accustomed to; was singing for her church, so she knew gospel songs as well as pop songs; songs she knew her church would appreciate. The setting at Fusion though was anything but holy, as a black skinny man took the microphone. The man's name was Flash D, a daytime radio personality and part time host/promoter.

"Ladies and gents we got a special night in store for you all. We got rappers, singers, spoken word artists and musicians all gathered here tonight in hopes of winning the prizes for this year's amateur night. So sit back and relax and enjoy all the performances tonight! Our first act of the evening hails from Elmhurst, New York. Give it up for Sly Sax!" he announced among cheers.

Sly Sax was the name of a local jazz saxophonist who performed in odd bands and also played for private parties. He played an old Stevie Wonder cover song and right away Andrea knew she had her work cut out for her.

Wow, he is really talented. This is not gonna be easy at all, she thought as Sly continued to play and she heard the positive responses from the crowd that was gathered.

Looking toward the opposite end of the club, she could see the judges, two men and two women, sitting across a long table with notepads facing them. After a few more minutes, Sly finished his selection and Flash introduced the next performer, an ebony girl with short hair by the name of Emiline, who slowly walked up to the stage. She had a slight frame and was short, barely above five feet. She wore a long blue scintillating dress. As the house band played behind her, Andrea soon recognized the song that Emiline was singing. It was a cover of Janet Jackson's single "Anytime, Anyplace." Her sultry voice when she sang each note seemed to raise the hair of every person in the building, whether it was a performer or a member of the audience.

Wow, she got an angelic voice, Andrea thought. She could feel doubt welling up inside of her. What if she didn't have what it took to give a legitimate performance? Emiline's perfect posture, her voice, her sighs at the most strategic moments were broken down to the molecule of the song. It was almost as if she had always performed in front of huge crowds. As soon as the performance was finished, Emiline received a huge ovation, even prompting a number of people to stand up.

After that performance, there really were no other performances that stood out. A couple other amateurs sang but they did not have the talented voice that Emiline had displayed. Then there was a rapper who performed one of his own songs, with the aid of his hype-man. The rapper was innovative, creative, and provided a great modern sound for the event. A few more performers came on stage and either played piano, sang and rapped. Then Flash approached the stage again.

"Ladies and gentlemen, it's always good when we have one of our own peoples from the block performing for us this evening. I want you all to give it up for Ms. Andrea!" he shouted.

Andrea heard her name but she was certain it wasn't her. Flash's voice sounded distant as she slowly rose up and approached the stage. Looking out at the audience, Andrea couldn't bring herself to move. She couldn't move her hands, her hips, or even her lips. A pair of eyes stared out at the audience as a million other eyes were staring back at her.

While Andrea stood frozen, paralyzed with fear, her eyes fell to Vanessa, who wore a look that said, "Girl, you lookin' like a straight chump. Come on, now get it together!"

Fortunately, the house band had already started playing, based on Andrea's recommendation. Andrea decided to do her performance on a cover song from Aaliyah. Closing her eyes, she imagined her sister watching her and whispering in her ear.

"Don't worry about them. I want to see you own this song, Drea'," Loree whispered in her ear.

Gathering strength from deep with her, she began singing. The judges wrote throughout the song, as Andrea performed. Other patrons listened to her song but there was no one more entranced with her singing than the lead producer of Metro Records.

Chapter Ten

Sitting at their tables, Julio and Craig took in the night's share of the most talented crop of singers New York offered during the event. They were taken aback by Emiline, who by Julio's standards; had performed a great rendition of one of Janet Jackson's songs. However, no other artist had stolen their breath more than the shy young lady who tentatively took the stage and overcame her fear to reveal the angelic voice within. Singing a song that had once been performed by another famous artist who hailed from New York, the young lady showed her ability to hold her voice in place and command the attention of the crowd in a way they had never seen before in such an amateur songstress. The other aspect of the performance that caught Julio's eyes was the youthful innocence she portrayed before she began to sing and with every passing note, she enticed the audience as a whole with her charm and her style. As soon as the young lady finished singing, Julio was convinced. This young lady would be a great compliment to De'Von's rough style and edge. There were other performers of course who performed after her but Julio wasn't giving them his full attention. In his mind he had already found his money singer and she was headed toward the back of the lounge, potential brimming from her very soul. Julio had to find a way to meet with the young lady as soon as possible.

He turned his head and he saw her entering a bathroom stall. With the performances still going, Julio got up and walked toward the same direction as he saw the young lady. Julio snuck around the indoor security and waited at the outside of one of the bathroom stalls. When Andrea emerged from the bathroom, she saw a middle-aged Latino fellow looking directly at her. At first, she didn't think anything of it.

Maybe he just wanted to congratulate me or something, Andrea thought as she attempted to make her way past the man.

But the man was persistent, blocking her only way back to her seat. "Excuse me," Andrea said politely, but the man did not budge.

"Your name is Andrea, right?" he asked. Andrea looked around nervously. She became suspicious. For all she knew, he could be working undercover, exposing all the underage patrons in the club.

"Who wants to know?" she asked.

"Hello, my name is Julio Vargas and I work for Metro Records. I just heard you singing over there and I have to say, your voice….I ain't heard anything like that in a long time," Julio said.

Andrea's eyes widened. "Wait, did you just say you were from Metro records?" Andrea asked but before Julio could answer her question, Flash D returned to the center stage.

"Ok folks, we've heard all the talented singers, musicians, and poets that the tri-state area had to offer. Let's give it up again for all the performers that came out tonight!" he said and the crowd broke out into applause.

One of the judges handed Flash the envelope. "Ok, so we have our grand prize winner of tonight's event. The winner, based on popular demand and judge's votes, will receive a thousand dollars in cash money and a possible recording contract with BHR or Metro Records," Flash announced.

"So the winner of tonight's event is Emiline Jacob!" he announced to the sound of raucous applause.

Andrea hung her head in disappointment. After all the work that she put forth in making sure she got out of work on time, preparing the song and performing it, it was all for naught. As Andrea watched Emiline walk up to accept her award, she thought that maybe Emiline did deserve the award. She sounded spectacular and she brought out the best in her song. Sighing, Andrea looked for her table. She could tell by Vanessa's wry look, that she wasn't pleased that Andrea hadn't won the amateur night.

"Well, there goes your winner right there. I think that's the girl you wanna talk to," Andrea replied, crestfallen before turning around to walk back to her table.

"No, don't worry about that. I had made up my mind even before they announced the winners," Julio replied. "Please, just hear me out for a second. You may have lost the contest tonight but you didn't lose the opportunity of a lifetime," he said to Andrea, who had initially begun to walk away from Julio, until he talked about opportunities.

She stopped dead in her tracks. "What chance of a lifetime?" she asked.

Julio came up to her. "Andrea, I could change your world faster than you can imagine. A talented voice like yours is hard to find and I was very intrigued by your style and by you," he continued. Andrea still wasn't sure but she decided to trust this madman for a moment. "When you sang the whole song, it felt like the heavens opened and God said, "she's the one!" Julio said.

Andrea smiled. It was the first time anyone had complimented her that way. "For real?" she asked.

"For real," Julio confirmed. "Now I have just one more thing I want you to do." He took a few sheets out of his folder. "This is a copy of the terms and conditions of the contract that we offer for Metro Records and if you'd like to do so, you can take it to an attorney or a lawyer to verify the legalities of our agreement," he said.

Andrea looked at him puzzled. "Lawyer? But I don't have a lawyer," she said.

Julio's eyebrows lowered in suspicion. "Really? How old are you, Andrea?" he asked.

"I'm eighteen years old, sir" Andrea replied. At this response, Julio gazed toward the ground. Oh no, not again. I'm doing it again. I'm about to sign a kid to a recording contract. When will I ever learn?

"So you mean to say that you shouldn't have been in here this whole time, hmmm?" he asked furtively.

Andrea hung her head in shame. "I knew it was a stupid idea and I didn't want to do it at first but my crazy friend kept tellin' me why I had to do this and we snuck in through the back. I understand if you change your mind and don't want to sign me," she said, in truth because the last incident she wanted was for the alarm to sound and for security and the huge bouncer to find out she was underage.

Julio wasn't the hollering type. "Hey, it's ok. Besides if you didn't sneak in, I probably wouldn't have given anybody this contract," he replied.

Andrea laughed. "Guess I was the lucky illegal, huh?" she asked.

"Guess so," Julio replied, laughing.

Andrea couldn't believe she was really talking to this man; this stranger who was offering her a recording contract. She had to blink and mentally pinch herself many times to convince herself that it was all true. Andrea certainly knew she couldn't jump at the deal without taking the first mature step in the decision.

"Mr. Julio, I'm flattered by the offer that you made to me but I really have to run this by my family so we can decide on if it's the best idea," she said.

"I see your point," Julio agreed. Then, out of nowhere, Julio hatched an idea. "Ok, what about if I help explain it to your family?" he asked.

Andrea agreed to have Julio visit her home and sway the family so they would have no choice but to let her join Metro. Besides, if her father decided to kill her for sneaking into a club, there would be a witness. As Andrea made her way back to the table where Vanessa and her cousin were sitting and waiting, Vanessa was the first to rise to her feet with a pained look on her face.

"Sorry you didn't win tonight," she said. To her surprise and amazement, Andrea laughed.

"Don't worry about that. I coulda done betta. You win some, you lose some right?" she reassured.

Vanessa looked at Irene, both wearing a perplexed expression. "Girl, you sick or something? You just lost money out there and you ain't even mad? I couldn't be in yo' shoes, that's for sho," Irene said.

"Mad about what?" Andrea asked Irene. Turning to Vanessa, she said "Girl, you was right. Coming here to sing was a great idea. I had nothin' to be afraid of," she said proudly.

As they spoke, they didn't notice that someone had approached their table. "Hey, Andrea I wanted to come over and say you got a great voice. I'm Emiline," the young winner said, introducing herself to Andrea. She spoke with a slight accent, which suggested that she was from the Caribbean Islands.

"Thanks. You sounded really good on your song. You can really go," Andrea complimented.

"Thanks. I didn't know what song I was going to sing tonight, then that one song came to my head. I wish I had thought of the song you sang though," Emiline said.

"You wish you thought of that song? I wish I thought of your song. You won wit' it so I say you chose the right song," Andrea replied.

As Andrea looked closer, she saw that Emiline's eyes were a soft brown. A girl with a nice frame and a great set of eyes to match that. No wonder she got the vote over me, she thought.

As Emiline walked back over to her own table, Andrea turned to Vanessa. "Listen, Nessa I've been offered a ride back home by this guy," she started.

"A man?!!" Vanessa exclaimed. "Ok you are gonna tell me everything about this so called 'man' of yours?" she asked. Andrea sighed for a second.

"C'mon Vanessa he's just another guy that sat and watched my performance. I'll call you lata," she replied.

Andrea decided she wasn't going to tell Vanessa about Julio or their conversation. She knew if Vanessa even got wind that Andrea just caught her break, she would make sure it would be broadcasted throughout the metropolitan area. She decided to keep it a secret until Julio spoke with her parents on the matter. Andrea found Julio waiting for her in the hallway.

"Ok Julio, I'm ready to go," she said.

"Great, let's go," Julio said as they walked back over to his table. "By the way, I want you to meet someone. Andrea this is my partner, Craig. He's also the producer and A/R at Metro records," Julio said as Craig shook Andrea's hand.

"I just want to say that you were phenomenal tonight and as Julio has no doubt informed you, we decided to sign you to our family," Craig said.

"I know, I'm still just trying to take it all in right now. I just can't believe this is happening," Andrea replied.

As they walked out of the club, Julio spoke quietly with Craig. "We gotta swing by her place to tell her folks about signing her," he said.

Upon hearing this, Craig laughed softly. "So you signed another baby, huh? First it was Miesha, then it was De'Von, and now it's this one. I thought you swore off kids, man," he said.

Julio scoffed at Craig. "Man, when it's babies that sound like that though, you gotta jump on that. I couldn't hold out another minute, man. Besides BHR already signed Emiline to a record deal and they could've walked up to Andrea and we woulda stuck out twice," he replied as they walked to their car.

As they drove to Andrea's home, they struck up a conversation with their new potential artist. "So Andrea, where are you from?" Craig asked.

"I was born and raised in Richmond Hill," Andrea replied.

"Oh ok. So do you like it out there?" Julio asked.

"Well, it ain't exactly downtown Manhattan or Broadway, but it's home. You know, it's a bit rough out there but I'll always rep it hardbody," Andrea replied.

"I hear that," Julio agreed.

"Man I went to high school in Queens, although it was before your time, and we would always beef wit' someone that claimed to be from Richmond Hill or went to Richmond Hill High School. There was never a shortage of drama ova' there," Craig said.

He doesn't know half of it, Andrea thought.

If there was anyone who knew about the constant drama in her neighborhood, it was Andrea. From casual drug-dealing in certain areas, to sparse levels of gang activity in other areas, and the fact that every time the six o'clock news was on, they were always the main story of the evening. Andrea sincerely hoped that this meeting with Julio and Craig was the beginning of the wheel of opportunity turning for her. Walking up to her duplex-styled home, she opened the door with her key and walked inside, gesturing for Julio and Craig to follow her inside. She heard pots and boxes in the kitchen and although it was late at night, she knew her mother was busy washing dishes. Stepping inside the kitchen doorway, Andrea greeted her.

"Hey Mom, what's up?" she greeted. Upon seeing her daughter back, Alisha ran and gave her a very soapy hug. After she let go of Andrea, she wasted no time jumping on her about her late night excursion.

"Honey, where have you been? Do you have any idea what time it is?" she badgered Andrea.

"Yeah, Mom I know. I'm sorry I came late, but believe me, you'll find out why soon enough," Andrea replied.

She invited Julio and Craig inside as Alisha walked out of the kitchen and she stared at the two men suspiciously.

"Hello, I take it that both of you came with Andrea today," she said. Julio stretched his hand out.

"Hello, Mrs. McAfee my name is Julio Vargas and I'm the producer and talent relations for Metro Records," he introduced.

"Metro who?" Alisha asked. Andrea rolled her eyes. She didn't have much time left. Craig and Julio had to be busy men and her mother was already working on a steady path of slow embarrassment by acknowledging that she didn't know about one of the best recording studios in New York.

"Where's Dad? I want you both to sit down and listen, because Julio and Craig have some big news for us," Andrea said.

Her mother seemed to understand. "Ok, so let me go get your father. He probably fell asleep in the bedroom in front of the TV again," she answered as she left the room to wake Amos up.

Andrea then asked Julio and Craig if they were thirsty and offered them a cold drink, which they both declined. Within five minutes, Amos made his way into the living room, where he saw two young men sitting on his furniture. Amos, as courteous as he was, shook both Craig and Julio's hand. As Amos and Alisha sat down across from their guests, Julio thought it was the best time to talk about his offer.

"Mr. McAfee, I wanted to talk to you about your daughter. We watched her sing earlier tonight at the Fusion lounge…." Julio began before being interrupted by Amos

"Wait a minute, wait a minute. You were at the Fusion lounge tonight? I thought you were at work tonight, young lady," Amos said sternly to Andrea.

"I know Daddy, but long story short, I was invited by Vanessa and she picked me up and drove us to the club," Andrea explained.

"That's another thing. What were you doing in a club downtown?" Amos asked.

"C'mon Daddy, that's beside the point," Andrea countered.

"No the point is that when I drop you off to go to work, that's exactly what I'm expecting," Amos countered.

"For your information, Daddy I was at work today but the store was so quiet that I got permission to leave early and go to Fusion. They had a talent show and I was signed to perform," she explained.

Amos made a sarcastic sound. "Oh that's just convenient. And where do you two guys fit into all this?" he asked Julio and Craig.

"Well we were at the club as well and we heard many performers but we've never heard a voice like your daughter's," Julio replied. "Although she hesitated a little bit before she got comfortable, she was able to relax and give an unforgettable performance," he added with a sly smile.

Andrea returned Julio's smile with a side smirk of her own. Although her parents were alarmed that she snuck into a nightclub without their knowledge, they seemed to be taking Craig and Julio rather seriously.

"As the A/R and the producer of Metro records, we would like to offer this very talented young lady a recording contract with us," Craig said.

Alisha looked at Amos with a bewildered look on her face. Andrea looked at both her parents, waiting for a response out of them but she couldn't hear anything.

"Well, we always knew Andrea had a gifted voice. From the time she was very young, she would sing all the solos in church with a high spirit in her," she said.

"I can tell she has a strong background in church and at home. That's why she would be a perfect fit in our family," Julio said.

Alisha looked at Amos again. "Well, Mr...." she started before her voice trailed off.

"Julio. Just call me Julio. All my colleagues call me that," Julio said before he turned back to Amos. "What do you say?" he asked Amos.

Andrea didn't have to be in her father's head to see the thoughts spinning for what seemed like an eternity. Her father stood up and shook his head slightly.

"Listen gentlemen, I'm grateful for the compliments about my daughter and I'm sure she's warranting of all the praise heaped upon her. "But she is still a student at school and I would like for her to remain in her studies," he said.

Julio looked at Craig. Don't worry sir, we will definitely take Andrea's education with high priority," Julio replied.

"Besides, come on, Mama, I'm graduating from high school, remember?" Andrea asked.

"I know, baby but what about college? What about graduate school?" Alisha asked.

"Mom, I can go to college anytime I want to. It's not gonna be the end of the world if I wait a semester or two," Andrea said.

"Andrea listen, that's exactly why I can't stress enough how important your education is. I don't want you wasting your years on this singing situation, either." Amos said.

At that point, Andrea knew she had to come to her parents with what she had left before her parents gave up on her altogether.

"Look ya'll I know I'm taking a big risk and this is a big step for me but I'm ready to take it," she said. "All my life, I've had to take a backseat to somebody else. I've always had to work for somebody else, always had to cater somebody else. Now here's my chance to sing in front of national audiences and make money through my music and you're asking yourself, did I know what was going to happen tonight? No, but it happened and if there was any perfect time to see what I can do, this is it," she pointed out.

Amos and Alisha looked at each other. Andrea hoped she had made a compelling argument that would swing the decision to her favor. Finally Amos stood up and he stared at Andrea with a stern gaze.

"Although I'm not too thrilled about what you did tonight to get this opportunity, I do understand the magnitude of this decision and the financial rewards that come with it," he stated before pausing for a moment. "But I leave the decision ultimately to you and your mother," he finally said.

Andrea smiled, because she knew that whenever her father left a decision to her mother, she normally sided with her daughter and in a moment of uncontrolled happiness, she hugged her father.

"Thank you Daddy, I'll make you proud. You'll see. I'll make everyone proud. I'll even make her proud of me," she said, gazing upward with tears rolling down her cheek.

Amos found himself almost unable to control his emotions because at that moment he knew Andrea was referring to Loree. Amos then turned to Julio and Craig.

"Even if she's working with you, she's still my daughter and she's the only one I have left. Promise me that you will do right by her and you'll treat her fairly," he said.

Craig and Julio agreed to treat Andrea fairly, especially during the distribution of royalties that Andrea would receive through sales, CD's, audio and music videos, and radio airtime. They discussed the contract, in which Andrea would be estimated to receive up to five figures during her current three year deal with Metro. Finally an agreement was signed by Amos to be the sole proprietor of Andrea's funds. At first Andrea resisted because she wanted to control the money she earned through her music but Julio warned her about other artists he signed at the same age who decided not to let their parents manage their money. The artists ended up making poor financial decisions which had cost them their endorsements, their reputation, and finally their contract. Under the circumstances, Andrea grudgingly agreed and the contract was signed in the living room, in the spring of 2009.

"Welcome to Metro Records. We are definitely excited to sign you to our family," Julio said.

Andrea still couldn't believe how fast it had all materialized. Yesterday she had been insignificant; working a simple job and going to school under a manufactured, flawed education system, and now here she was, Andrea, the professional singer.

The new princess of R&B, she thought, before she changed her mind. So the moniker needed a little work but she was excited nonetheless.

"Listen, until we get everything finalized and we get to work on some feature songs and ultimately your first album, I need you to promise me that you won't tell anyone about this," Julio warned.

Andrea was so excited about the opportunity that all she wanted to do was tell everyone she knew. "Why not?" she asked, disappointed.

"We have to remember, there are other people who would love to be in your place right now and they don't have the opportunity, so they hate on the person that has this chance. Hate always has a possibility of turning into many things. So I'm telling you for your own good not to tell anyone. At least not until the first EP drops and you go on tour," Craig replied.

"You'll continue to go to school, graduate, continue working, and when the time is right, we'll call you into the studio to get some work done, ok?" Julio asked. Andrea agreed and the two men thanked the McAfee family before heading out.

In East Tremont, Tico and JJ sat in their basement, wondering what had gone wrong in their performance at the Fusion Lounge. Tico, JJ, and NB went with what they were sure was a full package of a performance. Tico ignited the crowd with his lyrics and hooks which he believed would steal the show. However, when the winner of the amateur contest was announced, they were more than disappointed that it was not them but some dark skinned girl who sang some R&B song. The audience had been mesmerized by this young woman and it wasn't just the fact that she won. That had already infuriated them. It was the fact that they had actually witnessed the girl being signed by Big House Records that really galled them.

"I gotta tell it like is though, man. Girl got skills though," NB pointed out.

Tico scoffed. "Man, homegirl was ight, but she couldn't touch us, bro. We just got blackballed cuz they whole agenda was to sign a woman."

"They weren't thinkin' about us, man. We the victims of the mediocre talent that these people really want," NB replied. He sat at his mix tape table, clearly upset that he lost the contest. "Tony told me that Metro was supposed to be there too. I looked all over for them cats but I couldn't find them," he added.

They were expecting Tony soon, because he had told them that even if they didn't win the contest, he would still talk to the reps at Metro to secure a deal for a contract.

"Yo, but foreal though, forget the contest. I still blew it up onstage and I know them talent scouts were there," Tico said, before he heard a subtle knock on the door. JJ opened the door. Tony walked in, hands deep in his pockets.

"What up man?" he asked. Tico walked up to Tony, expecting to hear more about the possibility that they would be signed by a major record label.

"So did you speak with them upper levels at Metro? What'd they say?" Tico asked apprehensively.

Tony shook his head. "I tried runnin' them boys down to give 'em your demo after the amateur night, but they already bounced. Ya' bought it tonight, but they didn't even consider ya'll," he replied.

"What you mean, they ain't consider us?" Tico asked angrily. We killed it back thea' and you mean to tell me that I'm not gonna be getting' my shot but another chick is getting' a contract with BHR? You told me Metro was gonna be there," Tico said.

"Metro was there, homie," Tony said. "Those two guys that you saw near us were Julio and Craig and they work directly for Metro. I couldn't get close to their tables. Finally, when I asked to see 'em again, they left da spot," he explained. "I tried to talk with other people who knew those guys and word was that they signed someone new, the other girl that sang behind Emiline," he added.

"So, you tellin' me that two girls ended up getting' signed?" Tico asked. Tony nodded his head. There was no other way to break it to Tico.

"Yeah, man. I don't know what else to say bro," Tony replied. Tico got up and started pacing the basement.

This was the worst luck ever to hit Tico. He looked at the storage shelf which held tools, papers, and other supplies and Tico angrily reached inside the drawer of one of the shelves. Inside the drawer was his old cap, a bag of needles, narcotics, and other drugs. It also hid a small handgun, which wasn't loaded yet. He looked at his options. His money was running out and he was not left with other options. It didn't look promising but he would have to hustle and sell drugs again. The more he reflected upon that prospect, the more it infuriated he became. This was exactly what the system demanded of him. It was never meant for men like him to get a leg up to be successful in life, he rationalized. He hated that life. He hated when one of his kids would return home and talk about some high paying job that other kid's parents had while he was still out on the streets, making money illegally. It certainly wasn't in his grand scheme to continue hustling dope his whole life and he was not going to subject his children to the same lifestyle he had lived. He was going to do whatever it took to get into the corporate offices that had been closed to him. He was determined to get to the point where he could run the system and not be a slave to it.

"Is da block hot tonight?" he asked Tony and JJ as he stuffed the bag in his pocket and packed his gun in his back pocket.

"Hell yeah, fam. Mad cats comin' out lookin' fo' some. Tonight's definitely the night to make that money," JJ replied.

"light bet, dog. Next week, we bout to get back to the studio," Tico said as he headed out into the cool Bronx street.

On Monday morning, Andrea awoke and could barely contain her excitement. Today, I'm not waking up as Andrea McAfee the sad, sorry little girl. I'm now a recording artist with one of the most popular record companies in, New York she thought.

She had seen a picture of De'Von Franklin and wondered, perhaps even envied his success and crossover into being a known artist. She wondered if this was how he had felt when he got his break. Did he have the same felling about going to a high school class the same way she did? Now that she had a contract with Metro Records, Andrea felt it pointless to go to school. Why go to school when she had millions of dollars potentially waiting for her? Dressing in her favorite T-shirt and jeans she put on her black Nike sneakers and grabbed her book bag, which was hanging on the door handle of her room. She walked outside and no sooner did she approach the intersection following the next few blocks, then Vanessa ran to catch up with her.

"Yo Drea, what's up?" You left me and my cuz at the club on Saturday and you leave wit' some stranger, what's up wit' that? I thought we was girls," she said.

"We still are girls, Nessa what's going on?" Andrea replied. Vanessa shook her head in a gesture of regret.

"I shouldn't have asked you to sing on Saturday night. All that time we spent gettin' you out of yo' job and you ain't even win," she said.

Andrea did her best to contain her excitement, knowing that her contract was worth more than that of the actual winner of the competition. But she remembered what Julio and Craig had instructed her about telling anyone but she felt it was torture internally if she didn't tell anyone. Besides, Vanessa was starting to get suspicious.

"So who was that guy that you left with?" Vanessa asked.

If I tell you, you gotta promise me that you ain't gonna tell nobody," Andrea said.

"Why not? Is he yo' main squeeze for da night?" Vanessa teased.

"Nah, chill, Vanessa. Ok the guy that I was with was Julio Vargas, a producer from Metro Records. He heard me singing up on stage and he liked me. So we went over to my house and he signed yo' girl to Metro Record. But we still working on details now," Andrea replied.

Vanessa's eyes widened. "Oh my God, do you know what this means, girl?" she asked.

"Girl, I swear we can finally both go shopping, and not that cheap stuff, you feel me?" Andrea replied.

Vanessa shook her head, laughing. "I feel you Drea and I'm thinkin' this is gon' be a crazy ride," she said.

"I know but I want you with me every step of the way," she said.

"For real?" Vanessa asked. Andrea took another look at her best friend of over seven years. "Absolutely." she replied.

Chapter Eleven

At the entrance of the I-95 freeway at 96th Avenue, a police car sat in the middle of the road, checking for speeding cars and watching the streets. Officer Hawkins and Officer Anderson were the officers who occupied the car and as Officer Hawkins pointed the speed machine at the road, there were no cars exceeding the thirty-five mile speed limit. The day seemed to drag on and Officer Hawkins began to relax at the notion that he was dealing with a quiet neighborhood for once. His partner sat back, drinking his coffee and munching on some chocolate snacks. He attempted to offer some to Officer Hawkins but he refused. Officer Hawkins sat back in his seat. He tried to keep a positive attitude despite the issues that had been plaguing him. The most painful issue was the relationship with his son. He had tried to be more involved with his son's life, especially on days when he didn't have to work but he found getting along with Sean to be as hard as walking the New York skyline on a tightrope. He tried to talk to him about sports and although he didn't have any problems with his son, ultimately the icy indifference with Sean was paining him.

Another issue that bothered him was his position with the police force. He had recently applied for the position of a sergeant in the Queens precinct where he worked. The position had been held by Isaac Sands, one of the lead detectives in the NYPD. Since Sands had transferred to Staten Island, the sergeant spot remained open. Hawkins' wife, Kimberly, had been quite insistent about him getting the sergeant position because it meant more time behind his own desk solving mysteries and cases rather than being on the streets and potential danger. On the streets of Queens there was the daily fear of gunfire or other dangerous situations that confronted law enforcement. Officer Anderson noticed how quiet his partner was and he decided to find out why.

"Hey, earth to John, what's going on? You've been quiet since we've been sitting here man. Wanna talk about it?" he asked.

Officer Hawkins shook his head. "Nah, man. I'm good. It's just that things been a little rocky with my son lately. I don't know what it is," he replied.

"Teen boys. What else?" Officer Anderson replied. "They look up to you and want to hang out with you when they're little but once they discover the world of girls, rap music, and sports, dads often gets pushed in the back burner," he added.

"I guess, but it wouldn't hurt for him to acknowledge his old man once in a while," Officer Hawkins said.

"Agreed, but be grateful. A kid his age could've been caught up in God knows what out there. At least he's staying in school and out of them streets. He's got basketball and a scholarship going on for him. Many of these guys ain't got nothin' but bars to look forward to and I'm not talkin' bout a rap song," Officer Anderson replied. Officer Hawkins chuckled at his partner's clever line.

As they continued to survey the traffic, a gray Nissan Altima sped right past them, running a red light as it turned at the intersection. The speed detector began blaring as Officers Anderson and Hawkins suddenly shifted their patrol car into drive and turned on the sirens, so the other cars shifted to the side when they drove past. Officer Hawkins loved this part of the job because he always wondered what new level of stupidity these people were going to take. Most of them would comply and pull over to accept their inevitable speeding ticket, but quite a few times during his years in the force he'd seen people attempt to flee instead of pulling over. During those chases Officer Anderson and Officer Hawkins would make silent bets on how long the pursuit would last and how long it would take for them to apprehend the suspects. Officer Anderson always came closer to the most accurate time, which was usually about ten minutes after the car was sent to the precinct via radio and the car would be impounded upon arrest. However the driver of the Altima seemed to be more wise and level headed than most of his contemporaries and once he heard the sirens, he slowed down to a complete stop at a gas station. Officer Anderson and Officer Hawkins stepped out of their car to confront the owners of the gray Altima. Immediately the driver rolled his window down. Officer Hawkins noticed right away that the drivers were two black men wearing Nike shirts, backwards caps, and looks of surprise and anger on their faces for being pulled over. Officer Anderson approached the driver's seat.

"You fellas seem to be in a hurry this morning. Do you know how fast you were going?" he asked.

The driver scowled at the officer. "Come on, man I wasn't speeding. What you pull me ova' for?" he said.

Officer Hawkins appeared from the back side of the vehicle to offer backup for his partner.

"Come on, man I got shit to do, bro so if you can give me my ticket so I can get on my way," the young driver exclaimed.

"Shut up," Officer Anderson replied sharply.

"Hold up, who you tellin' to shut up? Man you ain't nothin' but a joke, bruh. If it wasn't fo' dat badge, you wouldn't be nobody!" the driver said.

"Hey, hey hey, we'll be doin' all the talkin' over hea'" Officer Hawkins said.

The driver turned to the passenger side where Officer Hawkins was standing, shaking his head. Officer Hawkins knew right away why the man shook his head. Most of the guys they had apprehended refused to believe that a fellow black man would subject himself to work for a corporation as corrupt in their eyes as the police force. As Officer Anderson went back to fill out the citation for the two men, Officer Hawkins stayed in front of the Altima side passenger door. After processing the ticket, Officer Anderson walked back to the car with a stern look.

"Gentlemen, you can go now. Watch your speed when you drive, boys," he said

"Whateva' man," he blurted, snatching the ticket as he drove away.

As they walked back to their patrol car, Officer Anderson spoke to Officer Hawkins.

"You see what I'm sayin'? These young men need to be disciplined in the society we live in. If their parents won't do it, that's where we come in. Without discipline, everything falls apart and what do you have? You got anarchy, chaos, and disorder," he said.

Officer Hawkins looked at Officer Anderson quizzically. Was that how he felt about all black kids? That they were simply an unruly bunch that needed to be disciplined and locked away like animals in captivity? Officer Hawkins always thought that Sean had it better than most kids in the neighborhood, because he grew up under the veil of law enforcement, while so many other kids grew up under the unwritten code of the streets that demanded survival at all costs. Those street codes meant opposing the police officers who were positioned to serve and protect their community.

As Officers Anderson and Hawkins drove through the busy Queens streets, surveying more traffic violators, they made their way back to the precinct. The police station was crowded with uniformed men and women handling cases and bringing in suspects handcuffed for different crimes. There were secretaries taking reports from attorneys and lawyers and as Officer Hawkins walked to the locker room toward the back of the station, he looked at the suspect processing area. It dismayed him when most of the people he saw were young black men. He wished fervently that his community wasn't responsible for over sixty percent of all prison facilities being full. He had joined the police force so he could make a difference and show others that they could be on the right side of justice. He so wanted to believe that he wasn't the only black man who had joined the police force to give his people a fair shake at justice. But the more black men he saw handcuffed, the more futile he saw his efforts. What good did it do him if he wasn't making a difference? Black men were always going to hate the police, no matter how many of them joined the force. Maybe that was the reason why his own son couldn't stand to be around him nowadays. In a world that revolved around public opinion and twisted values, Sean probably saw his father as merely an impediment to his individuality. He wanted to believe that age played a part as Officer Anderson explained, but what if Sean got through his teenage years and continued to isolate himself from his father? What if Sean always remained fearful of his peers perceiving him as being a sambo or a coon? Such thoughts were extremely hateful and counterproductive to what he was striving for, which was peace and harmony between the masses and the few police forces that resided in the area. But he wished that Sean would warm up to him and that he would understand the sacrifice he was making for the good of the community.

While his father worked, Sean stayed after school to work on his basketball game. Heading over to the gym, he took off his sweater and jeans. Underneath his clothes he wore Reebok shorts and a sleeveless T-shirt. He took one of the basketballs on the sidelines of the court and dribbled a couple of times between his legs and raised up to shoot the ball. Swish. He chased the ball down after he made the hoop and dribbled back even farther, behind the three-point line. Many of the other players including his teammates weren't comfortable shooting three-point shots but it never intimidated Sean. He squared up, locked his elbows in, and took the shot. Swish. He began dribbling back towards the opposite end of the court, dribbling low and looking ahead towards the hoop. He took two more shots, making them both. Sean was so immersed in his practice, he was unaware of being watched. Nathan Plummer, the high school varsity basketball coach, who was in his office printing out registration forms for the school's summer league program, heard someone in the gym, and he stepped out to see who was on the court.

"Hawkins, what's up son?" Nate greeted him. Sean heard him and stopped shooting.

"What's up coach? Sorry, I thought I was the only one in hea'," he replied. Coach Plummer laughed.

"Well, you're the only player in here. It seems that you're spending more time in the gym now more than you ever did during the season," he added.

Sean dribbled the ball. "I just got a lot on my mind, coach. I just came to do a little bit of practice, that's all," he said, hoping the coach wouldn't throw him out. Fortunately, Coach Plummer, who had been a high school basketball player himself, related to Sean's problem.

"Haven't heard from any schools yet, huh?" he asked. Sean looked at his coach. How did he know that no schools have contacted him? He shook his head, confirming that the coach was correct in his assessment. "Don't sweat it, son. I've been there before. I know how it feels to put in so much work and go through one hell of a season, only to not get any offers," coach Plummer, replied.

"I don't get it, coach. I thought this year I had would get me some shine wit' the recruiters, but it seems like I ain't done enough," Sean said.

Coach Plummer walked up to him and said, "Son, you've done more than enough for the team this year. You were third in scoring, fourth in rebounds and fifth in assists. Statistically, those numbers could get you into any college. Realistically, a lot of players who average more in points and rebounds probably won't see the floor again at a college level." Coach Plummer replied. "That's why it's always good to have a back-up plan. Go online and search for some academic scholarships. Get into a good school using what you have up here," he added, pointing to his head.

Sean shook his head and turned his back on the coach. "Coach, the only thing I've ever been good at since I was young was playin' ball. I can't even see myself doin' anything else," he replied.

Coach Plummer shook his head. Obviously this young man needed motivation that he wasn't getting at home. The last place Coach Plummer wanted to see Sean was in the streets, selling drugs like he once had, curtailing what could have been a promising career. Even though it was a different age and different generation, the game was still played the same way and the system was set up for young men to fail and to be marginalized by the use of drugs and violence.

"Hawkins, you're a smart young man. I want you to start looking for careers beyond basketball and focus on that going forward. Basketball opportunities will always present themselves but great career opportunities won't always be there," he said. Sean looked at his coach.

"So you don't believe that I'll get to college on a ball scholarship, is that it now?" he asked.

"No son, that's not what I'm sayin'," Coach Plummer said. "I'm sayin' that you have a world of opportunity in front of you and you have resources in other areas. I'm just gettin' you ready for the real world, Hawkins. Your father's a police officer in New York, so I know he's seen a lot out there. People throw their lives away after high school, because they've been sold a pipe dream about the NBA or even D1 college basketball," he explained. "I know because I'm one of those people, Sean. I had the skills, the determination, and I had the damn fire to keep it going. What I never had was a back-up plan in case all of that failed. Once I figured that I wasn't going to the NBA or even college, my world fell apart. I just don't wanna see that happen to you," he added.

Sean dropped the ball on the court. He took his clothes and put them in his book-bag.

"You sound just like my mom, coach," he said. "I just gotta keep workin' on my game and keep grindin' coach. You'll see," Sean added.

Coach Plummer walked up to Sean. "Hawkins, the one thing you gotta understand is that life's tough, especially with us. Nothin' comes easy. I'm just tryin' to equip you, so you'll understand where I'm coming from," he replied.

Sean took his book bag and left the gym. He didn't know why his own coach didn't side with him. He had to understand that basketball was all he had to get out of the 'hood. People didn't pick up young brothers because they knew science, math, or history. All those subjects were pointless because there was no way any college would pick him up for knowing who won World War II. No college was going to give him a chance because of the Pythagorean Theorem. He had to go out and make his future and that started with basketball.

"Seriously, we gotta come up wit' a dope stage name for you, girl," Vanessa told Andrea as they headed out the doors after the last school bell.

Andrea shook her head, although she was laughing slightly. She was beginning to regret telling Vanessa anything because her excitement was starting to get the best of her and she was attracting unwanted attention to herself.

"Come on girl, keep yo' voice down. I ain't tryin' to have the whole borough on notice yet. I'm still thinking about it," Andrea replied. "Although I don't really see nothin' wrong wit' my name," she added.

Vanessa looked at Andrea as if she had been dropped on her head at birth. "Seriously?" she asked. "So when you go to a large venue like Radio City or Madison Square Garden, hell even singing at the White House for the president, you won't care if they bring you out as ole' Andrea?" she asked laughing.

"I don't see nothin' wrong wit' using my own name. Artists do that all the time," Andrea replied.

One of the boys, the normal slackers who stood at the steps of the school, happened to eavesdrop on the conversation.

"I'll let you have my last name, Ma," he replied slyly as the other boys laughed.

Andrea normally ignored the crude sexist comments from the boys, but on this day, she was in a particularly good mood, so she decided to answer back.

"You betta' hope someone wants yo' last name," she cut back, among laughter from the other boys.

The boy laughed himself. "light, Ma you got it. Aye yo' I need to holla at yo' girl," he added, referring to Vanessa. "Word on da street is that you played Jimmy on prom night," he said to Vanessa. "Word was you dissed him," he added.

"I don't know where you get yo' facts from but even he know that's a damn lie," Vanessa bit back.

The boy turned back to his friends. "See, that's what I'm sayin'. Ya need to watch dem hoes, man. They gonna act like they don't want it, then when you give it to 'em, they gon' scream rape or some shit like that," he said.

Vanessa turned to reply, but Andrea coaxed her back around. "Girl don't even worry about 'em. They ain't worth the trouble at all," she said.

"Nah, you right. All boys gon' be hard-headed about what they hear. Neanderthal-lookin' ass," she retorted as Andrea walked away, laughing.

"So, you got work today?" Vanessa asked.

"Nah I gotta meet up with Dr. Jan today. I ain't seen her in a minute for our session," Andrea replied.

"Right, so are you gonna tell her the news?" Vanessa asked.

"Nah, still too early," Andrea said. "I shouldn't have even told you about it, but we girls, so you're a special exception," she added.

"Word? So if you blow up and make crazy money of yo' sales, you gon' hook yo' girl up?" Vanessa asked.

Andrea made a sound that resembled a scoff in her laughter. "Yeah, whateva," she said. Vanessa's face dropped. "Girl you know I'm just playin," she added. "You're already the first honorary member of my entourage," Andrea reassured Vanessa.

As they reached their respective corners, Vanessa turned off and headed for home and Andrea headed home to get ready to visit Dr. Ralwinski. Andrea's parents had given their approval for her to take the bus to get to the office. Andrea felt as though that her parents were being a little more lenient with her since she got signed. At first, she thought they had been trying to get into her good graces so she could give them money but Andrea hated to think of her parents that way. She liked to think that perhaps her parents were just proud of her and decided to give her a little bit of the freedom for which she so yearned.

After a couple of buses, Andrea arrived at the office about twenty minutes early. Dr. Ralwinski was not at the office yet. As she looked at her cell phone she read a piece of news that she found unsettling. Apparently BHR and Metro Records were more than rivals in the world of music. Their artists hated one another and on the previous night, it had all come to a head. A Metro Records employee and a BHR employee were at a club and exchanged brief, angry words and then a fight ensued. None of the artists were hurt but the two employees were arrested. Andrea hoped that she wasn't walking into the middle of a battle. As she continued reading the article, Dr. Ralwinski walked into the office.

"How are you doing, Andrea?" she asked.

"I'm doing good, Dr. Jan," Andrea replied as she took the food out of the shelf and fed the fish in the tank, as was their normal procedure.

The doctor sat in her chair, leaning forward a little bit, studying Andrea's body language. "You seem to be in a great mood today," she said.

Andrea knew she had to be careful not to let her emotions show too much because Dr. Ralwinski would be able to read it and figure out the happy news.

"Yeah, I've been doing really good lately. No complaints," she said.

"That's great, honey," Dr. Ralwinski replied. "So how did the prom go?" she asked.

The smile on Andrea's face evaporated quickly, as she recalled the night that started off so well, only to go sour when she nearly witnessed her friend getting raped.

"Actually, the prom didn't go too well," Andrea replied.

"Oh no, I'm sorry to hear that? What happened?" Dr. Ralwinski asked.

Andrea took a deep breath. "Well, it started off good. The limo ride, the pictures, the lobby where the prom was, everything was good. Too bad, I neva' realized that Vanessa's date turned out to be a jackass," she replied.

"Really? What happened between Vanessa and her date?" Dr. Ralwinski asked.

"Well, I was walkin' out into the hallway and I saw her date pushin' up on her and she was tellin' him to get off but he wouldn't stop. If my prom date hadn't arrived when he did, my best friend could've been raped," Andrea answered.

"Wow, it sounds like your date's a keeper," Dr. Ralwinski said. "It wasn't Sean, was it?" she asked furtively.

"No, it wasn't Sean, Dr. Jan," Andrea replied laughing. "It was a guy from one of my classes named Quentin," she added. "He saw what was going on and he got Jimmy away from her before it escalated," Andrea explained, the whole night flashing before her eyes again.

Dr. Ranlwinski looked at Amdrea with that familiar, sly look that indicated she suspected more than just friendship. "Thank goodness he was there in time," Dr. Ralwinski said. "So can you see yourself and Quentin together?" she asked Andrea.

"Nah. I' mean he's great friend and I owe him for coming to Vanessa's side when he did. But I don't see a future wit' him like that," Andrea said.

"Really? But you're so young. You might not feel that way about him now but things might change later, you never know," Dr. Ralwinski said. "One thing I noticed is that you've placed Sean on the backburner, huh?" she added.

Andrea laughed out loud, but secretly she was beginning to think Dr. Ralwinski knew too much. "There was no backburner for Sean to end up in, anyway. He's my friend and nothin' else," she said, squirming on the sofa, before lying back down again.

After a few minutes of silence, Andrea asked, "Dr. Jan, have you eva' wanted to be a star?" she asked.

Dr. Ralwinski was taken aback by the question. But she shared the names of many former teen artists who she had idolized in the years she grew. "At your age? Sure. I wanted to go be a Lena Horne or a Marilyn

Monroe. Trust me, I know exactly what you mean," Dr. Ralwinski answered.

"Ok, but let's say the road to being a star was much closer than you thought," Andrea replied, resisting the urge to tell her doctor how near she really was to becoming a star. Dr. Ralwinski adjusted the glasses on her face.

"If this opportunity is special to you, then you'd be a fool not to go for the money," she said, raising her eyes. "But I will say this. There are a lot of people who pretend to be best friends with one another and the reason for that is because they want what they can't have," Dr. Ralwinski replied. "Money is a powerful weapon Andrea and put in the wrong hands can be abused and people may take advantage of you. Most of the time I think that stars carry a bigger burden than we do because it's their families that are often threatened by others wishing to take this success away from them. Danger may be concealed within our own inner circles," she concluded.

Andrea thought about what Dr. Ralwinski said. Was she taking a huge risk signing with Metro Records, knowing that if news got out about her opportunity, she could be jeopardizing their safety? She hated comparing situations but it resembled finding out in the courtroom that Loree had engulfed herself within the gang who eventually killed her in their attempt to save some and to expose others. Was she putting herself in the same peril? Certainly there had to be special cases, such as De'Von Franklin. He has released an album that had gone gold and is currently working on his second album. He had already toured the country and his family was financially set. Besides, Metro seemed to offer plenty of protection, since she's seen De'Von surrounded by a number of body guards. She still wanted to tell Dr. Ralwinski about being signed by Metro but decided against it at the last minute as they continued their session.

On Saturday morning, Andrea's cell phone rang.

"What's goin' on, superstar?" Julio's voice blared out from the receiver. Andrea laughed.

"Nah, I ain't no superstar yet. I don't even know if I'm gonna be all that great," she replied.

"Aw, come on Andrea, don't tell me you're backing out on me now. Trust me, you are a superstar. I can see it now, and in due time you'll see it too," Julio reassured. "Anyway, just called to see if you were up cuz I wanna show you who we are and what we can do for you today," he continued. "Are you ready?" he asked.

Andrea jumped out of bed. She could barely contain her excitement. Julio was finally going to show her Metro Records. "Hell yeah I'm ready!" she exclaimed.

"Do you need me to drive ova there to meet you?" she asked, although she wasn't sure if her father would even let her use the car, since he normally handled chores and did volunteer work on Saturdays. She would have to coax him into using the car.

"No need," Julio replied. "I'm having someone pick you up right now. Just get ready and wait outside. Your ride should be there in about twenty minutes," he replied, before hanging up.

Andrea looked at the clock. It was seven thirty-one. She headed over to the bathroom to take a quick shower and got dressed in a Tommy Hilfiger T-shirt with jeans and blue and white Nike sneakers. She went to the dresser, which had belonged to Loree and she looked frantically for the piece of jewelry that her late sister often wore to parties and special occasions. She found it; a gold necklace with a single music note hanging at the end of it. Combing her hair until it fell just a little past her shoulders, she walked outside and waited for the car that was scheduled to picker her up. Her parents were still asleep and they probably wouldn't know she was gone, so she left a note on the fridge, letting them know where she went. Sitting on the front steps of her duplex-styled home, Andrea watched as different cars passed the next street and intersection. Finally, a 2008 Mercedez-Benz pulled up next to her house. As Andrea stepped closer to the car, she saw the window roll down slightly. A thick-bearded, heavy-set black man with a New York Giants cap looked back at her.

"Are you Ms. Andrea McAfee?" he asked in a serious tone.

"Yeah, that's me," Andrea answered, hoping that her doubt wasn't reflective in her tone. She thought either Julio or Craig would come pick her up but not this complete stranger. She stepped inside the car. "Who are you?" she asked.

"Marvin Pendleton, your personal driver, ma'am," he answered.

Andrea's eyes widened. She already had a personal driver? "Personal driver? Like just for today?" Andrea asked.

Marvin looked at her through the front-view mirror. "No ma'am. I'll be your driver for the duration of your time at Metro Records," he replied. Andrea looked at him, surprised.

"Seriously? You not playin' me or nothin' like that, right? You for real?" she asked.

"That's what my employers tell me, Miss. I was instructed to come pick you up here and drop you at the studio." Marvin answered as they drove to Metro Records.

Andrea never expected the location to be so far away but the trip to the studio took almost an hour and when they arrived, Andrea's jaw dropped. They arrived at a large eight-story building, with two outer doors, made out of steel and two inner doors made up of glass. Outside the building there was a huge neon sign, which was lit up at night but during the day it was just inscribed in big block letters, METRO RECORDS LLC. Andrea had to blink twice and pinch herself to make sure she wasn't dreaming. No, I'm not dreaming. This is definitely real and this is definitely happening, she thought as she gaped at the building.

Marvin opened her door and Andrea stepped out, looking up so high, she began to get a cramp in her neck. Marvin scanned what appeared to be an employee card on an outside scanner and the outside doors silently opened. Once inside, Andrea inhaled what smelled like fresh linoleum or carpet cleaner. Whatever it was, it smelled new. The lobby of Metro Records was filled with business men and women, whom Andrea took to be the execs.

"Right this way, Ms. McAfee," Marvin said as he pointed to a long, winding hallway that led to either elevators or a flight of stairs.

Andrea started to walk there, expecting Marvin to accompany her but was stunned when she realized Marvin stayed in the lobby. To her great relief, she saw Julio at the end of the hallway. He seemed to be taking some papers from one of the workers.

"Julio!" Andrea called out, waving her hand so she would get Julio's attention. When Julio turned her direction, he smiled and walked toward her.

"There she is! The superstar," Julio said. Andrea started to argue that she wasn't a superstar but then Julio spoke again. "So what do you think?" he said.

"This is crazy but it's off da chain. I like this," Andrea said, still at a loss for words.

"Welcome to Metro Records." Julio said again.

Chapter Twelve

Julio wasted no time in giving Andrea a tour of Metro Records in its entirety. From the wide conference rooms where the producers, executives, and television promoters met to the actual recording booths located in the back of the building on the first floor. As they walked through some of the meeting rooms and conference rooms, Andrea saw the shiny gold vinyl records that lined the studio walls. She later learned that Metro Records was largely responsible for not only honing new talent but providing key soundtracks for motion pictures and theme songs for television specials. Metro was totally independent, being a privately owned company. Metro Records had been founded in 1998 and had been a cornerstone for its community. Located in the corner of Broadway and 34th Avenue, Metro's strength was serving its community and provided job opportunities with no discrimation as to color, gender, or even age. Andrea followed Julio throughout the building and took everything in.

"So since I work with Metro now, am I gonna have to get one of those card swipe badges?" she asked Julio.

"Not necessarily. We believe that all our artists should have more freedom than other employees. Those card systems shut down at three-thirty AM for security reasons. Our last employee leaves around two-thirty. Some artists wanna come in later than that, so we actually provide them with their own key," Julio said.

Andrea could scarcely believe it. "My own key? Get outta hea'!" she said, not believing what Julio was telling her.

"I'm dead serious," Julio said. "Now I take it that you're familiar with some of the artists that work with us, right?" he asked.

Andrea hadn't known too many of them but with Vanessa's help in the past, she was able to identify a few artists.

"Yeah I know Miesha, Yolanda, Michelle, Bobby Smooth, and of course De'Von Franklin," she answered.

"Good job," Julio said as if she had just passed a pop quiz at school. "Let's go down to the recording booths, to see if anyone's down there now," he suggested.

Andrea followed Julio down to the recording booths where the artists worked. While they took the elevator back down to the first floor, Julio took the time to tell Andrea about their competitor, BHR.

"Andrea, I wanna point out that when we go on our next tour, there may be a slight possibility that we may be sharing a stage with an artist from Big House Records despite the fact that they are one of our biggest competitors. I've been around long enough to see tension build up between acts and there are fights that break out because you got different types of people that don't take opposition well. They end up getting into scrapes and fights because of it," he said. Andrea heard about the tension between the labels and although she was wary of possible confrontations, it didn't phase her at the moment.

"They are our biggest competitors for radio airtime, for television appearances, for sponsors, and for show guest appearances. As a matter of fact, they were at the amateur show where we saw you," he added.

Andrea finally understood why Julio ran into her after she just emerged from the ladies room. "Oh, so you were trying to get to me before they did," she confirmed.

Julio smiled sheepishly. "Exactly. I didn't want them to get their hands on you before I got a chance," he replied.

"It's ok, Julio. I think they were interested in Emiline more than with me," Andrea said.

"Don't worry about that," Julio replied. "To be honest, I think we're better off," he added.

Andrea smiled genuinely at Julio. She wasn't sure if Julio was just messing with her mind or if he really meant it. Emiline had a really great voice and Andrea couldn't help but think that if she hadn't gone to the amateur night, Emiline would have been on this tour of Metro instead of her. As they got out of the elevator, they heard loud music resembling drums and bass guitar in a rhythmic street beat.

"He must be here already," Julio said.

"Who's here already?" Andrea asked.

"The Bronx Flow himself, De'Von Franklin," he replied. Andrea started to feel her senses go numb again, the same way they had during their first meeting inside Johnson's when De'Von had purchased his shoes.

"Let's check him out," he added as they visited the booth where De'Von was working. As they accessed the booth, they saw four people inside the studio.

Andrea recognized Craig from the club and there was one other person, a white man who appeared to be in his mid-thirties. He was managing the sound board. As the beat continued playing, De'Von started rapping to the beat. His lyrics were methodical, quick, with subtle political references.

Call on da kid, they say he be low-low scheming/drinkin' the Hen when he needa be sleepin/They caught me catchin' a case like OJ/ I gotta press on, make da most of today.

Julio stepped inside the studio and convinced Andrea to follow him. Reluctantly, Andrea followed him. She found a place to sit down next to the third person in the booth; the boy who was with De'Von when he was shopping at Johnson's. It only took a moment but his eyes widened as the realization set in.

"Hold up. Stop the take," he said, as the sound man stopped the playback. "What's up, girl?" What you doin' hea'?" "We gotta stop meetin' like this," he said to Andrea.

Andrea just shrugged her shoulders, shyly. Julio looked between the two. "You two have met before?" he asked.

"Yeah, it's that chick that work at Johnson's. She the one who hooked me up wit' them Flights, man," he said, pointing to his feet. Andrea noticed that he was wearing his new sneakers.

Julio turned to Andrea. "Is that true?" he asked.

Andrea nodded her head to confirm De'Von's claim. "Yeah, I work part time at Johnson's and he came looking for the Flights. I helped him find a pair. It was no big deal," she answered.

"Yo, it was a big deal to me. Ya were the only ones who had 'em," De'Von said. "Anyway, what's up? You hea' for an autograph? I coulda hooked you up at Johnson's but since you was actin' all brand new, I guess you'll have to wait on that," he added a sly smile

"She ain't here for an autograph, superstar. I would like to announce that Ms. Andrea is part of the family here at Metro now," Julio said.

The other members in the studio clapped and congratulated Andrea. The white man who was working the sound board introduced himself. "Paul Waltzman, welcome Andrea. I hope to help produce some hits for you one day," he said.

"Hey Andrea, what's up? I know we met before but I wanna congratulate you once again on being a part of Metro We can't wait till you drop some heat for us," Craig said.

"Let's not wait then. Everybody hypin' her up like she already done sold a million albums," De'Von's friend said and from the tone of his voice, Andrea could tell right away that he wasn't too thrilled with her being part of Metro.

"Yo Slam, chill man. She just got hea' yo, let her breathe. This is like a trip to Disneyland for her," De'Von said, snickering.

Is he playin' me or is he coming to my defense? Andrea thought.

But Slam wasn't satisfied with De'Von's statement. "Nah nah, son. Let's see what she got. I've been around as long as you have and I've seen mad scrubs. Put her in front of the mike and let's see what she can do," he challenged.

"Come on Slam, De'Von got a track to finish. We ain't got time for this 'prove it' Don Corleone mafia nonsense," Craig said as he sat back down in front of the soundboard.

But Julio had other ideas. "No, wait. Ok, if Slam wants to hear our young new artist, let's give her a shot to show what she's got," he said.

Andrea looked at Julio, an expression of betrayal on her face. "You want me to show you now?" she asked nervously.

"Yeah why not?" Julio insisted. "Give non-believers like Slam and the others something to look forward to when you on da track," he added.

So De'Von stepped out of the sound booth and allowed Andrea to walk in. As she was walking in the booth, she could feel everyone's attentive gaze on her at that moment. She looked up at the overhead microphone, held by a suspended microphone stand. She stepped up the microphone and cleared her throat, when she heard laughter from the other side of the booth and Slam gave De'Von the smug look of confirmation that explained what he believed about her; that she was just a scared little girl who was in way over her head. It was Andrea's first time in a recording studio and it was very clear that she didn't know where to begin. De'Von stepped inside the booth again and showed Andrea where the headsets were.

"Here, put these on. It's so that Paul can get your voice on playback," he added.

"Thanks, De'Von. I feel so stupid," she added.

"Nah don't sweat that, I remember my first day in the studio. I had no clue where anything was and I never knew my cue to start rappin'," he said. "The main thing is to relax and take a deep breath and feel the track.

You got this," he added, before he stepped out the booth, leaving Andrea all alone in the booth.

"Aye Paul, give her an instrumental," Julio said as Paul switched taped and played an instrumental that sounded very familiar to Andrea.

It was a song that had been sung by another veteran artist from Metro records, named Melodee. It was a slow R&B song that Andrea was accustomed to listening to when she would be at lunch break at work or at school. It was one of her favorite songs entitled "Secrets of the Heart." As the playback began, Julio gave Andrea the signal to begin singing but to Andrea, it was as if she was back at Fusion Lounge. The lyrics seemed to be stuck on her lips and her tongue felt heavy. She attempted to open her mouth but no sound came out of her voice box. Singing at Fusion Lounge was easier because she was singing for a contest and it was showcasing in front of many people that she would probably never see again with other performers under the same pressure to perform. This was totally different. She was singing on an instrumental track in a booth all alone with all eyes on her. This was pure pressure. She felt her stomach churn and the sickening sensation of her breakfast threatening to come back up on her. Outside the booth, Slam was laughing.

"See, I knew her ass would freeze up," he said. Turning to Julio, he said, "You be so quick to throw money away, man. You think dis' chick's gonna help us? She can't even help herself," he added.

"Yo, why don't you shut da hell up and give her a shot?" De'Von replied angrily.

"Look at her dog. She looks like she needs a bucket in there, man. She ain't about this music life. Next," Slam said dismissively.

While all of these words were exchanged outside, Andrea could feel the producer's eyes boring through her and the red tinge of embarrassment start to creep over her face. At the same time, she felt a warm presence surround her. It was a presence that no one else saw but her. It seemed to whisper in her ear as she held both sides of the headsets.

Don't let them doubt you. Show them who you are. Represent for us. You can do it. The voice of her late sister always seemed to be there when she needed it, especially when she felt angry or nervous. She glanced over to Julio and with a quick nod of her head and twirl of her finger, she indicated to Julio that she wanted Paul to play the song back. As Paul started the song from the beginning, Andrea gathered herself and closed her eyes and felt the song she had been hearing for a long time.

There's a place deep inside me that longs for your tender touch/There's a feeling inside of me that adores you so much/I never thought I'd ever feel this way again/Started out as an acquaintance but more than a friend.

Andrea's rich tones and her vocal range astounded the people in the studio. Slam and De'Von stopped bickering long enough to hear the beautiful voice emerging from the budding songstress. Paul appeared to be in a state of shock himself as he continued the playback. As Andrea sang, her tones picked up through the audio, an idea flashed through Julio's head. The moment Andrea finished her song, the people in the studio applauded loudly. Craig turned around to face Slam, who appeared stunned at Andrea's dramatic emergence from her fear.

"And you were saying?" he asked Slam with a hint of sarcasm. De'Von was one of the people applauding the loudest.

"Yo, how come nobody ever told me she had a voice like that? She can get it," he said as they wrapped up the take.

Before De'Von stepped back into the booth, Julio called a meeting between him and Andrea in a separate room.

"Ok so while Andrea was settin' it off in the booth, I just got an idea. De'Von, you still got that song you wrote that needed a female hook?" Julio asked.

"No doubt," De'Von replied. I still got the instrumental on it but I thought we weren't gon' do that track anymore," he added.

"Oh, we're still doin' that track bro," Julio replied. "It looks like we found the girl with the right chops for it," he said gesturing to Andrea, who looked confused.

"But I thought when you signed me, you said I was going to be working on my own album," she protested.

"But you are working on your own album," Julio said. Andrea didn't seem to understand, so Julio continued. "My plan is to introduce you to our audience through being a feature on De'Von's next album. He got a song on his EP that needs a strong female voice hook. We've looked everywhere here and we haven't found anyone who's voice fits wit' the track. Until now," Julio said, winking at Andrea.

Suddenly his phone rang. Checking the screen of his phone, he excused himself and left Andrea and De'Von in the room. She could feel De'Von staring at her, like the one girl at a party that he admired.

"So what made you wanna sing?" he asked her.

Andrea shrugged. "It just makes me feel some type of way, you know? When I sing, I forget about all my pain, I forget all my troubles and I go into my own world," she replied.

"I feel you," De'Von replied.

"So what made you wanna rap?" she asked him.

De'Von didn't answer right away but he looked silently out a window for a moment.

"Just to let go, I guess, like you. I started rappin' wit' my older brother years ago and we used to go to every sock hop, every BBQ, any local place we could book for the day. We used to go up there and tear shit up, you know what I'm sayin'?" he asked.

"I feel you. So does your brother still rap now?" she asked. De'Von looked at Andrea.

"Nah, not anymore. He passed away almost ten years ago," De'Von replied. Andrea put a hand to her mouth.

"Wow. I'm so sorry to hear that. I didn't mean to bring up..." she began, but De'Von cut her off.

"It's all good. You ain't know about it. That's why I do my best to hold it down fa' him whenever I go on stage," he replied.

Andrea didn't tell De'Von right away but she certainly could relate with him coping with the loss of not only a sibling, but an older one. Maybe De'Von's older brother spoke with him while he rapped, just as Loree spoke to her before she sang. Andrea decided to lighten the mood up in the room.

"Bet when you met me at Johnson's, you ain't think that I could sing like that, huh?" she asked.

"Nah I had no clue. Besides I only had one thing in mind and that was getting' them Flights," he said. "You know you gon' have to quit that job now, right?" he asked, laughing.

Andrea laughed also. "Well, lemme see how this works out and when the time is right, trust and believe that I will be outta there," she replied.

"You must not like workin' there, huh?" De'Von asked.

"Well it's not that I don't like it. I've been there so long and it's just time for me to move on. Some of the people there be gettin' on my last nerve for real," she answered.

"Man, look. You best believe I would not stay in a place that I'm not wanted. I'd throw up dem deuces if I was you," De'Von replied.

"One day, man. One day," she answered. "Besides, before Metro discovered you, didn't you have a job?" she asked.

"Nah, I was still chillin at school and one day Julio came up to me, cuz he heard my demo tape and wit' me being from the Bronx, I guess my reputation traveled. So he called me and offered me a contract and the rest is history," De'Von replied.

"Must be nice," Andrea replied as she looked around the room. They were sitting inside what seemed to be an old recording room. There were old instruments, sound mics, soundboards and other items.

"So, Miss Andrea you got a man?" De'Von asked suddenly.

Andrea shook her head. "Never had much time to mess wit' anyone. If I'm not at school, I'm workin', she replied.

"Aww, so all work and no play?" De'Von asked.

"Yup. But I got the feelin' that you play all da' time," she replied.

"Hey gotta make room for celebration whenever your first album goes gold. Don't believe all the hype you read in the media," De'Von answered smling.

At that same moment, Slam came into the room. "Yo Von, we gotta get back to work. You can chop it up wit' Ms. Baby Blige lata' on," he said before closing the door behind him.

"Yo, what's wit' yo' boy?" Andrea asked.

"Who, Slam?" De'Von asked. "Nah he good people. He just be actin' like he got something stuck up his ass sometimes. Don't sweat him. He'll be cool wit' you too, eventually," De'Von replied, getting up to go to the studio. "So, I know today's a bit of an introduction and all for you, but you wanna chill in the studio while I work on my LP?" he asked.

"Hell yeah, I'll stay. Go tear it up," Andrea replied. As they went back to the studio and De'Von continued rapping his verse, Andrea couldn't help but feel a bit numb. Here she was, at Metro Records with one of the hottest young rappers out, and she would be featured on a track with him one day. It was just too much to handle.

"Man, I can't believe you was in the same studio as De'Von Franklin, girl," Vanessa said excitedly to Andrea that night over the phone. "If it sounds like I'm hatin' on you right now, it's because I am. You are so lucky," she added after Andrea told her about the tour of Metro Records and the events at the recording studio.

"I know, girl. It's all happening so quick. Julio didn't even come to pick me up. Guess who they had to come get me?" Andrea asked rhetorically. "A chauffeur, Vanessa. I had my very own driver, girl! He comes to get me and drives me to the studio or anywhere else I wanna go," she added.

"Must be nice," Vanessa sighed and Andrea could hear the longing of acceptance in her voice, as if she didn't want to get left behind.

"Aw come on Nessa, don't be like that. Remember, we in this together. I ain't gon' leave my prima behind. How about the next time we go to the studios, you come with me?" Andrea offered.

"Fo' real? You sure they gonna be cool wit' that?" Vanessa asked.

"Sure, why not?" Andrea replied. "I see artists bring in their peoples and their entourage's everywhere they go. If I eva' go platinum and they nominate me for best new artist or something, you gonna be there wit' me when I pick up my award," she added.

"What about when you go out to the clubs and all them expensive restaurants, I can kick it wit' you then, too?" Vanessa asked.

"No doubt. Girl I'm gonna need someone else to cover me when I go out on tour and I get mobbed by a bunch of over-hyped kids," Andrea replied before she quickly retracted. "Girl, I'm just playin'. You're more than a cover to me. When everything is right, I'mma have you wit' me in all the great places. From the beaches, to night clubs, to other spots, you gon' be rolling with me," Andrea added.

The promise seemed to galvanize Vanessa, who was starting to think that her longtime friend would leave her behind. "Yeah that's what's up. What about Sean?" Vanessa asked.

Andrea laughed. "What about him?" she questioned back.

"Well Andrea, he's been rockin' wit' us fo' years now and I think he should roll wit' us too," Vanessa said.

Andrea thought about the proposition. It wasn't ideal for her to have many of her other friends involved but Sean was like a brother to her. Andrea just couldn't leave him behind.

"I guess if he ain't too busy, he could roll wit' us too," Andrea said. "But you know how he is about ball, and he's so worried about that scholarship, so he might not get to roll wit' us," she added.

The phone was quiet for a moment, before Vanessa spoke again. "Ok girl, we really need to stop frontin' about and discuss your stage name, Miss Thang," she said.

"Well you go on and you think about your own name, baby cuz I got my name on deck already," Andrea replied, laughing.

"Really? So what you gon' call yourself then?" Vanessa asked.

Andrea recalled earlier that afternoon, before she had to work, when she had been thinking of the right name to give to herself. She didn't want a name that was too long or hard to recognize. She wanted a short, sweet, yet significant name in case she had to answer to it in interviews.

"You can call me Adia," Andrea replied.

"Adia?" What does that name mean anyway?" Vanessa asked.

"It means, "gift from God" in African-Swahili and Indian dialect," Andrea explained.

"I love that name, it sounds very exotic," Vanessa said.

"I love it because of what it means to me and what it can mean to people who listen to my music. It is a gift from God and I don't think of it any different," Andrea said.

"That's what's up," Vanessa said. "Now Adia, since you had the experience of being inside Metro Records, who else did you meet today?" she asked.

"Well I met another producer, a soundman and I met De'Von's friend, Slam," Andrea said.

"Slam? What kind of name is that?" Vanessa asked.

"Girl you askin' the wrong one," Andrea replied. "Anyway I don't know what's up wit him but I don'think he's feelin' me too much. He thinks Metro wasted their time on me," she added.

"Don't even worry about that girl. I mean, it ain't like he an artist or nothin' like that, so what right do he have to step up to you, actin' like he know all about you?" Vanessa asked.

"True. If you want my opinion, it seems like he livin' on De'Von all day and I'm not sayin' anything about it, but I don't trust him," Andrea replied.

"Well, you already know I ain't gon' do you like that. We friends before anything else. We were girls before the money started rollin' in and we gon be girls even after the money's gone," she added.

Saying goodnight to Vanessa, she hung up and got ready for bed. Looking at the dresser that had belonged to Loree, she could sometimes picture her sister poring over the drawers looking for her clothes or jewelry and see herself sneaking a piece she would wear during the day. She knelt down in front of her bed and said a prayer before going to bed.

Andrea had a very strange dream when she crawled into her bed. It was downright eerie. She was seated in the back of small blue Honda accord and was strapped in tightly by her seat belt. There were two dark figures in the front of the car and at first Andrea couldn't make out who the two boys were but her heightened sense of fear increased when the two boys came into focus. Both boys were talking frantically and Andrea couldn't decipher what they were saying. As the scene shifted into focus, Andrea realized in horror that the two boys who sat in the front of the car were gangbangers by their durag bandanna colors and tattoos. Looking closer, Andrea saw that one of the gangbangers was tall but still had a boyish face. The other boy in the car was lighter in skin tone and had a small amount of peach fuzz underneath his nose. Both boys were strapped with guns and heavy rap music blared in the car. Both boys seemed to be arguing non-stop and the passenger appeared to be a great deal of panic.

"Man, forget what Tadarius said. We ain't gotta to listen to him," the boy in the passenger seat argued as the boy driving gave him a look that threatened to kill.

"Listen to yo' punk ass now," the driver said. "All this time you talkin' bout wantin' to roll wit' his crew and now you startin' to punk out. You lettin' dis one get to yo' head too?" he asked as both turned around to face Andrea.

Andrea tried to speak but no words came out of her mouth. Nonetheless, the driver informed Andrea to shut up, as if she said something that he didn't want to hear. Andrea decided to occupy her time by looking out the window. She saw they were driving down Parsons Boulevard and were heading towards Guy R. Brewer Drive. Andrea looked at the glass and realized where she was and more importantly, who she was. A gaunt, thin, and exhausted Loree looked back at her. She couldn't believe it. She was Loree and Loree was her. Andrea then realized that she was seeing Loree's final hours in this world. She didn't know what trick the universe was playing on her but she instinctively knew she was about to be shot in a matter of seconds and she couldn't do anything to prevent that outcome. Just as Andrea wondered when it was going to happen, the car suddenly braked to a halt.

"If you gon' keep bitchin' and whinin', get outta hea' then," the driver said.

"Ain't nobody whinin' but I ain't down wit' this no more man. Let me outta hea," the passenger said.

The driver pulled over to the sidewalk near a secluded area and the passenger opened the door. The driver glowered at him.

"When Tadarius hears you punked out, he gon' track yo' sorry ass down. You'll see, watch," the driver said ominously.

"I don't care what he said man. I'm done wit' this. I'm out," he said as he stepped out the car and started walking the opposite direction.

As if instinctively, Andrea moved to the passenger seat. Andrea tried yelling to her sister's subconscious, telling her to get out of the car as quickly as possible but it was to no avail. Without warning, the driver grabbed Andrea's hair and pulled it roughly.

"Antonio was always a sucka. So I see you gave Tadarius that work earlier. When is it my turn?" he asked aggressively and Andrea yelled out from the pain she felt from the boy's fingers pulling each hair follicle at its roots.

She couldn't tell if it was her own strength or Loree's strength in her last bid for freedom, but she suddenly saw the boy fly back into his seat. She then unlocked the door and started running down the street. She didn't even have a chance to turn back before the bullets from the boy's gun ripped through her chest. Waking up in a cold sweat, Andrea rubbed her hands over the spots where the bullets penetrated her in her dream. She felt moisture on her shirt but was relieved to find out that it was only sweat. What had just happened to her? Was she really thrust in Loree's last hours on earth? Her hand still massaging her chest area, Andrea could never forget the sharp pain she felt from the gunshots, a feeling of skin and flesh being ripped into, and the force of hitting the ground face-first. Andrea always remembered that when Loree was found by a motorist at the time, she was described as being fatally wounded but she still had enough in her to walk to the end of the block before collapsing. She had believed Loree to be superhuman when Andrea learned that Loree had nearly survived the shooting. Unfortunately, she had lost too much blood so there was no chance of recovery. The most important information Andrea took from the dream was that neither of the boys resembled David Anderson, Loree's estranged boyfriend, who had been initially accused. She knew they were gang members. The identical tattoos on their arms, the guns, and the same black shirts with the blood spots and the dollar bill sign on them. Andrea got out of bed and went to the bathroom to splash cold water on her face. She looked in the mirror as her eyes asked the same longing questions. Why was I in the car? Why was Loree in the car? Could she have gotten away?

These were questions that lingered in Andrea's head. A visit to Dr. Ralwinski was definitely needed. Maybe she could explain what Loree was subconsciously trying to tell Andrea. She whispered a little prayer to herself, got back into bed, and rolled the sheets back over her head.

Chapter Thirteen

School dragged on for what seemed like a day of slow motion for Andrea. She walked to school, showed up in her classes, ate lunch, and basically did what she normally did on an average day but Andrea was still distracted. It was the dream that had her floundering. She found herself thinking about it constantly and she couldn't shake it off her. She was so preoccupied that during British Literature class, the teacher called on her to read a passage of one of the stories they were reading and Andrea was so lost in thought that the teacher called her name four times before Andrea finally responded. She had to apologize to the teacher for not paying attention. Vanessa, who was thinking only of the exciting prospect of Andrea being a signed artist, was oblivious about anything bothering Andrea.

"So, Ms. Adia, when do you return to the studio to record?" she whispered silently.

"I go back next weekend," Andrea replied, more nonchalant than she had intended.

"Ok, try not to look so excited. I know I would be if I'm about to work with Metro's stars such as Miesha, Michelle Brown, and let's not forget the leading man there, De'Von," she said, trying to pump Andrea up but it just wasn't working. After a while, Vanessa realized that Andrea was distracted.

"Ok Drea, what's up? You've been quiet all day today. Is some-thing bothering you?" she asked.

Andrea found herself at a crossroads. She really wanted to tell Vanessa about her dream because if there was anyone who knew what she had endured since Loree's death, it would be Vanessa but Andrea didn't want to bring Vanessa into her head about it. She had her own life to live and her own situations.

"I'm all right. I just got a lot on my mind right now. I'm definitely ready for this Saturday, no doubt," Andrea replied.

Vanessa smiled at her in confirmation "There you go. That's the Andrea we're waitin' for," she replied. As they walked down the hallway, they ran into Sean, who was talking to some friends and former teammates.

"What's up Andrea?" he asked casually.

"I'm good Sean, nothin' much. So I don't be seein' you that much nowadays. What's goin' on?" she asked.

"Oh well, you already know me, always workin' at the gym. The game neva' stops for me," Sean replied.

Andrea snickered. "True but once the game begins for you, everything else just don't matter, including catching up wit' yo' friends," Andrea said, raising an eyebrow to Sean. "So what's up, is yo' father comin' to pick you up today?" she asked.

"Nah, Pops is locked in some cases right now. Some idiot left about three grams of weed on a floor stoop, so now the police department's searching for the buyers and suppliers of the pack," Sean said.

"So your dad's got his hands full, huh?" Andrea asked.

"No doubt," Sean confirmed. "Anyway I gotta bounce. Gotta get home to check to see if any letters from any colleges made its way ova to my crib," he said as he walked off, saying goodbye to Vanessa as he walked out of the school.

Andrea turned to Vanessa. "Man! Being a son of a cop can't be easy at all, especially in New York," she told Vanessa as they walked out of the school doors.

On Saturday Andrea was back at Metro and now that her paperwork had been processed, she knew that she would start working. Julio and Craig had written an R&B song that featured De'Von as a rapper. It was well known that De'Von had been working on the song for weeks but they hadn't been able to find the right voice for the hook of the song. Since Julio suggested that Andrea be the voice to the song, it would be a great way to introduce her to the mainstream audience and once she got their attention with her voice, they figured she would be the perfect contrast to De'Von's rap style. Andrea made it clear that she wouldn't start recording until they approved her new stage name. When she announced it, she received mostly approvals and nods of support. Of course, Slam was the only one who was sarcastic about it. De'Von was of a different mindset.

"Not bad. I can dig it," he replied. Craig stepped up to the microphone that was mounted just outside the booth.

"Adia featuring De'Von, take one," he said, before Paul played the song back. De'Von started rapping and Andrea was impressed by the speed of De'Von's rap. She found herself bobbing her head to the beat and before she knew it, the break was coming. Andrea geared herself up for it and once her cue came, she took herself to the place where she was alone with the music and she sang the hook line to DeVon's verses.

I know exactly what you want/You know exactly what I need/You a man that's a different kind of breed/ Just take my waist and let's proceed.

Andrea's voice was smooth, seductive, and at the same time it had the vocal power needed to lift the single to another level.

As they were working, Andrea looked at the corner of her eye and she could see Julio smiling. She also saw Paul, Craig, and a few of the other artists who had made their way to the studio bob their heads to the beat and enjoy the song. When the take was finished, everyone in the studio applauded.

"Andrea – or should I say Adia – great job on the hook and De'Von, you killin' em as usual," Julio said. "As a matter of fact, I have another idea. Why don't we make this song a music video to promote your next album?" he asked.

Andrea's mouth dropped. "A music video? Are you for real?" she asked.

"Definitely," Craig replied. A hot track like this could easily make the Billboard's top one-hundred in about a week. I don't see why not," he added.

De'Von clapped his hands. He hadn't had a bevy of music video opportunity. He had only appeared in a couple and those were features for more seasoned artists but he was excited that he would get to be the main act in the video along with his new singing partner.

"Yeah a music video would be dope," he agreed. "What you think, dog?" he asked Slam.

Although he was still suspicious of Adia, even Slam had to admit the song was a hit. "Yeah I can't lie homie, the song is fire," he said, dapping De'Von and Andrea.

As the studio wrapped up the song, De'Von looked at Andrea. She was talking with Michelle Brown, who had walked into the studio after her own session.

"Yo, dog, you think she got a man?" he asked Slam.

"Hell if I know, man. If you feelin' her, go for it. Even if she does got a man, what he got ova you right now?" Slam asked.

"True that," De'Von laughed as he dapped Slam another time.

Tico stood outside a housing project in East Tremont. Blue box-like structures had been placed above the heads of the pedestrians so the material from the fallen debris would not land on passersby. It was a lovely night; the breeze of the evening cooled off the heat of the day. He wore an athletic parka with track pants and the latest sneakers available. Counting his drug stock, Tico saw that he had about twelve grams of marijuana, four needles, and a few packs of PCP. He had enough to make a few hundred dollars if he sold the entire stock.

Unfortunately, Tico could tell by the small number of people walking that the night would once again be slow in terms of sales. Leaving his two kids in the care of a family friend, Tico looked at his supplies and shook his head. This was not the plan that he had for his family at all. He was humiliated that he had to return to what he knew, which was hustling and selling drugs. The way he saw his situation, nobody understood him, not even his family or his friends. He really believed he had a chance with Metro Records and that he would get his shot but it clearly wasn't meant to be. People like him didn't get a second chance. Anticipating another slow night, Tico got his cell phone and to make a call.

"Hello?" Tony replied on the other line.

"What up, man?" Tico replied.

"Nothin' much man. You out on da block today?' Tony asked Tico.

"Yeah man. Ain't nothin' else to do man. Bills due by the end of the month and I gotta feed my kids too, ya know?" Tico said sadly. "Yo man, that's actually why I call you. Block definitely ain't hot tonight and I got that rent due in four days, Can you spot yo' boy a couple hundred bucks?" he asked.

He could hear Tony let out a small sigh on the other end of the line. "Alright man, I got you. Stay on da block, I'll be there in over an hour," he replied.

"light cool, I'ma be hea," Tico replied as he hung up his phone.

Standing outside the housing project, he saw a small group of people forming a line on the block across from where he stood. Tico knew he wasn't the only drug distributor outside tonight; there were plenty of others in the same neighborhood. Tico realized quickly that this particular throng didn't appear to be seeking banned substances. It was a good distance from him but Tico could hear it. He heard a rhythmic beat, like an instrumental because there were no artists featured on the song itself. Tico finally understood what was going on. From the instruments being played, the people gathering around (both men and women), and the sound of a strong MC Tico knew, as he chuckled to himself. It was Aaron Sealy, known by his street handle, A-Run. A known freestyler in the Bronx area and also a resident of East Tremont, A-Run was known to have clever punchlines, hurling insults at his opponents who would be unfortunate enough to find themselves going up against him in a freestyle battle. Luckily for A-Run, he had not gone against Tico yet, and that was good because Tico wasn't in the mood to embarrass the young man in front of his friends. But while he was watching the movement of the people to the beat, he noticed a few of them turning around to look at him, laughing.

Tico shrugged his shoulders at them, as if to say, "What's so funny?" Instead of replying, they turned back around to listen to the performer. Tico decided to walk over to the next block himself to find out what was being said about him. Joining the throng, he arrived to hear A-Run's last few verses:

You can hea' him comin from a mile away/Comin' to get his ass whupped like Kunta Kinte/Listen to the play-by play from the Run/ I ain't neva gon' front till my diss is done.

He ended his freestyle amidst cheers and admiration from the onlookers who just realized that Tico had just joined them. Apparently A-Run had done exactly what Tico wished to avoid. He challenged Tico to a freestyle battle. Now the challenge was put down. Tico looked at A-Run.

"Ayo, run that shit back. I got something fo' you," Tico said, while the crowd egged him on to accept the battle. The instrumental was played again and Tico proceeded.

I hate comin' to remind you what you already knew/If you screw wit' my crew, my head's comin' for you/These playas round hea' know I'm da truth, like Pierce/ My lyric's fierce, bet ya thought yo' boy was through/Damn A-Run, it's kinda late, ain't you past yo' mama's curfew?/So next time ya roll up with ya beats on blast/ Just keep that weak shit in a cast, cuz I just ethered yo' ass.

The crowd roared themselves into a frenzy as Tico made a motion of leaving an invisible mike hanging. A-Run came forward and dapped Tico. Even though it was a rap war, they still respected each other's skill. A-Run informed Tico that he would be ready next time and walked off into the night. The crowd dispersed into the cool night and Tico began to walk back toward his block, when he felt someone tap his shoulder. Turning around, he saw it was a white man in a blue blazer and striped pastel.

"What's up?" Tico greeted.

"How you doing, sir?" the man greeted. "My name's Sam Dolson and I represent the talent A/R from BHR."

"BHR? Big House Records?" Tico replied.

"The one and only," the man confirmed, giving Tico his card. "I was on my way home and I heard that little go-round with the young gentleman back there. You have exceptional skills. Do you have a few minutes to talk?" Sam asked.

Tico nodded , saying he was all ears and the negotiation was set up. "No offense to you or your peoples, but I was actually hopin' to talk wit' someone from Metro," Tico said, before wishing he hadn't said it at all. Here was a man willing to take a chance with him and he mentioned another label. He wanted to put his foot in in his mouth. But Sam seemed amused.

"Ah yes, Metro. It's funny because a few of the artists that we signed started out with Metro and most of them, if not all of them, ran into some type of money issues," Sam said. "Metro has a funny way of breaching their contracts and not telling their artists the whole deal. Most of the artists that are there now, will probably end up broke five years after their contract's up," the man continued.

"How do I know you won't screw me ova' the same way?" Tico challenged, clearly not sold by the man's sales pitch.

"I'll make you a deal," Sam said. "If you sign with us, you'll receive a signing bonus that guarantees you three times as much as anyone and once your EP reaches gold status, we'll pay you over half of the share of profits made from the record," he said.

Tico thought it over but in all honesty there wasn't much to think about. Metro never approached him and from what Tony had told him, there were never signing bonuses from Metro. Sam stuck out his hand.

"Do we have a deal?" Sam asked. Tico, smiling broadly, shook Sam's hand.

"We definitely have a deal," he said.

"Great. Meet me at our facility tomorrow so we can discuss the specifics," Sam said.

"Will do, sir" Tico replied.

After Sam walked away, Tony appeared to be coming from across the block. "What's up man?" Tony greeted as he dapped Tico. "What did that guy want?" he asked, gesturing to Sam who just walked away from the scene.

"That was the dude from Big House Records, man. They just heard me spittin', wit one of dem local fools hea' and they offered me a contract," he said.

"BHR? But what about Metro, dog?" Tony asked.

"What about them?" Tico asked, annoyed. "Ya' had yo' shot at da kid and ya blew it," he said. "I got mouths to feed and I can't keep waitin' on ya'll to get yo stuff together, man," he added.

"Lemme at least get one more shot to talk to brass at Metro, man," Tony said but Tico refused.

"Nah man, don't even talk to dem bustas' anymore. I got my deal, so I'm good. If you want, why don't you roll wit' me man?" Tico offered. But Tony knew he couldn't leave Metro.

"Nah son, it's all good," he replied.

"You sho' man?" Tico asked. "I mean ya can't keep on ridin' De'Von's sack for the rest of yo' life, man," he continued.

"Yeah but BHR and Metro got dis beef, man and wit' De'Von's status growing as it is now, everyone in the media's watchin' my move. I can't be seen wit' dem cats, man," Tony said.

"light, man. Take care of yourself, homie," he said, dapping Tico before walking off into the night.

With the prospect of the music video becoming a reality for Adia and De'Von's new single, "What You Want", the promoters and producers at Metro records were hard at work trying to push the single to be played in radio stations across New York City airwaves. Andrea found herself enjoying the studio presence more and more. As days passed, she felt herself getting comfortable in the recording booth. It was an exciting time for Andrea because they were finally beginning to work on her own EP, which was due to come out later in the summer. Julio was her main point of contact, who reminded Andrea that she had a photo shoot scheduled or a visit to make at a venue where she would be expected to perform. On the following Saturday, Andrea decided to do what she promised and brought Vanessa over to Metro Records. During the entire ride to Metro, Vanessa acted like a kid in a candy store. She gushed over everything. From the limo ride, to Andrea's chauffeur, and when they finally arrived, her eyes sparkled as she saw the huge "M" on the side of the building and the shiny double-doors. Andrea took her key out her pocket and opened the doors herself to let them in.

"Ok, this is a good deal. You betta' not screw this one up, Drea'" Vanessa said. As they walked down the corridor, Vanessa gasped as one of her favorite artists walked her direction.

"Oh my God, girl that's Michelle Brown! I can't believe Michelle is walking this way!" Vanessa said excitedly. Andrea laughed.

"Calm down girl, you look like you bout to go on yourself. "What's goin' on Michelle?" she greeted.

"What's up, Adia?" Michelle greeted brightly. She was wearing a silver, sparkly blouse with green capris and designer sandals. Vanessa could hardly contain herself next to Andrea, looking as if she might explode.

"Oh I'm sorry Michelle, this is my best friend, Vanessa. Apparently she's a huge fan of yours," Andrea said, laughing. Michelle shook Vanessa's hand.

"I could tell," Michelle said, laughing as well.

"Are you headed down to the studio?" she asked Andrea.

"Yeah, I'm gonna start workin' on my first one," Andrea replied.

"That's what's up. I remember my first album. It's a lil nerve-racking at first but it's a lot of fun. Maybe I'll get to feature in one of yo' tracks," she said.

"That would be dope," Andrea replied. Looking between Vanessa and Michelle, Andrea asked while rolling her eyes. "Look, do you mind takin' a picture wit' Vanessa? It might last longer," she added.

"No I don't mind at all," Michelle replied. Andrea used her cell phone to take a couple pictures of Vanessa and Michelle.

Then the three of them headed down to the studio level. "So Michelle, what's it like doing a music video?" Andrea asked.

"Oh music videos are fun. It's like you're filming a mini-movie and the best parts are the edits and the jump-cuts between scenes, that keeps the video rollin'," Michelle replied.

As they walked inside the studio assigned to Adia, they saw a couple of people there. One of them was a girl who looked to be in her mid-twenties. The other was a black man who looked as if he was in his mid-thirties. He had glasses and large headphones over one ear. Andrea walked in and introduced herself. The young woman was Patti LeMay, a well-known songwriter for Metro records. She had been responsible for creating lyrics for the other artists such as Miesha, Michelle and others who had worked for Metro. The man introduced himself as Andre Graham, the producer and arranger for those songs. They had both been hired by Julio to create the sound and the quality of Adia's first album.

"I've heard so much about your ability to sing and move a crowd. I'm hoping we can move a generation with your music," Patti said.

"I hope so too," Andrea replied.

"I heard the track with De'Von the other day and I gotta say, the track was fire," Andre said. "So what I was thinking, we should fuse the same energy that you used on De'Von's album and we shift it over to yours. That way you'll have a total of ten tracks on your debut, six uptempo songs and four ballads, or just as you young people like to call em now, slow jams," he continued.

"Am I gonna have any features on the track? Andrea asked, hoping that she could have Michelle on one of her tracks.

"Absolutely! But only on a couple tracks because we don't wanna cover your whole album with different artists, at least not yet. We want the fans to hear what you're made of and then once the first album hits, your next album will have hella features," Andre confirmed.

"Cool," Andrea replied.

"Check out the first track of your album," he said as he played the instrumental of the first track.

The song was a unique mix of an uptown beat, similar to certain songs from earlier in the millennium. Michelle and Vanessa bobbed their heads up and down. Andrea loved the beat and couldn't wait to get started. Patti went to Andrea with the lyrics to the song.

"The name of this song is "I Got Your Love." It's a very sexy track and fast paced. I want your first song to jump out the box. Be a party smash. Something for all the clubs and radio stations across New York. Then once it expands, it'll spread throughout the US. Before you know it, you are gonna be worldwide, baby," Patti said.

Andrea smiled at Vanessa, who smiled back at Andrea. Her best friend was about to be an R&B singer. She could scarcely believe it was happening. As they studied the first song, Vanessa sat with Michelle while they took in the full session. Andrea's voice sounded so flawless and crisp.

"Yo girl sounds like the real deal," Michelle told Vanessa.

"Yeah she is. She started out singing in her family's church," she replied.

"That's what's up. She got a bright future ahead of her," Michelle said as the session continued.

After a couple of hours, they broke to take a break. Walking back up to the main floor, Andrea looked at the gold records that lined the hallway.

"One day, I'll have an album that sells so much, they gon' give me a gold record, too," she told Vanessa.

"No doubt, once that happens, you gon be runnin' the show," she said.

Andrea paused. "You think so?" she asked.

"Hell yeah," Vanessa replied. "You might as well not show up to school after that cuz once word gets out, everyone gonna be all ova' you from the get-go," she warned.

"I know, it's gon' be crazy," Andrea agreed. "Not even Sean knows about this, or Quentin," she added.

"Well, eventually they're gonna find out, once they hear your music on the air," Vanessa said.

They were heading outside the studio, when they ran into De'Von and Slam. "Ladies, ladies we have got to stop meeting like this," De'Von said confidently. "People might talk, you know," he added.

Andrea stood close to De'Von's ear and although she didn't know it at the time, she turned him on.

"Let 'em talk," she said as seductively as she could.

"What's the name of homegirl ova there?" he asked.

"Oh, this is ma girl Vanessa. Vanessa, I believe you know De'Von," she said.

Vanessa had her best smile on display for the artists she knew the best.

"So where ya comin' from?" he asked them.

"Nothin'. Just workin' on my first track. We were just takin' a break," Andrea replied. "As a matter fact, looks like it's time to head back," she added while walking back to the studio, pulling Vanessa with her, who was still looking at De'Von with awe.

Vanessa wasn't the only one staring. Slam apparently had his eye on Vanessa. "Yo, shorty got ass on her, I ain't even gon' lie. I'd like to tap that one day," he whispered to De'Von.

De'Von looked at Slam. "C'mon man. You just met this chick a few seconds ago and besides she wasn't even lookin' at you," he replied.

"I know, I know. She was scopin' you, money but she feelin' me too. She just don't know it yet," Slam replied.

"Man, make your corny ass useful and get me a bottle of water. We got work to do, homie," De'Von said, laughing as they headed down to the studio.

On their way down, Vanessa said to Andrea, "That Slam guy is not as bad as you make him out to be. He a bit creepy though. I don't like the way he looks at me."

Andrea laughed. "Aw, you go girl! He's checkin' you out. Why don't you give him some play?" she asked Vanessa.

"Ha, very funny, remind me to laugh," Vanessa said not laughing at all.

The televisions above the studio normally displayed news and commercials but Andrea saw a specific piece of news from the music television program. An interviewer, name Leena Sarunas, was interviewing a black man seated across from her. He was dressed in a regular sweater that was half-buttoned and a gray Nike t-shirt. He had a few gold necklaces and gold rings on his fingers. Andrea could immediately tell he was a CEO or a member of exclusive management. Leena started to address the public.

"Good morning folks! Welcome to Music Hype, your source for new music news. Today I have music mogul, producer, and sound dresser, Mr. Jamar Russell, the founder of Big House Records, or BHR, as they are better known today. Mr. Russell, we are so glad to have you here with us today. So what can we expect for new songs this year?"Leena asked.

"I think we can expect some new material. I've spoken to all my peoples and I'm sure this will be a strong year for Big House. We have signed some exciting new talent to lift us over the hump," he replied.

"Ok great. So I understand that you have had some altercations with your rival, Metro Records, because of the history between the two record companies. Do you still believe that they are your competitor for radio airplay, tour dates, guest appearances, and other events?" Leena asked.

"Of course we still view Metro as a competitor but I don't like to go into too much history between us," Mr. Russell said. "Our goal is to record and make music for everyone to listen to and enjoy. I hold no ill-will against Metro Records or their staff. I'm sure they're working hard as we are right now." he concluded.

"Well, we've heard that BHR has recently signed a couple of new artists onto its label. Do you think signing them will push you over the hump for a gold or platinum award?" Leena asked.

"Absolutely," Mr. Russell replied. "I don't wanna spoil everything but we are happy with the new additions that we've recently signed and we expect nothing less than greatness with them," he continued.

"Ok folks, you heard it here first. Mr. Russell from BHR Records has spoken. Thank you for watching this minute of Video Hype," she said.

The program ended and most of Metro's artists just shrugged off Mr. Russell's words. "So why do everybody got beef wit' Big House Records?" Andrea asked.

"They just a bunch of lames who just be copyin' what we do. If we perform at Madison Square Garden one day, the next few days, we would hear that they performin' there too," De'Von replied.

They have no originality and the rappers who roll wit' them like to act like they hard and they always got beef with someone," Michelle answered.

"Have ya ever had, like, physical fights wit anyone from their yet?" Andrea asked.

"It's neva gotten that far yet, but watch. It's only a few days, or a few weeks away," De'Von replied. Man, but as long they don't mess with me, I ain't about to get myself arrested." he said.

De'Von and Adia's single began to pick up steam in the upcoming weeks, just as Craig had predicted. With the aid of various radio stations that picked up the song and put it on constant rotation for airplay, the song, which had started at number twenty-three on the music billboard, slowly began to move up on the chart. It was peaking at number six in the chart for pop and R&B releases. Andrea herself had not heard the song yet but she had been informed by Julio that the song was breaking ground and had people anticipating De'Von's upcoming EP. As Andrea continued to work on her own album over the weekend, she still had to carry on her normal life of school and work at Johnson's, which was becoming more and more unbearable by the week. Gloria has increased her attack on the other employees during a staff meeting by calling certain employees out on their lack of diligence and dedication to their task. Andrea, whose work quota had dropped significantly since being at Metro, received most of the blame. The following Saturday, Andrea was put at the front register with Cindy. It was at that same exact time that Gloria came in from her lunch break.

"There go the Wicked Witch of the West right there," she said.

What happened next was very instantaneous, so quick that even Andrea couldn't explain. The store radio, which usually played old songs from the 1970's to the 1990's played new releases occasionally. On that particular day, Andrea was talking with Cindy when she heard her song with De'Von for the first time on the radio.

I know exactly what you want/you know exactly what I need… She couldn't believe it. It was her voice on the store radio. It was surreal. Andrea turned excitedly to Cindy.

"Oh my God, Cindy that's my song! They're playin' my song!" she exclaimed excitedly.

"Girl, I know! It's my song, too," Cindy replied humming the song.

"No I mean, it's really my song. I made this with De'Von at Metro," she blurted out. Cindy looked at Andrea.

"You mean, you're Adia? That's you on da' radio?" she asked, bewildered.

"You already know!" Andrea exclaimed and both girls yelled.

"Hey, hey what's with the yelling over there?" Gloria barked out. She walked over to Andrea and Cindy.

"Cindy, you need to be calling customers to your register since you not busy and Andrea, you're already on thin ice. I need you in the fitting rooms to clean the pile of clothes there. C'mon let's go!" she barked.

Andrea started to go, but then a thought dawned over her. That was her voice on the radio. She didn't have to take it anymore.

"Oops, guess I fell through the ice then," she replied sarcastically to Gloria, throwing her badge in Gloria's direction, while walking out the door. "I quit," she added.

Chapter Fourteen

Amos was none too pleased when he heard that his daughter had quit her job at Johnson's Department Store. After she had begged for independence and he had pulled strings to make sure that Andrea secured the part-time position, it was now all for nothing. When Andrea called her father and told him what she had done so she needed a ride home, Amos was furious. He was so angry that he refused to speak to Andrea during the entire car ride home. The mood was tense with uncomfortable silence. When they finally arrived home, Andrea opened the passenger door to escape to the house but Amos told her to stop.

"When you go inside, we're going to discuss this with your mother," he said. Andrea rolled her eyes as she walked inside. Alisha was inside preparing for dinner.

"Hey honey, how are you? You're home early today. Did the managers let you leave early again?" she asked, eyebrows raised.

"Yeah, Mom they gave me the rest of the day off. I'm on a permanent vacation now," she replied. Alisha looked up at Andrea.

"What?" she asked. Andrea sighed in exasperation.

"I quit my job at Johnson's today," she said, looking down.

"Why did you quit, honey?" Alisha asked.

"There's no reason to explain why she quit, other than it was out of pure laziness and ungratefulness," Amos said heatedly as he walked into the kitchen.

"Dad, please let me explain. You don't even know half of it," she started to explain.

"No I guess I don't know the half of it," Amos argued back. "I don't how I managed to help you find a job to help teach you responsibility and accountability and then you lose it all in one day," he added.

"Dad, I was miserable over at Johnson's. I hated it," Andrea said. "The managers and floor supports were mistreating us. I mean, I'm takin' on a lot with the whole school, work, and studio thing. I felt it was time to leave Johnson's anyway," she explained.

"Ok understood, sweetie, but what you should've done was to write a two-week notice and hand it to your manager if you wanted to leave," Alisha said. "At least that shows character and professionalism. You don't just walk away."

Andrea looked at the ground. She knew her mother was probably right but she still didn't understand the magnitude of what she had done.

"Mom, I know. But when I heard the song I made with De'Von on Metro Records on the radio at work, I was getting yelled at instead of getting any type of credit," Andrea replied. "You're right, though. I shouldn't have quit the way I did but I felt some type of way when I heard my song playing on the radio. It felt like despite everything I went through, I finally made it," she said.

Alisha walked up to her daughter. "Honey, you did make it but not because you signed the contract with Metro. You made it because you're a positive influence on everyone that you come in contact with and you overcame so much at a young age," she added.

Andrea understood what her mother was saying at that moment and immediately she regretted what she'd done. Eventually she would have quit her day job because her career at Metro had been quickly shifted into high gear. She couldn't really explain it but she had been having fun in the recording studio. She had been working on her EP and exploring different instrumentals and sounds in the studio. De'Von's second album had finally been released and the song that featured her was was still picking up steam. While working on her EP, Andrea learned that De'Von would be featured on one of her tracks and she would be teamed up with Miesha on another track. Before going to bed that night, Andrea received a phone call from Vanessa.

"Yo, I came to Johnson's lookin' fo' you today and I couldn't find you. Then Cindy told me that you quit. Is that true?" she asked.

"Yeah it's true. So they were playin' that track that had me and De'Von on it at the store today...." she started to explain, but then Vanessa cut in.

"Oh you mean that dope track that had De'Von flowing and you come through wit' dem sexy ad-libs? Yeah, that's my song too," she said. Andrea laughed.

"Anyway, can I finish explaining what happened? So I'm hearing the song and I'm so excited and guess who comes to steal my shine? Gloria. You already know what she about. So my song is playin' and me and Cindy were gettin' live and she comes in threatening me, sayin' I'm on thin ice or whatever. So I quit and I threw the badge at her triflin' ass," Andrea explained.

"Wow. What did yo' parents say about that?" Vanessa asked.

"Well, you know, they weren't too thrilled about it or whateva' but they understood that at the end of the day, I made the best decision for me. I didn't do it for nobody else, and besides, the way De'Von's song is blowin' up right now, when my EP drops, who knows how good that might do?" Andrea asked.

"True, but you know what I can't wait for?" Vanessa asked.

"No, what?" Andrea wondered.

"Graduation from high school," Vanessa said.

"Yeah, I feel you girl. Glory Hallelujah, no more Richmond Hill High School. I'm so ready to get up out of there too," Andrea agreed.

"So you thinkin' about college? Or you gonna continue this music thing?" Vanessa asked.

Andrea hadn't really given a thought about college while recording in Metro but she decided to leave it up to the performance of her first album before making that important choice.

"Girl, I've already been accepted to some colleges, but if this music thing takes off, I gotta ride this wave. I can't stop now," she replied.

"Girl, you already know you bout to be on every billboard, every commercial, every movie. Yo, you might get some calls to appear in some sitcoms on TV next to someone like Chris Rock or Tyler Perry," Vanessa exclaimed excitedly.

"Yeah, right. First I gotta make sure this whole music video thing works out and that I'm photogenic enough to even be displayed on screen," Andrea pointed out.

"Girl, you'll be fine! And the best part is that you'll have more time to work on the video since you left Johnson's." Vanessa said.

"That's true. Damn now you got me all excited about this music video girl. Lemme go to sleep before I get in trouble talkin' to you," Andrea laughed before she ended the call.

The music video process was the most exciting part of being a recording artist for Andrea. From promotion to make-up to trying on different outfits that she couldn't wait to wear on set; the whole experience was exciting. From what she had been told informed by Craig and some of the other producers, the video itself would be filmed outside a Manhattan nightclub. Over the next couple of weeks, Andrea found herself busy learning the choreography of the video. Since the video was for an R&B song, there were a few subtle dances that were required to maximize the appeal. Long-time choreographer, Joanne Hutchinson, who had worked with many different artists over the years, grew more exasperated by the minute as she watched Andrea try to master a dance move.

"No, no, no Adia it's like this. You have to drop, pop and lock at the end," she explained, while Adia did her very best to follow Joanne's moves and rhythm.

It wasn't as if Andrea couldn't dance. The truth was that she was basically well coordinated and she picked up moves fairly quickly. The other back-up dancers just seemed to have picked up the routine quicker than she had. By the looks on their faces, they were amused by Adia's attempts to master the correct moves.

"Sorry Joanne. Let's go again. I think I can get it this time," Andrea insisted.

"Ok we'll take it from the top again," Joanne called out yet another time.

As soon as she started, Andrea had her most successful turn yet. She performed the dance routine exactly as Joanna had instructed and she began to understand the timing of the songs versus the timing of when to step in and perform the routine. It took hours of back-breaking, knee-bending, butt-shaking repetition but it had all been rewarded. The backup dancers were finally becoming impressed with Andrea's moves. They stopped laughing and began to introduce themselves to her. There was one dancer in particular who caught Andrea's attention. She looked older than the others; probably in her mid-thirties. She sat rubbing her feet from the aches of repeated dancing and footwork. Andrea found that the dancer's name was Susan Palgray and she has been a back-up dancer for over seventeen years. Andrea was impressed by her skill, endurance, and her swift moves – especially for her age.

As the session ended, Andrea walked out of the dance studio when she heard a voice calling to her "Good work today, Adia," the voice said. Andrea turned around and saw that it was Susan.

"Thanks Susan. I know I suck right now but I'm real new at all this," Andrea replied.

"It's ok. You'll get better. Trust me, being in this business as long as I have, I've seen other artists start out worse than you did. At least you got rhythm," Susan said as she put her sneakers on.

"Thanks. I just hope I don't make a fool of myself when them cameras roll," Andrea replied.

"Girl, by the time that happens, this will be almost second nature to you." Susan replied, as she grabbed her bag and headed for the exit.

"You know, you're cool to talk to, Susan. You ain't like the other back-up dancers. You straight," Andrea said.

They exchanged phone numbers and contact information. Later on that day, Andrea rode with De'Von, Slam, producers Julio and Craig, as well as the video director Roy Phipps. They were on their way to the location where the video would be shot. De'Von wore blue and white sneakers with what looked like dry-fit track pants of the same color and a sleeveless Nike T-shirt. He had two gold chains hanging from his neck and his New York Yankees baseball cap was worn sideways on his head.

I'm not gonna lie. De'Von looks so good right now. Swagged out in his lil outfit, he got it goin' on, Andrea thought before she put her mind right back on the video.

She had to stay focused. She couldn't afford to look star-struck. She was the star too and she had to keep that thought in mind. As the limo approached the outside of the club where video would be shot, Andrea's mouth dropped. Apparently, those who had been assigned to keep the location of the music video under wraps did a poor job. There were scores of young fans outside, waiting for De'Von to step out. He hesitated for a moment to look at Andrea who returned his gaze sarcastically.

"Well, what you waitin' for superstar? Go out there, your public awaits," Andrea said hotly and De'Von stepped out of the limo. There were huge cheers from the young girls and guys all hoping for the chance to get De'Von's autograph.

Andrea stepped out of the car and she expected a few people to recognize her but she certainly didn't expect the reception she got. Before both her feet landed on the ground she heard the chants "ADIA! ADIA! ADIA!"

Andrea was stunned. She had only made one song and that was a feature with De'Von. How had she become so recognized? Andrea felt like a major superstar. She signed autographs for kids and adults alike. Finally, security placed silver barriers around the club and the crowd was informed that it was a closed set and forced the dispersal of all the fans.

The video had a pretty simple concept. It started with De'Von's arrival to the club shortly after midnight and while he rapped his verses, he would step into the club. Once inside the club, his eyes would fall on Adia, the sexy vixen with a voice to match. The chemistry between them had to be as strong visually as it had been heard on the radio. Each day, as they worked on the music video, Andrea found herself enjoying the cast of the video more and more and especially with De'Von. She never knew how he could do this on a regular basis and make it seem so routine. He was loose and even joked around on set during the video's many takes.

After two and a half weeks of shooting, the video was finally done. The magic words from the director as he said "That's a wrap folks," evoked huge sighs of relief from Andrea, De'Von, and the rest of the cast.

Although filming the video had been a fun process, it had been arduous. It had been especially difficult for Andrea because the video had been filmed primarily at night, so she would work until three and sometimes four in the morning. After a long night of filming, she would get barely three hours of sleep before dragging herself to school. There had been more than a few times when Andrea would be caught sleeping in class, often causing her to be called out by the teacher in front of the class. Vanessa noticed that the video was taking a toll on her friend's stamina and strength but quitting just wasn't an option. Andrea was pleased that she was able to purchase her own cap and gown for graduation, which made her realize she was actually going to graduate high school in less than two weeks.

"It's still so surreal," she told Vanessa after school when she left the store where she had purchased her cap and gown.

"I know right?" Vanessa agreed. "Seems like yesterday we were just comin' in hea' as two lil scared freshman girls and now we are about to leave it," she added.

Andrea remembered those days very well. She had first set foot on Richmond Hill's hallways two years after Loree passed away and back then, she remembered how she struggled to push those memories behind her. What made the experience worse was that during that very first semester, all of her teachers had taught Loree at some point. Andrea had always felt they were not as tough on her as they were with other students. She was grateful for all the attention she received but she grew tired of it after a year or two because she wanted to pave her own way and she couldn't do so if she was always stuck in Loree's shadow.

"So how's the video shoot going?" Vanessa asked Andrea.

"We wrapped yesterday, so we just makin' some final edits and touches to it before the world premiere on Friday," she replied.

"That's what's up. I know you gon' be hype as hell when you see yourself in a music video," Vanessa replied.

"Girl, you already know," Andrea confirmed. "I probably won't even recognize myself. All the makeup they put on me and the different outfits I changed into on different takes, hopefully it's all worth at the end of the day," she added.

"Girl, you know it'll be all well worth it at the end. You'll be gettin' paid for this," Vanessa reminded Andrea.

"Yeah, and I'm workin' on my first EP, so once that comes out, I should be workin' on another video soon. If it blows up, then you know what time it is. Tour time," Andrea replied.

Walking through the school hallways, they saw Sean taking some books from his locker. "Let's go mess wit' him," she told Vanessa and they both walked up behind him and Vanessa placed both her hands on Sean's eyes.

"Guess who, balla?" she asked. Sean didn't crack a smile, which was odd because Sean was usually an upbeat individual.

"Chill, Vanessa. I ain't feelin this today, ok?" he replied angrily, slamming his locker.

"What happened? You ok?" Andrea asked.

"I don't know. Maybe my superstar friend knows what's wrong wit' me," Sean said, looking Andrea up and down as if he didn't know the person standing right in front of him.

Andrea closed her eyes and shook her head. She had planned to tell Sean about her current situation sooner or later but the right moment never seemed to present itself.

"So you know?" she asked sheepishly.

Sean nodded his head. "Of course I know. A couple people I'm cool wit', told me they saw you and De'Von outside Club Rebel the other night shooting a music video. They came to me talkin' bout, 'yo did you see yo' girl?' and all that shit. So I had to hear it from other folk before I heard it from ya'll, right? I thought I was yo' boy, Drea. That's messed up," Sean said, walking away.

Andrea looked at Vanessa, who shrugged before they ran to catch up to Sean. "Sean, I was gonna tell you, but…" Andrea began.

"….But what?" Sean challenged. Turning to Vanessa, he asked. "How long did you know?" he asked her.

"She actually knew about it weeks ago," Andrea admitted. "As a matter fact, if it wasn't for her, I probably wouldn't be at Metro Records right now. If people knew about me, they would start treating me differently. Askin' me for money and other stuff. I just didn't know who to trust telling," she explained. Sean looked at Andrea, his eyes intense.

"So you couldn't trust tellin' me? I had to find out from two strangers that Andrea and Adia are one and the same?" he asked.

"I'm sorry Sean, I really am. You were just so busy with your basketball thing and I figured you wanted to focus on that," Andrea said.

"I feel you, but what you think I was gon' do? Keep moochin' after you for money? Nah I wasn't gon do you like that, but you need to be real though. Stop playin games wit' people's minds, yo," he said. Andrea nodded her head. She knew Sean was right.

"Ok check it out. This Friday, there's gonna be a viewing of the world premiere of the song I sang with De'Von. He's having a review at his place. I was gonna invite you and Vanessa to come. You down?" Andrea asked.

Sean thought about it for a moment. Although still upset that Andrea kept her singing career a secret, Sean agreed to attend the premiere night. After the exchange, Sean turned to his own block to go home, while Andrea and Vanessa walked in the opposite direction to their homes.

"That boy been trippin', lately," Andrea said of Sean as they walked home.

"He's been dealing wit' some stuff right now," Vanessa explained. "For starters, that lil hoochie mama that he went to prom with, ended up stabbin' his back and was caught sleepin' around wit' another boy. Then you got the whole basketball situation about him tryin' to get a ball scholarship," she added.

Andrea shook her head as Vanessa revealed Sean's stress and personal level. Sean needed his friends more than ever and she had repaid him by nor telling him the truth about her own life changes.

"Well, we bout to go to yo' honey De'Von's crib this Friday for the music video premiere," she said, attempting to entice Vanessa.

"He ain't my honey," Vanessa replied. "Not yet. Besides I'm waiting and I'm biding my time. My boo know what time it is," she added dreamily. Andrea laughed

Yeah, time for you to give it up, girl cuz knowing De'Von, he ain't gonna give you any play, any day, she thought quietly but was careful about keeping her thoughts to herself. She didn't want to dash her friend's hopes, no matter how far-fetched they were.

Andrea's personal driver arrived at eight o'clock on Friday night. By that time Sean and Vanessa were at Andrea's house and the television in the family living room was already switched onto the music channel, as they waited for the special that would premiere her music video. Since the premiere wasn't scheduled for another hour and a half, they got into the limo.

"light, Drea I see you," he said.

Andrea and Vanessa rolled their eyes at the same time. "Whatever, Sean. Anyway, yeah Marvin can you take us over to 311 Park Avenue?" she asked her driver.

Marvin nodded as if to say he understood, before engaging his personal navigation system.

"I heard this cat De'Von live in some type of deluxe apartment or something like that," Sean said.

"Apartment?" Andrea repeated, laughing. "No boo-boo. De'Von stay in a penthouse suite, worth over three million," she replied as Sean's job dropped.

After about an hour of driving and maneuvering through Manhattan traffic, they finally arrived at their destination. Vanessa, Andrea, and Sean all let out a collective sound of amazement. The building was at least fifty stories high and the sides shone as the backdrop of the setting sun reflected in its black chrome. Andrea wasn't sure which suite was De'Von's penthouse but she was sure that wherever he was, he had a great view of the New York skyline.

"Yo, I take it back. This man is livin' large," Sean said.

"You ain't neva' lied," Vanessa replied. Andrea took out her cell phone and called De'Von's number. After two rings he picked up.

"Yo, what's up?" he responded. "Yeah, it's Adia. I just got hea'. What's yo' suite number?" she asked. After De'Von told her, Andrea gestured to her friends. "C'mon, let's go," she said as they entered the building.

They took the elevator up to the fifth floor. Once the elevator opened, they turned around and looked for the suite. They followed the noise as the sound got louder and louder. Andrea knocked on the door but unfortunately she had to knock more than once because the noise coming from the inside of the suite was almost deafening. Finally Slam opened the door when he saw who was there and invited them inside the penthouse suite.

"What's up Adia? You ready for da premiere?" he asked.

"You already know. I came in ready," Andrea replied.

The house was full of middle aged men and women who had already arrived to watch the video premiere. In the center of the room, Andrea could see that De'Von had a large table with plenty of food and below the table was a cooler with all the wine coolers, beer, and juice. The suite was filled with people whom Andrea recognized at once from Metro records. Some of them were executives and others were in-house musicians, those she had worked with previously, all gathered in the location as well. Julio and Craig were noticeably absent. Andrea speculated that they might be at the studio working. They looked for De'Von, who was sitting in a chair on the upper deck of his penthouse and he wasn't alone. He had three girls surrounding him and he was dressed all in white; from his blazer to his jeans, every piece of clothing was white. He even wore a white fitted New York cap and white Nike sneakers. Spotting Andrea, he stood up from his area and walked downstairs to greet Andrea.

"Yo what's up Adia?" he greeted.

"What's up De'Von?" she greeted back and couldn't help but notice how ripped he looked in the white t-shirt he wore under his blazer. Gathering her thoughts to remember exactly why she was there, she introduced De'Von to her friends.

"I believe you already know Vanessa. This is my homeboy, Sean Hawkins," she continued. Sean stepped up to De'Von, dapping him. Andrea could tell that Sean resembled a little boy at the candy store, giddy at the very prospect of meeting his idol.

"Yo, what's up man! Yo, I got that first album. It was hittin'. You did your thing on that, man," he said.

"Thanks man," De'Von replied, looking at Andrea with a side-eye.

"Breathe, boy. You look like you bout to pass out," she informed Sean, who glared at Andrea.

As they introduced themselves to the rest of the people at the party, Andrea saw it for the first time. A group of boys, perhaps in De'Von's entourage, had small piles of what looked like twigs but they were longer and more defined. Next to them was a small bag of a green leaf-like substance and they had ashtrays where they would place the stubs. Andrea knew right away that these guys were smoking weed.

As the air grew more pungent with the smell of fresh marijuana, one of the girls in De'Von's entourage shouted, "light ya'll, the video's finna come on. Watch yo' boy work," she said.

The premiere began and on the fifty-inch television screen they watched the long stretch limo pulled up outside the nightclub at the beginning, as the camera showed a closeup of De'Von's silhouette as he started rapping.

She got me feenin' as I'm schemin' my next move/Sippin' on dat boo, watchin' her hips groove/Damn right I'm lookin' for a good time/Got me so turnt, my mind done skipped the line....the lines continued to proceed and as he entered the club. It was made clear to the viewers that although there were other people dancing, De'Von had his eye on one girl and she was at the center of the dance floor. Dressed in a sexy halter top that bared her midriff and showed a bit of cleavage, Adia made her entrance in the video. As Andrea watched herself sing the hook lines to the song, she was transfixed, as though she was watching someone else. This fiery, sexy, outspoken, knockout of a young woman could not possibly be her. She saw members of the entourage look back at her and nodded their heads at her positively. Some of them even made comments.

"Ok, Ma do yo' thang," one of them would say. "Yo she killin' them dance steps and she can sang? It's a wrap," others would say.

As the video went on, Sean and Vanessa found themselves in awe as well. "Drea', you lookin hot in that video," Vanessa said.

"You ain't lyin'," Sean said in agreement. "If I didn't know dat girl on da video, I woulda tried to hit that," he added without kidding.

Andrea and Vanessa looked at Sean in disgust.

"light, I'm just playin'. I don't mean it like that. But still...." he said with his voice trailing.

"Girl, I just can't believe that it's me in the video. I'm still wonder-ing how I eva got to the point of makin' videos," she said to Vanessa.

"Well, I might've had something to do with that," Vanessa said furtively.

"No doubt," Andrea replied.

When the video ended with Andrea dancing with De'Von, the screen went black. Everyone in penthouse cheered for Adia and De'Von, dubbing them hip hop's couple of the year. Andrea could scarcely believe that she was part of Metro and she could only wonder about the reception she would receive when she returned to school Monday morning. Each person made a point to shake her hand and congratulate her on doing an excellent job on the video. As Andrea spoke with the members of De'Von's entourage, De'Von looked at her. Slam noticed his friend staring at Andrea.

"Yo dog, if you feelin' her, why don't you just ask her out already?" Slam asked.

"Nah, bro" De'Von replied. "She ain't like other chicks. I saw that in her when she was workin' at that department store. She ain't petty, bougie, none of that, man. She's real," he added. "I don't know why you all up on mine, B. I know that you feelin' her friend, though," he said to Slam.

"I ain't gon' front, she looks nice up front if you know what I mean, and I know she a closet freak. My instincts can sense those things," he replied.

"Shut up, man!" De'Von countered, laughing as they returned to the viewing party.

Chapter Fifteen

Once the music video aired, the popularity of the song caught on, especially with the teen demographic, which was Metro Records' aim when they released the track. Since the day it had premiered, the song had become a regular on the music television's morning programs, often appearing in the video countdowns, and twice the video had been nominated for best new video. Of course, as many times the video played, it was nothing compared to the royalties that came with it. De'Von, who was used to being paid enormous amounts of money, didn't see it as different from the norm but the same couldn't be said for Andrea. She had never seen so much money in her life. The first check she received, she counted five zeroes on her first royalty check. Andrea looked at the check early the next morning, which she had placed on the bed across from her. She could feel tears beginning to drop down her cheeks. She could buy her way out of her neighborhood and take care of her parents as well.

As school dwindled down into late June, Andrea saw her fortunes change at school too. A couple days after the music premiere, Andrea and Vanessa walked to school as usual and when they arrived, they heard a young sophomore boy shout, "There she go! That's Adia!"

Before Andrea and Vanessa had a chance to blink, they were surrounded by at least forty students who complimented her on the video, asking for autographs and pictures to be taken with them on their phones. Never had Andrea received so much attention in her life and she now understood how other stars felt. It was like a whirlwind. As she walked up the steps of her school, the boys who normally hung out on the steps, looked at Andrea.

"What's up superstar? Dope track but can you figure out what I want and what I need?" one asked, making a clever reference to the song.

"You need to stop sweatin' her so much, cuz she ain't fo' you," Vanessa replied.

Even Andrea's teachers began to make references to her rising stardom and her video. One teacher, Mrs Gibson, caught up to her after class and asked for an autograph, which caught Andrea totally by surprise.

"It's only because my youngest daughter loves you and I told her that you attended here. I wouldn't have bothered you with it, but she is only twelve," Mrs Gibson said as Andrea respectfully agreed to autograph her daughter's picture for her.

Wherever Andrea walked throughout the school, she could hear Julio's words echoing in her ears as prophetic as they sounded. Her life had changed and it had been quicker than night and day. She had also begun going to the studio after school to continue working on her first EP. She never had as much fun before as she had whenever she was working on another song. The part of her contract with Metro Records that she really appreciated was that she was allowed to write her own lyrics and she would have any help she needed with the arrangements and the background music. She only had two features, which included a song featuring De'Von and another song which featured a duet by one of Metro's smoothest, silkiest voices, Bobby Smooth. The song was a ballad, in which Bobby Smooth and Andrea sang in different rounds throughout the song, which explained an outlook of love from the female and male psyche. Patti had done an excellent job overseeing the production and the recording of the songs on the EP. Andrea was learning a lot about production and which buttons were used to alter natural sound and which controls were used to add the latest auto-tune sound to the tracks. She absorbed it all like a sponge. Patti was an esteemed veteran and the more she worked with Andrea, the greater potential her album had to make sales.

Big House Records stood on the other side of the borough in historic Brooklyn between a pizza place and a gyro stand. Heavy beats and instrumental beats could be heard from the studio. Tico was busy at work on his first album, which was the beginning of his recording with BHR. The other signed singer was nicknamed Queen Sheba, otherwise known as Emiline. All of the BHR artists had been called together to discuss upcoming tours and concert dates. Dru Simon, one the producers at BHR and their talent scout addressed the rest of the group.

"Ok guys, our sales aren't doing too bad but as you can see, Metro made a huge leap this week with De'Von's new track featuring newcomer, Adia," he said.

"I saw the video. They sounded good. Adia is a strong singer," Emiline said, as she remembered their first meeting at Fusion.

"She's phenomenal, Queen but so are you," Dru replied. "Now we just signed another artist to the team, named Tico. The boy is a dope lyricist and a freestyle king," Dru added.

"You know this, man," Tico replied, smiling.

"Ok so what we need to do is get some tracks going. Emiline, can I count on you to write a banger?" Dru said.

"Ok cool. Don't worry about it, I'll definitely get crackin' on something new," she replied.

Dru turned to Tico. "Can I count on you to bring it to the studio as well Tico?" he asked.

"Of course. All day, every day," Tico replied as he played his track over the airwaves at his studio.

"Metro has been out-selling us for a long time and we need to get back to being on the top of the billboard," Dru continued.

"I don't get it. Why can't we collaborate with Metro? They got some great singers over there and Adia sounds like she's gonna be the future ova' there," Emiline explained.

"I don't wanna touch anything that Metro execs has touched," Dru said, disdainfully. "Besides you got more experience in the music business than she does, right?" he asked.

Emiline didn't agree nor disagree on Dru's take but she was beginning to wonder if it was worth the battle.

The day of Richmond Hill's high school graduation finally arrived as the huge auditorium in Queens College was adorned in the dark red color of the Richmond Hill Lion logo. Excited seniors sat on the wide stage as they listened to their principal speak. Andrea sat in her cap and gown. This was it. She was finally done with high school. Four years seem to have flown by so quickly she barely noticed it through all the grief, drama, and triumph that surrounded her scholastic career. Yet she still felt the familiar pang of guilt and sorrow. She was the first McAfee daughter to graduate high school and that harrowing reality never left her. She wished that her sister had the chance to graduate and that she had been there to witness Loree's graduation. Just as her mother had told Andrea before the ceremony, Loree was there in spirit and she was celebrating the moment with her. As the ceremony proceeded, they began calling the names of the graduates. Andrea saw very quickly that the ratio of high school girls graduating exceeded that of the boys. She had heard rumors that it was because Richmond Hill High School faced potential closure in the near future.

Maybe if these guys actually went to class and stopped trappin' and cuttin' classes, maybe they would be walking today, she thought.

She heard the principal call Sean's name as he walked to the opposite end of the stage to get his diploma. Sean's parents stood up and cheered, while his father took a picture with his digital camera. It seemed like an eternity but finally her row stood up at the side of the stage where they waited for their names to be called. Then she heard her name.

"Andrea McAfee."

She walked up to the principal to get her diploma but what she didn't expect was the loud reception she received from the crowd of parents, as well as her classmates. Among the cheers she heard many different words of congrats.

"You go, girl!" "Go get it, Adia!" "Represent fo' da Hill, Adia!"

Andrea was stunned when she heard those remarks from her classmates and although she was grateful, she knew she wouldn't have received the same acknowledgement if she hadn't been a recording artist. She walked back to her seat and as the ceremony continued, Vanessa's name was called. As she walked up to the stage to receive her diploma, her parents stood up and cheered and there were more than a few catcalls from the boys in the graduating class, no doubt alluding to the rumors of her and Jimmy on prom night. Andrea shook her head.

They are so childish and ignorant. I'm so happy high school is over. I'm ready to move on, she thought.

As the last student in the graduating class was called, the parents all stood up and cheered loudly. The ceremony concluded and Andrea tried to get to her parents in the audience but found challenging. Nearly every student she passed either wanted her autograph or for her to sign their yearbook. It took almost thirty minutes before she found her parents talking to other parents. While they were talking, she heard someone call her name.

"Andrea!" The voice sounded familiar and Andrea turned around to make sure the voice she heard was not her imagination. Smiling at her from a few feet away were Shania Hillman and her fiancé, Trevor McClain. Andrea's eyes were open in shock as she ran to hug her longtime friends.

"Yo, what are ya doin' hea'? I didn't know you were comin'," she said.

"What, and miss my little sista's graduation? No way. I had to be here," Shania replied.

Andrea looked at Shania. Her long black hair was tied in its traditional ponytail and she was still slender as usual. Trevor had developed a little more muscle during his time overseas, but overall he hadn't changed too much, with the exception of a small patch of facial hair.

"So Trev, how's the goatee comin' along?" she asked, laughing.

Trevor laughed, while stroking his small beard. "It's comin' along just fine, thank you. It could be longer though, and bushier," he replied.

"No it's fine the way it is. I like it this way. Don't encourage him," Shania warned Andrea.

"Ok I won't," Andrea laughed as Trevor made a gesture behind Shania's back to ignore what his fiancé was suggesting.

There was no yardstick on earth that could measure the depth of love Andrea had for Shania and Trevor. If it hadn't been for them, Andrea's life might have fallen apart but Shania and Trevor had stuck by her and guided her through her tragedy. Andrea also wanted to believe that she was part of the reason Trevor and Shania were together. She mentally reminisced about the phone call from Shania wondering if Trevor was really the right one and her response that yes, he was certainly the right man for her. Andrea's face broke into a smile at the thought.

"So what's this I'm hearing about you being a music diva and all? I thought I was yo' girl. You could've put me on, at least," Shania expressed in a fake sympathetic voice.

"Yeah, I'm sorry I didn't tell you earlier, but yeah, I was signed by Metro records a few weeks back and I've been working on my first album," Andrea said.

"Yeah, I peeped the music video," Trevor replied. "At first I said, 'Can it be?' then I was like 'nah'." he said, grinning.

"So what gave me away, Sherlock?" Andrea asked, jokingly.

"To be honest, it was the forehead. I can't remember seein' another girl with a forehead as big as yours and you know how TV magnifies everything," Trevor laughed.

Andrea hit Trevor's arm playfully. "Shut up, fool" she laughed.

"So with your life being so busy now, you probably won't make the wedding, huh?" Shania asked.

"Are you kidding me? Of course, I'll be there. I wouldn't miss it for nothin'" Andrea emphasized.

"Really?" Shania asked.

"Yes Shania. I'll do whateva' it takes to be there," Andrea confirmed.

While they were talking, another girl from her graduating class walked up to Andrea and asked her to sign her yearbook. While she was signing, Trevor said to Shania, "See baby? I told you she got this whole superstar thing down. She can be down and still sign autographs."

Andrea looked at Shania while rolling her eyes at Trevor's joke. "You gon' keep yo' man in check right?" she asked Shania.

"Oh you ain't gotta tell me twice," Shania said, looking at Trevor.

Vanessa began to gesture for Andrea to come over to her. She was taking pictures with her parents and some friends.

"Look, I gotta go but I'll talk to you later. Thanks for coming again," Andrea said as she left Shania and Trevor, who went to catch up with some alumni while Andrea walked over to Vanessa.

They took a few pictures together and soon Sean joined them and the three of them took pictures. It was the greatest time for Andrea, cherishing moments with her friends that may never come again. Vanessa had been accepted at Stony Brook University where she planned to major in journalism. Sean had received a few letters and offers from small technical colleges and CUNY John Jay where he planned to major in political science and law but he had yet to receive the elusive letter from an NCAA Division I basketball school. Andrea knew that the time with her friends was limited and she had to value them. Unfortunately she wouldn't get the opportunity that day. Her cell phone rang and she saw that it was De'Von on the other line.

"Yo Adia what's up?" I was workin' on this dope-ass track wit' Patti today. She got the lyrics and I got the instrumental all done. Can you get down to the studio to work?" he asked.

"What, on the day of my high school graduation? Come on, there ain't another day that I can work on it?" Andrea asked.

"Well the session's already paid for and this track is hot. But if you can't work on it, I'm sure Miesha or Michelle wouldn't mind takin' it," De'Von replied.

Andrea thought about it for a moment. Her album was coming along just fine but the word around Metro was that Adia was lacking that one hit that would catapult her EP to popular status. De'Von not only rapped but produced his own songs and had worked with other artists. If he had a hit on his hands and he gave it to the other artists, they would capitalize off it instead of her. Andrea knew her chance of getting a billboard chart song would be minimized if that happened.

"All right, I can be at the studio in about an hour. Is that cool?" Andrea asked.

De'Von agreed and Andrea ended the call to find her parents. "Hey Mom, Dad they need me at the studio right now, so I'm gonna have to go," she told her parents.

"Wait. On your graduation day?" Don't these people have respect for family time?" Amos asked.

"Dad, look they wrote this song for me and they want me to work on it. So I'll see you later," Andrea said rushing out the doors to call her chauffeur. On her way out she bumped into Quentin, who had been walking back inside to find some friends.

"Oh what's up Andrea? Or should I call you Adia?" he asked, with his eyebrow slightly raised. Andrea smiled furtively.

"So you know about me too, huh?" she asked sheepishly.

"Yeah I know about it. It's not everyday someone turns on a TV and they see their prom date on a music video," Quentin replied.

Andrea looked into Quentin's eyes. She wasn't sure if he was joking with her or if he was also disappointed that she hadn't told him sooner, like Sean had been. However, Quentin appeared to be in good spirits, so Andrea decided to keep the conversation friendly.

"It just all happened so quick, Quentin. Sorry for not sayin' nothin' but even I don't know how long this will last," she replied. Quentin nodded his head, as if he understood.

"Well, the music business is a beast. Just don't let nobody change you over there," he advised Andrea before one of his friends called him. "Anyway, congrats and I wish you the best in your career," he said as he walked over to join his friends.

Andrea watched him walk over to his friends. Quentin was a very unique individual. She was surprised that he didn't even ask for an autograph or ask for any piece of profit from her instant stardom. She kept that little detail in the back of her mind as she waited for her driver.

At Metro Studios, two hours after her high school graduation, Adia was in the recording booth waiting for the instrumental to begin. A fast moving drum beat, combined with the autotune synthesizer came into play. Looking down at the lyric sheet Patti had given her, Andrea closed her eyes so she could let Adia burst forth and she began singing.

Boy, you know I got you in a trance/On the dance floor I can feel your glance/The excitement in yo' eyes tells me what I know/Come wine wit' me as we let da music flow.

The song flowed through her and she felt as if she was singing the song to a boy standing right next to her. Different images of men flashed before her. Gary from Johnson's crossed her mind; his shirt off and his biceps glistening in sweat. His dark mysterious eyes would look through her and undress her with just one stare. Gary's lips touched hers and they shared a sweet passionate kiss, her eyes closed. When she opened her eyes, Gary was no longer there and he was replaced by Quentin. He wasn't wearing his glasses and he was wearing a tight Polo shirt that showed his muscles and chest. Quentin touched and massaged her face in a soft, seductive matter. She closed her eyes again and when she opened her eyes, De'Von was there wearing the latest sneakers and walking in his familiar swagger. Patti and Paul, the sound tech recorded the song and were nodding their head as if they knew it would be a hit. De'Von was in the studio as well, hanging on to every beat and every lyric. The recording was a success and the song was placed on the EP. At the same time, Julio walked into the studio, followed by Slam.

"What's going on everybody?" he greeted. "I got some great news. We got an invitation to perform at an HBCU next week. Howard University just finished its graduation commencement and they're holding a benefit concert. They've invited Metro records to perform," he announced.

Everyone in the booth cheered and clapped. Andrea didn't know what to expect. She had performed in front of live crowds but Howard University had thousands of people who attended and she knew all of them would be hardcore hip-hop fans.

"For some of us, this is the first tour trip with Metro recording artists," Julio said, looking at Andrea. "So I wanna go over the rules once again for those who are joining us for the first time. "There will be no drugs or alcohol of any kind consumed on the bus or on tour. Everyone will be given a schedule with the time of performance so that you will know your cue when to go on stage," he added.

"I bet you and I gon' be the first ones up there," De'Von whispered to Andrea.

"Shut up!" Andrea whispered back. Andrea knew that De'Von was trying to feed into her fear of crowds, in an attempt to psyche her out.

"Furthermore," Julio continued, "we will be rooming at the Radisson Hotel just a few miles off campus. No funny business, no parties with alcohol, drugs, or any element that could be detrimental to your performance. We are going there to put on a show and we have to be as precise and as professional as possible. Howard's been a great host to Metro and other record labels in New York and I want that relationship to stay intact. Does everyone understand?" he asked.

The artists acknowledged that they understood the rules but Julio gave them all a hard copy form and had them sign a contract stating that they had received a copy of the rules and regulations of the tour. Andrea knew that with the release of her first EP coming up, it would be imperative for her to be on top of her performance game. She wasted no time. During the days leading up to the trip to D.C., she spent as much time as she could in the studio and in the choreography room. She was slightly jealous by how easy De'Von had it. Not only had he toured before but he was the type of artist who didn't seem to need any practice on dances or stage presence. All he had to do was show up on stage and start rapping. No complicated dance steps to rehearse and no waiting on cues from other artists. All in all, De'Von had it easy but this time she would be performing on stage with him.

Looking at her program, she saw that the show would end with her and De'Von. Miesha would be the artist starting the show with two songs from her third EP. Once Miesha finished her selection, Bobby and Michelle would make their appearances and sing selections off their albums. After they were done, they would introduce the main act, which was of course, De'Von. He would take over with three of his songs from his new EP, one of the songs being the collaboration with new artist Adia. She would close the show with a song from her upcoming EP. Everyone knew their roles in the performance and for many of them, it was a performance that would determine their futures. They would learn from this one perfomance if they would have more work to do, or if they were ready to take their show on the road. Julio stated told them that they were allowed to bring a couple friends along. De'Von took the message to heart, inviting three of his friends whom Andrea recognized from his house during the video premiere. She also knew that they were the ones cutting up weed at the premiere as well, so it would be very interesting to see what unfolded, given the rules. Unfortunately, Andrea found out that her own friend wouldn't be joining her on her tour.

"What you mean you won't be able to come?" Andrea asked Vanessa in shock.

"I know, right. I wish I could go. But my mom's been on me lately about getting a job over the summer and raising some money for college and all that. So I've been applying to many places, I got a couple interviews coming up," Vanessa explained.

Andrea went to Vanessa's house the day before she was scheduled to leave town. "Aye, I feel you girl, as long as you don't work at Johnson's," Andrea said, laughing.

"Nah, Johnson's ain't fo' me anyway. Besides all them stories you told me about Gloria and the way she did you, you can best believe that if she cross me like that, I would check her ass," Vanessa said as Andrea laughed.

"Aye look, she gave me no choice. I was sick of her ridin' me all that time. So now when she see me blowin' up on TV and on radio, she gon' wish I still worked there," Andrea said. Vanessa looked at Andrea as though she couldn't believe what she said.

"Anyway, guess who tried to talk to me, sayin' he apologize for what he did? That bum Jimmy," Vanessa said disdainfully.

"What did you tell him? I hope you ain't accept his apology, cuz he's doin' that to save face. I can't forget what he almost did to you," Andrea replied angrily.

"Right?" Vanessa agreed. "I don't know how that fool found my phone number but I told him he betta' not hit my line up again or I would block him," she added.

"I would block him anyway. Just stay away from him while I'm gone, ok?" Andrea asked.

Vanessa agreed and Andrea hugged her friend. She didn't know how she was going to make it through three days without her best friend on the road.

The day finally arrived and the large tour bus pulled up to the front of Metro Studios where all the artists' bags and personal belongings were stowed. As they loaded up the bus, many thoughts swirled around Andrea's head. Her parents were aware of the tour trip but were very annoyed that Andrea was putting her college education on hold. They had an argument about whether it was best for Andrea to remain with Metro.

The argument ended when Andrea stormed off into her room without addressing her parents on the matter. As far as she was concerned, they knew what she was getting herself into and they knew school was going to have to take a back seat. While buried in her thoughts, Andrea heard someone call her name. She turned around and saw that it was Miesha.

"What's wrong, Adia? What, yo' girl ain't comin' wit' you?" she asked in a tone that suggested false concern.

Andrea chose to ignore her. Many of Metro's resident artists had begun to warm up to Andrea, and even Slam was not as sarcastic, or uncaring as he had been when Andrea had first arrived at Metro. But Miesha had remained cold and bitter toward Andrea, as if she had taken something or someone that had belonged to her. It was no secret that Miesha and De'Von had been involved romantically at one point, even having recorded some songs together in the past. Andrea's arrival seemed to complicate that dynamic and she didn't know if Miesha was jealous or if she just didn't like Andrea. Since Miesha hated being ignored, she stepped up to Andrea. She was older and slightly taller but Andrea didn't care. If their situation escalated into a fight, Miesha didn't know who she was messing with when it came to Andrea.

"I asked you if yo' girl was coming or not, didn't you hea' what I said?" she asked grabbing Andrea's right shoulder sharply.

"Don't touch me," Andrea warned, her eyes locked into Miesha. "I don't know you like that," she added bitterly.

"I know exactly who you are though," Miesha continued. "You're just a useless, lucky-ass pretty girl who got this big break and just because you scored a hit with De'Von, you think you a diva now. I still run this, you feel me?" she asked.

"Whateva' just stay away from me. I ain't in da mood to start nothin' wit' you," she replied to Miesha, who was flanked by her childhood friends, Phoenix and Maria.

Before they could berate Andrea any further, Julio walked outside with Craig and they decided to go inside the bus. Julio walked up to Andrea.

"Are you ready for this?" he asked Andrea.

"I don't know. This is my first time traveling out of New York. I don't know what to expect," she replied.

"Well I ain't gonna lie. Howard's got a pretty rough crowd when you sound terrible but remember to stay calm, represent, and do what you do," he advised her.

Andrea took the advice to heart when she entered the bus. Looking inside the bus, she was amazed. The inside had a small kitchen with drawers and cupboards with plenty of storage. She picked out a nice quiet seat near the back window and sat down waiting for everyone to load up.

Amos sat in the kitchen, reading a copy of the New York Post. Alisha was in the kitchen as well, making coffee for herself and her husband.

"So did you see Andrea off this morning?" she asked.

"Yeah, I dropped her off today with her bags. She kept insisting she was ok and there were people that could help her but what kind of father would I be if I didn't drop her off for her first road trip?" Amos asked, browsing through the sports pages and looking at stats. He sighed when he saw the baseball recap and box scores. The New York Mets had lost another close game. What else is new? Browsing through the sports pages and leisure living page, he made his way back to the world and local news section at the beginning of the paper. There was some other miscellaneous news about raising money for the public school system, the trade deficit and some other Wall Street news. Suddenly his eyes fell upon a side article on page A3 of the paper. At first he barely glanced at the story and was prepared to turn the page but then he saw an image that he had been seeing in his dreams for over six years. The face of his daughter looked back at him from a small photo. The article explained that the lawyer for Loree's convicted killer, Terrell Taylor, was appealing to the New York State Court for a possibility of parole due to lack of evidence tying his client to the crime. According to Terrell's lawyer, the testimony provided by Antonio Franks had been coerced, fabricated, and wrought out of fear and there was no real evidence tying this testimony to his client. A mug shot of Terrell was at the bottom of the article. Looking at the smug, yet emotionless face was all it took for Amos to slam the paper down angrily on the table.

"Honey, what's wrong?" Alisha asked. Disregarding his wife's request for an explanation, he walked out of the kitchen, leaving Alisha stunned in the kitchen.

Chapter Sixteen

The raucous crowd at Howard University's amphitheater was deafening as scores of students chanted at the top of their lungs, "METRO! METRO! METRO!"

The stage props, the pyrotechnics, and the sound system were operational and advanced technicians had tested all of the equipment forty-five minutes before curtain and all systems were go. Andrea sat on a small stool near the side stage as all the other artists stood at their designated location underneath the stage. Metro provided in-house musicians that would be playing a version of their most popular singles. Andrea peeked through the small middle slit of the curtain. She could feel her stomach churn as she saw what felt like a billion students out there. Andrea felt a surge of apprehension and fear. Sensing her nervousness, Michelle approached her.

"You ok, Adia? You don't look so good," she remarked, upon seeing Adia's pale expression.

"I'm ok," Adia lied. Michelle sat in the stool next to Andrea, clearly not convinced by her fellow musician's tone.

"It's absolutely normal to be nervous. I remember my first show," Michelle recalled. "We were performing at Radio City Music Hall and I had just released my first album that year. Man, I remember how big that crowd was and mind you, Howard is big but when you perform in front of millions of people at the Hall you can get so nervous, you forget your place, what song you're supposed to sing. It all becomes a jumbled mess in your head," she added.

"That's the way I feel now," Andrea admitted.

"Don't let your thoughts run with you, Adia. That's the way most newcomer's get cold feet and they end up quittin' right there, boo. You way too talented to let that happen to you," Michelle assured Andrea. "Just pretend you're back at the studio and go out there and have fun. Remember the only person that can stop you is yourself," she added. "Well I gotta go get ready now. They're callin' me to go on now. Good luck, girl!" Michelle said as she stood at her spot.

Each artist had a designated spot where a small platform would be rising from under the artists' feet, guiding them to above stage level. Michelle stood on her platform and the other artists dispersed to make way for Michelle as she rose up. One of Michelle's tracks started to play as the in-house band played. Michelle greeted the audience as the roar got even louder. As she began to sing, the other artists ran over their stage cues they had practiced for only a day before had they arrived at Howard. As artist after artist ascended the platform, Andrea felt herself getting even more nervous. This time, De'Von stepped up to her.

"Adia, you got this. I'll be up there wit' you. Just breathe, listen for the transition in song, and do you. This ain't nothin' but another day at the studio, baby," he said with a sly smile.

Andrea smiled back. "Yeah, you right. But one thing, though. I'm not yo' baby," she replied back with her eyebrows raised.

"But they don't know that," De'Von said, pointing to the direction of the crowd. "It's all showbiz, girl. It's fo' the fans. We gotta make it look real, you feel me?" he asked.

"Yeah ok, I got you," Andrea replied as the she heard a deep roar from the crowd.

Sensing that his time to appear on stage was approaching, De'Von stepped on a platform. Slam stepped up to De'Von and began to do his usual "hyping up" routine for him.

"light son, it's all you. Make 'em feel you. Let 'em know who you are. Can't nobody do this betta than you. You da king. Show em why," Slam said as he dapped De'Von, just when the stage platform started to rise.

It didn't take long for the Howard University audience to erupt into loud cheers and screams from the girls in the audience as De'Von took to the stage. He had total command of the stage from the minute he grabbed the mike.

"What's up Howard?" he asked the audience. "I said, what's up Howard?!" he asked even louder as the fans roared.

As the music started for one of his first tracks, Andrea took her place at the platform that would raise her up to the stage. However, she would be introduced differently. While all the other artists were raised to a blinding spotlight that would allow them to be seen immediately by the audience, Andrea's platform was going to be raised while De'Von performed in the dark, concealed by half a curtain. There she would stand, until De'Von introduced Adia to the Howard audience. As the stage platform rose into the shade of darkness, De'Von continued rapping his first number to the crowd and as he came to the end of his song, De'Von turned to his right, where he knew Andrea would be standing. It was time.

"Ya know it takes a savage to make it in this game, but even a savage gotta have a chick who's down wit' him. Sing to me, baby," he said.

Andrea instantly disappeared as her alter-ego, Adia, took center stage, singing the break to their hit song.

I know exactly what you want/You know exactly what I need/You a man that's a different kind of breed/ Just take my waist and let's proceed.

As her angelic voice began to sing, the spotlight shone on her and the crowd roared themselves hoarse. Adia stepped down from the platform and started to walk the stage toward De'Von the way they had rehearsed it. Her moves were hypnotic and the male population oat Howard University was transfixed by Adia's beauty and soulful lyrics. She stepped up to De'Von and began dancing with him as the female population of the audience cheered. After the song ended, the crowd applauded for five solid minutes and the curtain closed, allowing De'Von and Andrea to retreat backstage, where the other artists were waiting for them. The performance had been a huge success and all the performances were considered amazing but there was no question that De'Von and Adia's performance had been the most scintillating. The other artists applauded backstage as Julio walked forward.

"Ladies and gents, that was one hell of a show! You guys showed everyone what Metro was all about and you repped hard tonight," he complimented as everyone cheered their success. "For one of us, this was her very first show and if I may say, she put on a very convincing performance tonight. Let's give it up for our Metro Princess, Adia!" he exclaimed while everyone clapped their hands in support.

Slightly embarrassed, Andrea stood there accepting the accolades. She still noticed that Miesha and Slam were only partially clapping but she was relieved to realize that she didn't care. Haters always gonna hate, she thought as she made her way outside to the bus.

Before the artists stepped outside, a huge number of security offers surrounded them so they wouldn't be accosted by the audience, who had begun to crowd the exits. They called everyone's name as they entered the bus but Andrea heard her own name through the frenzy of chanting that evening.

"ADIA! ADIA! ADIA!" They continued chanting her name, even after the bus pulled out of the campus.

"Damn girl, they really sweatin' you," Michelle remarked.

"I know," Andrea replied. "I've never seen or heard anything like that before," she added.

It was true. Andrea never had people outside of New York fawning over her before. She couldn't wait until her EP dropped because she was sure it would only propel her newfound stardom.

"Ok, ok let's not forget who discovered her and made her who she is," De'Von said, gesturing to himself. Andrea rolled her eyes, laughing

"You must be talkin' bout Julio, cuz you did not discover me. Matter fact, you saw me before I blew up and talked about being too big to handle," she replied back to De'Von, who chuckled upon reminiscing their first meeting at Johnson's.

"Bet they wish you was still ova' there now," De'Von said, referring to Johnson's.

"Well, I'm still there, in spirit," Andrea replied. "They can always think of me when my songs play on their airwaves," she added.

"I know that's right, girl," Michelle said.

As the bus headed back to NY, a thought crossed Andrea's mind. Does it only get better from here? Could she rise even higher? Or would people judge her based solely on her first album and then consider her to be nothing but a flash in a pan? As they made their way back north, the excitement of the Howard performance abated and most of the artists fell asleep in their seats, except for two of them. The two who were awake could never hope to find peaceful sleep because they had witnessed the cousin of sleep; death. Sleep was elusive for them. De'Von found his mind, as usual, wandering off to thoughts of his late brother. His mother always believed that Mason was always watching over De'Von. De'Von had never been as spiritual as his mother and he often wondered if he was actually living Mason's dream or his own? It was difficult to tell because there were days De'Von wanted to quit the rap game. He rationalized that there was too much competition, too many guys wanting to be the best MC. De'Von sometimes found himself wondering if it was worth it all; the money, the gold chains, and the fame. He knew that he was trying to push away the fear that he was merely living the dream that his brother once had before his untimely end.

Andrea's reason for being wide awake was similar. She also thought about her late sister, Loree. The images from her dreams had never left her but Andrea feared she was walking the same dangerous path as had her sister. One of the traits that Andrea lacked was the sensuality that her sister possessed. It was no secret that there had been many boys who coveted Loree and most of the time she got her way with them. She had a charm about her that drove men crazy. Andrea didn't have that innate allure but playing to the crowd as her alter ego, Adia, gave the illusion of seduction. The music video had been exotic and the clothes Andrea had worn on the video and on stage were sexier than her personal taste. They were provocative and although Andrea understood that Metro was trying to sell her as a songstress who had both street appeal and sex appeal, she still wasn't comfortable with it. Andrea was resigned to Adia being seen as a a repressed version of Loree. As Julio had said to them, it was clear that the chemistry between Adia and De'Von on stage was magic but she it wouldn't be long before magazines and modern media bagan speculating about an actual relationship. Andrea searched for the small remote that controlled the television set on the bus. When she found it, she turned on the set and switched to the music channel. A video music premiere had been scheduled for that evening. Curiously, Andrea stayed on the music channel to watch the premiere. She was surprised to see the girl from Fusion Lounge, Emiline, in the video. She had been called Queen Sheba on the music video. The setting appeared to be an Egyptian-retro style theme and she was wearing Egyptian garb. The song featured rappers DFM (Driven For Money) and new rapper Tico, whom Andrea had also seen at Fusion. The video was very professionally done since BHR flaunted their wealth in props and scenery, showing their expertise at taking visuals to a higher level. Andrea found herself bobbing her head to the song before she heard someone speak.

"Who da hell is that?" Miesha asked. She had woken up and unbeknownst to Andrea, was watching the video as well.

"It's the new song from BHR," Andrea replied.

"Who's that chick, laying there like she queen of the Nile?" Miesha asked.

"Her name's Queen Sheba. She's a new artist," Andrea replied.

Miesha continued watching the video. "Song's aight, but the video's wack. Even the rappers they got ain't that good. De'Von can run circles around any one of them fools," she replied.

"The video's okay and De'Von's not the only rapper out hea'," Andrea said defensively.

"Oh so you tellin' me you like the garbage that BHR puts out? Maybe you should go roll wit' them," Miesha bit back.

"Just cuz you hate 'em don't mean I got to hate 'em," Andrea replied angrily. "I got a mind of my own so I can like who I want, when I want. Nobody dictates that, not even you," she told Miesha firmly and gradually she could sense the fight go out of Miesha.

"Whateva' but that new girl they got, Queen Sheba or whatever her name is, don't even look that good. Ugly concept, ugly girl," Miesha cracked gleefully.

The only ugly that I see around here is you, Andrea thought but she certainly didn't say it aloud. It wasn't worth arguing with a person who was determined to have hate in her.

Andrea was relieved when she finally saw the New York skyline as the bus made its way through the pay tolls, the Midtown tunnel, and the familiar busy streets of Manhattan. While she had enjoyed the road trip, Andrea also couldn't wait to get back to Queens, back to her home. Many times, she had grown weary of her environment; the crime, the grimy sidewalks and streets, and the girls her own age selling their bodies for money. It wasn't living at all. Yet in a strange sort of way, Andrea found herself homesick and she couldn't wait until she told Vanessa about the success of the road trip. She didn't know why Vanessa hadn't spoken with her since she had left for Washington. She had tried to call Vanessa from her cell phone but had been unable to reach her. Vanessa had never been one to ignore any phone call, whether from Andrea or anybody else.

After the bus arrived at the studio, Andrea was driven home by her chauffeur and arrived at home at six thirty in the morning. She pored herself into her own bed and after getting a few hours of sleep, Andrea woke up and decided to go to Vanessa's house to see her. She walked the few blocks to Vanessa's house and knocked on the door. Vanessa's mother answered the door.

"Hello Andrea. How are you?" Sylvia Roberts replied as she held the door.

"I'm doin' good Mrs. Roberts. Is Vanessa home by any chance?" Andrea asked. Mrs. Roberts shook her head.

"No she isn't home now. She's at work. She works at Romana's restaurant in Cambria Heights now," she replied.

"Oh ok. I didn't know she worked there. I guess you miss a lot when you're out on the road," Andrea said.

"Oh yes. I remember Vanessa telling me that you're a recording artist and you're on TV most of the time now," Mrs. Roberts said. "How is everything going for you?" she asked.

"Well everything's going ok. I'm getting used to the music industry and everyone treats me nice over there at Metro. Well mostly everybody," Andrea corrected herself, thinking about Miesha. "Ok, well I'll talk to Vanessa later. Thanks you Mrs. Roberts, I'll see you lata'" she said as she started walking home.

Andrea went back to work at Metro Studios to put the final touches on her first EP. She decided to name her EP Simply "Adia". It was due to be distributed in only three days. Normally her recording sessions had been fun. Patti and De'Von were easygoing people and they made the recording process as fun as possible. De'Von was known to be a practical joker so there would be days when Andrea was recording that she would glance down and see a hideous black rat with red beady eyes staring up at her. Andrea would shriek in horror, until De'Von calmly walks over and picks up the rat, showing Andrea that it was just a stuffed animal or a pet chew toy. Overall though, when he wasn't playing pranks, De'Von had been nothing but helpful in the creation of Adia's feature EP. He had shown a natural ability to mix instrumentals and beats that captured the mood and the vibe of the songs. One song that Andrea liked in particular was Queens Love, which was a track that had been penned by Patti and Andrea and arranged by Paul and De'Von. It was also the song that they decided to release a music video, which would feature Andrea and an as yet unknown male model or actor. Filming the video would be exciting for Andrea. The video itself would be filmed in various parts of Forest Hills and Adia had scenes in which she would ride a motorcycle, clad in black leather. The concept of the video centered around Adia leaving a party, which would have cameos of Metro Record's artists. She would drive the motorcycle (not really driving it of course, as the director would use a green screen for special effects. She would drive the motorcycle home which was a building suite, not too different from where De'Von resided. Adia would start to unlock her door in the video and she would show shock when her door already ajar, fearing a break-in. She then would go to the security system and find a rose petal trail, leading to the living room. Her video boyfriend would be waiting, shirtless. There would be two takes in which the actor would have to caress Adia on her shoulders and upper body.

When shooting began and actor James Sessions was cast, De'Von couldn't help but feel a pang of jealousy. It should've been him in the video, not the black Fabio-like man who had his large hands draped around Adia. During outtakes of the video, Andrea and James would laugh raucously at the outtakes of the video, but De'Von rarely cracked a smile. On the final day of filming, De'Von barely said a word to Andrea as they prepared to finish the song. Noticing his strange behavior, Slam walked up to De'Von.

"Yo, what's good dog? You cool?" he asked.

"Yeah, I'm straight, man. I was just thinkin' it was more live makin' this song in da studio instead of makin' it a video. I just ain't feelin' this video," De'Von admitted.

Slam laughed. "Nah that ain't it. You just not feelin James. Lookin' like Idris Elba out there, touchin' up on yo' woman, I know what you feelin' bruh," he said. "You need to stop wastin' time and handle that before another James comes ova and claims that ass," he added.

De'Von looked at his friend but didn't reply. He knew he was right. Adia had been gaining tremendous public appeal with hip hop and R&B fans. Her popularity might even surpass his own one day and he had to prepare for that reality. After days of filming, the director, Guy Poleski, finally called it a wrap, cut, and print. Michelle walked over to Andrea. She had been one of the cameos in the video as one of the party guests.

"Yo, nice video Adia. I gotta give it to you girl. You're gettin' better at this singing thing. I might have to get yo' autograph one day, that's fo' damn sho'," she said as Andrea laughed.

"I'm just doin' my thing. I'm still tryin' to get the hang of it," she said as she headed back to her dressing room to change out of the leather costume she had worn throughout the video.

It looked great but she realized right away that it was really uncomfortable. She wasn't used to wearing leather all the time and she couldn't get used to the clinging sensation of it, especially when she was sweating from all the choreographed dancing that she was doing. While she was in her dressing room, Miesha who also had a cameo in the video despite the wishes of both Miesha and Adia, walked off the set. Metro producers wanted as many Metro artists in the video as possible for promotion reasons, so they were stuck. Miesha walked up to Michelle.

"Yo' lemme holla at you real quick," she said to Michelle.

Michelle followed Miesha as they walked around the block. As soon as they were out of earshot of the cameras, producers, and director, Miesha said, "Ok, be up front wit' me. Why are you being so nice to Adia for?" she asked.

"What you mean?" Michelle asked.

"I mean the way you proppin' her up and suckin' up to her like a lil' fangirl. 'Oh I wanna get your autograph one day' star struck shit. What's that all about?" Miesha asked.

Michelle then glared and Miesha. "What's your problem with her anyway? She ain't done nothin' to you, so why you hatin' on her?" she asked angrily.

"Open your eyes, girl!" Miesha replied just as angrily. "Can't you see what's happening?" They proppin' her up to be the next princess of R&B right under us. They givin' her more videos, more interview appearances, and more exposure. So where do you think that leaves us?" she asked.

"Ok you need to chill. I don't know what the hell you're talkin' about. I'm still sellin' my music and I'm still makin' dough. You're makin' money too, so you need to chill wit' the Adia hate," Michelle said.

"Look, I been in the game longer than you. I've seen this scenario unfold before," Miesha argued back. "They gon' make her the face of Metro Records and when it comes down to contract negotiations, guess who they gon' pay more money to? That's right, Ms. Adia. Meanwhile, everyone gon' see you as old news and you start losin' sales; so they won't renew yo' contract. Trust and believe that as quickly as Metro signs you, they will drop yo' ass in a heartbeat," she added.

"You trippin', Miesha." Michelle answered.

"Oh I'm trippin?" Miesha bit back. "Ok watch when this propped up princess blows up and all these extra endorsements roll in for her and you don't get a dime," she said.

"Ok so let's say for the sake of your argument, you're right about everything you said. What can we do about it?" Michelle asked.

"I already got it figured out. We ask Metro to release us from our contract and we sign with another label. My cousin out west started a record label and she just told me that they can pay us twice as much as Metro can," Miesha said.

"So your answer to this whole thing is to dip out on Metro?" Michelle asked.

"Better to dip out now then later," Miesha said. "All I know is I ain't waitin' for my check to start losin' zeroes to make a move. I already peeped game and it's about time you did too," she added, before walking back to the video set leaving Michelle to her thoughts.

The following Friday arrived, which meant that it was the night that Adia's solo music video would premiere around the world. Andrea initially thought about going to De'Von's place to watch it but decided she wanted to keep it a small private affair. She invited her friends Sean, Vanessa and even De'Von and Slam to watch the music video with her at her house. Alisha cooked comfort food, chicken mashed potatoes, rice, and macaroni and cheese for the family. She was especially excited to have De'Von at her home for the first time.

"De'Von, I wasn't sure which beverage to buy, either fruit punch or Sprite or ginger ale, so I brought them all," Alisha said, putting all the drinks on the kitchen table.

"It's ok, Mrs. McAfee. You don't have to go through all the trouble. Water will be fine, thank you," De'Von replied in a kindly manner.

Andrea turned to De'Von, a look of pleasant shock on her face. For a moment, De'Von acted as if he actually had home training. "What about you, Sam? Water too?" she asked Slam.

"Uh, I'll take a Sprite actually. Thanks," Slam replied.

Finally the music video began and Adia started to speak in the video and the scene began when Adia was at the party where all the Metro artists were.

"Look at that man, De'Von sittin' wit two girls on him. True G style," Sean said.

"You already know," De'Von replied, dapping Sean.

Andrea rolled her eyes as the song started. I've heard about real love but what do it mean?/Is it a love that longs to be felt and seen?/What I gotta do to show you how I feel/I'm ready for deep love that's real…Adia's tones and lyrics were piercing and precise.

As she appeared to drive the streets on the motorcycle, De'Von couldn't take his eyes off the image of Adia on the screen. Then came the scenes he hated; the touching and groping scenes between James and Adia. De'Von wasn't the only one who didn't appreciate the scene. Amos had emerged from the kitchen to the living room where they were watching the video. As he watched, he certainly wasn't pleased with either content or the costume choice for his daughter.

"I don't get it. Are they tryin' to turn my daughter into a dominatrix or something?" Amos asked.

"Daddy chill. It's just a music video. Adia is just a character. She's the sexy leather woman, not me. You gotta be able to see it that way," Andrea explained. But Amos didn't seem to be listening to her as he continued to watch the video.

"And who is this man who got his hands all over you? Look at the way he's touching you!" Amos added.

"Oh ma' gosh Daddy it's nothin'!" Andrea replied, exasperated by her father's lack of understanding the concept of a music video. "There's nothing going on between me and that man offscreen," she said.

"Heeey, but there's plenty going on between Adia and that man onscreen," Vanessa said.

Andrea glared at Vanessa. "Not helping," she said. Vanessa smiled and shrugged sheepishly.

"I might have to go down to that studio of yours and talk about the clothes they makin' you wear in these videos," Amos said sternly

. Andrea got up from the couch. "Daddy, listen to me. It's not a big deal. It's not like I'm naked onscreen or anything. Julio sees to that. But Daddy, don't you see the only way I can sell records is be a little risqué in these videos? I mean, sex sells. I'm sorry but it's the truth," Andrea explained.

De'Von and Slam were still watching the video but they were watching the argument between Andrea and her father as well. De'Von didn't make his thoughts known to everyone but he was pleased the video wasn't more provocative than it might have been. In an odd sort of way, he found himself agreeing with Mr. McAfee. Andrea should not be overexposed to the public, just to fit the agenda of certain recording labels. Not everyone deserved to see Andrea in all her naked glory. He was not the type of man who liked to share, anyway. When the video ended, all five watchers applauded.

"Andrea that video was dope. When the album drops, people are gonna be lining up to get their hands on one. You know I'mma cop an album," Vanessa said.

"I got you too," Sean said.

"Aye make sho' when ya get the album, listen to track four," De'Von said.

"What's so special about track four?" Sean asked.

"It's because this fool is on that track wit' me," Andrea replied, laughing.

"Aye, gotta self-promote sometimes. We ain't all as big as you are," De'Von said.

"Get outta hea' De'Von," Andrea replied. "People know your name. They chant it everywhere we go. You still da superstar at the end of the day," she added.

"Well, not to toot my own horn but..." De'Von started to say but Vanessa and Andrea finished it off by making tooting sounds, similar to a freight train.

"Every time you speak, you tootin' yo' own horn," Andrea said, while Vanessa laughed.

De'Von turned to Sean. "Yo bruh, is this what you deal wit' on a regular?" he asked pointing to Andrea and Vanessa.

"That, and then some," Sean confirmed, while Andrea and Vanessa jokingly punched Sean. Suddenly the doorbell rang.

"I'll get it," Amos said as he walked to the front door. Staring at the door keyhole to see who it was, Amos opened the door. "Hello, Mr. Hawkins. I presume you're here to pick up Sean?" he asked.

"Yes sir, how's your night been?" Officer Hawkins asked as he stepped inside the home upon Amos's invitation.

"Oh it's been a quiet night thus far. We were just watchin' our baby daughter on TV tonight," Amos replied.

"Oh, that's right," Officer Hawkins replied. "Word on the street's that your daughter is becoming quite the music star these days. Make sure she's got my autograph ready," he added. Amos led Officer Hawkins into the living room.

"Hey kids, what's up? Sean, you ready to go?" he asked.

"Yeah Dad, in a minute," Sean replied. "Yo De'Von, I'd like you to meet my father, George Hawkins," he said.

Officer Hawkins went over to greet De'Von but when De'Von turned around to see who Sean's father was; all it took was one glance. The blue shirt, tie, and blue pants with black stripes. The silver badge that was pinned to his shirt. The police hat had the emblem of the New York Police Department printed across the top of the brim. It was the same uniform the officer wore when he gunned down Mason. The sadness and the primal sense of fury started to rise up in him again. Officer Hawkins had his hand out to shake De'Von's hand.

"How are you? My son's told me a lot about you. He says you're his favorite rap artist. It's nice to finally meet you," he said.

De'Von just stared at the outstretched hand. It was a black hand but it was the same treacherous hand that had taken the life of one of his own. Slam, who saw the tension mounting in De'Von's eyes, shook Officer Hawkin's hand instead.

"Excuse, my friend. He's uh, not feeling too well right now. We were actually leaving," he said as he and De'Von stood up and opened the door to leave, thanking Mr and Mrs. McAfee for the invitation.

Officer Hawkins just stood there puzzled. "Was it something I said?" he asked. Even Sean couldn't explain DeVon's odd behavior that night.

Chapter Seventeen

Adia's first EP was released by Metro Studios and Andrea was free to do whatever she pleased. No practice, no studio sessions scheduled. She knew the music video would give her EP a huge push in terms of sales, so she didn't have a worry in the world. She decided to go to the studio to help or watch other the artists' record. Julio wandered into the studio booth where Andrea was talking with Michelle. Michelle was still working on her third EP and she was singing a very loud piercing hook line when Julio walked inside the booth. Michelle stopped singing at once.

"Oh yeah, Michelle that sounds really great. Awesome, I hope your next EP is comin' along just great," he told Michelle. "Adia, can I speak with you for just a moment please?"

"Yeah, sure boss. What's up?" Andrea replied.

"Well, I got some excellent news. As you well know, your first EP dropped today. From what I'm hearing in radio reports, your song is becoming one of the most popular hits out there," Julio said. "So it's climbing up the music charts as we predicted. Anyway, I wanted to let you know to be ready because you has an album signing at the Sony music store on the corner of Legacy and Park Ave." he added

"You mean I'll be signing autographs at Sony today?" Andrea asked excitedly.

"That's right," Julio confirmed. "After watching your premiere yesterday, Sony Music store was so impressed that they want you to come in and sign your EP for customers today," he explained. He stepped forward and took Andrea's hand encouragingly. "See it's finally happening, just like I said it would," he said. Andrea knew what he meant because there had been a time not so long before, when she never would have believed she would get to this point. "Anyway, your ride is leaving at around noon today, so get ready to meet and greet your fans," Julio said before heading back upstairs into his office.

Andrea could hardly contain herself as she walked back into the studio where Michelle was recording. "What was Julio telling you out there?" she asked.

"The Sony store in Manhattan wants me to come by and sign my EP for fans," Andrea explained.

"That's what's up!" Michelle said, giving Andrea a hug.

"I can't wait, but I've never done anything like that before. What's it like?" she asked Michelle.

"Oh it's pretty cool. Of course signing autographs for two or three hours can be boring as hell after a while and your hand starts crampin' up and all that, but you meet some pretty interesting people and who knows, maybe a movie star or two might pop up in there and get them an Adia CD," she replied.

Andrea couldn't wait to go and she knew that once the EP started gathering steam, it would allow her to go on tour to promote it nationwide. Adia started to branch out on social media as well, starting up a Facebook celebrity account that had gathered well over ten thousand followers. Friend requests were flooding in every minute, so much that Andrea had to put her phone on silent, so the ringtone wouldn't disturb her every time she received a new friend request. The studio door suddenly opened behind her as De'Von and Slam made their way over to the sound booth. Andrea walked over to De'Von.

"What's up? So what was last night all about?" she asked.

De'Von made a sound of sucking teeth and raised his eyes as if discussing his strange behavior the past night at Andrea's house wasn't on his mind.

"Last night was about nothin', ok?" Don't worry about it," he replied.

"What you mean don't worry about it? One of my best friend's father comes to meet you and you dead left him hangin'. Why?" Andrea asked.

"Why you sweatin' me so early in the mornin' for?" De'Von asked vehemently.

"I'm sweatin' you cuz what you did to my friend's dad wasn't cool. Now you might have all these people round here fooled, thinkin' that you got all that privilege, but whenever you step out wit me, that's the real world, you feel me? When you hurt one person in my pack, you hurt me," Andrea said.

"Man, it ain't got nothin' to do wit' privilege. You just ain't tell me that Sean's daddy was five-oh when you invited me ova to yo' place," De'Von said.

"Why does that matter?" Andrea asked.

"It matters to me," De'Von replied angrily. "Maybe where you at, you see all cops with halos on they heads and shit but I don't see it the way you do," he said.

"What you talkin' about? Officer Hawkins is good people," Andrea argued back.

"Yeah, good people workin' for the man," De'Von bit back. "Adia, lemme drop some knowledge on you, real spit. Cops ain't nothin' but corrupt, violent tools of the system meant to keep us black folk in line," he added.

"I'm tellin' you, Sean's dad is not like that," Andrea argued back.

"So ask him, then. How many black people did he arrest this year alone?" he asked her.

"How should I know?" Andrea answered back. "All I know is that Officer Hawkins is good people. That's all I need to know," she added.

"Whateva' Adia. You can think all you wanna think about five-oh, but I ain't changing my mind about the way I feel about 'em," De'Von replied to Andrea before walking off to greet the other artists.

Andrea shook her head. Prima donna pretty boy, Andrea thought cruelly. She had believed De'Von was more than a jerk but maybe she had been wrong about him all along.

The limo arrived outside of Metro studios for Andrea as the makeup crew put the finishing touches of lip gloss, mascara, and blush on her face. It's time for Andrea to make an exit and Adia to make her appearance, Andrea thought as she stepped inside the limo.

After the forty-five minute drive the limo arrived at Sony Music store and Andrea's jaw dropped. The line waiting for her to sign albums stretched outside the store and almost around the entire block. As soon as Andrea alit from the limo she waved to the fans who were screaming themselves hoarse while she entered the store from a back door. Two bodyguards, Kenny Pizzario and Ray Sykes, who had been hired by Metro, protected her as she walked into the store. Waving to her fans, the manager of the store showed her to the table where she would be signing copies of her CD. Overall the entire experience was totally numbing. The fact that people were screaming for her and wanted her autograph was still a very foreign concept to Andrea. For three hours, Andrea signed autographs and took pictures with all different types of people. She was surprised that her music did not stick solely to one demographic. There were older people, young people, black and white people and people from nearly every country, China, India, and South America in the line. Although she must have signed over three hundred autographs that afternoon, she remembered a few people that stood out to her. One of them who stuck in her mind was an adorable little girl. She was white, thin, and very frail with a long ponytail flowing down her back.

"Hi little girl, aren't you the cutest thing? What's your name sweetie?" Andrea asked.

"Sylvia Caroline, I live in Hempstead. I love your music," she said.

"Thank you, Sylvia." Andrea replied as she signed a CD for her, making it out to Sylvia. As they posed for their picture, Sylvia reached over Andrea's table and hugged her tightly, tears streaming down her pink cheeks.

"One day, I wanna be a singer, just like you, Adia," she said. It was then that Andrea realized that Adia was a role model to young girls her age and whatever she sang or expressed in front of her audience spoke volumes. It was a feeling she vowed she would never forget.

Another memorable customer happened to be a familiar one. A young woman about the same age as Andrea, maybe a little older, emerged from the line and Andrea had to do a double take, so she could make sure she wasn't losing her mind.

"Cindy?" Andrea asked in shock, as her old co-worker from Johnson's Department Store greeted her with a hug. "Girl, what are you doin' hea?" she asked Cindy.

"Girl, when I heard that you was comin' out here to sign copies of you first EP, you knew I had to jump on that right away," Cindy replied.

"I feel you. So how's everyone at Johnson's?" Andrea asked.

"Girl, a lot has changed since you left," Cindy replied. "First off, Gloria got the boot," she said. Andrea looked at Cindy, stunned

"Gloria got fired?" she asked.

"Yeah girl, it all happened so quickly. Upper management called her in and she was in the admin office for well ova an hour. When she came out, she was so upset, banging into everything that she walked past. I looked close and realized that she didn't have her badge on her and I put one and one together," Cindy explained.

Although Andrea couldn't stand Gloria while she was working at Johnson's, she hated seeing or hearing about anybody losing their job. But corporate America wasn't a joke and it was unfortunate that it happened.

"Mmm, well I hope she gets back on her feet as quickly as possible. Maybe she'll find a heart," Andrea said. "What about Gary?" she asked.

"Gary is still there. If I'm not mistaken, I think he got promoted to the position that Gloria had," she said.

"Good for him. He really deserves it. Hopefully he won't be as much of a jerk as Gloria was," Andrea replied.

The people in line started to get restless because Cindy was holding up the line, so eager were they to get an Adia autographed CD.

"Girl, here lemme sign my EP for you before they leave you for dead," Andrea laughed as she signed a copy for Cindy. Cindy thanked Andrea for her copy and head out the door while Andrea continued to sign more albums for her fans.

Upon hearing the small buzzer sound, Julio entered the CEO's office at Metro Records. The room was semi-dark for a moment. Julio could barely make out the desk and the chair at which Mr. Morgan sat. Smoking a cigar and drinking a gin and tonic, he gestured for Julio to sit down.

"You wanted to see me today, sir?" Julio asked.

"Yes, sir." Mr. Morgan replied confidently. "I wanted to congratulate you on a job well done in developing these young artists this year. I look at the billboard chart and I'm impressed by what I see, especially from our newest addition, Adia," he said.

"Yes sir. She's been making a lot of strides this year. Her EP just dropped today and it's among the highest sellers in our teenage and young adult demographic." Julio replied.

"That's great. However I still look at the charts comparing us to other record labels and BHR still has our number from a sales standpoint. So I think it's time we up the ante a little bit, don't you think?" Mr. Morgan asked.

"What do you mean, sir?" Julio asked.

"Well, I loved the video that Adia did with the motorcycle and the love affair with a TV model. All that's well and good but Andrea has the potential to push the envelope a little bit, you know what I mean?" Mr. Morgan asked.

"I don't know sir. She's still eighteen years old and very new to the game. If you're looking for her to be more exposed in her videos, I don't think that's a good idea as of yet," Julio countered.

"And why not?" Mr. Morgan asked, almost in a testy voice that exposed the nerve that Julio had to speak up in front in him. "Sex sells, Julio. You and I both know that. Now you've been putting her on the same track as De'Von these days. You saw how people responded to their chemistry onscreen," Mr. Morgan said.

"Yeah, sir. I do see that but I hardly take it as meaning we need to sexify Adia any more than she already is," Julio said.

"Julio, I hired you to produce and to cater to new artists at Metro. We've seen a fair share of people come and go because they havn't performed to the best of their abilities. I love the work that you've done so far but we still have more to go than just leather suits and motorcycles. We need to make Adia one of the sexiest artists in the world and I trust that you will see to that. If I don't see better results from you, you better hope there are other labels lined up ready to accept your services," Mr. Morgan warned. Julio stepped out of the office. With that distinct warning, his jaw went taut. So the new goal was pretty clear. Make Andrea look sexy or he'd lose his job.

After her signing event at the Sony Music store, Andrea could tell her popularity was increasing because she heard her songs everyday on the radio. People were requesting it and wanted to get to know her. She was finding it much more difficult to leave home without being barraged by people in her neighborhood wanting an autograph. She was spending an abundance of time in the studio, which concerned her parents because they still were concerned about her future and wanted to know what she would study, if music happened to fall through. Andrea would always argue that there was plenty of time to go to school but music opportunities came once in a lifetime. Andrea realized it was time to leave Richmond Hill and its streets of small dreams behind. Checking her finances, Andrea certainly had enough funds to rent a luxurious apartment in Manhattan. She immediately began her search for her own home.

Her chauffeur came to pick her up as usual but instead of heading to Metro Studios, he took a detour. Andrea didn't recognize the route at all and she had half a mind to ask her chauffeur where they were headed. She didn't panic yet. After all, it may have just been a shortcut to the studio that she was not aware of yet. Finally they reached what appeared to be a stretch of new brownstone homes built next to each on the block. The street had a small sign that read Briarwood Brownstones: Welcome Home. The car suddenly slowed to a stop as they approached Julio, standing on the steps of one particular brownstone. It was dark red brick with orange coming down the sides of the home. After her chauffeur parked, Andrea stepped out the car.

"Julio what is this?" she asked.

Julio smiled widely before putting his hands inside his pockets. When he took his hands out his pockets, Andrea saw that he was holding a pair of keys.

"Adia, you are doing so well with Metro and you've been such an integral part of the family, that we would like to say thank you and this is a sign of our thanks. Welcome home," he said, placing the keys in Andrea's hands.

"Are you serious?" Andrea asked in shock.

"Absolutely, this is our way of thanking you for everything you do. Here. Take a look inside," Julio urged Andrea as they opened the door and stepped inside the brownstone.

The living room was very spacious and the kitchen was painted bright white. After walking around exploring the kitchen and the living room, Julio took her upstairs where there were two bedrooms and a bathroom. After getting a thorough tour of the home, Julio asked, "So what do you think? Do we have a winner here?" he asked Andrea.

Andrea could still scarcely believe that she was walking in what would be her future home. "Yeah, I'm feelin' this. I could definitely get used to this," she said.

"All right, I knew you would like it," Julio said. "I've spoken to the realtor and it's yours," he added.

Andrea was still breathing deeply, trying to take it all in. Adia was going to be on her own. No mother to look after her, no father to argue with whenever he disagreed on a certain subject. She would finally be a homeowner with the final say-so about what she allowed in her own home. Julio then brought out the title deed on which she would sign her name as the homeowner.

"Julio, I don't know how to thank you enough for this," Andrea said as she signed and looked around.

"No thanks needed. Just keep the hits comin' and everything else will follow," Julio replied.

A few days later, Andrea took Vanessa and Sean to see her new place.

"Yo, this place is fresh G," Sean said as they walked around the home. "Damn they really take care of you ova there, don't they?" he asked Andrea.

"Just a little bit," Andrea replied, downplaying the reward. Vanessa and Sean stared at each other, shaking their heads.

"Whatever, Drea. I'm so hatin' on you right now," Vanessa said wistfully as they looked at the enormous bathroom.

"I was thinking about putting some rose-colored drapes there. I think it brings out the color of the bathroom," Andrea pointed out.

"Oh come on, are we really discussing drapes now?" Sean asked in a fake exasperated voice. "Look at this space ova hea, son. Yo' when you plan that housewarming, make sure you let a brotha know," he said.

"Are parties all you care about?" Andrea asked.

"Ain't nobody said nothin' about no party," Sean replied laughing. "All I was talkin' about was a housewarming. You know, a get together, with a few people, maybe some Richmond Hill fam, and if some of your people from Metro wanna come to kick it too, the more the merrier," he added.

Andrea rolled her eyes. "Yeah I should just start makin' party cards now and start stockin' up on food. Nah, ain't nobody got time fo' dat now and besides, with my album blowin' up, Julio said not to be surprised if they announce tour dates for me," she replied.

"Where you gon' be goin' when you on tour?" Vanessa asked.

"Girl all over. They sayin' North Carolina, Atlanta, Detroit, LA, Tennessee, Philly. Places like that," Andrea replied.

"I know you excited girl," Vanessa said.

"Traveling all over the U.S.? No doubt," Andrea confirmed. She looked outside her window as the sun's rays shined on the leaves and trees. It was as if God was confirming her future and it looked bright.

"Another tour so soon?" Alisha said as Andrea told her the news over the dinner table.

Andrea was still living with her parents, although she had started packing all of her clothes, posters, and other belongings in her room that she was going to bring with her. At first her parents were not thrilled by the label's move to get Andrea her own place. Not only was it too early but they thought it was suspicious that they would help her get a house if they didn't want anything in return.

"Mom, last time I just went to Howard University. It was just one place. This time I'll be traveling state to state. I might be gone as long as three months," Andrea replied.

"I just don't like it," Amos said. "Don't you think they're moving just a little too fast here? I mean you just had one album out...." he started.

"...and that album is blowin' up right now," Andrea interrupted her father. "Dad the only way I'm gonna build on this momentum is to travel and get my music and my brand out there. Julio and Craig said it's better to take advantage of opportunities right now," she added.

"But you have priorities to take care of this summer," Alisha pointed out. "You got to decide on college and you also have Shania's wedding to go to," she added.

Oh no, the wedding! I completely forgot about Shania's wedding, Andrea thought. She didn't give school a second thought. "Look Mom, I know I promised I would be at the wedding but things are happening right now and I can't blow off this tour now," she said.

"But you could blow off a wedding that you promised Shania you would go to?" Alisha asked.

"I'm not blowing it off on purpose. I'm sure once she knows how many things I got on my plate, she'll understand," Andrea replied.

"She's gonna be crushed," Alisha said.

"You don't know that," Andrea argued back. "She's understanding and she knows how busy things get fo' me. Believe me, I had my whole heart set on going to her wedding too but this could be my only chance," she added.

Alisha stood up and walked across her kitchen. "You know, you're the only part of Loree that she has left and I know Loree would've wanted you to go to the wedding because she would've gone to support her best friend," she said.

"So what does that mean to me? That I'm not a good friend to Shania?" Andrea asked.

Getting up from the table, Andrea made her way to her room where many of her belongings were packed away in bags and boxes. She had the choice of packing before her tour but she had so much clothes and shoes, some of which had belonged to Loree, that she decided to finish packing for her new place after the tour concluded. Her mother was wrong, she demanded to her subconscious mind. Shania might be a little disappointed but she knew that the life of an R&B singer was not easy and certain appointments would be broken. She hadn't been able to see her therapist, Dr. Ralwinski in weeks but she knew how busy Andrea had become. She would have to call the doctor and after that she would have to call Shania to break the news to her.

As the artists and other producers loaded up the tour bus outside Metro Records, Andrea looked around to make sure she wasn't missing anything. She was probably missing her comb; which was in her bag; packed away with the rest of her belongings. Her hair was a sweaty, matted mess because she had helped the bus loaders with the luggage, although she certainly wasn't required to help. De'Von and Slam hung outside the studio, laughing at some old joke. Andrea looked at De'Von. He hadn't been acting his normal, smooth overconfident self lately. Andrea noticed that during the past few studio sessions, De'Von hadn't played any pranks. He had been tediously serious about his work but continued producing tracks. The friendly relationship that had existed between Andrea and De'Von had dissipated and they had become quite distant, almost as though each time they saw one another it was for the first time each time. De'Von had never explained his odd behavior at Andrea's house when Sean's father attempted to greet him. He wouldn't explain why he had such total disdain for law enforcement but after several attempts, Andrea decided to let it go. As they made final checks as all the artists entered the tour bus, Andrea walked up to Michelle, who was talking with a couple of her friends.

"Hey Michelle, what's up girl?" she asked.

"Hey what's up," Michelle greeted back but Andrea sensed an icy indifference in Michelle's voice.

"You good?" Andrea asked. Michelle rolled her eyes as if she couldn't believe she was being interrupted again.

"I'm chillin'. I'm sure you're doin' hella fine," she replied, unable to hide the contempt in her voice.

Andrea couldn't understand why Michelle was replying to her in that tone. She was one of the only other artists who had been supportive Andrea. "What's that supposed to mean?" Andrea asked.

"It must be nice to have a label that gives the new bitch whatever she wants. I don't remember gettin' a nice house after just one album," Michelle replied. "You know I had to bust my ass to release four albums before I could even afford a place to call my own. I actually had to work to get to where I am," she said.

"So you think I ain't work for what I got?" Andrea asked, her own anger starting to build up as well.

"Not as long as I have, boo, and not as long as Miesha has. We both worked really hard early and wouldn't see a dime for weeks. Meanwhile, you just come out of nowhere and release an album and that wack song with De'Von and all of a sudden you got yo' own crib," Michelle said. Andrea was stunned that Michelle turned on her.

"Don't be mad because I sound betta' than you. I can't help that," Andrea replied before realizing she may have gone too far. Michelle started to walk toward Andrea with violent intent in her eyes. The two girls had to be separated by Michelle's other friends.

"Whateva. You ain't worth my time and I'mma be done wit' this anyway," Michelle said as she headed toward the bus.

Andrea waited for her and her friends to enter the bus before she entered herself. Feeling betrayed by one of the only label mates that she thought believed in her, she found a single seat in the back of the bus, near the bathroom and sat by herself. Andrea was so furious that she had totally forgotten one of the most important days in her friend's life.

White and light blue streamers were decorated across the walls of the Rock of Jacob Baptist Church on 101s Avenue. It was a bright early Saturday morning as the wedding guests made their way to their seats. The first four pews were reserved for family and relatives of the bride and the groom. Alisha and Amos made their way to the church where they hadn't stepped foot in nearly six years. Many of the church members greeted them as if they were regular members, expressing how much their presence had been missed and told them about the changes that had taken place since they left. Amos never thought he would be back in the sanctuary where he and the pastor had shared so many wonderful moments before their split. Another presence the church hadn't seen in quite some time was a woman by the name of Isis Samuels, who had once stirred controversy in the church when it was rumored (and discovered by one of the church members) that she and the bride's father, who was the pastor of the church, had been involved in an extramarital affair. After nearly making what could have been a catastrophic mistake, Pastor Mike Hillman had been able to make amends with Isis and her son Jamal, who was currently playing basketball at Syracuse University. Jamal also happened to be at the wedding as one of the groomsmen for his old friend Trevor McClain. His best friend Omar Keaton was also one of the groomsmen in the wedding. Omar also played college basketball at Iona College, located upstate. The two friends had remained close over the years. Although their teams had never faced one another, they always bragged about who would beat the other. Among the other groomsmen were old high school friends and teammates of Trevor's, Edward Brannon and Jonathan Thomas. The bridesmaids included Amy Thomas, Jonathan's younger sister who was a junior in high school and Lisa Chen, who had been Shania's high school friend and teammate on the track team. Lisa was currently at Molloy College, where she was studying to become a nurse. The other bridesmaids were Dorothy Woods, Megan Brown, and Victoria Campbell, all whom attended Richmond Hill High School and went to Queens College, where Shania attended after high school. The groomsmen and bridesmaids had endured hours of practice to walk slowly and gracefully to walk to the altar before the bride.

At last, the wedding began. Jamal and the rest of the groomsmen were on one side of the aisle while the bridesmaids were on the other side. Jamal glanced at his aisle partner, Megan Brown who stared back and smiled. Jamal leaned forward and whispered to Omar.

"Yo, you seen Shania's friends? They fine, right?" he whispered. Omar, whose partner was Victoria Campbell, nodded his head in agreement.

"Yeah, I know. Vicky's got body fo' days," he whispered. "Huge upgrade from Patricia, right?" Omar added, laughing as he referenced Jamal's old girlfriend from high school, Patricia Cuevas. Jamal laughed upon the reference.

"Nah chill wit' that homie," he laughed.

The little ring bearer and flowergirl made their way to the front of the church, with the flowergirl throwing rose petals everywhere. Pastor

Whitefield performed the ceremony since Pastor Mike was busy giving his daughter away. While Shania and her father were waiting at the side of the church, getting ready to enter, Shania's eyes welled up with tears. It wasn't because of the emotional moment of her marriage but because one of her friends who should have been her main bridesmaid, was not with her. Shania had certainly noticed that Andrea wasn't present at the rehearsals and she had tried to call Andrea but none of her calls were returned. She finally called her parents, who had to break the news to her that Andrea wouldn't be able to attend the wedding or be a part of it. Shania was devastated. Andrea was the only part of Loree still remaining and without her, she felt as though she couldn't walk up to the alter. Now, on her wedding day, Shania was surrounded by family and friends but she felt a huge part of her was missing. Mike was there to wipe his daughter's eyes with a tissue.

"Hey sweetie, don't worry about it. God is with you and I'm sure wherever she is, she's here in spirit and she's walking with you today," he whispered.

After the groomsmen and bridesmaids walked up the aisle, Shania took a deep breath and walked down the aisle with her father. She looked into the eyes of her future husband who was smiling and waiting for her; to touch her, pull her veil back, and touch her lips when they would be declared husband and wife.

Chapter Eighteen

The Metro tour bus drove swiftly throughout the Northeast region. The artists had already performed in venues located in New York, New Jersey, Pennsylvania and they were making their way towards Boston, Massachusetts. Wherever they had performed, the Metro artists were cheered upon arrival but none of the artists received a bigger ovation than Adia. She had stolen every show with her rare music tones and her stage presence. Adia had begun to receive offers from television and movie producers who wanted her to star in their productions. Andrea was still shocked at the vast number of adoring fans she had amassed. Kids in middle school and high school carried designer book bags adorned with Adia's picture and were ecstatic when Adia signed them. Adia had become uncomfortably aware that as big as her name had become, the more resentful the rest of her label mates were. Michelle and Miesha both sang on the tour but neither were pleased that Adia had gotten most of the recognition and they were stuck in what amounted to be mediocrity. What had once been theirs – the crowds cheering themselves insanely and endorsement deals – were gone and Andrea was reaping the benefits of their failed sales. The tension increased when Andrea sat in her familiar back corner of the bus.

"How's that tour life, princess?" Miesha said, laughing.

"The tour life's good," Andrea replied in a casual flippant manner. As the bus made its way toward Boston, De'Von stole a glance at Andrea, who was sat quietly and alone, looking out the window.

With a feeling of regret, De'Von got up from his seat, where he had been sitting next to Slam. Slam was sleeping soundly so De'Von was awake and bored, so he decided to join Andrea in her lonely back seat. Andrea, who had been in her own world, was startled by the presence next to her. When she saw it was De'Von, she rolled her eyes.

"And is there anything I can do for you?" she asked De'Von.

"Nah, I'm good," De'Von replied. "Yo, you killed that performance back in Philly though, foreal," he said.

"You really think so?" Andrea asked.

"Yeah. You blew everyone's mind ova thea'," De'Von added.

"Yeah, well there are other people who don't even see it that way," Andrea replied as she stared at the front of the bus. De'Von followed her gaze over to the front where Michelle, Miesha, and a couple of their friends talked animatedly and gossiped.

"Oh them?" he replied. "Look don't let 'em get to you. They just hatin' cuz you the one getting' all da' shine now," he added.

Andrea couldn't deny that De'Von was right. She had always heard that money was the root of all evil. Andrea knew it wasn't just her fame but pressure of maintaining that success which was the most challenging.

"Yeah, I ain't got nothin' more to say to her. I mean it ain't my fault I got da juice, you know?" she said.

"Miesha need to get herself a man, that's what she need," De'Von laughed.

"Oh yeah? Why don't you take her for a ride, yourself?" Andrea asked De'Von, laughing.

"Nah, been there, done that. No need to get back up on that train, you feel me?" he replied.

"So what happened between ya two? I mean, like why didn't it work out?" Andrea asked.

De'Von took a deep breath, as though he was reflecting on what had once been the best moment of his life.

"It was just too complicated between us. I mean, when we first hooked up, it was cool, you know what I'm sayin'? She was chill, laid back, all of that," he replied. "Then later on, she started trippin' about any and everything, fussin about everything, from a song that I would write for her to where she wanted to go on a date, she was drivin' me crazy," he continued.

"So then you broke up wit' her after that?" Andrea asked.

"Yeah, we broke up. We just couldn't stand each other anymore," he answered.

"Oh ok, I thought you might've broken up wit' her because she had a family member who was a cop," Andrea said, referring back to the night at her house during her music video premier.

"You still remember that, huh?" De'Von asked.

"Uh, yeah I still remember. I think Sean is still tryin to figure out what his daddy did to you," Andrea answered.

Suddenly, De'Von's face grew serious, almost angry. "I ain't have no beef wit' Sean's pops. I just hate cops, period," he replied.

"But why? Why do you hate cops so much?" Andrea asked.

"Because they nothin' but crooked officials workin' fo' the man and the white establishment. They tryin' to wipe us out," he continued.

"I feel you, De'Von. But not all cops are like that. There are some who are legit," she countered.

"Really? Tell that to my older brother. He was shot dead by a cop like a dirty dog in da street ten years ago," De'Von replied. Andrea put her hand to her mouth in shock.

"I-I didn't know that," she stammered, struggling to find words at the moment. "I'm so sorry," she replied feebly.

De'Von shrugged as if he was tryin' to shake his emotions off but found himself brushing away a tear, angrily.

"You know, if it wasn't fo' Mason, I wouldn't even be a rapper today. I got everything from him. My style, my wordplay, my clapbacks to certain disses," he said, his eyes reflecting those days. "I would perform everywhere wit' him. We were a team, Adia. Then one night, some dumb-ass cop took him from me. The worst part is that he wasn't even indicted for the murder. They acted like the fool defended himself and my brother was a savage black man," De'Von continued.

Andrea listened. It was easy to feel sorry for De'Von because he was a performer, so he kept all his emotions bottled up inside him.

"I know how you feel, De'Von. I lost my older sister six years ago," she said, without thinking. Normally it had been a part of her she didn't to share with others, but at that moment, De'Von needed someone who understood his loss.

"Foreal? What happened to her?" he asked.

Andrea sighed. "She was shot by a member of MOB six years ago," she replied. De'Von shook his head.

"That sucks. I'm sorry you went through that. I've heard about MOB in the past. They some ruthless bastards. My brother had some dealings with them," De'Von said. "What was her name?" he asked.

"Loree McAfee." Andrea replied.

"Oh yeah, I remember seeing the news about that on TV six years back. MOB ain't nothin' but some punks. Always gotta kill somebody to make a damn point. Then you expect the cops to protect you when you need it and they kill even more of us. It's a jacked up world we live in," De'Von said.

"You ain't neva lied," Andrea agreed. A moment of silence passed between them as the bus continued on toward its next destination. "I feel so bad right now. One of my friends got married this weekend and she wanted me to be part of the wedding. But I had to do this tour. I want to call her but I wouldn't know what to say," Andrea said, breaking the silence.

"What, you missed yo' girl's wedding? You could have told Julio and might've pulled some strings for you. He probably would've delayed the tour for another week or two," De'Von answered.

"I thought about askin', but Julio, Craig and the rest of Metro Records already done a lot for me and I ain't even been signed six months yet. They pulled enough strings for me already, I'd prefer not to annoy 'em any further," Andrea said.

"Girl, stop. They would've done it for you. Hell could freeze over right now and Julio would still bust his ass to make sho' he takes care of you," De'Von said. "He need to chill though. He could be puttin' his job on the line playin' wit' fire though," he added.

Andrea turned to face De'Von. "So now, I'm the fire right? Well somebody needs to put me out before I burn outta control," Andrea said, batting her eyelashes.

She didn't know why but she found flirting with De'Von so exciting. De'Von was certainly attractive. Sometimes, when she'd had been recording in the studio she would find De'Von staring at her from the sound board for minutes at a time. He wouldn't react, he would just stare.

"So who qualifies to put out Adia's fire?" he asked, although he wasn't sure if it was meant to be a rhetorical question or if he was waiting for an answer from her.

"I'll let you know," she said, smiling.

"You really enjoy doin' this huh?" De'Von said.

"Doing what?" Andrea asked with a fake tone of innocence.

"You love leavin' me hangin'. It's like you wanna get me to sweat you or something," De'Von replied.

"Maybe. Is it workin'?" Andrea asked.

"I'mma let you know. I shoulda known there was something bout you, since I met you at Johnson's that day," he said.

"Oh God, are we really gonna bring back Johnson's again?" I swear you can neva' let that image of me go," Andrea said laughing.

"Well that was the first time we met, Ma and they always say that first impressions last a long time," De'Von said. Andrea didn't let it show right away but she could feel herself blushing.

De'Von had been a rap star who had made millions and had all the females eating from his fingertips. Andrea knew that firsthand when they had toured through Pennsylvania and New Jersey. After a stellar performance, the Metro artists had been leaving the stage. Normally when they exited they were surrounded by security and bouncers who would separate them from the screaming crowds and audiences. One very courageous young woman had somehow gotten through security and ran up to De'Von. Without warning, she pulled off the spaghetti-strapped top she had been wearing. Andrea was shocked when she saw the girl's breasts fully exposed as she hugged De'Von, kissing him all over until security finally arrived and pulled the young lady off. He wore a wry, sheepish grin after security guided the lady away.

"Must be nice," Andrea said to De'Von as they had entered the bus after the incident. It was those situations that reminded Andrea that De'Von would never be the type of man who would ever settle down. His life moved too fast and he was always looking for the next big break in his career. As tempting as a relationship with him might be, it wasn't worth the pain that Andrea was sure she would eventually incur.

"Can I be real wit' you?" De'Von asked.

"Yeah, what's up?" Andrea replied.

"Have you eva' thought how life would've been if yo' sister was still here? Like would she support you in your career? For me, even though Mason's gone, I feel like if he was hea', we woulda blown the top off this game. We woulda been two of the hottest MC's," he said.

Andrea thought about it for a moment. She never really gave it a second thought. "She definitely would've been my number one fan. She would've been part of the entourage, you already know," she said.

"What, you don't think she would've been up on da stage witchu?" De'Von asked.

"Nah, singing wasn't really her thing. If anything, she loved fashion and modeling. She probably would've helped me create my own clothing line. You know, shoes, blazers, shirts, bras, panties, you name it. We would make stuff that girls could wear," Andrea said thoughtfully.

"I feel you," De'Von replied.

"So if you never started rappin' wit' your brother, where would you see yourself?" Andrea asked. De'Von shook his head and it was clear to Andrea that nobody had ever asked him that question.

"To be honest, I don't even know. When my brother started rappin', he was sellin drugs out on da block. He started rap battlin' on dat same block and that's where he realized he had skills. He was the one that honed it in me, he taught me the tricks of the trade. I guess the one reason why he wanted me to rap was because he ain't want me livin' the life he was livin' out there in the streets," De'Von replied.

"My sister just couldn't stay away from the streets. It was like she was married to it but she was tryin to break away from it," Andrea said.

"I feel you. My brother was the same way," De'Von said. "The night he got shot, he was payin' back one of his homeboys. He had to sneak out the window so my mama wouldn't catch him. He thought I was asleep but I wasn't. I thought this would be like them other times where he would come back, but he never did," he added.

Andrea listened to the story with a pained heart. It must've been awful for De'Von to have seen his brother in the last minutes of his life. It was an image Andrea was sure De'Von could never escape. She could still see her sister in the hospital bed, tubes sticking out everywhere, with doctors desperately trying to revive her. Eager to shift the subject from their deceased siblings, Andrea looked outside.

"Check it out, we just hit Massechussetts," she said as they just passed the welcome sign on the interstate.

Minutes before arriving at the venue, Andrea overheard Julio talking on his cell phone. This wasn't unusual, since he was always busy and always planning the next events. However, Andrea noticed that Julio was talking on his phone angrily, not in his usually calm voice.

"How could you let this happen?" Julio asked the club promoter over the phone. Julio sounded furious. The club promoter, wanting to book more events at Phoenix Landing had accidentally booked the Metro artists on the same day that he booked the artists from BHR. "Look, man you had only one job to do. To see that we weren't overbooked or sharing the stage with anybody. Don't you understand what could happen?" Julio asked frantically.

"Look, Julio we'll get it straightened out. Now I spoke to the producer for Big House, and as upset as he was also, he also promised that there would be no problems. He's aware of the issues between you two," the club promoter assured Julio on the other line.

"I don't know," Julio said. "BHR's artists are abrasive and confrontational and they don't give a damn about who they hurt," he said. "I've been in this business for too long and I know what can happen," he added.

Ending his call, Julio turned to face the rest of the bus. "Ladies and gentlemen, we got a little situation. We were booked at the same club as BHR today," he said.

There were exasperated groans and many heads were shaking. "Are you serious? So you mean we gotta share the stage wit' them bustas?" Bobby asked.

"I'm afraid so," Julio replied. "Look. They will be performing before us and as soon as they're finished, we're up, so make sure your mind is on the show tonight. Don't be distracted by the BHR artists and don't let 'em throw you off your game," he said.

"Easier said than done," De'Von said and the rest of the bus nodded their heads in agreement. "It's all good though. They're just saving the best for last," De'Von added, laughing.

Before long, they were in the city of Boston and they reached the Phoenix Landing Club. Sure enough, there was another tour bus parked along the side of the building.

"Look at their raggedy-ass bus. Hopefully they could finish their set before we get to ours," De'Von told Bobby as they walked out of the bus.

Hoping that the security would be adequate, Julio stepped outside and walked inside the club where BHR was finishing up a song. Andrea saw Emiline on the stage with a rapper whom she's seen before but wasn't able to place where she has seen her before.

Emiline has a great voice, Andrea thought as Emiline sang.

I want to be your black queen of the Nile/Giving you all my love for more than just a while/When I look at your eyes, I see what they're sayin/ Gimme your love boy and don't keep playin.

As soon as they finished their selection, the BHR artists walked backstage amidst the applause and the cheers for encores.

"C'mon Adia, let's get ready," Michelle told her as they walked backstage. The general plan was to take a different route backstage so they wouldn't run into the BHR artists.

As Michelle, Andrea, Bobby, and De'Von walked backstage, a BHR rapper by the stage name of DRA (Dopest Rapper Alive) noticed Andrea walking toward the back of the club.

"Ayo Ma, what's up?" DRA asked Andrea. "You feel like doin' somethin' lata? Check it out, we got a party goin' on at da Ritz Plaza tonight. You can come, as long as you bring yo' sexy ass only instead of yo' wack crew," he added.

Andrea took one look at DRA, rolled her eyes the same way Loree would have whenever she was dismissing a man. Ignoring him, she continued walking but DRA would not give up easily. He walked up to Andrea, and grabbed her arm.

"Yo, didn't you hea' me back there?" he asked, grabbing Andrea's arm roughly.

"Nigga, if you don't let go of me…" Andrea started to warn but looking at DRA's eyes, she could tell he was drunk. De'Von heard the commotion and turned back towards Andrea.

"Yo DRA, let her go dog," he said.

"Hold up, this ain't none of yo' business, pretty boy," DRA replied.

"Well, I'm makin' it my business now. You betta get yo' ass back to the bar wit them wack punchlines," De'Von replied.

DRA loosened his grip and Andrea yanked her arm out of his grasp but he wasn't done yet. "Oh shit. So Casanova got jokes now, right?" DRA said in mock tones and without warning, he shoved De'Von hard.

De'Von shoved him back. "You betta back up off me or BHR's gon' be one artist short, you feel me?" he replied.

Tico and Bobby ran to back up their respective parties. "Yo, DRA. Now's not the time man," Bobby said.

"You De'Von's bitch now?" Tico asked Bobby. "I thought that was her job," he added, pointing at Andrea.

"Who you callin' a bitch?" Andrea challenged.

Tico may have been from the hood, but Andrea wasn't a model of restraint herself. Security was notified of the stand-off and immediately ran to the scene and separated the five artists. Watching from a distance was Emiline, who Andrea noticed before she got into it with Tico. She noticed that Emiline was trying to avoid any confrontation.

"All right, all right let's break it up folks, let's break it up," the security guards said as the BHR and Metro Record artists walked their separate ways.

As soon as they were backstage and preparing for the show, Andrea turned to De'Von. "Thanks for the backup," she said.

"Don't even sweat that. We label mates, we gotta have each other's back, especially out on the road," De'Von replied.

As the host of the event introduced them, the show went on as normal with all the Metro artists singing their signature songs from their albums. Finally Andrea was up. Once again, she closed her eyes and channeled her inner performer and Adia burst forth onto the stage. As she sang her number, Adia's voice captivated the crowd as much during the ballads as it had during the uptempo songs. Finally she reached the song that she shared with De'Von and the crowd went crazy as the two performers traded verses and bars perfectly. As the show neared its close, something happened that Andrea couldn't explain. While De'Von spoke to the audience about how much love he had for Adia, she realized he was doing more than playing a role for the crowd as artists; he was implying that were lovers.

"Fellas, when you've found dat one chick, keep her by your side cuz she gon' ride wit' you all da way," he said to shouts of agreement and applause from the audience. "Finding the right girl takes a certain type of ambience and patience and persistence," he walked over to Andrea who was still holding her micropone.

"Baby you da only one that can have me feelin' some type of way," Adia replied. "Ain't nobody gon' come between us, baby," she added as De'Von stepped even closer.

As the lights on the stage began to dim, De'Von drew closer to Adia. She didn't know how it had happened but De'Von's lips found hers. The girls in the crowd yelled and the boys were hooting and cheering for De'Von. The kiss had taken Andrea totally by surprise, as they certainly hadn't rehearsed it and he had never kissed her onstage before. It happened at the spur of the moment and because they were on stage, Adia had to continue with the show but the feeling of De'Von's soft lips pressing up against hers was unexpected. De'Von immediately continued with the show. When the show finished, both artists retreated backstage. Andrea only had time to say a few words to De'Von and it was only a question.

"What was that?" she asked. De'Von found himself momentarily quiet. It had not been planned to display a kissing scene on the stage.

Could it be that his pentup feelings for Andrea had surfaced and it had just manifested on stage? Or was it Adia he had kissed and just part of the show?

"I don't know. I guess I got caught up in the moment. My bad," De'Von apologized. As soon as they reached backstage where the other artists were, there were catcalls, whistles, and clapping when Andrea stepped into the room with De'Von. Slam immediately walked over to De'Von.

"Yo man, what was that at the end?" Slam asked.

"I don't know what happened, dog. One moment I'm talking to her like I normally do during our takes, but this time was different bro. She was standing next to me and I don't know dog. I lost control of myself," De'Von explained. Slam laughed.

"So I see, and now the whole city of Boston saw it too," he replied.

While the producers, security, and others congratulated Andrea on a great performance, she still had the kiss on her mind. De'Von had never pulled that stunt before on any other tour stops. Regardless, Andrea couldn't help but feel the heat of that kiss. He hadn't gone too far and he wasn't sloppy. It had just been sweet, yet she felt electricity between them. As they headed back to the bus to head to the hotel, Andrea sat by herself again, while De'Von went back to join Slam. Michelle had her little group of friends with her and Miesha had her two close friends. All of them glared at Andrea. Andrea didn't know if the faces were judgmental or envy. Miesha had a right to feel jealous, since De'Von had dated her.

As they reached the Four Seasons, Andrea grabbed her own suitcase and went directly to her hotel suite. The news magazines and the tabloids would certainly have their juicy gossip of the week. Andrea could just picture the title of the magazine. QUEENS SONGSTRESS ADIA AND RAPPER DE'VON SHARE PASSIONATE KISS ONSTAGE. It was not the type of publicity she wanted. She wanted to be known for her music not for swapping spit with De'Von.   Andrea started to lie down on the bed, stretching out, when she heard a knock on her hotel door. Opening the door, she saw that it was De'Von.

"Can I come in?" he asked.

Everything in Andrea's mind told her that this would not be a good idea but Adia was of a different mindset.

"Yeah, come in. What's up?" she asked.

As soon as he closed the door, he started to talk quickly.

"Yo, Adia I'm sorry for what I did on stage today. I know we didn't rehearse it and we probably gave everyone something to talk about for the next couple days. I don't know what came ova' me, you a great singer, artist, and one of the most realest, down to earth chicks I've ever met. I guess I ain't know how to say it," he said.

Andrea turned away from De'Von to act as if she was staring out her window, but she didn't want De'Von to see the color rise in her cheeks. Was De'Von, the great rapper and young lyrical genius, admitting to getting tongue tied around her?

"Well that kiss took me by surprise, and we never rehearsed it that way. I never knew improv was part of the show," she said.

De'Von looked down at the ground, looking apologetic. Andrea saw his reaction and walked over to De'Von, placing her hands on his shoulder.

"But it was nice though," she added. De'Von looked up and his face resembled a kid on Christmas morning who had received every gift he ever wanted.

"But you know people are are gonna talk," he said.

"I don't give a damn if people talk. They've been talkin' about us before so now we gave them something else to talk about," Andrea said, shrugging her shoulders.

"Yeah, you right," De'Von replied.

"So what do we do now?" Andrea asked. De'Von just sat there at the opposite end of the room.

"Well I got a couple ideas," De'Von replied with a smart look on his face. "You know, if you check the bottom of the small fridge in the kitchen, they left a bottle of Merlot," he said as he walked to the refrigerator.

He poured a glass for Andrea and afterwards he poured a glass for himself. Andrea was not accustomed to drinking alcohol, even if she had been to many parties and club events, so it was relatively new to her. She remembered Julio's rule, but at that point it didn't matter, as she took a sip of the Merlot.

This is not so bad, she thought. Andrea and De'Von sat in the guest room laughing. After three hours, the wine bottle was nearly empty.

"So that's what happened when I tried to cut school that one time," De'Von finished, telling Andrea some of the stories he lived through as a child.

"Man, my girl Vanessa got so many similar stories to that, it ain't even funny," Andrea said.

De'Von laughed. Andrea didn't know what it was, but she was even happier than when she was on stage. "De'Von, lemme ask you a question, foreal, foreal. Why do ya hate each other so much? I mean BHR and Metro. How far back does that go?" she asked him.

"I don't even know," De'Von replied in a short but slightly slurred voice. "BHR and Metro been throwin' hands since prehistoric times. Nah, but seriously, both companies always bumped heads. When Metro signed me, they was still beefin'," he added.

De'Von looked at the clock. He saw that it was almost two in the morning.

"Well, I better go. Bus leaves at nine AM," De'Von said, heading over to the door. Andrea walked up to follow him.

"G'night De'Von," Andrea said, reaching over to hug him. "Thanks again for backin' me up," she told him, looking at his eyes. Oh no! I can't allow myself to look at his eyes. That boy got brown chestnut eyes, she thought, but she couldn't take her own advice. It must be the buzz.

De'Von's eyes were enticing and she was drawn to his warmth and his laid-back personality. De'Von felt his heart rate gallop and his mouth began go dry. He saw Andrea in her flannel pajamas and her usual headwrap. Right there, in the privacy of her room, she arched her head up and kissed him again. De'Von returned the kiss, more vigorously this time. Their lips were locked from what seemed like an eternity until De'Von broke off.

"Damn, girl. You makin' it hard for a brotha to leave this piece," he said, smiling while Andrea caressed the back of his head. She didn't know what had come over her but she had to have De'Von and she couldn't wait another day or another minute. She couldn't wait another second.

"Then don't leave. Stay with me," she whispered in his ear.

De'Von felt a warm sensation on his earlobe where Andrea had her mouth just a moment ago. Finally unable to hold back, De'Von gave in and kissed Andrea even deeper. Andrea took De'Von by the front of his shirt and dragged him to her bed. In the back of her mind, she feared what she was about to do. Was her sister this spontaneous sexually? She had never been in a releationship this deep with anybody before. She couldn't proceed until she was certain that De'Von was serious. She suddenly broke away from the kiss, her headwrap halfway unraveled and her flannel almost undone.

"Wait, wait. Do you have something?" she asked. De'Von raised his eyebrows in confusion at first; unsure of what Andrea was referring to. Then realization set in as he reached into his wallet in his back pocket and pulled out a condom. Smiling mischievously, Andrea continued to kiss him while she unbuttoned his pants for him to slip on his protection. Pushing him onto the bed; she proceeded to pull off his shirt, while he pulled off her pajama top. Giving into their passions, they surrendered to the sensation of their bodies as they intertwined.

Chapter Nineteen

Students began to file out of the classroom doors at Stony Brook College. Vanessa Roberts had been in college for eight months and had asked a question of the professor about a humanities assignment. She quickened her pace so she could reach her dorm and get started on her assignments since she had an event with her sorority group that evening. Her parents had been against her joining a sorority, but Vanessa had been looking forward to the experience, mostly because she felt so isolated at the college. Sure, she had made a few friends, but it hadn't been easy. She had always believed that a certain old friend would be with her at college, but her best friend had been too busy becoming a superstar, so college had been her lowest priority.

In less than a year, Adia's popularity had skyrocketed, and her music career had opened even more doors and avenues. She was the face on every teen and young adult magazine, and she has even been featured in music videos with other artists. She had used her endorsements and other deals to multiply her funds and expand into millions. With all of Adia's success, Vanessa no longer had direct access to her best friend. Whenever she tried calling, her call would be forwarded and a strange woman would answer the phone, stating that she was a representative of Adia. She tried to contact her online, but Andrea had transferred her personal Facebook into an Adia celebrity page with well over sixty thousand other followers. Vanessa just couldn't find a way to contact her friend. Vanessa also discovered through the tabloids that Adia and De'Von were currently an item. The paparazzi had spotted them together walking through parks, going to public events, and kissing romantically. They always appeared together at award shows, concerts, and public venues. Vanessa didn't even care so much anymore. Andrea had been a friend for many years, but it seemed that her own fame had overwhelmed her because Andrea had neglected important events in her personal life such as weddings, funerals, and family cookouts. It wasn't as if this unparalleled rise to the top was unknown.

As Vanessa opened the door to her dorm room, she saw that her roommate, Ingrid Rosmanov, who was Russian-American; was not in her room. "She must've gone to class," she said to herself while she sat down on the couch and turned on the television in the living area. Flipping through channels Vanessa finally landed on the music channel where Rose Wright, one of the reporters of the music news was interviewing none other than Adia. Vanessa rolled her eyes, and every instinct told her to change the channel but curiosity got the best of her and she watched the interview.

"So Adia, in less than a year we have seen your music career explode. Two albums, both of them went gold and you have ten songs from those albums on the music billboard's top twenty. How did you manage to succeed in this industry and who do acknowledge being your biggest inspiration?" Rose asked.

"Well, it wasn't easy, but it took a lot of work, perseverance, and love from my fans who continue to come out and support my music," Adia replied. "I have a lot of friends back in my hometown of Richmond Hill, New York. They've always encouraged me to sing and to share my God-given gift to others. I took their advice, and the rest is history," she added.

"That's wonderful," Rose gushed.

Vanessa felt as if she might gag. Andrea know she dead wrong for this. I was the one that got her ass in the music business. If it wasn't for me she would still be a nobody working at Johnson's, she thought.

"So who would you say was your biggest inspiration?" Rose asked. Adia was silent for a moment as if she was unsure of how to answer the question.

"I would say the biggest inspiration for me is my late sister, Loree McAfee. She always encouraged me to follow my dreams and she has always been my guardian angel. She still is," Adia replied.

Rose nodded her head as if she understood but Vanessa knew Rose couldn't possibly understand what it was like for Andrea to lose someone so valuable to her.

"Yes, that's right. Your older sister, whose life was tragically cut short at the age of eighteen, is that correct?" Rose asked.

"Yes, that's right," Adia answered.

"I know how emotional it must be for you to continue working and still have that memory linger. How do you manage to stay strong through it all?" Rose asked.

"I've found inner peace and take solace in knowing that she's still here and my boyfriend and producer De'Von has been my rock as well. Sometimes I've been overwhelmed with her memory but when I remember what she has inspired within me, it motivates me to keep going," Adia answered.

"There are rumors swirling that you would like to collaborate with Queen Sheba, another established R&B singer, who has songs that have charted high as well. Do you foresee this union happening, especially given the background of both music labels?" Rose asked.

"Yes Rose, I still can envision me and Sheba doing a song together. We both burst onto the music scene at about the same time and we both admire the other's voice. To sing with her would be a tremendous honor and despite the differences in our recording labels, I would be happy to put it aside to work with her," Adia answered.

Rose then turned to the camera. "Well, this is the great Adia once again joining me this afternoon. Stay tuned, we'll be back after a quick word from our sponsors," she said.

Vanessa turned off the TV. Not once had Andrea or "Adia" mention her name or Sean's name as being the ones who had stuck by her side and who had supported her music. Vanessa never thought the day would come where her once best friend would forget about her, but it seemed as if the day had arrived.

At Metro Records, Miesha was recording a slow R&B ballad in the recording booth while Paul and De'Von worked on the sound and the beat of the song. After strong consideration (and plenty of convincing by Craig, the head producer) Miesha had decided to stay at Metro. She never intended to leave the only home she had ever known. She decided that the good memories and the potential of greatness within Metro, was worth another shot. She had become more tolerant of Adia, although since she and De'Von had become a couple, their public displays of affection had been, at times, more than she could bear. She still couldn't see what De'Von saw in a young girl who was only nineteen years old, impressionable, and in her personal opinion, spoiled. She believed Adia had De'Von in her pocket. They appeared in more videos together, they showed up at events together, and they publicly displayed their regard for each other. Miesha had begged De'Von to spare her feelings whenever Adia was around. Unlike De'Von, Miesha wanted to keep the memory of their brief relationship alive. Although it hadn't lasted long, it had been one of the best times she had ever had known.

As they began recording, there was a loud noise and inside walked Adia, flanked by her two bodyguards, Ricky and Tony. She came in wearing Jimmy Choo shoes and a dress that had several side slits. Her hair, which Miesha had always considered to be unruly and messy, was now flowing silkily down to her shoulders. When she arrived at the studio booth where De'Von was, she walked inside. Miesha watched as they shared a passionate kiss. Paul let out a low whistle, laughing as Miesha stopped recording.

This girl really have no idea who she messin' wit', she thought as she walked out of the recording booth. They were still kissing as she approached them both. "If you ain't too busy, we got work to do. Can't you take your lil freak show somewhere else?" she said adamantly. Andrea smiled brightly at Miesha.

"Chill Miesha, we doing good now. I got my man by my side and we feel like we could conquer the world," she said.

"What ya' need to do is to conquer a bedroom. Yo De'Von' whats's up man? I told you to keep ya hands from each other," Miesha said angrily, as she tried to walk between the two lovers.

"My bad Miesha. You right, I gotta fight these urges whenever my girl comes over," he said while holding Andrea's hand.

"I think I'm gonna be sick," Miesha said in disgust as she re-entered the recording booth.

"Well where were you, baby?" De'Von asked Andrea as she took a seat on his lap

. "I know I'm late but I've been talking to the representatives for Queen Sheba and she agreed to collaborate with me on a song," Andrea said.

De'Von looked at Andrea, eyes more intense and serious than ever. "You sho' bout this? I mean, I don't think it's a great idea. These folk at BHR are greedy. They'll let you in, but what if they want something from you? What if they want you to sign with them?" he asked.

"C'mon baby, it won't be all that. Besides, I still got the contract ova here, so trust me, nothin's gonna happen," she assured him.

Walking out of the college atrium, Sean Hawkins made his way over to his borrowed Honda Civic that was parked on campus. He attended Queens College where he had finally won a spot on the basketball team as a walk-on. Unfortunately, he hadn't made the rotation and he had been forced to redshirt for his freshman year. The team was sub-par, finishing just one game above .500, and they had been knocked out in the first round of the regional tournament. Relieved that his nightmare season had come to an end, Sean just wanted to focus on school and college fun. He had pledged Kappa Alpha Psi, and joined the brotherhood of the fraternity where they did charity work and held events all over the tri-state area. They were also known for throwing the most raucous parties and which Sean was all too familiar with them. He had his pick of women at those parties and the ones girls he had chosen had been all too accommodating. With classes coming to an end for the semester, Sean decided to take a trip home to Richmond Hill. As he wandered onto the parking lot where his car was located, he heard someone call his name.

"Yo Sean, what's up dog?" Sean looked around for the source of the greeting and saw a familiar face of a friend that he hadn't seen in over three years.

"Vince Edwards, is that you?" Sean asked.

"You already know bro," Vince confirmed, laughing as Sean dapped his old friend.

Vince had also attended Richmond Hill High School but through an unfortunate set of circumstances that included drug possession and firearm possession, Vince had been arrested during his sophomore year of high school. Sean had not seen him since then.

"What's up son? What you doin out hea'?" Sean asked.

"What, you ain't heard? I go to school here too, man. While I was in juvey I was able to get into a work-study program and earn my GED. So I decided to try out this college thing, you know," he said. "So what's up, you played ball this year? I know you was killin' it back in Richmond," Vince added.

Sean looked at the school and sighed. "I know bro. I ain't had too much of a chance to do nothin' out hea. It was a jacked-up year for me, man," he admitted.

Vince patted his shoulder. "Yo, don't even sweat that, homie. You got three more years. Shit, I'm just tryin' to get through this year," he said laughing.

"I feel you, man." Sean said.

Vince looked around. "Yo, a whole lot's changed since I've been in lockup. I seen yo' homegirl Drea on TV now. She's a artist, is that true?" he asked.

Sean nodded shook his head. "Yeah it's true but I don't know much more than that. We ain't talked since after high school," he said.

"Sound like she went and left all us lil people behind," Vince said, laughing.

"You already know," Sean said, laughing. "Yo, I'm bout to grab a bite to eat, you got plans? We could catch up," he offered.

"light cool," Vince said as he followed Sean to his car.

At BHR Studios, DRA and Tico were going over the layout for a new track they had released. Emiline sat in the couch just outside her studio, pen and paper in hand. She was mulling over a less than perfect studio session earlier in the day. While Emiline, recording as the Queen of Sheba, had been recording a song for her third EP entitled "Feelin' Imperial", she had failed to reach her octave at one point in the song. She coughed clear her throat and continued again but her voice still failed to reach the highest point. Emiline was in unknown territory. She had never failed to perform to her fullest potential but she felt it was starting to fail her. The producer at BHR, Rod Birchfield, noticed that the Queen was off. While Tico and DRA continued working on their song, Rod approached Emiline.

"There goes our BHR Queen, Emiline!" Rod greeted.

"Hey Rod," Emiline replied, without emotion. Rod decided not to waste any time discussing the studio session and he cut to the chase.

"So word is out that you want to collaborate with Adia, is that true?" Rod asked.

"That's true. Adia is a wonderful talent and we both got signed at the same time. It seems only right to do a song together," Emiline said. She was fed up with people at the label who had been against Queen Sheba collaborating with an artist from an opposing label. Emiline, however, didn't care and she had never been more determined to do the song with Adia then she had been recently.

"But Queen, she's with Metro Records and right now she's breezing through the charts with her songs," he said. "This collaboration could be an excellent idea, though. When you record the song with her, tell her da 411 on BHR," he added.

Emiline looked at Rod with an incredulous stare. "So you want to use me go to Metro Records and recruit Andrea?" she asked Rod.

"Look, it's no big deal, I can give you the paperwork and you just run 'em by her when you girls relax," he said.

Emiline shook her head. This wasn't the way she wanted to work with Adia. "Look, Rod, I love this label and I love everyone who paved the path for me but I'm not gonna rip Adia away from her label. I couldn't do that," Emiline told Rod. "I'm not gonna co-sign into doing that. This whole Metro and BHR beef has gone on too long. Maybe by singing together, we can bridge the gap between both labels," she added.

"Whateva you say, Queen. But I'm tellin' you it's not gonna work," Rod said.

"Anything is possible through God. Just believe it and you'll see," Emiline said but no sooner had the words left her mouth, she began coughing again.

Tico and DRA looked up from their track, "Yo Queen, you good?" Tico asked.

"Yeah I'm ok," Emiline replied. "Never better," she added as she headed over to the restroom.

Finishing their session for the day, Andrea and Emiline left Metro's booth and went to a restaurant to have some dinner together.

"See Andrea when you put your voice up a little now, you gotta remember to build before you hit that high note," Emiline advised.

"Yeah you right," Andrea said. "You know, I've been doing voice exercises every day and drinking plenty of tea," she added. Andrea never loved to drink tea before, but she learned that when one was in showbiz, there was always a way to spice up tea.

"Oh yeah tea is good for it. Even if it does make you pee every twenty minutes," Emiline said. Andrea laughed. Emiline was down to earth, laid back, and knowledgeable about the business. Of course it also helped to be three years older than your competition.

"I just wish this whole Metro and BHR stuff ends cuz I would like all of us to work with each other," Andrea said.

"Me too," Emiline agreed.

Andrea enjoyed herself as she ate and talked with her new friend. However she couldn't help but notice a slight change in Emiline's appearance. Back when they had first met at the Fusion Lounge, Andrea remembered how much she had loved her voice and she knew that this was a person with whom she had to work. Emiline had never been big. She had been petite and beautiful. Since then, it appeared that Emiline had lost significant weight.

"Anyway this song's gonna kick ass when it hits the airwaves," Andrea said.

"I couldn't have said it betta' myself," Emiline said, as they ordered mimosas and toasted to their upcoming success.

"Can I ask you a personal question, Queen?" Andrea asked.

"Girl, now you know you don't have to call me Queen. Call me Emiline. We're practically family now," she said. Andrea smiled.

"Alright cool. So how long have you been singin'? When did you know that you had this gift?" she asked.

"Well I used to sing at my parents church every Sunday when the pastor called," Emiline said. Andrea was shocked.

"That's exactly how it started for me, too. I sang in church every Sunday," she said.

"Yeah, sometimes I miss that experience. No bickering labels, no long tours, no money involved, and no drugs. It's just you, the Lord, and the music. I miss that," Emiline said.

"I feel you," Andrea agreed. It had almost been a year since she has attended church and through no fault of her own. She had been busy with promotional visits, tours, recording, television appearances, and other engagements.

"I got an idea. Why don't we visit my church this Sunday?" Emiline asked. Andrea almost spit out her mimosa.

"What? Look Emiline, I would love to but we're on a tight schedule. We gotta get this track out as soon as possible," she said.

"Oh come on, please? I'll introduce you to my family. They've been waiting to meet you," she said.

"Really? Your fam wants to meet me?" she asked.

"Yeah, my three brothers, two sisters, and my parents," Emiline said.

"Dang, you got a big family," Andrea said.

"Tell me about it. Oh, and by the way, when we get there, make sure you sit by me, cuz you might have trouble keeping up with the service," Emiline said.

"What you mean? Trust me, I understand what goes on in church," Andrea said. "What makes it so different?" she asked.

She had spoken too soon. Upon entering Bethesda Missionary Church in Woodhaven on Sunday morning, Andrea realized that Emiline had taken her to a Haitian church. She passed a couple of members who were busily talking in a strange language. She leaned over to Emiline as they walked up the stairs that led to the sanctuary doors.

"What language are they speakin'?" she asked.

Emiline laughed at the expression of confusion on her friend's face. "They're speaking Creole. It's a form of French, Spanish, and African dialects," she explained.

Right away Andrea could tell that most of the adults didn't recognize her as Adia. Andrea had grown so accustomed to people dropping everything just to shake her hand, take a picture, and get an autograph. Although the Haitian community wasn't starstruck, they were very welcoming. Emiline shook the hands of nearly every member of the deacon board and was pleasantly surprised by how warm and receptive they were. When Emiline walked into the sanctuary with Andrea, many people proceeded to hug her as soon as they got the opportunity. Andrea looked around. The church was similar to the one she attended with her parents, with an upper level and a lower level. In the corner of the church, the musicians played an upbeat song until service started.

Wow, their band is pretty good, Andrea thought. But it only took a couple minutes, before she heard the familiar words, "Oh my gosh, is that Adia?" The voice seemed to come from a small group of Haitian-American teen girls.

A group of at least eight kids ran over to Emiline and Andrea and they signed a few autographs for the crowd of kids gathered around them. Suddenly the children took their places as the leader of the service took his stand at the pedestal. He was speaking Creole so quickly that Andrea found herself turning to Emiline, who was listening intently.

"What did he say?" she asked.

"He said that it's great when brothers and sisters gather together to worship our Lord and Savior," Emiline translated.

As the service continued, Andrea found these people were enthusiastic and full of life. This was not a church of people who simply stood and read hymn books like a bunch of zombies. Indeed, these people were totally different from the church in which Andrea had been raised. During a portion of their service, many of the adults stood up as the music steadily became more upbeat. They had been playing a type of music she had never heard before. The drummer hit his cymbals harder and the beat became louder and the pace quickened even more. The congregation included some adult women who wore what appeared to be a shawl over their heads. They stood up and began dancing in the aisles. They sang a song from one of the pamphlets that had been handed out to the congregation before the service. Andrea looked at her copy. She might as well have been reading Chinese, for she couldn't understand a word on the paper. The crowd sang, "Toujours, Toutours, je chanterai ton grand amour!"

Andrea leaned over to Emiline again, but before she asked the question, Emiline answered. "It means, always, I will sing about your great love," she replied.

Then the song ended and the leader of the service, sweat pouring down his face, shouted, "Beni soit L'Eternel!" The congregation repeated those words.

"Beni soit L'Eternel!" They repeated the same cycle for seven times.

"They're saying praise the Lord," Emiline explained.

The leader of the service then asked the congregation to sit down. He called on Emiline to introduce her guest and once she stood up, Andrea stood up as well and the congregation cheered. Then he called Emiline to come onto the stage. Emiline walked up on stage, whispering some instruction to the musicians, who nodded and when she came up, she waitied for a moment while the musicians began playing. Then Emiline opened her mouth and the angelic voice emerged from the depth of her heart. It was a familiar gospel song that Andrea had heard before. It brought Andrea back to the simpler days when her family was free of grief and heartache and they had still been whole. Emiline's voice carried itself into the consciousness of every member of that congregation. It brought Andrea back to the heart of worship within herself. She had almost forgotten where and why she had started singing in the first place. She thought of her sister, who would be sitting in the first few rows of Pastor Mike Hillman's church with Shania. Shania would have taught her Sunday school class. As Emiline finished her song, the crowd applauded as did Andrea, tears streaming down her cheeks. Through all the songs that Emiline had sung as Queen of Sheba Andrea was convinced that this was the most beautiful of Emiline's songs. No studio, no money, no drugs, and no revealing clothes. It was just her and the music. After that, the pastor approached the stage to preach and he preached in Creole but thankfully there was a young man who translated the message into English. It was a message that made Andrea think of her purpose in life. She had always believed that she had to do whatever the studio told her to do – all for money. As soon as the service was over, Emiline introduced Andrea to her family, her five siblings, who were all Adia fans. She signed autographs, took pictures, and shook hands with them. The pastor was the last one to greet her as she left. They welcomed her to come back whenever she could.

As the friendship between Andrea and Emiline continued to develop, the media wasted no time covering the story. There were times when Andrea would walk down her street and she'd see the head of a photographer hiding behind his parked car. Andrea understood that it was the media's job to cover celebrities but she felt like she was dealing with a pack of vultures. Many headlines surfaced, some of them with Andrea and Emiline at the front cover walking together without a care in the world.

"ADIA AND QUEEN SHEBA: FRIENDS OR FOES?" Other headlines exaggerated their union, stating," ADIA AND QUEEN SHEBA REPRESENTING THEIR LABELS? I THINK NOT" Andrea did what she always did when she felt pressured by the media: she ignored it.

Andrea wouldn't answer any phone calls for fear that it might be a media member or someone from Metro calling to reprimand her about her strange partnership with a client from the opposing record label. One day, while in studio, De'Von took the chance to speak to her about it.

"Adia, word on the street is that you're hangin' out with Queen Sheba and ya puttin' a track together," he said.

"Yeah so what about it?" Andrea replied.

De'Von looked at her, his eyes serious with intent. "So you still think it's a good idea? She might be using you to spy on us so she can give an advantage to BHR," he said.

Andrea rolled her eyes. De'Von could be enlightening sometimes but other times he could be aggravating in his outlook.

"C'mon De'Von that ain't fair," Andrea pointed out. "It wasn't just for me. It was for Emiline also. We wanted to make a song together since before you signed me," she replied.

"But trust me, some moves are bad to make just because of history. I'm just asking you to peep game, ok," De'Von said as he approached Andrea and kissed her.

Andrea couldn't help but notice that De'Von had been distracted lately. Maybe the pressure of his next album was getting to him. De'Von's last album hadn't reached the level of success of his past album. Feeling that his next album had to exceed expectations set by Metro execs, De'Von had spent many nights at the studio, mixing beats and instrumentals with his rap. The song had been looking good but he needed more sound. He decided to have both Miesha and Adia sing on his album. They hadn't initially agree to do it since there was still a rift between Miesha and Andrea, but they had finally put their differences aside to help De'Von since they both cared about him and his future in the industry.

"Anyway once the album drops, I'm hosting an album release party at Club Max in downtown Manhattan. You'll be there, right?" he asked.

Andrea walked up to him and stroked the back of his head in the loving way she always had. "You already know, I got yo' back, baby." she said.

Sean followed Vince to his place on 102nd Ave, just a few blocks away from Richmond Hill High School. Vince said he had a new car but there might be a problem with the engine and none of his friends or family could figure out the problem. Sean, who considered himself knowledgeable when it came to cars, followed Vince to his home where his car was parked.

"It's an '05 Mustang. I got it at a price of a thousand nineteen," Vince explained.

Sean drove his own car to his home first then walked with Vince to his home so he could help fix his car. They arrived at what appeared to be a small one-story house with only two side windows. There were three boys sitting outside the stoop of the house smoking cigarettes and drinking beer.

"What's up, Big Pete?" Vince greeted as he dapped one of the larger boys on the stoop. "Yo, this is da homie Sean from Richmond Hill High. Sean, meet da homies, Big Pete, Drew Townes, and Stone Brown," Vince introduced Sean to his friends.

After Sean dapped all three boys, he followed Vince to the front of the house, where his car was parked. Sean popped the hood open and began to look for the problem with the engine. While he was preoccupied, Vince left his side and went inside his home. Sean thought he might have gone inside to grab a cold drink. He checked the battery for any corrosion, leaks, or any signs of damage but there didn't appear to be a battery problem. When he checked the oil, he even saw it was full. So if there was nothing wrong with his car, why did Vince invite him to come to his place?

"Yo Vince, everything looks okay here, man. What did you say you wanted me over again for?" he asked.

"Aight cool, but I got another question fo' you," Vince replied.

"What's up?" Sean said, as he closed the hood. Suddenly he heard a clicking sound next to his ear. Stiff as stone, Sean turned around and saw three guns pointed at him.

"I wanna see how fast I can unload dis clip into yo' ass," Vince replied.

Chapter Twenty

It only took seconds for Sean to realize that he had walked into a trap. Vince's car never had any engine trouble. He had used the car as bait to lure him to his place. "What the hell is this?!" Sean exclaimed in a mixture of anger and fear.

"Welcome to Club Payback, fool," Vince said as his two friends took Sean by his arms and dragged him over to the hood of the car where they slammed his upper body down. Sean's forehead hit the hood cover, opening a small wound on his forehead. As the blood poured down his head, Sean felt the cold steel of the gun's barrel on the left side of his temple.

"Yo man, why you doin' this? I thought we was boys!" Sean bellowed.

"What made you think I would eva' be cool wit' a sucka like you?" Vince asked, gun still pointed at Sean's head. "Because of your pops, I spent three years in juvey upstate. I lost my girl, lost my mama, I lost everyone," he said.

Sean then realized that Vince had been one of the kids caught in the drug ring and that the officers who responded included his father, who was responsible for arresting Vince. His father had explained the incident to Sean that evening and Sean suddenly remembered what he had thought that night. He had hoped Vince wouldn't get out soon because if he made the connection between his father and him, Sean would be in a world of trouble. That trouble was now pointing a gun at him.

"When five-oh came and busted shit up, I was pissed off. The po-po came and started cuffin everybody and this one man comes up to me and tells me to put my hands behind my back," Vince explained to his friends. "I said no and he slams me against the wall and cuffs me. I took a look at his badge and I read his name. Hawkins. It was then I knew that this cop was related to this nigga. I remember seein' him coming to all the ball games," he added.

Sean was held at gunpoint and he closed his eyes. He might as well resign himself to the fact that the bullet was surely going to snuff the life out of him because if he knew anything about Vince, it was the fact that he was mentally unstable. He now remembered the violent spells in high school when he fought other kids who had dared to mess with him. It had never been confirmed whether or not Vince was associated with any gangs but Sean wouldn't doubt it.

"Look man, I had no idea that my pops locked you up. Please man, let me go. I won't say shit, I promise," Sean pleaded with Vince.

"See I wish I could take you at yo' word, but I can't afford to be soft on you now. They sho' wasn't soft on me when they locked me up," Vince said. "You wanna know what hell feels like, Sean? Hell is waking up in an eight by ten cell every day, eatin' only three times a day. Hell is hours of doin' nothin' but hard labor for nothing.' Hell is havin' to watch yo' back every day so someone don't stab yo' ass and fightin' every day to get respect. Well now, I'm gon' give you a brand of hell," he said insanely.

Sean could feel the tears falling down his cheeks. He couldn't help crying because he was sure that his life was coming to an end.

"Please man, I'm sorry for what happened. Please don't," Sean pleaded. Vince thought about it for a moment. Then he decided to spare him.

"Get him up," Vince ordered his friends and they took Sean and dragged him to the front of the house. "This ain't ova yet. I better not see yo' father by himself, cuz if I do, I'm gettin' rid of him and you," he threatened. "So hea's what you gonna do. I'm seein' yo' homegirl Andrea doin it big lately with singin' and stuff, and I know she swimmin' in dough right now," he added.

"What's that got to do wit' me?" Sean replied, realizing that he might have spoken too soon. Vince and his friends were still armed.

"I need you to get me the autograph of Adia for me. I'm hustlin' random things online and out in deese streets. I would say, given how much she makes, the autograph falls under the ballpark of about two thousand," Vince said. "So here's what I'm gonna tell you to do. Call yo' homegirl and ask her if she could get me an autograph copy of her last CD and nine-hundred dollas. If you do that, we'll let you go. But if you play us and call the cops on me and my boys, first thing I'm gon' do is track yo' ass down and when I find you, I'm gonna finish what I started today. If you get the money and the autograph, I might let you and yo' pops go and drop da whole thing," he added.

Sean glared at Vince. This was a new low for someone he thought he knew well in high school. Vince, although unstable, was no idiot. He understood Sean's connection to Andrea since high school and since she started making money, he had begun plotting a strategy that would assure his ultimate revenge and also ensure guaranteed money in his pocket. .

"Look man, I don't even talk with Andrea anymore like that. She changed her number and been on tour mad times. I ain't seen her in months. What if I pay you the money?" Sean asked, hoping Vince would meet him halfway and show him mercy. Unfortunately mercy was not in Vince's vocabulary.

"Nah, I want that autograph, fool and you got a week to get that and the money. After that, if I don't get neither, you betta' watch yo' back cuz I'm comin at you wit' straight heat," he threatened. "Don't even think about tryin' nothin' stupid like fakin' the autograph. I want the real shit, you feel me? I got eyes all ova Queens, boy and if I hea' you playin me, you betta start pickin' out yo' gravestone," he added.

"Ok I got you, can I go now?" Sean asked, clearly shaken up. He had never had his life threatened before and now with the noose just inches away from his neck he had to find a way to get the autograph before Vince finishes him. Vince gestures to his friends to let Sean go. Sean stumbled out of the halfway house and begins to walk home, trembling from head to foot.

At Metro Studios, Andrea waited outside the office of the CEO of Metro, Mr. Morgan with Julio and Craig. Andrea had demanded to see the CEO due to some costs on her paycheck. The tour that had grossed Metro over five million dollars, had only paid Andrea four hundred thousand dollars. Reading the details of her paycheck, she saw that tax, travel, hotel stay, and all the drinks from the after-parties had taken a huge chunk of her check. Andrea was not stupid at math. She knew that despite those expenses, she should have received at lease one million dollars. The numbers simply hadn't added up.

"I don't know why you want to see Mr. Morgan. He's a very busy man," Julio said as they waited together outside the office.

"I don't care, Julio." Andrea replied. "I've made millions of dollars for this label and I'm only getting ten percent of that? Where's the rest of the money?" she asked Julio.

Fifteen minutes later, they were all ushered into Mr. Morgan's office. "How's my R&B sweetheart doing today?" Mr. Morgan asked.

"I ain't doin' too well, sir. What's this?" Andrea asked, holding her paycheck in her hand. Mr. Morgan took the statement and held it in his hands.

"Well I would say that's a reward for the fruits of your hard work," he replied.

"Nah, this ain't no reward sir. This is minimum wage," Andrea replied.

"What do you mean?" Mr. Morgan said as he looked over the statement.

"Adia has performed at over fifty venues across the U.S. promoting her first and second albums. I believe she deserves a higher cut than what's been given to her," Julio explained.

Mr. Morgan stood up from his chair. He walked around the square table in the center of the room.

"Do you believe so, Mr. Vargas? Do you believe that Adia deserves more money?" he asked. "Well, tell me now, what do you believe about Mr. De'Von? Or Ms. Michelle? Or Ms. Miesha? Do you believe we should pay them all more from their tours?" Mr. Morgan asked.

Julio was not sure if the question was rhetorical or not, so he avoided answering the myriad of questions that had been hurled at him.

"We have a motto here, Mr. Vargas, and it is the fact that we are a family. I believe a family should share an equal piece of the pie. If I start paying an individual more money than the others, we lose order, gentlemen. Order is the standard that we stand by." Mr. Morgan explained.

"But I've had to do so much more than they had to do," Andrea said, her voice slightly rising in anger. "I've had to modify my wardrobe, I've had to make TV appearances and interviews, I've had my name attached to gifts and I've had to go around promoting you. I did all that," she added.

Julio gestured to her to calm down and turned to Mr. Morgan with a fiery glare in his eyes.

"You're right Mr. Morgan, order is the standard that we stand by. Is that why you ordered us to modify Andrea's style, so we can sell to billions, only to see nothing?" he asked. Craig tried to get Julio's attention with his eyes, but Julio wouldn't look in his direction, therefore he continued his banter. "Is that why you went out of your way to promote De'Von last year when his first album exceeded all expectation, despite how the other label mates felt? With all due respect sir, the fact that we are family rings true for us. We all have our favorites," Julio said. Mr. Morgan now stared at Julio, the happy flicker from his eyes gone.

"Very well, Adia. I will see what I can do for you. You may leave now. Julio, remain here in my office. I need to discuss some matters with you," he said in a voice that was surprisingly dry for an enthusiastic chief executive officer.

Craig ushered Andrea out the door while taking another glance back at Julio. Andrea wasn't sure if she had imagined it, but she could've sworn she saw Julio wink at her as she left. A wink that said, keep being you, no matter what happens or the circumstances. Andrea left the office, not knowing what would happen next.

A few days later, Adia was in the studio polishing her song with Queen Sheba. Andrea felt as if she couldn't sing anymore. A few hours earlier she had heard the news that Julio Vargas had been unceremoniously fired from Metro Records. Andrea couldn't prove it, but she believed it had been due to her confrontation with the CEO about her check and that Julio had been fired for coming to her defense. Craig had taken over most of the production, but the sessions hadn't been the same without Julio. Julio had been admired by so many people at Metro Studios and his absence had created a gaping hole in the emotional chemistry. After the session, Andrea sat outside the studio booth with Emiline. Emiline had grown to be somewhat of an older sister to Andrea. She would never replace Loree but the bond they shared in music and in life was like no other.

Andrea had gone to Emiline's house in Forest Hills, New York. Her mother had made a delicious dinner for her, and it had been the first time she had ever eaten Haitian food. From the rice and beans to the macaroni and cheese, to a tasty beef that she heard the Haitians refer to as griot, the meal had been wonderful. She spent time with Emiline's siblings and was pleased that all of them knew her music. Andrea was becoming more and more worried about Emiline's health. During dinner she had asked to be excused to use the bathroom several times and Andrea couldn't help but notice how frail Emiline looked. She had dark circles under eyes as if she hadn't slept in days and her facial features looked sunken. She would try to hide behind her makeup, but it didn't work. No amount of concealer covered her emaciated appearance. When Andrea asked if Emiline was ok, she would simply say that she was never better.

"You gotta leave Metro," Emiline said to Andrea after she told her about the meeting with Mr. Morgan.

"I don't know, Emiline," Andrea replied. "Without Metro, I wouldn't be where I'm at now. I'm finally livin'," she said.

"But you're being cheated on. The CEO is greedy and you know it," Emiline said.

"Well how would you know?" Andrea asked, challenging Emiline.

"Cuz BHR's the same way," Emiline said. "They're not what I thought they were. I'm not getting' any money from them either. So I'm dippin' out on 'em too," she said. "Besides, I was thinkin' about switchin' to gospel," she added. Andrea thought about that.

"Gospel? I heard there's barely any money in that," she said.

"But you said it yourself in church that day. You wished music was more about the spirit of the song than about contracts and money," Emiline said. "What you said got me thinking. Maybe I should do something different with my music. Maybe you should too. Don't lose yourself in this business."

As soon as the words had left Emiline's lips, Andrea suddenly recalled the dream she had about of Loree and the words Loree had said as she stroked Andrea's hair: Don't lose yourself. Not only was the message eerily similar but so was the manner it which it had been said; gentle and concerned. It felt like Loree was speaking to her through Emiline.

Andrea thought about all the promises she had broken. She had promised her friends Vanessa and Sean that she would take them for the ride but once she was actually on that ride, she had left them behind. She had promised Shania and Trevor that she would be at their wedding and she had reneged on that promise, too. She realized she had been totally caught up in her glamorous life, so much so that she began to lose sight of what was really important to her.

"You're right Emiline," she admitted. "I have been losing myself in this business. When you have high expectations from your label and you have to play a role for fans all over the country, it's tough," she said. Andrea had been slowly disappearing performance after appearance and Adia had taken over.

"I know. I've been there. I'm still there now, tryin' to get out. The Queen loves her fans and she loves the limelight, but Emiline just likes the simple stuff," Emiline said. Suddenly she started coughing again.

"Hey, are you ok?" Andrea asked.

"Yeah, I'm fine. Don't worry about me," Emiline said but Andrea was getting more and more worried. Emiline wasn't coughing lightly; she was coughing as if her throat was on fire. They were becoming coarse and hacking.

"I'ma go get some water. I'll be right back," Emiline said before getting up and walking back inside the building.

"Ok, girl I'll be hea' if you need me," Andrea replied. She sat on the bench for a few minutes, thinking about what Emiline had said. She had hurt people she loved but was it possible to make amends with her friends and family? She took out her phone and scrolled down her contact list. Many of the phone numbers were other artists or celebrities in the music business. After four minutes of scrolling, she saw Shania's phone number. Maybe it was not too late to repent.

I just hope she hasn't changed her number, Andrea thought. Unfortunately Andrea had been forced to change her own number because she had gotten so many calls from fanatic fans, many of whom were vulgar and lewd in various ways. She called her old friend and silently prayed. After several rings, she heard a woman's voice answer the call.

"Hello? Who's this?" the voice asked.

"Is this Shania Hillman?" Andrea asked.

"Yes, this is she. May I ask who's speaking please?" Shania asked.

"It's Andrea McAfee," Andrea replied.

There was silence on the other line for a moment. At first, Andrea was afraid that Shania didn't believe her and had hung up on her. She was relieved when she heard Shania reply.

"Hey, how are you Andrea? Or should I say Adia?" she asked with a laugh.

Andrea was relieved to hear the joy in Shania's voice when she replied on the other line. "Girl, just call me Andrea. You ain't got to use my stage name. We're practically family," she replied.

"Practically family?" Shania asked. "Are you sure about that? Cuz normally family members attend special occasions for other family members," Shania replied while oddly still pleasant. Andrea sighed deeply into the phone.

"Shania, I'm so sorry I didn't come to the wedding. You trusted me and I let you down. It's just this music thing got me so wrapped up and I tried to make time but I was on tour after tour and shooting videos all the time," she explained feebly.

"I understand," Shania replied. "I'm not gonna lie, Drea. I was really upset when you didn't come to the wedding. It shook me up so much that I barely made it to the alter," she added. Although Andrea couldn't see her, she was positive, given the quivering voice and silent sobs between words that Shania was crying.

"You know, when she was alive I made a promise with your sister. We promised each other that we would always be there for one another, no matter what," Shania said. "That promise included parties, family support, and weddings. We always dreamed about going to each other's wedding and we promised each other that we would be maid of honor for the other. I asked you because you were the closest thing to Loree that I had left. Looking at you and sometimes talking to you, I saw her," she added.

Andrea felt tears starting to well up in her own eyes. She never realized how much it had hurt Shania that she hadn't been there, to keep the memory of their promise alive.

"Please forgive me," Andrea pleaded.

"I forgive you, sis." Shania replied. "Sometimes I forget how young you are and you got caught up with all this superstar status. I know how overwhelming it must have been. But be careful because there are people who say they are one person and when you look again, they turn into someone completely different," she said.

"Tell me about it," Andrea replied, thinking about Mr. Morgan and how he had refused to pay Andrea her fair share of the money from the tour. She heard the door open behind her and realize that Emiline was making her way back over next to her.

"I'm sorry, Shania but I gotta go. Thanks for forgiving me. I promise as soon as I can, we'll chill together," Andrea said.

"Ok cool," Shania said, before hanging up.

"Who was that?" Emiline asked Andrea.

"Oh, just an old friend," Andrea replied. "Are you ok?" she asked Emiline.

"Yeah, I'm good. We should really head back to the studio to finish the track," Emiline said. As she got up to follow Emiline inside the building, she scrolled down her phone and her eyes fell upon Vanessa's contact number. She had managed to mend one friendship and now it was time to mend another one.

After the studio session with Emiline, Andrea drove over to De'Von's apartment. She knocked on the door several times but nobody replied. She knocked again even harder.

"De'Von, it's Andrea. Come on, open up!" she exclaimed as De'Von looked through the door peephole. Andrea's testy eyes met his. Andrea saw on the other side through the peephole that De'Von was on the phone, which explained his late arrival at the door. He finally got the door opened.

"Damn, what took you so long to open the door for me?" she asked as they gave each other a hug and she kissed him on the cheek.

"Nothin' I was just on a call baby," he said.

"With who?" Andrea asked.

"It was actually Byron Caine, a movie producer who I'm cool wit," he replied. "He's tellin' me that based on the sales of my last album, there are talks to cast me in a movie next year," De'Von said excitedly.

"For real? That's what's up. You deserve that opportunity," she said. She was sincerely happy for De'Von. He had another EP release in two days and he could possibly be cast in a movie.

"Do you have any idea what the movie's, gonna be about?" she asked.

"Well the details are pretty dry right now, but once I get more details, I'm definitely puttin' you on," De'Von said. "Anyway, make yourself at home. I'll be right back, ok?" he confirmed to her.

Andrea sat down on the couch to wait for her boyfriend. When she sat down, she felt a vibration next to her. De'Von's cell phone was ringing. She looked at the caller ID on front of the phone. When she saw who was calling, she felt a stab of jealousy and anger. It was Miesha's name on the screen. Andrea just didn't understand. What did De'Von see in Miesha that he couldn't see in her? As soon as De'Von emerged from the bathroom, drying his washed face with a towel, Andrea stood in front of him, holding his phone.

"You mind explaining this?" she asked. De'Von looked at Andrea with a look that resembled a deer caught in headlights.

"What you talkin' about?" he asked.

"I'm talking about Miesha. She just tried to call you. Was she the one you've been talkin' to?" she asked.

"No, I told you I was on a business call," he replied but under Andrea's glare, he continued explaining his case. "Ok, the truth is Miesha's been blowin' up my phone lately. She's tryin' to get me to hang out with her or whatever but I haven't answered it. I told you, ain't nothin' goin' on wit me and her," he explained.

Andrea tried to look into his eyes to see if they were shifting, trying to avoid her own. But De'Von's gaze was intent and he looked sincere, so she decided he was telling the truth.

"Ok, De'Von, I'll take yo' word for it," she said.

"Cool, so what you plannin' on wearin' tomorrow night at my EP release party?" he asked teasingly. Andrea laughed. "Is it something that I could see through?" he asked slyly.

"It ain't none of yo' business, that's what it is," she answered. De'Von walked up to her, caressed her smooth face and put his hands on her hips.

"Maybe I should make it my business," he said before moving in for a kiss. De'Von's lips tasted so sweet to Andrea and he never rushed his display of affection. He took his time, which was what Andrea liked about him.

"I was gonna step out for a minute but plan's changed," he said, going over to the door to make sure it was closed. He didn't want an audience. Andrea laughed as they kissed each other on the way to the sweet seclusion of bedsheets and pillows.

The lights at Club Allure on Queens Boulevard illuminated the skies as musicians, artists, and celebrities made their way to support the release of DeVon's third EP. Photos were taken between the people of high status and regular music fans who were able to attend. Adia was busy signing autographs and taking pictures with countless. De'Von was dressed in a white suit, a black shirt that sported gold buttons, and he wore at least three gold chains. Adia wore a half-white half-black dress with a sheer slit cut on the side to compliment her boyfriend who was the reason for the occasion. Her hair dressers had done an exceptional job designing Adia's hair and as Adia walked with De'Von signing autographs, he said, "Damn you look fine. "I might have to wife you one day," he whispered in her ear.

Andrea couldn't imagine why he would want to marry anyone other than her. Andrea had managed to invite Vanessa to the party. She called Vanessa and reconciled with her. She completely understood why Vanessa was angry at her too. Where old wounds were still open, the healing process had begun. Andrea was happy to have her best friend by her side once more. Vanessa wore a short blue sequined dress that showed off her long legs and an enormous smile on her face.

"Girl, this party is turnt up. I think I see Bobby waving at me. How I look?" she asked Andrea.

"Girl you look hot. Be careful who you take home, now," she said, laughing.

"Shut up!" Vanessa replied, laughing. "I'm comin' back, I'm bout to go use the restroom," she told Andrea and she walked to the ladies' room, unaware that someone was following her.

A few minutes later, Vanessa stepped out of the stall to wash her hands when she was suddenly confronted by Slam. Judging from his hazy eyes and unfocused expression, Vanessa knew he was drunk.

"Slam, what the hell are you doing in hea'? You know this is a female bathroom, right?" she asked in an alarmed voice.

"What's up baby? Long time no see," Slam replied in his laid-back bravado. He didn't seem to care one bit that he was in the ladies' room. "You've been playin' hard to get since I first met you," he added, taking a step towards Vanessa.

Vanessa now was more than a little alarmed, she was sure Slam was losing his mind from the red in his eyes to the way he was attempting to grab her.

"Look, I don't know what you're playin' at, but you betta' get out of hea now," she said.

"Nah, nah,nah, I ain't goin' nowhere till I get what I came for," Slam replied. "De'Von look like he havin' fun out there wit' his girl right now, so I'm guessing I can have fun wit' her sexy friend," he said.

Vanessa tried to maneuver her way around Slam but to no avail. Slam's frame blocked her path to the door.

"You're sick, you know that?" she said angrily.

Slam suddenly grabbed her with such force as she struggled against his tight grasp. "How am I the sick one, sweetheart? De'Von got everything, nice big house, money, women, and commercial deals wit' his music. What do I got? I ain't got nothin' but his scraps, year after year. His deal should be my deal. His money should be my money. Why you think De'Von and yo' girl ain't gettin' as much money as they expected from Metro? You wanna know why? Cuz, I'm callin da shots, all the money goin' to me," he added and Vanessa, for the first time saw who Slam really was; a jealous maniacal psychopath who had been riding De'Von's coattails to the top for years. He was supposed to be De'Von's best friend but he had really only been looking out for himself.

"I hooked up my own bank account with De'Von's and whatever he gets, I take about sixy percent of it all. I get my money in cash and I do what he was supposed to do; give back to the Bronx and help other cats get theirs," Slam added.

"So you've been pretending to be his friend, just so you can get yo' cut?" Vanessa asked. "I always knew you was triflin,'" she added.

"Damn girl, you make it sound like a bad thing," Slam said, amused. "Check it out, nothin' personal, but it's just business. Ain't no friends in this industry. It's all about da green, baby. Oh and by the way, you can call me the dude formerly known as Slam. My name's actually Tony Wadell," he said, laughing insanely.

Vanessa backed away from who she was sure was a madman. She tried to sneak past Tony, but he grabbed her forcefully and thrust his lips against hers. She slapped his face in retaliation, but she would soon realize it would cost her. He slapped her back even harder. Vanessa fell back and she could taste the blood in her mouth. He grabbed both of her arms violently and slammed her against the wall near the back stall. Vanessa's head jerked back from the force and hit the wall. Reeling in pain, her sight became blurry, and she slumped down, unable to fight off the monster who was now lying on top of her, taking full advantage of her vulnerability. She felt her dress go up and her underwear was being slid down her legs. Alone, helpless and defenseless, Vanessa succumbed to the forceful entry of her attacker.

Andrea and De'Von mingled with party guests, danced and partied for most of the evening, unaware that their friends were involved in such a violent ordeal. After twenty minutes, Tony walked out of the bathroom, still stumbling from the effects of being enebriated. He walked up to De'Von.

"Ayo, man I'm wiped. That last drink got to me. I'm bout to dip out of hea' ight?" he said.

"'Ight, man. Get some sleep homie. Your head gon' be bangin' in da mornin'" DeVon said laughing.

"I know," Tony replied before leaving the nightclub. Andrea, although enjoying herself, was beginning to worry. Vanessa had not emerged from the restroom. She excused herself and went to the restroom to check on her friend. She opened the door but couldn't see anyone.

"Vanessa, you ok?" she asked.

Small sobs were heard from the back stall. Andrea ran over to the stall and saw Vanessa crumpled on the floor. Her dress was disheveled, she had small cuts and welts on her arms and legs, her makeup was smeared, and her panties were lying on the ground beside her. It was obvious that her best friend had been raped.

"Oh my God, what happened?" she asked. Vanessa looked at Andrea's face, her eyes reflecting the horror that had so recently been inflicted upon her.

"You weren't hea'," she said, crying. Andrea hugged her best friend. "You weren't hea'...." she repeated.

"I'm here now, girl. I'm here," Andrea replied, tears streaming down her face as she attempted to comfort Vanessa. After a few minutes, they walked out of the restroom. Walking over to De'Von, she said, "Hey baby, I gotta go. I gotta take Vanessa to the hospital. Someone attacked her tonight," she said while still holding Vanessa's hand.

De'Von saw Vanessa and he was stunned. "Who did that to her?" he asked.

"I don't know. She didn't tell me. But I'm gonna find out," she said before walking to the exit. Before she could leave, the club bouncer walked up to her.

"Adia? This young man came up to me, asking for you. Says he wants an autograph from you and that he knows you personally. Do you know this guy?" he asked.

"What guy?" Andrea asked, clearly distracted by Vanessa's ordeal. The bouncer stepped aside and Andrea looked and saw that it was Sean Hawkins.

Chapter Twenty-one

Andrea looked into the eyes of her oldest friend, with whom she had not spoken to in nearly a year. She smiled at him, which relieved Sean, who knew he was not going to be thrown out by the bouncer.

"It's ok, he's wit' me," she confirmed, and the bouncer moved his wide frame aside so Sean could enter the club.

"Yo' Drea I gotta holla at you right quick about something…." he started to say before he noticed Vanessa's condition.

"It's gon' have to wait, Sean. I gotta take 'Nessa to the ER. Someone attacked her tonight, and she hasn't told me who did it yet," Andrea replied.

Sean's concern for himself suddenly took a backseat to the situation in which he was confronted. He focused solely on helping Andrea and Vanessa.

"Damn. Should I call 9-1-1?" Sean asked. Andrea looked at Vanessa for confirmation. Vanessa knew who had attacked her and she feared implicating the perpetrator due to the strong possibility of retaliation. Andrea did manage to talk Vanessa into going to urgent care and filing a report to the police for the case. Sean headed out of the club and followed Andrea as she drove her friend to Queens Hospital Center in Parsons.

Not this hospital again, she thought. This was the place where her world had crashed down around her seven years ago upon hearing the news that her best friend and sister had died. If a piece of her heart had been left anywhere, it had been left in the waiting room at Queens Hospital Center. Surrounded by two of her bodyguards, Andrea walked into the hospital after parking the car. Strangers gathered around surrounded her, interested only in Adia. To them held the hand of some random girl. Many of the kids wanted autographs but Andrea refused since her only concern was getting her friend attended to by a doctor.

After a thorough examination by the doctors, Andrea and Sean were grateful that the wounds on Vanessa's body were superficial and were treated immediately. However, the doctor stated that since Vanessa had been the victim of rape, the psychological damage could affect Vanessa for years. As they waited outside the room for the police to take her statement, Vanessa, finally broke her silence about her attacker. She explained how Slam deliberately walked into the girl's room and looked as though he had been drinking. She also explained the confession Slam had made to her before he assaulted her. Andrea listened and with every vivid detail of the attack, she grew sicker and sicker by the minute. By the time Vanessa finished recounting her story, Andrea stood up, her eyes filled with fire. She tried to make amends with Vanessa after she had left for her tour and she believed she had been on the right track until this horrible event. She wished she had thought to check the restroom sooner and gotten De'Von who would have no doubt confronted his friend.

"Does De'Von know what kind of snake he has hangin' with him?" Andrea asked.

"No, he doesn't know. He's using him, Drea and he's been taking money from him and from you too," Vanessa replied.

While she waited for the police to file a report, Andrea turned to Sean. "So what is this about an autograph that you wanted from me?" she asked him. Sean looked at Andrea straight in the face.

"Yeah, you know. My friend Andrea is doin' it big and I wanted to show my roommates that I know you," he said.

"So you want my autograph to show off to some other men in the dorm room? You ain't tryin' to make money off me, aren't you?" Andrea asked, her eyebrow slightly raised.

"Nah, nothin' like that," Sean lied.

"So why do you need my autograph for? We were cool before all this happened and we still gonna be cool when it's all over wit'," Andrea replied.

"Look, I just need the autograph ok?!!" Sean exclaimed loudly. A couple of the doctors, who were passing by looked at the raised voices. Andrea turned to the doctors.

"Everything's fine," she said to them, and they continued walking. The bodyguards stood nearby. "What's wrong, Sean?" Andrea said quietly. Sean proceeded to explain the visit from Vince at his school and how he acted as if he was a friend only to fool him into coming to his house and threatening him and his family if he didn't come up with the autograph.

"Vince? Are you talkin' bout that guy that cut classes and was arrested in tenth grade for some drug money?" she asked.

"Yeah that's him. He said if I don't come up wit the autograph and the money in a week, he gon' cap me," Sean explained.

Andrea puts her face in her hands. She couldn't believe what was happening. Life was beginning to spiral out of her control. First, the dispute about her financial situation at Metro had cost one of the best producers in the business his job. Then Vanessa had been attacked in the shadow of her celebrity and she hadn't been there to protect her. Now Sean had an impending death sentence on his head unless he could provide her autograph and a large sum of cash to a guy fresh out of jail. Life had become completely overwhelming for Andrea.

Does your dad know about this?" she asked.

"I didn't tell him, cuz Vince has guys all ova' da place. He's probably watching me now," Sean said. "Besides all this was because of my pops.

He was the one that arrested Vince and sent him off to juvey, and now he's takin' it out on me," Sean said. Then he stood up. "Listen, if you don't wanna help me, whateva. I just gotta face it like a man," he said before Andrea stopped him.

"Wait, I got an idea," she said as she whispered her plans in his ear.

Early the following morning, Andrea went to Metro studios, her eyes narrow and focused. She was supposedly off for the day but she was going to confront Vanessa's attacker. As she stepped out of the elevator to the recording booths, she saw De'Von recording. Slam worked on the sound and bobbed his head like he usually did. Andrea strode past Michelle and Miesha, who watched the session and walked directly into the studio before Slam had a chance to say a word. Andrea slapped him squarely in the face as hard as she could, causing Slam to fall back against the speakers.

"That's for puttin' yo' slimy-ass hands on my friend, you sick excuse for a man!" she yelled.

Michelle, Paul, and De'Von did their best to separate Andrea from Slam. Slam got up from the speaker set he had fallen on during the confrontation. Andrea could see a red mark across his cheek and the bridge of his nose where she had struck him.

"I don't know what the hell you talkin' 'bout, bitch," he replied. The statement set De'Von off and he stepped up to Slam. Both men were almost nose to nose.

"What did you say?" De'Von asked. "Slam, you my boy but if you call her a bitch again, I'ma whup yo' ass," he warned.

"He ain't yo' boy!" Andrea shouted, still being held back by Michelle and Paul. "All this time, he's been playin' you. He takes yo' money after tours and he raped my best friend," she added.

The effect was instantaneous after Andrea made those shocking confessions. De'Von's face reverted from anger to confusion. He had clearly been caught in the middle. Andrea was his girlfriend and they had been dating for almost a year, but Slam had been by his side since before first signed with Metro, which had been four years ago. He didn't want to believe his best friend had been stealing from him. He turned to Slam, who was rubbing the spot where Andrea hit him.

"Is that true?" he asked.

"His name ain't even Slam!" Andrea shouted.

At this, all the artists and sound engineers looked at Andrea, as if they couldn't believe what she had just said. Then they turned to Slam, who at this time starting laughing smugly.

"You mind tellin me what's so funny? Did you rape Vanessa?" De'Von asked angrily. Slam shook his head, laughing hysterically.

"This is funny though. You got this broke-ass ho' comin' into this label because she won some talent show and after a few million dollars, she think she God. So she starts spewin' random stuff cuz she crazy like that. As far as Vanessa goes, we were both drunk and one thing led to another. You know how it be," Slam said. "Who you gon' believe?" he asked De'Von.

De'Von looked between Andrea and Slam. "Go ahead Slam. Tell 'em what yo' real name is," Andrea demanded, fearing that De'Von wouldn't believe her and would side with his main man. Instead, De'Von looked back at Slam for an answer.

"You heard the lady. What yo' real name, nigga?" he asked Slam furiously. Slam threw his hands up, as if to suggest that he surrendered but he wasn't going down without a fight.

"All right, the truth is what you want right?" he asked. "You want truth? Aight, hea's da truth. Yeah my name ain't Slam. It's Tony Wadell, 'ight? I'm from the same block in East Tremont like you. I knew yo' brother and I seen you two perform and I knew once he passed, you were gonna drive yoself to make it, and you did. But then, you forgot about the block," Tony said. "You forgot where you came from and you forgot who the hell put you on. So I talked you into sharing an account and did I take a few dollas? Yeah, I did, but I only did it to give other peeps from da hood the same chance you got. I had to sit through your prima donna attitude and do all that rich shit because you did it," he added.

De'Von's eyes widened, and he shook his head solemnly. Andrea knew that he was blaming himself for not seeing through Tony's façade.

"So all this time, you played me?" he asked. Tony laughed even more once the realization of the truth dawned on De'Von.

"Like a Gameboy, man. You know what else? Since we on a truth-tellin' flow, maybe it's time for me to spill a lil truth to your lil side ho' right hea'" he said gleefully, pointing to Andrea.

"Who you callin' a side ho'?!" Andrea shouted. "In case you ain't notice, I'm his girl," she added.

"That ain't da way Miesha sees it, right?" Tony said. Andrea turned around to Miesha, who stood outside the booth. She had walked in when the whole confrontation had started and remained quiet, not wanting to bring attention to herself.

"What the hell are you talkin' about?" Andrea asked. Clearly Slam, or Tony, was losing his mind every minute.

"Tell 'em dog," he said to De'Von, who suddenly turned pale and very silent. "Tell 'em how you was doin' Miesha behind yo' girl's back. Tell 'em bout the session last week when Miesha stopped by yo' crib that night and didn't leave till eight in da mornin'." Tony said.

While Tony was confessing all of De'Von's transgressions, the elevator doors opened and two NYPD officers walked out and made their way to the studio. Andrea looked at De'Von, hoping he would deny what Tony had said but De'Von simply hung his head in guilt. Andrea knew that De'Von wouldn't say anything in his defense.

"Is that true, Dev?" she asked him.

"Yeah, it's true," De'Von started to explain but Andrea decided not to hear any more. She walked out of the booth at the same time that the officers entered.

"There's yo' man, officers," she said, pointing to Tony. Then she turned to De'Von. "It's over," she said, before walking out out of the booth. The officers arrested Tony on counts of assault and battery but the real damage had already been done. As they handcuffed Tony and walked him out of the building, De'Von followed Andrea out the door.

"Look Drea, I'm sorry. I ain't mean to hurt you. It was just one night and all the old feelings came back. I was gon' tell you, but…." he explained but Andrea cut him off.

"But what?" Andrea asked angrily. "You slept wit' yo' ex and you didn't tell me shit. So now you expect me to take it like it's ok? You can have her back now," she said walking out. She passed Miesha and expected to see a smug reaction on her face, as if to blatantly say the best woman had won but she also wore a face of sorrow and regret.

"I hope you and De'Von are happy together hea. Sorry I came and messed things up for you two. I guess I was just sloppy seconds," she said, before walking out the door.

De'Von tried to call her back and apologize but Andrea was already in her car and she was driving away from the Metro building. As she angrily brushed a tear away from her eye, she thought about how Julio had said they were a family but once De'Von slept around and Tony stole money from his own label, she realized how right Emiline had really been. They could no longer be a family and this was a business that she no longer wanted to be a part of in any way. De'Von watched from front of the building as Andrea drove off.

Vince and two of his friends waited outside their home, talking excitedly to themselves. Sean had just called Vince and informed him that he had the stuff he wanted. Vince was beside himself with the joy of retribution. That boy worked quickly, he thought as he waited on the front porch with Pete and Drew. Finally, they saw Sean as he walked around the corner and greeted them as soon as they came within sight. A generic white car pulled up next to Vince's residence. Vince didn't think twice about the car because after all, it was a public street and many cars drove by or stopped and parked. The windows were tinted so they couldn't see the driver.

"So, you got what I asked for, boy?" Vince asked, while Pete and Drew chuckled softly. Sean scratched the back of his head sheepishly.

"Well, I actually don't have the autograph that you asked for," he replied. The smiles and jovial grins disappeared and Vince felt his anger rise. He could not believe the nerve of this guy who had strolled up to him at his home and not met his demands.

"What did you say?" he asked as he reached into his pocket for his gun. Sean surprisingly showed no fear like he had the last time he had been threatened. "You just wasted our time, kid. Now you gonna pay for that, permanently." Vince said grimly.

"You didn't let me finish," Sean said.

"Ain't nothin' to finish. I asked you for two simple things and you couldn't do it. I hope you bulletproof, dog," Vince replied but Sean put his hand up to stop the imminent threat to him.

"What I meant to say was I don't have the autographed CD with me but here's someone who does have it," he said, walking over to the white car, which had parked less than a foot away from the residence. Sean opened the passenger seat and out stepped Adia. Pete and Drew nodded at each other excitedly.

"Hello Vince," Adia said in her most flattering voice. She wore her best Givenchy outfit with designer shades and shoes.

"What's up Adia? Long time, no see. High school, I think," he said.

"I know. So I heard you want an autographed CD and some cash, is that right?" she asked. Vince smiled and put his gun away in his pocket.

"Yeah, if you don't mind. I'm just a big fan of your music and I wanted to get your next CD and Sean also had a business arrangement with me," he replied.

"Yeah, I heard about that too. I actually got the money and the signed CD inside the car. Your car," she said, throwing the keys over to Vince and both of his friends looked at the keys to the new car that was given to him. "Look in the backseat, and you'll see the signed CD and the nine hundred dollars in a small envelope," she said.

Vince was ecstatic, because not only had he gotten the signed CD and the money, but he also got another car. It was a new model, which made his old car look like a boxcar.

"Let's check it out, man," Vince said and they all walked over to the back of the car and opened the backseat door. Just as Adia promised, there was signed CD and an envelope which Vince assumed was the money. They also saw some far less pleasant items; a badge and two blue shirts and hats that read, "New York Police Department."

"What the hell?" Vince asked as he realized his blunder.

"Nice to meet you again, Vince," Officer Hawkins said stepping out of the car. Pete and Drew started backing away from the car, looking around as if they were deciding how to make a clean getaway. "So, threatening my boy with that weapon of yours? Sounds like assault with a deadly weapon to me," Offiver Hawkins said.

Sean grinned widely as he saw the look on Vince's face. It was the same confused expression that he wore when he had walked into Vince's trap earlier in the week. Now the shoe was on the other foot and Vince was the one who appeared shell-shocked.

"Tell yo' friends they betta' not even think about runnin," he warned, before reading him his Miranda rights and placing him under arrest. "I heard you're a fan of Adia. Don't worry, I'll pop her CD in my car so you can listen on your way to the precinct," Officer Hawkins said. "I believe that belongs to me sir," he said to Vince, gesturing to the key that Adia had given him. Vince dropped the key and Officer Hawkins picked it up. "Trust me, where you're goin', you ain't gon' need a car anyhow," he said.

Sean and Adia laughed as the three perpetrators were arrested and driven over to the precinct. Vince glared his most venomous glare at Sean and Adia. He knew this wasn't over and the first act on Vince's agenda would be to exact retribution, but Sean wasn't worried. As the white car drove away, Andrea turned to Sean.

"I guess he probably won't be a fan of my music for too long," she said as Sean laughed.

"I know right?" he said laughing. "Man, Drea. You really came through. I appreciate the backup. Thanks," he said. Andrea hugged her best friend.

"We're friends, no matter what. I know I messed up a lot but I'm tryin' to fix it," she promised.

"How you gon' do that?" Sean asked. "Rumor has it that Metro's been rippin' you off and you thinkin' about leaving," he added.

"Well I gotta do something," she said.

"I feel you," Sean said. "Hows Vanessa doing?" he asked.

"She's hangin' in there. Tryin' to take it one step at a time, you know," Andrea replied, hoping that her friend hadn't been traumatized beyond repair by the incident.

It was blatantly obvious to Andrea that the atmosphere at Metro Records would never the same after the ordeal between Tony Wadell, De'Von, and Andrea. The laid-back family atmosphere that had been so prevalent throughout the studio had been replaced with a quiet awkwardness. The remaining artists still went to work every day and continued to record their albums, except for De'Von. He had mysteriously disappeared from work since the fallout between him and his supposed friend, as well as the revelation about one night he had with Miesha that had destroyed his relationship with Andrea. Days passed and there was still no sign of De'Von. Andrea and Emiline were able to finish the song they had been recording together and were waiting for the results. Andrea still signed autographs for fans and she was always happy to take pictures with them but she no longer had a desire to represent Metro Records. Despite the many times she had appealed to Mr. Morgan for a new contract, Mr Morgan kept avoiding it. She felt more alone than ever with De'Von gone and Vanessa still going to the hospital to check on the injuries she had sustained from her attack. Emiline remained her friend and she often spoke with one of the hired backup dancers, Susan, who always listened to her patiently whenever Andrea had the need to vent her emotions. Andrea expressed her desire to leave Metro to Susan who agreed wholeheartedly to follow Andrea out of Metro whenever she decided to move. One day, while at the studio testing sounds and playing back her song with Emiline, Craig walked in.

"Hey, Adia. How've you been?" he asked. Andrea shrugged her shoulders.

"All right, I guess," she replied with a cold indifference.

She had never spoken to Craig in that manner before because Craig had been one of the few people who had been on her side when it came to re-negotiating her contract, as Julio had been. But Craig was always busy searching new talent or kept himself alone in his office the rest of the time. Andrea guessed that Mr. Morgan purposely kept him occupied because he knew that Craig sided with Andrea for an improved contract and the more, he kept them apart, the more he could prevent any type of mutiny among the other artists.

"Listen Andrea, I know you're still fed up about not getting a better deal and I know you've been going through personal things too," he said. Andrea guessed by 'personal things', he meant her relationship with De'Von. "Anyway, I wanted to let you know that I'm still on your side and I want what's best for you but you gotta do what's best for you too. So whatever you decide, I'm behind you one hundred percent," Craig added.

"Thanks Craig," Andrea replied. She wondered if that was all Craig had come to tell her. But she realized Craig had more to say.

"I checked with De'Von's family. They tried calling him and they couldn't reach him. Sources around him are saying that he's going through a really rough time right now," he said.

"And that's my problem because?" Andrea asked disdainfully. Craig shook his head.

"You don't understand Andrea. De'Von's own mother said that whenever De'Von was stressed, sad, angry, or upset, he would withdraw to himself and wouldn't talk to anybody or eat anything," Craig said. "It's like he goes into a depressive state. He went through that for weeks after his brother passed," he added. Andrea had enough. She had problems of her own and she didn't feel like hearing De'Von's sob story.

"Look Craig, I understand. But it ain't none of my business. We broke up cuz he was seein' his ex behind my back. How do you think that makes me feel?" she asked.

"Look, I'm not makin' excuses for him. He messed up and he gotta own up to that. I get it. But imagine losing a lover and a best friend in the same day, not to mention record sales plummeting for him. His songs on his new EP are not even hittin' the billboards," Craig explained.

"What can I do about that?" Andrea asked.

"You could talk to him. I'm not saying that ya could patch it up. But right now, he needs a friend, and he needs someone to talk to, so I'm asking you, please talk to him before he throws his whole career away," he replied.

Andrea glared at Craig. He couldn't be serious. What would her talking to De'Von accomplish? But she remembered when they had been on tour for the first time and at a sad moment when she had felt totally alone, he had sat next to her on the bus and spoken candidly with her. She knew with that on her conscious, she couldn't let De'Von drown in his depression.

"All right, I'll talk to him. But knowing me, I might make things worse," she said.

Andrea went to De'Von's penthouse and knocked on the door but nobody answered. She tried knocking his door again. There was still no reply or response.

"De'Von c'mon, I know you in there," she said.

She didn't know what led her to do so but she turned the doorknob and the door opened. De'Von never left his door unlocked; he was very sensitive about his security and privacy. As Andrea walked into the suite, she saw the dining room and kitchen were a complete mess. It was as if a tornado had swept through the whole suite. Liquor bottles,beer cans, pizza boxes, and little joints with blackened tips littered the room. The mess showed Andrea that De'Von held plenty of private parties and had been doing a lot of drinking, eating, and smoking weed. The messy trail led to a space where his bedroom was located. Andrea was certainly no stranger to his bedroom. She walked in and there she saw her ex-boyfriend, slumped in a corner. His hair had grown and it was disheveled. He had a five o'clock shadow around his face and judging by a curved tube and a bag of white powder in the corner of his bed, he had been freebasing. This was the worst condition Andrea had ever seen De'Von in. She internally reminisced about the days before Metro when she had borrowed a De'Von CD from Vanessa and she had seen his fresh face, great smile, and youthful exubererance. That image stood in great contrast to the pitiful being she saw in front of her. Andrea walked over to him – as close as she could get due to pungent odor in the air. Apparently De'Von had not bathed in days either.

"De'Von, get up, c'mon man. I can't see you like this," Andrea said. De'Von's eyes, which were staring at the wall, as if hypnotized, found their way over to Andrea.

"What you doin' hea'?" he asked in low tones.

"De'Von, we haven't seen you in days. Look I know you tore up cuz of what went down between Tony and us but you gotta shake it off, cuz they miss you over there at Metro," Andrea said.

"Miss me?" De'Von asked. "Man, nobody misses me. I mean, how could everything that was goin' so good, end up like this? I mean, homeboys comin' from da block, actin' like like they was my friends, when they were really using me," he added and Andrea knew that he was alluding to Tony, who now faced two counts of assault and battery charges and one count of embezzlement. Once Metro had found out that he was stealing money from them, they had filed their own lawsuit against Tony.

"Then I lost you," he continued. "I really wanted it to work between us. Go out together, see the world, make money, and just chill. But Miesha came back and as hard as I tried to resist her, she made it impossible," De'Von explained and Andrea had the sudden urge to stand up and walk away because she didn't really want to hear about De'Von's infidelity. However, she decided that De'Von had no one to turn to, so she stayed.

"Miesha came by one day and we were watching movies, laughing, and crackin' jokes like old times. Then we came back and even though I tried to stop it, we couldn't hold back on each other. Next thing, I know, her lips was on mine and one thing led to another," he said.

Andrea looked away from De'Von. She felt the familiar pang of jealousy and anger she had felt when she first heard the story through Tony's lips. She managed to calm herself down and reminded herself that it was over and she had her own career to think about.

"So, do you love her?" she asked De'Von. The disgraced rapper straightened himself and with a groan, got himself off the floor.

"She's very important in my life. I do have feelins' for her," he admitted.

"That's what I thought," Andrea said, more harshly than she had planned. Taking it as her cue to walk out, De'Von tried to stop her.

"But I love you, though. When I met you at the store that day, there was something real about you and I knew I wanted to share whatever that was," De'Von said. Andrea closed her eyes and laughed as she recalled the first meeting between them at Johnson's when he was looking for the Flights.

"Yeah, I remember. I remember when you also said that you were too big to handle," she said and De'Von laughed. Andrea was relieved. It was good to see De'Von crack a smile.

"Yeah, me and Slam. We were like a duo together. He was my boy, then I found out that he really wasn't my boy at all," he said.

"De'Von, you gotta forget about that guy. He played you. I don't agree with what he did, but I saw why he did you dirty," she said.

De'Von looked at her with a disparaging look in his eyes.

"What are you sayin'? So you agree wit' him takin' money from me?" he asked. Andrea shook her head.

"That ain't what I'm sayin'. I'm sayin' that sometimes you got to look around and realize you got it made. But there are other cats on the same block, another lil' De'Von waiting for his chance but he can't afford it. Sometimes you got to give back to yo' community," she said. De'Von thought about what Andrea said for a moment.

"You're right. It's crazy, cuz Mason always said that when he made it, he was gon' leave the Bronx behind, to get my Mama outta there, all that. I guess I was tryin' so hard to get da hell out of there too. It's almost like I was tryin' to live for my brother," he said.

Andrea understood what De'Von was saying, because she felt the same way about Loree.

"Anyway, I gotta go," Andrea said, heading for the front door.

"Do you think things are gon' get betta' between us?" De'Von asked.

"I don't know," Andrea replied. "I think we need to give each other a bit of time, you know. Maybe we should just focus on our careers," she said as she walked out of his suite.

Andrea was back in the studio, running playback on the song she had done with Emiline. It was a song with powerful lyrics about sisters staying together and having fun together. Andrea very much would have liked to have done a music video for the song but Metro and BHR were still concerned about their feud and their public image and were both advised that doing a music video would only spark tension between the two labels. As she was replaying the song, Paul came into the booth.

"Hey Adia, what's up?" he greeted.

"What's up?" she greeted back. Paul was normally in good spirits, but he sounded distressed.

"You ok? What's going on?" Andrea asked.

Paul shook his head. "I was on the lobby, checkin' my phone when I got in and I got an alert from Music News online that I couldn't believe," he said.

"What alert?" Andrea asked. Paul sighed deeply before replying.

"It's about Queen Sheba. She was found unconscious in her bathroom this morning. She's at Northshore Hospital," he said.

Chapter Twenty-two

Andrea drove to Northshore Hospital in Long Island as fast as she could. She probably went over the speed limit a few times on her way there but she didn't notice and didn't care. When Paul had broken the news to her, she almost blacked out herself. It was like a hideous deja-vu from seven years ago, when she had been told that Loree was in the hospital. She took two of her bodyguards and they accompanied her inside the hospital after she parked her car. As soon as she stepped inside the doors, she groaned. There were twenty members of the media already inside and the moment she stepped inside, cameras started flashing and reporters began trying desperately to ask her questions.

"So Adia, when you heard about Queen's condition, what was your reaction?" one of them asked.

"Do you think the members of BHR would let you visit her given your past feuds?" another one asked.

"Listen, please no questions," Andrea replied as she frantically made her way through the throng of reporters in the lobby to get to the receptionist.

"Quite a circus, huh?" the receptionist asked as Andrea reached the desk.

"Tell me about it. What room is Queen in?" she asked. The receptionist gave her a pass.

"She's in room 0128," she replied. She pointed in the direction of the room, which was down the hall. Andrea walked down the long corridor to the room. One of BHR's bodyguards guarded the doorway and folded his arms almost defiantly, as if he would not allow Andrea to enter the room.

"Look, I'm a friend of Emiline. Please let me in, I gotta see her," Andrea asked.

The bodyguard just stood with a stoic expression and Andrea thought she had failed in her attempt at convincing him to let her in the room. Then he suddenly stepped aside and gestured to the door.

"Thank you," Andrea said, and she opened the door.

She saw Tico and another artist she'd never met before but had seen on music videos in the past. Andrea remembered her name, which was Ruby D. and that she was a female rapper with BHR. As soon as she saw Andrea she stood up from her chair across from the Emiline's bed.

"What's Metro doin' hea'?" she asked harshly. She started to walk toward Andrea but one of Andrea's bodyguards who walked in with her, stepped in front of Andrea to prevent any physical altercation.

"I'm here to visit my friend," Andrea replied.

"Your friend?" Ruby replied.

"Let her stay," a weak voice replied and Andrea realized that it was Emiline. Upon hearing the voice of her fellow label mate, Ruby slowly walked back to her seat. Andrea walked up to the bed.

"Hey honey, are you ok?" she asked, stroking the top of her head.

"Oh yeah, I'm fine. You already know da Queen will be back in full effect soon," Emiline replied.

Andrea laughed as a small tear rolled down her cheek. It was great that Emiline still kept her bright personality despite the circumstances. Andrea could see the pain in Emiline's eyes.

"I got this rare lung disease, or so they say," she whispered matter of factly, and Andrea put her hands over her mouth. She knew that a condition of that magnitude could not only end her career but could evolve into a life-threatening situation. Andrea looked at all the tubes going into Emiline. She couldn't bear seeing her this way.

"You know, I've been goin' over that song that we worked on and I think we got a real hit," she said.

"I know we got a real hit," Emiline corrected. "Our vocals go well together. I don't know why we don't collaborate more often," she said.

"I know that's right," Andrea agreed.

"Just remember, I could still sing yo' ass out of the studio," Emiline said, laughing feebly.

"Whatever. You know I got skills," Andrea replied laughing as well. The mood soon became serious after the exchange.

"You know, I was thinking about what you said. You know, leaving Metro and do my own music," Andrea said. Emiline lowered her gaze.

"I'm sorry I told told you that. I know they're like family to you and it was rude of me to interfere in that," she said.

"But you made sense. Some stuff went down over there, and now I don't even know who to trust. It don't feel like family anymore," Andrea admitted.

The nurse abruptly ended the conversation by telling all visitors to leave so she could administer some medication for Emiline. Andrea promised Emiline she would visit her daily before leaving the room. Walking outside into the waiting room, Andrea saw Emiline's family who were waiting for updates on her condition. Andrea suddenly flashed back to her own family in the waiting room at Queens Hospital sitting with Shania, waiting for news. She saw herself as the same misty-eyed twelve-year-old who held onto the hope that somehow her sister would survive and then remembered when reality had set in. Shania had taken the loss hard and Andrea remembered how she had run for seven miles, while she cried as hard as she ever cried before. Andrea now began to reflect on her music career. Was it worth it? Was her going to countless recordings in the studio booth, signing autographs, doing concerts all across the country, was it all worth it? Life had been much simpler when she had been able to grieve on her own and nobody knew her name.

Now that she was worth over two million dollars she could probably feed every child in the hood but her life had become complicated. She had complex relationships and had been spoiled by the lavish lifestyle she had been living in for the past year. Her parents continually tried to convince her to go to college and initially she had wanted to do just that. Then she had been corrupted by the music industry. Andrea drove home and she looked for her keys to unlock the front door but she was shocked to find that her front door was unlocked. Her eyes became wide open with alert, as she reached into her purse to take out her mase. Who would know where she lived and how would they be able to enter her house? As soon as she entered her living room, she saw someone sitting on her couch, and it was the last person she ever expected to see in her home.

"How are you doing, Ms. Adia?" Pastor Whitefield said with a huge jovial grin upon his round face.

"Pastor Whitefield, I ain't expect to see you here," Andrea said. Pastor Whitefield laughed.

"If I could just take a picture of your reaction right now, it would be a priceless suvenir for me," he replied.

"How did you find out where I lived?" Andrea asked suspiciously.

"I spoke with your parents and they said you livin' out here in the 'burbs now. So I see you've moved on up, like the Jeffersons," he replied, looking around. "You know, you should really remember to lock your doors, sister," he added.

"And you should really learn how to call before showing up," Andrea retaliated, before she instantly regretted what she said. "I'm sorry, pastor," she apologized. "I'm just going through a lot right now and the last thing I wanna do is drag Mama and Daddy and you into this," she said.

"I know, sister. It's all over the music news and the magazines. Adia's in financial disputes with Metro Records. Adia is working with rival label. Adia caught in love triangles," the pastor reeled off.

"So you know, huh?" Andrea asked.

"Well, we all know what Adia's going through. Does anybody know what Andrea's going through?" the pastor asked.

Andrea didn't understand what the pastor was asking. She knew that during his sermons he had the ability to speak in second and third person to make references to his messages and conclusions drawn from the Bible.

"I don't know pastor. Even I don't know what Andrea's going through," she admitted, sitting in the small couch across from Pastor Whitefield.

"Your parents were starting to worry about you. They've stated that at times they called you and you haven't answered. You've been moody and sullen as of late and you haven't given a thought about life after music," he said.

"They told you all of that?" Andrea asked.

"Oh, that's just the tip of the iceberg. Trust me, there were more things they told me but all the same, they wanted me to pay you a visit," he replied.

"Well you've already let yourself in," Andrea said. She stood up and walked to the window. Looking outside she said, "Pastor, I never thought in my wildest dreams that I would be here, living like this. Being an R&B star that people listen and look up to. I've worked so hard to get what I want. This is supposed to be what I wanted, right?" she asked.

"Not if it's tearing you apart inside," Pastor Whitefield replied.

Andrea hated to admit it right away, but she knew the pastor was speaking the truth. One of her friends was lying in a hospital bed and another friend had his life threatened solely because of his association with her. Her best friend had been raped by a man who wasn't even the person he claimed to be. Her boyfriend had cheated on her so she had dumped him, only to see him going through a horrible downward spiral.

"I don't know if I want this anymore, pastor," she said.

"You always have a way out of this," Pastor Whitefield said. "It's time to stop feeding your flesh and it's time to start feeding your soul," he continued.

"But the people want Adia. The sexy R&B princess," she said.

"But is being Adia, the sexy R&B princess, fulfilling to you?" the pastor asked.

"No it isn't. But I can't give it up now. This is what I do. I gotta fight through this and keep going," she said. Pastor Whitefield stood up from the couch and looked directly at Andrea.

"I remember your sister, Andrea," he said. "I remember how full of life she was and I remember her selflessness and her compassion for her family," he said.

"What's your point?" Andrea asked. The pastor continued, as though he hadn't heard Andrea interrupt him.

"But I also remember her struggles. I remember when she tried so hard to be someone she wasn't. She had a void that needed to be filled inside and the void was self-acceptance. She never was comfortable with what she was involved with and who she was involved with. She was mired in self-conflict with and eventually it cost her," he said.

Andrea, still looking out the window, began recalling the testimonies on the witness stand in court the day those revelations had been made that Loree was involved with gang members but eventually sought a way out for herself and for others. She remembered the shock that went through the courtroom when it had been discovered that Loree had been living a double life in her final days. Looking at her own life, Andrea saw that she had been living through Adia all this time and she forgot the essence of who Andrea really was in her soul. Her soul had a void, perhaps the same void that her late sister had.

"You know pastor, I only told my therapist this but I had a dream that Loree came to me and she told me not to lose myself," she said.

"Mmmhmmm. And what did you take from her warning?" Do you think she knew what you would be going through right this moment?" he asked.

"It's hard to say," Andrea said, not wanting to sound crazy for thinking her sister may have spoken to her from the grave.

"Maybe she's telling you not to forsake yourself for the sake of others," Pastor Whitefield said. "What shall it profit a man if he gains the whole world and loses his own soul? That's found in the Gospel of Matthew, chapter sixteen verse twenty-six," the pastor said. He stood up and shook Andrea's hand. "I pray that you find peace in the Lord, sister and when you do, listen to His voice and what He's truly calling you to do," he said and silently made his way to the front door.

"Pastor Whitefield," Andrea called. The pastor turned around.

"Yes, sister?" he replied. But Andrea was at a loss for words at that moment. Then she rushed forward and hugged him.

"Thank you, for everything," she said.

"You're welcome. You have a wonderful day," the pastor said as he left. Andrea closed the door, very positive of the next move that she wanted to do.

The very next day after her encounter with Pastor Whitefield, Andrea walked to the Metro Records building. Her eyes were burning with intent about what she wanted to accomplish. She walked past Bobby, who tried to greet her but she ignored him. She had one destination in mind and that was Mr. Morgan's office. Walking directly into his office without an appointment, she could see Mr. Morgan surrounded by at least five other executives and judging by the stunned looks on their faces, she knew she had interrupted a very important meeting.

"Adia! Here is my sexy vixen," Mr. Morgan greeted cheerfully. "What can I do for you today?" he asked. Andrea wasn't in the mood for pleasantries. She knew what she wanted to do.

"Mr. Morgan I came here to inform you that as of today, I'm resigning from Metro Records. I want a contract buyout and freedom to negotiate with other labels," she said. Mr. Morgan stood up from the table. His smile now dissipated, he looked at Andrea as if she was mentally insane.

"Adia, you are one of the most beautiful and compelling artists we have here. You're talking about leaving a multi-billion dollar label. To shop around would be foolish on your part because no label will pay you as much as we do," Mr. Morgan said.

"I don't care," Andrea replied fiercely. "I want out and if you even think about suing me, I will counter-sue for breach of contract and embezzlement," she added. With the other executives watching, Mr. Morgan walked over to Andrea.

"You were nothing when we discovered you. You wanna take a walk? Fine. But remember that I have access to the media and when they hear what an ungrateful little girl you are, you'll be lucky to find a mediocre label that'll sign yo' ass," he threatened.

"You think that scares me?" Andrea challenged. "You'll be lucky as hell to find another girl that can sing like me," she replied and with that, she left Metro Records for good.

It wasn't long before the news broke that Adia was no longer signed with Metro and many people on music media and news speculated that Adia would fall off the map and she would never reach star status again. Andrea didn't care how she looked to the media. She spent her days visiting Emiline in the hospital. Unfortunately her condition continued to deteriorate and Andrea almost couldn't believe how quickly her friend was fading away before her eyes. The doctors didn't give her much longer, but Andrea still prayed and held out hope.

Finally one day, Andrea came back to the hospital and when she asked to see Emiline again, the receptionist bit her lip and said, "I'm sorry, Adia. Emiline is no longer with us. She passed away this morning."

Those words, those very words struck Andrea like an arrow that pierced her heart. It was the very same feeling from the very day she prayed she would never have to relive. She walked inside the room anyway and saw the empty bed in which Emiline had once laid. Andrea sobbed as hard as she ever had in her life, clutching the sheets that had once kept her dying friend warm.

Chapter Twenty-three

 was laid to rest at Edward D. Lynch Funeral Home in Queens Boulevard. Scores of family members, friends, and others in the Haitian community attended the funeral. Emiline's younger brother, Vladamir, performed the eulogy and to the surprise of many, they chose Adia to sing a song at the funeral. It wasn't a big surprise to Andrea, as she had been approached by Vladamir and the rest of Emiline's family to ask Andrea to sing at the funeral. At first, Andrea was taken aback by the request. Emiline's family could have asked anyone to sing at her funeral. There were various artists at BHR that were more than qualified to sing at the Queen's funeral. But when her family insisted that Adia sing she agreed to do so out of the goodness of her heart because Emiline had been her friend and had so closely resembled an older sister more than anyone had been to Andrea, aside from Loree. While Andrea sang the beautiful a gospel song she suddenly broke out into the hook of the duet that she had made with her late friend.

Got my girl's back, no matter the cost/Try to play us both, you've already lost/We sing a different tune than all the rest/I got many friends but only one that's best.

As Andrea sang, she felt her voice crack and she paused for a moment. Silence and quiet sobs could be heard throughout the congregation that had gathered outside the funeral home. Tears rolled down Andrea's face as the congregation comforted her from their seats and encouraged her to keep singing. Gathering her strength as much as she could, Andrea found the motivation to finish the song. As soon as the song was over, the congregation rose up to clap their hands for the girl who had befriended their favorite daughter. When the funeral was over and the guests were leaving after paying their respects, Andrea turned to leave also, but she was stopped by Vladamir.

"I can't thank you enough for what you did for our family today," he said.

"Oh please, it was nothing," Andrea replied.

Vladamir sighed deeply, looking at the sky and the horizon. "Everything just happened so soon. One day, she's the house, joking around like she always does and on the other day, she's gone," Vladamir said. He was a year younger than Emiline but he was still older than Andrea. "Anyway I got something to give to you," he added as he took a small post-it stamp out of his pocket. "Before she passed, she wanted me to give you this," he said handing the paper to Andrea before going to greet other people.

Andrea looked at the small stamp in her hand. On it was the phone number for another record company that promoted gospel artists by the name of Omega Studios. Andrea was confused, until she learned that this was the recording studio Emiline had wanted to sign with onced she finished her contract with BHR. It was as if Emiline was passing the baton to her to continue her dreams. She saw the address and the phone number for the company. She decided to call them immediately to set up a meeting with the local execs. She went into the meeting and she was astounded by how welcoming they were. From the CEO Chris Henderson, to each and every gospel artist who greeted her, they were all kind and generous. They discussed her contract, the money she would make, and promised Andrea creative freedom to write and produce her own songs. The only stipulation was that her songs would be tasteful and that they maintained Omega Studio's moral standards. Andrea was actually pleased about the clean image restriction. She had already done too many songs and videos that had been anything but clean and she wanted to re-invent her image. The deal was finalized and Andrea found herself an artist of Omega Studios.

Later that day, Andrea drove back to Metro Studios. Although she no longer had a key to enter, some of the employees who recognized her let her in. Andrea took the elevator at the far end of the building to go to the dance rehearsal room. She had another promise to keep. Opening the door to just enough to see inside, Andrea saw Miesha working on dance moves for her next video. Most of the moves involved the constant gyration of the dancers' rear ends and it was so repetitive that Andrea was amazed at how they still kept up the pace. After the session ended, Miesha walked to the other door, which served as an exit so while Miesha left the room, Andrea walked in so she wouldn't be seen by her ex-labelmate. Susan, one of the dancers who Andrea had met while rehearsing for one of her videos, sat and rubbed her sore feet. She was one of the older dancers, so the constant performing had taken a toll on her.

"Hey mama," Andrea greeted. Susan looked up and smiled gleefully when she saw Andrea. They ran and hugged each other.

"Oh my goodness, it's been so long, how you been?" Susan asked.

"I've been doing great. How about you?" Andrea asked.

"I'm okay. You know, just tryin' to get these steps down but I'm not as young as I used to be," Susan said. "So I heard you signed with another label after you left? Is that true?" she asked.

"Yeah, I signed with Omega Studios in downtown Manhattan," Andrea said. Susan smiled widely.

"I'm so proud of you baby," she said.

"Thanks, Susan." Andrea replied. "Yeah, so they want me to start working on my EP right away and I was looking for backup vocal singers," she added.

"Really?" Susan asked.

"Yeah, and I remembered hearing your voice after that rehearsal the other day and how you loved singing, and you were the first person that came to mind. I was wondering if you wouldn't mind singing backup for me on my next album," Andrea asked.

Susan looked like an overjoyed child on Christmas day. "No, I wouldn't mind at all. I would love to sing with you," she replied.

Andrea smiled and she helped Susan gather her belongings and before long Susan also became an ex-employee at Metro Records.

Dr. Ralwinski arrived at her office building at ten-thirty in the morning. After parking her car, she walked inside the building and was surprised when she saw a huge group of people gathering around someone. She assumed they were patients or worse, people who didn't even have an appointment scheduled. Fighting through the throng of people, she saw Andrea in the center of the melee signing autographs. After she had handed her CD to a young boy, Andrea looked up and saw the woman who had helped her stay sane for the past several years.

"I should've known it was you," Dr. Ralwinski said, smiling. Andrea smiled sheepishly.

"Sorry about this, Jan. I promise I'll leave in a few minutes. I just wanted to see how you were doing," she said.

After signing a few more autographs, Andrea walked into her former therapist's office. Since the previous visit had been shortly after she had signed by Metro Records, Andrea hadn't been able to visit Dr. Ralwinski in almost a year. She felt a sense of nostalgia as she walked into the office, pausing at the fish tank where she used to feed the fish before their sessions. Looking at the tank, she noticed that Dr. Ralwinski had added a couple more fish to the existing group. She also noticed that the huge book shelf that had been on the right side of the room was now on the left side. Aside from those minor changes, the office looked the same.

"So I see things are looking up for you," Dr. Ralwinski said.

"Yeah, everything is going as planned. I finally understand what my sister was trying to tell me all this time," Andrea said.

"That's great. I'm so happy for you that you found your place of happiness," Dr. Ralwinski said. "You're happier now than I've ever seen you, especially after seeing all those pictures of you in the magazines. You smiled in those pictures, but I had a feeling you still weren't happy," she added.

"Well, I have God to thank and I have you to thank also, Jan," Andrea said. Looking at her watch, she realized she had to leave. She had a recording session at Omega. "Thank you Jan, for everything," she said.

"You're very welcome dear," she said, hugging her fellow patient. "You know how you could repay me? You could hook me up with your next album and maybe some tickets to your next show," Dr. Ralwinski said, laughing.

Andrea laughed as well. "I got you, Jan," she said as she walked out the door.

A year later, Andrea was at Radio City Music Hall performing five songs from her second EP at Omega Studios. Although she had been on stage many times as the sultry songstress Adia, for the first time in her life she felt completely free from anyone's control and any doubts that she had were gone. She felt an immense amount of pressure lifted from her shoulders. She no longer had to dress provocatively, and she didn't have to memorize choreography show after show. It was only her and the music, just as Emiline said. No drama from label mates and no disputes about money. It was peace of mind, and she was happy that she was finally able to sing what she was born to sing. She ended the show with the following lines from one of her songs:

If it wasn't for Him, I would still be crying/I can't deny my love for Him, I'd be lying/I'm trying to live my life without dying/It's not what I'm looking for, but it's what I'm finding.

As she ended her show and the curtains began to descend she saw the crowd standing up in a standing ovation and for the first time, she felt the audience was impacted by Andrea, the girl who sang to escape her pain and her sorrow to bring forth happiness and joy in others. An hour after the show ended, Andrea was still signing autographs for fans and supporters. Susan walked up to her.

"You did very well tonight honey," she said.

"Thanks, mama. You were great tonight, too." Andrea replied as Susan hugged her and left to help the musicians pack up their instruments.

As she continued to sign autographs, two young black women followed by a black man walked up to her table. Right away, Andrea knew that they were from her block by the way they spoke to each other. One of the women, who appeared slightly older, seemed to be talking with her man and by the way she was holding his hand, she knew it must be her boyfriend. She appeared too preoccupied with him to pay attention to the other young lady, who was about twelve years old. They stood in front of her table.

"Hi, what's your name, sweetie?" Andrea asked. The young girl cast her eyes downward, not out of disrespect but nervousness.

"My name's Kira," she replied.

"You are so cute," Andrea said while she signed a copy of her CD and handed it over to her.

"Thank you," Kira replied. Andrea saw the man and woman still busily talking to each other and they were holding up the line of the other fans who wanted autographs.

"Is that your older sister?" Andrea asked Kira. Kira nodded, although she didn't seem too enthusiastic about admitting it. The woman finally stopped talking to her boyfriend long enough to finally greet Andrea.

"Hey Adia, what's up girl? My name's Chanté and this is my boyfriend, Wallace," she said hastily, speaking to Andrea as if they were lifelong friends.

"Nice to meet ya'll," Andrea replied.

"All right girl, so level wit' me real quick. Do you really wanna stick wit' this tired gospel gig? Tell me you don't miss all that money you was makin' up at Metro," she said.

Andrea thought about her statement before she responded. "Well I'd be lying to you if I said I didn't miss it at times but just because you miss something doesn't mean you have to spend your whole life thinking about what could've been. Sometimes we have to move on and start fresh," she replied.

"I think you're better now than you were before," Kira said. Chante looked at her little sister with a disparaging look.

"Oh, you was quiet when you first got hea, and now you wanna talk," Chante said with a tone of annoyance, and Andrea could tell that Chanté s abrupt tone was upsetting Kira and with one glance at Kira, Andrea saw herself at the same age.

"You know, you should treat your sister better than that," Andrea said, looking at Chante.

"What?" Chante asked.

"With all due respect, Kira looks up to you. She lives wit' you and she sees what you do and how you talk to others. Be the best example for her. You never know how much longer you'll have each other," Andrea said.

Chante looked up as if she couldn't believe how Andrea had spoken to her. Not wanting to cause a scene, she just nodded her head.

"Kira's a bright young lady. Treat her as your best friend," Andrea added. She then signed Chante and Wallace's CDs and they walked off.

A few days later, Andrea drove back to Richmond Hill near 101 Avenue, returning to her old haunts. Ever since she had signed with Omega Studios, Andrea realized she could no longer afford the elegant home she once owned in the most exclusive part of Queens. Not to be deterred, she found an affordable apartment near Flatbush and had lived there ever since. Due to her busy schedule and shows, she hadn't had the time to visit her parents or the neighborhood where she had grown up. She finally listened to her parents' advice and enrolled at CUNY John Jay, which was a college system in New York. Most of her classes were online, which worked in her favor because the schedule never interfered with her touring or her show dates. Alisha had called her daughter to give her some exciting news that Shania and Trevor McClain wanted to share with them. Although Andrea already had an idea what the surprising news was, she wanted to be there in person. Since missing Shania's wedding, Andrea made a vow to never allow her busy schedule get in the way of family. As she drove past familiar blocks small duplex homes, she saw a young man walking in the opposite direction. At first, she didn't think anything of him until she looked closer and recognized him immediately.

"Oh my goodness, is that Quentin?" she asked herself as she slowed to a stop and pulled up close to the sidewalk. Indeed, it was Quentin, although anyone who went to high school with him might not have been able to recognize him. Quentin had changed so much in appearance. His hair was cut even shorter and he no longer wore glasses. He even looked stronger than his high school years. Andrea could tell he had buffed up in college. She wasn't complaining at all though. He had been a grade A stud, much like Gary, her old co-worker at Johnson's. As the car approached Quentin, he stared at the driver questioningly.

Rolling her window down, Andrea shouted, "Quentin, what's up? It's me Andrea, you remember me?" she asked before she instantly regretted the question. She used to be on every music channel known to man, so certainly Quentin might have seen her at some point at Morehouse College. Still, he remained suspicious until he looked closely at Andrea and suddenly he recognized her.

"Andrea, what's up? Long time no see. But I can tell that you stay busy," he replied.

"Yeah, I've been extremely busy," she said.

"Yeah, I've peeped you in a couple music videos back in da day," he replied. "But the move you made to get outta Metro when they was cheatin' you out yo' money was dope though. I respect that," he added.

"Really? Cuz everyone seems to think that I made a mistake leavin' Metro," Andrea admitted.

"Don't even sweat that," Quentin said. "I seen what all them magazine articles said. You did what was right for you. I woulda made the same move if I was in yo' place," he said and as he looked at Andrea, she noticed his brown eyes. It was funny how she never noticed them when he had his glasses on.

"Thanks Quentin, I really appreciate that. So what you doin' ova hea? Don't you still go to Morehouse?" she asked.

"Yeah, I'm still there. I just came back for the summer after semester ended," Quentin replied.

"Oh ok. You look good, you know that?" Andrea said, and she felt the color rise in her cheeks out of embarrassment. Why couldn't she ever keep her mouth shut? "But you probably got a girl down there in Atlanta anyway," she added. Quentin laughed.

"Nah, I been too busy grinding in school fo' that," he said. There was a brief moment of awkward silence between them. "Listen, if you ain't doin' nothin' lata', maybe we can go out sometime, you know, catch a movie or something," he said as casually as he could but secretly hoping he didn't sound too desperate. What were the chances of a recording artist ever going out with him? Not to mention the previous time he attempted to ask her out, she turned him down, and she wasn't even famous yet. But to his surprise, Andrea accepted.

"I'd love to go out wit' you," she answered, smiling.

"Iight, cool. But first, we gon' have to find you a dope disguise so that we don't get ran over by your fans," he said in his semi-serious tone. Andrea laughed.

"Whateva, you so stupid," she replied.

After exchanging numbers, they went their separate ways. After a few minutes, she arrived at Shania's parents' house. She remembered where the Hillmans lived, because she had visited their home. Pink balloons were tied by the string to the front door, the mailbox and the lamp post. After parking her car, Andrea walked up to the door and rang the bell.The door was opened promptly by Mike Hillman's wife Robyn.

"Hi sweetie, look at you!" she exclaimed as she hugged Andrea.

When she stepped inside the home and walked up the stairs, she saw that Mike was there along with his brother-in-law, attorney Arthur Blaylock. A large paper sign hung across the hallway wall arch between the kitchen and the rooms. The sign read: CONGRATULATIONS, IT'S A GIRL! Andrea stepped into the kitchen and finally she saw the newborn child, in the arms of her mother and her father, who was standing behind his little family. Shania had given birth and she had just been discharged from the hospital. Trevor, who had been in the midst of a summer league tryout with the New York Knicks of the National Basketball Association, had rushed to the hospital when he received word that his wife was in labor. He was able to get to Shania's side on time, and today they were happy parents to a little girl. Shania saw Andrea and she smiled widely. Andrea looked at the baby. She was so tiny; wrapped up in white blankets and her eyes were still closed as she took the first few breaths of life.

"Shania, she's beautiful," she said.

"You wanna hold her?" Shania asked.

"Yeah, I'd like that," she answered and Shania gently handed her over to Andrea.

"Watch the head now," Arthur said cautiously.

Gently holding the newborn while supporting her head, Andrea asked, "So what's her name?"

Shania and Trevor looked at each other. "Her name's Loree Emiline McClain," Shania answered.

Hearing that, it took all Andrea had within her, not to break down and sob. Shania had not only named her baby after her physical sister but she also named her after the surrogate sister that Emiline Jacob had been to her. Trevor then excused himself from his family. Calling Andrea, he gave her his phone which had his Pandora music app playing. Andrea handed the baby back to Shania and followed Trevor out into the hallway. He pulled out his headphones and gave them to Andrea so she could listen to a specific song.

"Check it out, it's yo' boy. Looks like he broke out of his funk," he said. As Andrea listened, she realized the song was a new rap single by De'Von Franklin, his first release in more than a year. Between depression, drug rehab, and fan disinterest, De'Von had significantly fallen off the music map but he appeared to be making a comeback with his current single entitled "Thanks, Baby," She listened closely as he rapped the following lines:

I was so hardheaded right from the start/But baby, I know you had the keys to my heart/If I knew it then, I would do it all again/You was right baby, now yo' boy's on the mend.

Andrea smiled as she listened to his words. She knew the relationship between them would never be the same but she was hopeful that De'Von would find the new beginning that she herself had sought and had been fortunate enough to find. As the baby slept in her mother's arms, Andrea looked at her and saw through baby Loree Emiline that true joy was not in what she had lost but the new life that had emerged from her losses and an assurance that her future would continue to show the fruits of her inner growth.

About the Author

"Marc A. Beausejour"

Marc A. Beausejour was born on July 28, 1987 in Queens, New York to Haitian parents Jean and Lineda Beausejour. He discovered his passion for writing at the tender age of twelve, with poetry becoming his initial artistic expression. Beausejour showcased his poetic talents in various school talent shows and poetry reading events during his time at North Cobb High School and later at Kennesaw State University after moving to Kennesaw, Georgia in 2001.

Throughout the years, Beausejour continued to hone his craft, writing poems for diverse occasions such as weddings, funerals, and church events. In 2011, he took a significant step by self-publishing his first book, "Words on High," a compilation of spiritually inspired poems from his formative years. Building on this success, Beausejour released his second poetry book, "Rising Higher Than Ever," in 2015.

In the same year, he ventured into a different literary landscape by writing and publishing his first urban novel, "The Preacher's Web." This gritty morality tale marked a departure from his earlier poetic works, showcasing Beausejour's versatility as an author. Expanding his literary horizons, he created the *BlackCyrano* series, demonstrating a wide-ranging creative skill.

While continuing to share his literary work on blogs and social networks, Beausejour remains committed to his education and promotions, earning his associate degree in marketing management from Chattahoochee Technical College in 2018. As a multifaceted writer, Marc A. Beausejour continues to captivate audiences with his words across various genres and platforms.

Also by. Author

"Marc A. Beausejour"

Title: The Preacher's Web | Publisher: SHE PUBLISHING LLC | ISBN: 978-1-953163-91-2 (paperback) Publication Date: February 2024 (*Second Edition*)

Set in the heart of the city, "The Preacher's Web" unfolds a gripping narrative of former All-City quarterback turned pastor, Mike Hillman, whose dedication to preaching love and forgiveness in Queens, New York is challenged by the return of an old friend seeking revenge. Amidst a community grappling with the scourge of drugs and gangs. As Mike puts his reputation on the line to testify for a young man accused of murder, the story converges with the adolescent struggles of Jamal Samuels on the basketball courts of New York City.

Now, standing at the crossroads of faith, family, and societal challenges, Mike faces a pivotal choice. Will he risk more than his reputation to uphold justice and fulfill his role as a public servant and father? The pages of "The Preacher's Web" beckon you to explore the complexities of morality and redemption. Can Mike Hillman rise above, or will he be consumed by the web of his past?

Title: Fires of Justice | Author: Marc A. Beausejour | Publisher: SHE PUBLISHING LLC | ISBN: 978-1-953163-93-6 (paperback) | Publication Date: February 2024

English professor Levell Thomas is ecstatic when he receives the opportunity to teach in a metro Atlanta high school. A native of Queens, New York, Levell moves to Georgia with his family and as they settle in their new home, Levell meets his neighbor, a mysterious girl named Raven Roberts. Despite being underaged, she doesn't hide her desires for Levell and pursues him relentlessly. Levell refuses her advances but would soon pay dearly for his decision. The spurned teenager accuses Levell of assault after a physical confrontation and Levell is found guilty in the court of law. Detective Isaac Sands leads the investigation to expose a plot of false accusation and imprisonment in a race against time. Will Sands help prove Levell's innocence by finding the conspirators, or would he put himself in harm's way?

"The controversies confronted, stirred, and then addressed in this story have no choice but to awaken you to new perspectives that might not have ever crossed your mind. Readers, all I can say is be prepared to feel the fire that Beausejour has ignited in this suspenseful masterpiece!"

—D.A. Goodwin, author of The Offender I Once Defended

Title: Split Decision | Author: Marc A. Beausejour | Publisher: SHE PUBLSIHING LLC | ISBN: 978-1-953163-94-3 (paperback) | Publication Date: February 2024 (*second edition*)

Prepare to enter the ring as cultures clash in this adrenaline-filled drama! Under the tutelage of experienced trainer Jim Shaw, young boxer Sylvio Dominique has taken the middleweight class division by storm, winning bout after bout. Nicknamed "Wolf" for his boxing style and aggression in the ring, Sylvio works hard in the ring and plays even harder out of the ring and there is no shortage of women. Reuniting with childhood friend Valentina Cruz, the two become involved in an intense romance. But as Sylvio falls deep in love with Valentina, he realizes that she is more than what she seems. With a fight against the undefeated Dominican champion Felipe Maximo looming, secrets are revealed, and friends turn to foes as Sylvio later discovers that he may not be fighting only for the middleweight crown, but he may also be fighting for his life.

Title: Split Decision II - The Comeback | Author: Marc A. Beausejour | Publisher: SHE PUBLISHING LLC | ISBN: 978-1-953163-95-0 (paperback)| Publication Date: February 2024 (*second edition*)

After Sylvio Dominique's sudden retirement from middleweight boxing following a close brush with death, the former champion hangs up his gloves to continue running the Shaw-Dominique Community Center in Queens, New York. When Sylvio's hometown rival and current middleweight champion Barry Taylor; asks him to help train for his title defense against new contender and former MMA fighter Jun Zhang, Sylvio agrees to the proposition. But Taylor is defeated handily, and when Sylvio suffers a tragic death in the family and the center struggles financially, he makes the decision to return to the ring. Meanwhile, his girlfriend, Valentina Cruz find success as an actress and her relationship with Sylvio begins coming apart at the seams. Sylvio's trainer, Jim Shaw is reluctant to help Sylvio, as he finds himself struggling with his own personal demons. Jun Zhang then challenges Sylvio to fight him for the crown. As he prepares for his toughest ring battle yet, can Sylvio and Jim find the fortitude to emerge victorious while putting all their struggles behind them?

Title: Street Retribution | Author: Marc A. Beausejour | Publisher: SHE PUBLISHING LLC | ISBN: 978-1-953163-96-7 (*paperback*) | Publication Date: February 2024 (*second edition*)

New York City attorney Edward Reed harbors a secret. He was once known as Antonio Franks, a member of M.O.B., the most dangerous gang in Queens, New York. He was also the key witness in the trial that exonerated another ex-gang member, David Anderson, when he was falsely accused of murdering his girlfriend, Loree McAfee. But years later, both men's lives are in danger, as other former gang members are slain under mysterious circumstances by a femme fatale, prompting rumors that M.O.B.'s ruthless gang leader, Tadarius Hill is seeking revenge on those that turned on him and his organization. Will Edward and David survive the bounty, or will they fall victim to the code of the streets?

Title: Divine Vengeance | Author: Marc A. Beausejour | Publisher: SHE PUBLISHING LLC | Publication Date: COMING SOON!

After the murder of David Anderson, LaToya Richardson awaits her day in court while attorney Edward Reed receives a warning from Tadarius Hill, the gang leader of M.O.B. and sexy femme fatale Tina, who gives him an ultimatum. Realizing that he cannot use conventional methods to combat the tactics of his former gang, Edward pulls out all the stops to prevent Tadarius from wreaking havoc in the city. LaToya's son, Chris adjusts to his new home and new school while staying with David's family. Andrea McAfee's relationship with her boyfriend Quentin comes apart at the seams as lust and infidelity threatens to tear the couple apart. Can Edward, Chris, and Andrea summon the strength amidst the chaos in their environment to secure their futures?